praise for Denise Hildreth Jones

THE FIRST GARDENER

"This tender and uplifting read . . . should find its way into the hands of readers who like the Southern novels of Rebecca Wells."
LIBRARY JOURNAL

"A heart-wrenchingly believable story . . . Jones's novel offers comfort and challenge, and readers will find it lingering in their hearts and minds long after the last page has been turned."
PUBLISHERS WEEKLY

"Full of drama and emotion . . . *The First Gardener* is a story of love, loss, and faith . . . that will have you reading through your tears. . . . Denise Hildreth Jones is a rising star on the literary scene, and this book is an indication that she will be around for some time to come."
JACKIE K. COOPER, *Huffington Post*

"Reaches into the depths of the reader's soul. . . . [Jones's] ability to convey real-life emotion without sugarcoating, yet still providing hope, elevates this novel above the rest."
ROMANTIC TIMES, 4½-star Top Pick review

"With the perfect balance of tender and intense moments, [Jones] tells this heart-wrenching tale in a way that will not allow the reader to put down the book. . . . Genuine and

honest . . . a perfect story for any woman looking for a good book with a positive outlook on life."
CHRISTIANBOOKPREVIEWS.COM

HURRICANES IN PARADISE

"Magnificent reading. . . . Hildreth writes her books with an open heart and a generosity of spirit."
JACKIE K. COOPER, *Huffington Post*

"[A] winning combination of humor, spiritual insight, and true-life characters has widespread appeal."
ROMANTIC TIMES, 4½-star Top Pick review

"Hildreth has done a masterful job of creating realistic, unforgettable relationships interwoven in a wonderful story line of real-life struggles, heartaches, and hurricanes, showing that with God's help, we can survive even the strongest storms of life."
CBA RETAILERS + RESOURCES

"A great story with so many twists and turns that just never stopped getting intriguing. The end leaves you just begging for more."
EXAMINER.COM

"Soaked with sun, wit, and heart, this is a story of healing and the hope that, sometimes, surviving the storm has its rewards."
PATTI CALLAHAN HENRY,
New York Times bestselling author

FLIES ON THE BUTTER

"Hildreth's latest shines with humanity and originality. . . . Keep tissues handy for the emotional conclusion."

ROMANTIC TIMES

"[N]othing less than a spiritual odyssey of inner reckoning."

SOUTHERN LIVING

"Beautifully portrays how looking back thoughtfully has the potential to powerfully transform one's future."

ANDY ANDREWS, *New York Times* bestselling author

THE SAVANNAH SERIES

"[*Savannah from Savannah* is] smart and witty."

LIBRARY JOURNAL

"Reading *Savannah Comes Undone* is like taking a virtual vacation. It's a quirky, fun foray into life in the South. . . . You won't be disappointed."

KATHY L. PATRICK,
founder of the Pulpwood Queens Book Club

"An engaging read of real-life vignettes and relationships. I read it cover to cover. As Savannah discovers her beliefs, values, and passions, the reader will be looking into their own 'mirror of truth.'"

NAOMI JUDD

secrets
— over —
Sweet Tea

a novel

DENISE
HILDRETH
JONES

Tyndale House Publishers, Inc., Carol Stream, Illinois

Visit Tyndale online at www.tyndale.com.

Visit Denise Hildreth Jones's website at www.denisehildrethjones.com.

TYNDALE and Tyndale's quill logo are registered trademarks of Tyndale House Publishers, Inc.

Secrets over Sweet Tea

Designed by Jennifer Ghionzoli

Edited by Anne Christian Buchanan

Published in association with the literary agency of Daniel Literary Group, Nashville, TN.

Secrets over Sweet Tea is a work of fiction. Where real people, events, establishments, organizations, or locales appear, they are used fictitiously. All other elements of the novel are drawn from the author's imagination.

Library of Congress Cataloging-in-Publication Data

Jones, Denise Hildreth, date.
  Secrets over sweet tea / Denise Hildreth Jones.
    p. cm.
  ISBN 978-1-4143-6684-5 (sc)
  1. Secrets—Fiction. 2. Friendship—Fiction. 3. Franklin (Tenn.)—Fiction. I. Title.
PS3608.I424S43 2013
813'.6—dc23   2012030519

Printed in the United States of America

19 18 17 16 15 14 13
 7   6   5   4   3   2   1

also by Denise Hildreth Jones

FICTION

Savannah from Savannah

Savannah Comes Undone

Savannah by the Sea

Flies on the Butter

The Will of Wisteria

Hurricanes in Paradise

The First Gardener

NONFICTION

Flying Solo:
A Journey of Divorce, Healing, and a Very Present God

Reclaiming Your Heart:
A Journey Back to Laughing, Loving, and Living

To any heart that is tired of saying,

"Those were the best years of my life."

acknowledgments

Many thanks to my Tyndale team: Karen, Stephanie, Babette, and Andrea.

To my wonderful editor, Anne Christian Buchanan.

To my agent, Greg Daniel.

To my family and friends for their continued belief in my stories and the never-ending supply of wonderful material.

And to my heavenly Father—thank you for yet again giving me one more story to tell and for finding my heart so worth fighting for.

{ *Chapter 1* }

SCARLETT JO NEWBERRY'S lime-green flip-flops smacked the
sidewalk loudly as she walked through her neighborhood. Her
prayers were sometimes just as loud—or sometimes she prayed
them in her head. Sometimes she'd hum gently, and other times
she'd belt out a song at the top of her lungs.

She didn't mind the stares or the comments. She was used
to both. Some folks had trouble with her love of bright colors.
Some disliked the noise her five children could make. Some
thought she strolled the streets talking to herself. But Scarlett
Jo hadn't simply survived her life. She had learned how to live
in spite of it—and not to worry too much about the perceptions of others.

This early morning routine of part prayer, part recalibration was pretty much a daily occurrence. Every day except the rainy ones. Rain messed up her hair. But with her hectic household, she needed a set of new mercies as often as possible.

She started humming that old song again, the one from *The Sound of Music* that listed "my favorite things." Watching the sun rise was one of her own favorites. So was walking. And praying. And with all those things in this one beautiful morning, she had that song on her mind.

If anyone had been listening, they might have hummed along. But most people weren't listening. If they were jogging, they passed her by with things stuck in their ears, pumping music in so fast and furious that she didn't know when they'd last heard all the beautiful music that life made right around them.

She passed Sylvia Malone's house and prayed for her. Sylvia needed a lot of prayer. Sometimes Eugenia's house next door wouldn't even get prayed over because Sylvia needed so much. But Scarlett Jo tried to cover every house if she could, including her own. Talking with her Father that way made all of life better. And so would the pastry she'd grab from Merridee's Breadbasket over on Fourth Avenue South when she was done.

Scarlett Jo reached beneath her double-Ds and adjusted her underwire. Then she reached into the pocket of her hot-pink terry-cloth shorts and pulled out the small pencil and notebook she kept stashed in there for moments just like this. For distractions.

She wrote, *Visit Victoria and get a new secret.* She giggled. Jackson would like that. A lot. That special connection of theirs had helped make her the wife of one good-looking preacher and the mama of five amazing boys.

She stuck the notebook back in her pocket and continued on her morning walk. Franklin, Tennessee, was just starting to come alive. But Scarlett Jo Newberry had been marvelously alive for years.

Despite what many believed, she'd never been out for attention. Her oversize personality just seemed to attract it. And Scarlett Jo didn't mind because she knew she'd eventually earn entry into people's hearts. Experience had taught her that many who initially disapproved of her would eventually want her on their committees and include her at their functions and parties. Maybe the fact that she wasn't the skinniest or the quietest girl in the room helped them feel better about themselves.

But Scarlett Jo thought it was something else. It was because, for the most part, she was nothing but herself. What you saw was what you got. It had taken her a long time and a lot of pain to get there. And people responded to that.

Not everybody, of course. A lot of those she knew weren't quite there yet. And she was trying to learn patience about that. Trying to learn when to speak up about what she saw—she was pretty good at that—and when to shut her mouth and wait—which was still a challenge. She knew she stepped over the line a lot, that people weren't ready for her to let it all hang out. Every day she asked God to show her the fine line between being herself and simply being too much—and to please keep her from hurting Jackson's ministry by saying the wrong thing.

Not that Jackson would ever tell her to do anything for the ministry's sake. He was crazy about her just the way she was. But Scarlett Jo had been involved with churches long enough to know that folks could be as bottled up and closed off and easily offended in church as anywhere else. Maybe more so in church than anywhere else. Which meant the state of Tennessee must be chock-full of the bottled up, closed off, and easily offended because churches were as plentiful here as ants at a Sunday dinner on the grounds. Why, right here in Scarlett Jo's little part of Franklin you could find Church of Christ, Presbyterian, Methodist, nondenominational, and Catholic. Probably more.

Sometimes she wished their church had confessionals like the Catholics did. With a confessional, at least for a few brief minutes, you had a soul vulnerable, available to the kind of honesty that could heal. And if they weren't being honest, you could simply jump out of your side of the curtain and grab them before they got away.

The nondenominational church she and Jackson had started two years ago didn't have confessionals. What it did have was people hungry for something real. That was evident by how quickly the church had grown. But though Jackson tried with all his might to get their people living out of their "authentic selves," it hadn't been as easy as he'd expected. It wasn't easy for people to be authentic—or appreciate authenticity—when they hadn't seen their authentic selves in decades.

Still, Scarlett Jo had hope. She was a woman on a mission for her city whether they knew it or not. So each morning after her walk, and after all five of her boys got out of the house and on their way to school, she'd curl up in her hot-pink robe on the small sofa in her sunporch, sip a glass of sweet tea, and watch men and women as they scurried up the streets with their coffee. Or ran behind baby strollers. Or walked like half drunks with their eyes glued to a screen no wider than her big toe as if everything in life depended on reading the latest tweet. She'd watch them all and pray a little more.

What she really longed for was to be the kind of person who, when people wanted prayer—the real kind of prayer that reaches down to soul places and up to heavenly places—they'd know to come straight to her. Unfortunately that had only happened one time in the two years she and Jackson had lived here. Proving that sometimes denial is a strong-willed companion. Or that she still had some growing to do. Probably both.

"Scarlett Jo, seriously. I've told you—no woman your age or your size should be in hot pink. You look like an overgrown bottle of Pepto-Bismol."

Scarlett Jo walked to the edge of Eugenia Quinn's yard, two houses down from her own. "Eugenia, if those aren't the loveliest peonies I have ever seen."

"Well, they would be if Jeremiah would quit messing with them. I told Gray if he started sending that man to me, he'd spend the rest of his life all up in my business. I'm a prophet!" Eugenia used the back of her wrist to push at her bleached-blonde locks, the palm of her gardening glove almost as black as the soil. Her bob bounced right back into place. Good hair was about the only thing she and Scarlett Jo had in common.

"Well, it's good you have Jeremiah taking care of things for you now that you're going to DC so much." Scarlett Jo leaned in. "I heard the White House is beautiful. Is it beautiful, Eugenia?"

Eugenia bent over her peonies again and swatted at Scarlett Jo. "It's big and it's white and it has pictures of dead people everywhere." Her tone softened. She couldn't help it. She was about to speak of the people she loved most. It always shifted here. "But my family is there in Washington. And my grandbabies need their Gigi."

"They sure do. How are they adjusting?"

"They're the smartest children you'd ever find. And very well-mannered." Eugenia raised her eyebrow at Scarlett Jo.

Scarlett Jo got Eugenia's message and completely ignored it. Her five boys burped, passed gas, and rode skateboards and bikes all over the place. They were loud. They fought. And they were totally and completely alive, just the way she liked them. "And how are Sam and Lola?" she asked Eugenia. "The pictures I've seen look like they're growing like weeds."

"And jabbering up a storm. I'm crazy about them."

"Of course you are, Eugenia."

"I see you killed those trees I gave you for your front porch."

The little potted trees had been Eugenia's welcome gift when Scarlett Jo and Jackson moved into the storybook stone cottage up the street. Scarlett Jo twitched her nose and pushed out her lips. Her weight rocked slightly on her flip-flops. "If your thumb is green, Eugenia, mine is—"

"Hot pink! You spend more time focused on looking like a neon sign than taking care of plants. Heaven knows I should have gotten you silk ones. But then the town would be downgraded from the twentieth best place to retire to number twenty on the tacky meter."

"I told you when you gave them that I'd do better with some cinnamon buns."

Eugenia raised her eyebrow again and opened her mouth.

"Don't say anything! I'm going to go back to praying. Anything special you need today?"

Eugenia looked at Scarlett Jo, obviously thinking. "I need life to slow down. My friend Dimples to speed up. Jeremiah to leave me alone. And God to keep the cicadas from hatching. Got that?"

Scarlett Jo nodded. "Got it. Are those cicadas really as bad as everyone says? Swooping from the air? Screaming in your ear?"

"All that, baby girl. All that."

Scarlett Jo shivered and finished her prayer with an added bonus for the cicadas.

❀ ❀ ❀

Jackson came up behind Scarlett Jo and wrapped his arms around her waist while she stood with her nose almost touching the glass pane of their sunporch. She noticed his hands didn't make it quite as far around as they had twenty-five years ago, when she was eighteen and he was twenty. But neither one of them minded. It hadn't been their figures that had attracted them to each other in the first place.

She patted his hand. "Morning, sugar. Rest well?"

He breathed his words across the base of her ear. "I'd recognize that Mississippi drawl four states over."

His breath gave her chills. She tried to squirm free. "Jackson, you just made the hairs on my legs grow."

He laughed. "I know." He finally leaned back, patted her rear, and came around next to her. "Who are you spying on now?"

"New neighbor. Four doors down." She motioned with her fingers in the direction of the house as if she were engaged in some covert mission.

He played along. He always played along. "Well, that does happen when people move out. Usually someone moves in. Think they're terrorists?"

She slapped at him without turning his way. "I think they're from up North somewhere. They drive one of those Prius cars."

7

Sylvia Malone could be the neighborhood watch committee all by herself, but Scarlett Jo couldn't resist helping her out now and then.

"They do sell those now in the South, you know."

"I know that. But I watched them take in most of their clothes too." Her sigh came out heavy. Did this man not pay attention?

"Of course you did. And you started this surveillance activity when?"

"Two days ago. They started Saturday. And had everything in by yesterday." Her next words came out in a whisper. "Their clothes were mostly black. Only people from New York or California dress in all black." She took a long sip of her tea.

"We'd better hide the good china." He shivered as he spoke. "Plus, all this time I thought you were out there praying in the mornings."

"Don't mock me, Jackson Newberry. Northerners are a different breed, baby. They don't like you to touch them. They don't want to be called sugar or sweetie or honey pie or darlin'. They've never heard of lard. They have no clue on God's green earth what *fixin' to* even means. And if you say *y'all*, they look at you like you probably marry your second cousin or something."

His phone rang from his pocket. He leaned over and kissed her before he pulled it out. "I've always wondered about your cousin Thelma Lou."

She swatted at him, and he laughed. "What I know about you, Scarlett Jo, is you can make even Northerners fall in love with you. I'll see you tonight. And please, don't take them anything at least for a week. Let them get settled first. Visit them next weekend."

She started to protest, but he shook his ringing phone in front of her and walked from the room. She sighed. People thought pastors were like God—needed to be accessible at all times. She turned back toward the house down the street that seemed quiet after yesterday's busy activity. She breathed a prayer for the hearts that would now live inside. Then her mind began to rummage through the selection of baked goods at Merridee's. She'd find out what these Northerner newcomers were really like. And she had every intention of finding that out today.

$\{$ *Chapter 2* $\}$

HE KISSED HER SOFTLY and rolled over. "That was just what I needed this morning."

Her words brushed softly against his ear. "Me too." She pulled the sheet around her and snuggled up under his arm.

"I've got to go," he murmured. "It's time to really get this day started."

"No, not yet. This has been the perfect morning."

He kissed the top of her head. "I know, babe. But I've got to get some kind of run in before I head to the office." He moved his mouth closer to her face. "But we will pick up where we left off later. How's that?"

Her lip poked out in a soft pout.

He walked into the bathroom and grabbed his running

shorts and T-shirt, which were haphazardly thrown over the side of the tub. After he slipped his running shoes on, he returned to the bedroom.

She looked beautiful lying there, her dark-brown hair scattered in waves across the pillow, the filtered sun lighting her flushed cheeks. He went to the side of the bed and leaned down and kissed her. Her lips were warm and soft and inviting. Her arms came up around the base of his neck, and he chuckled through the kiss.

"Seriously, I've got to go. If I don't go now, I won't have time to exercise today."

"I hope you have a great day then." Her words dripped with confidence, a certainty that he would never leave. He shook his head to dislodge his emerging thoughts. If he didn't get outside right now and run, he wasn't going to leave this house all day.

"You too, babe."

He left the bedroom and headed through the kitchen to the door that led out to the small garden. He turned the knob and entered the warm May Tennessee morning. As he came to the edge of the fence, he looked quickly to see if any cars were on the streets. All was still quiet, so he jogged across and settled into a pace that was certain to produce a sweat fast.

The streets of downtown Franklin formed a grid of sorts. Main Street ran down the middle, crossed at regular intervals by numbered avenues. First Avenue, on the northeast end of town near the Harpeth River, bent around to form Bridge Street, parallel and north of Main. Third Avenue met Main at the town square, with its stately Confederate monument. And the entire downtown district came together southwest of the square, where Fifth Avenue met Main and a diagonal street called Columbia Avenue to create Five Points. This star-shaped junction could take you any direction you wanted to go—Murfreesboro, Nashville, Bellevue, Thompson Station, or Brentwood. But it also invited you to stay because all of town life intersected at Five Points. A post office anchored one corner; a church sat on another. Then there was a Starbucks and an ice cream parlor, and the Williamson County Archives building finished it off.

This one little section of town could fulfill just about every need a person had—spiritual, emotional, physical, and relational. And yet Zach Craig had never felt so unfulfilled in his life. A bead of sweat dropped into his eye as he reached Main Street and turned east. Already the lift from his morning tryst—that *alive* feeling—was draining away. His run wasn't helping much either. He couldn't outrun the truth of what his life had become.

He and Caroline had been married for fifteen years now. The twins were almost fourteen, and the estrogen in his household was off the charts. The girls cried over almost everything, and when they weren't crying, they were simply nasty. He didn't know where his sweet little girls had gone. And Caroline wasn't much better. With her, you never knew what you were going to get. Each morning you could throw a feather up in the air, and where the wind would take it was usually more dependable than Caroline's moods.

A sneeze that tickled his nose almost forced him to stop running. Spring had arrived with a vengeance, and the allergies that had tortured him since he moved to Tennessee now bloomed to life with the flowers and the grasses. His other faithful companion, shame, was about to settle over him with a vengeance as well. So he shifted his thoughts quickly to the cases that lay before him that day. He let them play through his mind as he continued down Main and skirted the square.

He had been predominantly a divorce attorney for the last five years—more out of necessity than choice. Title closings had been his real expertise, but when the real estate market tanked, he'd had to find something that was steady. And divorce certainly seemed a dependable source of income, especially in the Nashville area. He had actually read in a magazine that the city had been given the grade of D in marriage survival. Almost the worst grade you could get. Bad news—unless you made your living off those who flunked out.

He saw all sides of divorce—the ugly, the uglier, and the ugliest. One of his current clients was convinced his estranged spouse had just killed his dog. The man had come into his office sobbing, certain the dog had been poisoned. The vet was doing a necropsy now. That was a new one for sure. It never ceased to amaze him how minuscule the line was between love and hate.

Zach's legs burned as his feet pressed harder into the unforgiving concrete of the sidewalk. He ran down First Avenue and rounded the corner onto Church Street. A large moving truck sat on the opposite side of the road. More new neighbors, it looked like.

Franklin had become an attractive place to live for people from both coasts. Nissan's decision to relocate its entire California operations to middle Tennessee a few years ago had helped the lagging economy, but not by much. Finances were tight for a lot of people these days. Even divorce attorneys.

Zach ran past the first few townhomes that sat at the corner of the neighborhood—his neighborhood now. The brownstones at First and Church looked historic, but the entire community was actually less than a decade old, built to blend in with the quaint downtown. He stopped at a fenced courtyard and opened the gate. A large iron fountain flowed just as it had when he'd left it earlier that morning. The brick walkway and four park benches that circled the fountain pretty much made up his front yard.

Caroline had fallen in love with this "urban development" from the moment construction began back in 2005. The houses were at peak market value then, way past Zach's budget. But Caroline was determined to own one. He resisted for two years, though it cost him a few trinkets in between. Then the market dropped a little and he relented. But he'd bought too high nevertheless, and he was still trying to figure out how to pay for his wife's dream house.

He paced the courtyard for a few minutes with his hands on his hips, sweat dripping from his brow as he tried to slow his breathing. He raised one hand and rubbed at his face, the weekend growth rough against his palm. He walked toward the front steps and leaned against the wrought-iron rail. It was already warm beneath his touch. There were days when he wondered if Tennessee even knew how to cool off.

He turned the handle on the wood-and-etched-glass door and reentered his three-story world. He found the twins perched at the kitchen counter eating cereal.

"Morning, Lacy." He leaned down to kiss her cheek.

She swatted at him. "Gross, Dad. You stink."

Joy held up her hand before he even got near her. "Don't even think about it, Dad."

He laughed. "Good morning to you too. Where's Mom?"

"She's on the phone, I think," Lacy answered.

"Want me to fix you some French toast?"

Joy dug a spoon into her cereal for one last bite and then hopped off the barstool. "We've got to go get ready."

Lacy followed quickly. "Yep. See you, Dad."

"Hey, I love you."

"You too, Dad!" Joy hollered. He was almost certain that Lacy grunted as she headed for the stairs.

He grabbed a water bottle from the refrigerator and headed upstairs. He could hear Caroline going at it with someone over the phone. The peacefulness of his morning was obviously over.

"Well, you didn't fix it." She stood in the middle of the bathroom floor and scolded as if talking to a six-year-old. "It still isn't working. So I want someone over here today, and I don't want some four-hour time slot that you *think* you might be able to honor. I want to know exactly when you will be here. I am just as busy as you are, and if this isn't fixed by the end of the week, I'm calling the Better Business Bureau."

Zach leaned against the counter. When he left his wife sleeping early this morning, she had looked so peaceful and serene that he almost changed his mind about going out. No more. Her brow was furrowed, which was hard to believe possible now that she had started getting Botox. She was still two years from forty, and yet she'd thought she needed it. He hadn't argued. Not because he agreed, but because he was simply tired of arguing.

"I'll see you in one hour then." Caroline hung up the phone. She looked at him and brushed at her bangs, which had fallen in front of her face. "You sure got out of here early this morning."

He walked over to her and moved long strands of auburn

hair from the shoulders of her workout shirt. "Yeah, I knew if I didn't, I wouldn't get a run in."

She squirmed away from him. "You stink, Zach."

He moved back. "I've been told that already."

"Well, I've got a busy day today. I'm going to drop off the girls and then come back to meet the electrician. Then once he gets through, I'm heading to the store. I've got two clients coming in to be styled for photo shoots, so I won't get to the new inventory until tonight. I probably won't be home until pretty late."

He went to the shower and turned on the water. "Why can't Kristin help you today?"

She turned toward him, frustration in her green eyes. He knew he was forgetting something, but he just couldn't bring it to mind.

"Summer internship in Paris, remember? I've only got Kelly and Amy available, and they need to work while I'm doing the styling."

"By the way, why do our girls have school today?"

She shook her head in that way she had, as if he'd just spoken in a foreign tongue. "What?"

"Well, I have this, um, friend who took his kids to visit their grandmother. They didn't have school today. Why do ours?"

She gave herself one last glance in the mirror. "It's probably a private school, public school thing. Even their spring breaks are different."

That made sense. "So the girls and I are on our own for dinner?"

She nodded. "You can take them out or something. They love that."

"Yes, they do," he mumbled as she left. "They enjoy their mother's presence too." She never heard that part.

Zach climbed into the shower and let the water wash over him, allowing his mind to retreat back to this morning: the shining dark hair, the deep, dark eyes, the desire, the longing, the actual awareness of his presence.

He decided he might take a run again tomorrow morning. Yep, he was pretty sure he'd run all week long.

{ *Chapter 3* }

GRACE SHEPHERD slid the earpiece from her ear and pushed away from the desk in front of her, the wheels of her chair rolling back smoothly as she did. She stood and picked up the final pages of her pink notes from the desk.

Leo Tanner, her producer, burst out of the control booth, licking his fingers. Everything about him was accentuated by speed and volume. "Great job today, Grace. Great job."

She stepped over the cord to camera number one and dropped her notes into the trash can on top of an empty Krispy Kreme doughnut box. When she moved from the bright television lights into the shadow of the studio, her body seemed to cool instantly.

"Thanks, Leo." She patted him on his thick football-player's shoulder. He had been a linebacker at the University of South Carolina and still loved to go around shouting, "Go, 'cocks!"— especially now that he was a Gamecock in Tennessee territory. The man had given his life to sports and to broadcasting. Worked as a sportscaster in Columbia, South Carolina, for quite a few years, then moved to the Nashville market and worked here until his gut got too big for the camera. That was when the gold *Producer* placard took its place on his office door. Producing was a perfect job for him because he loved to tell people what to do.

He followed her out of the studio. "I told you to take the week off, Grace. It would have been okay."

"Leo, if I took a week off every time we moved, I would run out of vacation time. And listen, you should lay off the Krispy Kremes. Honestly, you know what the doctor has said about your diabetes."

He tucked in a corner of his blue button-down that hung beneath his navy blazer, the bottom three buttons of the shirt stretching across his girth. "You brought 'em. Though they're nowhere near as good as your homemade cinnamon rolls, so I'll be glad when this move is over and you can get yourself back in the kitchen. And don't you worry about my diabetes. That's why they have medicine. As for the vacation thing—you know you never take one, so you're not about to run out of time. And you have to be exhausted."

"I am." She sighed and reached for the door of the ladies' restroom. "I'll take a nap this afternoon."

"Think that husband of yours will let you live in this house for a while?"

She patted Leo's dark-brown cheek, smooth beneath her

hand. "Thank you for your concern, but you know we do this for investment purposes."

"Gotcha one of those foreclosures, huh?"

She smiled. She couldn't help it. "We got a really good deal. Now I need to go so I can get home and unpack boxes."

He took the door handle, opening the door for her. "You're just as stubborn as me, Grace. Must be why I keep you."

She laughed. "I'm sure that's it. What are you doing today?"

"You mean aside from making the other networks weep by producing an amazing morning news show? Well, I'm going to a Rotary club lunch, and Sissy starts soccer this afternoon. Papa's got a full day. Now, go sleep so you can get up in the middle of the night tonight and do it all over again."

"Technically it will be tomorrow morning."

"Grace, if it's dark, it's night. We work at night. Don't fool yourself."

She smiled. "Okay, well, I'll see you tonight." The restroom door closed slowly behind her as she walked past the three bathroom stalls and into the small dressing room at the back. She pulled the second door closed behind her and turned to study herself in the mirror. She straightened the red jacket that Tyler had picked up for her on his last New York trip. He'd said the color would be good on the air, striking against her shoulder-length blonde hair and light-brown eyes.

He also said the new house was a good deal, that buying it was the right thing to do. For them. For now. She reminded herself of that as if saying so would convince her.

She pulled gently at the skin around her eyes. They did look tired. And just thinking about the boxes that awaited her made her even more tired. But this was part of the job. Both jobs—news anchor and wife. She began collecting tubes and brushes from the vanity, tucking them away in her cosmetics bag. She had been packing up makeup for the last ten years, ever since they upgraded her from reporter to anchor. The job had come the same year as her wedding. At the time, she'd been sure she needed nothing else. She had officially been granted the perfect world— a wonderful job and a good-looking, talented husband.

A soft burst of air that was half laugh, half pain came out of her nose. Like most fairy tales this side of Walt Disney World, that one had evaporated, leaving her with one less glass slipper and no sign of Prince Charming.

She dropped the Bobbi Brown mascara into her bag and tried to distract herself by thinking of all the viewers out there who thought she was like one of those major anchors who had someone to do her hair, brush her teeth, and wipe her nose. Wouldn't they love to know that she drove herself to work at two thirty every morning, dressed herself, did her own hair and makeup, and wrote her own teleprompter notes? It had taken her three years of begging before Leo finally agreed to put makeup lights in here so she could actually tell what her face would look like on camera. Before that it had been a case of trial and error. Mostly error.

She stuffed the workout clothes she'd worn to the studio into a bag, grabbed her purse, and headed out into the morning sunshine. Most people were just getting to work about now. Her workday was over.

She yawned as she beeped her car open and strapped herself in. The drive from Nashville to Franklin would take her thirty minutes. She used the voice command to wake up her cell phone. Rachel would talk her home. She always did.

"I can't believe you went in this morning." Her friend's voice sounded in her ear.

Grace was almost too tired to laugh. "It's my job, Rachel. And unlike you, I'm not a big vacation taker."

"Hey, hey, now. Play nice. I worked full-time with one kid and another on the way. I needed those days off."

Grace and Rachel settled into comfortable best-friend chat as the miles sped by. After almost thirteen years, they could practically finish each other's sentences. They'd met at the television station fresh out of college—but different colleges. Rachel took pride in being a Carolina Gamecock like Leo, though she had graduated quite a few years behind him. And she always pointed out she and Grace were friends in spite of Grace's University of Tennessee diploma. But Rachel still refused to go out with Grace if she wore UT orange. She insisted that Gamecocks gagged at the color because it represented the two teams they hated most, Clemson and Tennessee.

Rachel had risen to producer pretty quickly and was a huge advocate for Grace's getting the anchor chair. The two of them were called chocolate and vanilla around the station. Rachel's smooth brown skin, raven-black hair, and matching black eyes next to Grace's golden skin, blonde locks, and chestnut-brown eyes had heads turning wherever they went. When baby number two arrived, Rachel had opted to stay home. But she and Grace still talked at least once a day—and almost always on the drive home.

"I hope you didn't bake Leo something."

"I just moved, Rach. I haven't even unpacked my pans. I brought Krispy Kreme."

"The man needs a Krispy Kreme like he needs a comb."

"It's not nice to make fun of bald men." Grace laughed.

Rachel did too. "So I'd offer to come help you today, but you wouldn't let me."

"You're right. I wouldn't."

Rachel was silent for a minute. They'd had this conversation before. Finally Rachel asked, "How was Tyler this weekend? If he's yelled at you once, I'm coming over there to slap him myself. And why you let that man make you move again is beyond me. A woman needs to nest. She needs to plant roots. She needs to—"

"You can breathe, Rachel. It's key to survival."

"Well, that man just infuriates me. How can one living creature infuriate someone so much?"

"Rach, stop."

She could hear Rachel's buff-colored nails tapping on her countertop. She knew they were buff-colored because that's all Rachel wore. And she always talked on the phone in the kitchen near food. Rachel loved food. They both did. They claimed it was part of being a Southern woman—okay, any kind of woman. Women bonded over food. So Rachel felt they were closer if she was in the kitchen eating something while they talked.

"Tyler's my husband," Grace reminded her friend.

"Yes, he is. He is your husband. And usually I am an advocate for your husband, just as you are for mine. You know Jason always says you're the best friend of this marriage. But when Tyler doesn't value you like you deserve to be valued, Grace . . . well, it makes me angry. Anyway, I'm through venting. No more venting."

"Good. Now, you have successfully talked me home. Can I go now?"

"You can go. But please, please be kind to yourself this week. I love you, girl."

"You too," she said as she rounded the corner and reached for the garage door opener. "Bye."

Grace pushed the button to open the garage. Boxes were stacked floor to ceiling in the back. Tyler had promised to move some into the house so she could start unpacking this morning.

Not one had been moved.

Grace's body ached just looking at them. All she wanted to do was get unpacked and back into some kind of normal routine. For a moment she was grateful she had waited to open the garage door until after she had hung up with Rachel. She was too tired for another comment.

Miss Daisy greeted her at the door. "Hey, beautiful girl." Grace slipped her hand down into the champagne fur of her shih tzu and rubbed. Miss Daisy's moans came out soft but clear. "Oh, I know. I know."

The dog wriggled free from Grace's hand and went to stand by her bowls. Grace followed her. Both were empty. "Didn't Daddy feed you this morning?"

Miss Daisy looked at the bowls and then back at Grace, her meaning clear. Grace set her stuff down on the kitchen counter and filled the bowls, then left to the sound of slurping. She made her way down the unfamiliar hallway to the bedroom. Tyler was still sleeping. No surprise. That's the way she found him most mornings lately.

At thirty-three, Tyler was considered old for professional hockey. Hockey wasn't an old man's game. Few players stayed around until their forties. Or rather, she should say, few were *kept* until their forties. About the time Tyler hit thirty, he'd started getting yearly renewals in place of the multiyear agreements he'd signed before. The three years since then had been a spiral down to painful places.

Grace moved quietly to the closet for her pj's and her black ballerina bedroom slippers. After she had changed, she walked over to the bed. Tyler never stirred. His sour-sweet breath seemed to fill the room.

Her feet moved slowly back to the kitchen, where she poured a large glass of sweet tea. Her mother had always made sweet tea so thick it practically oozed out. Grace didn't think the recipe needed changing. Since turning thirty-five, she had thought occasionally about switching to an artificial sweetener, but then she'd decided there was enough in her life that was artificial. This was the one place she was going to let the real thing have its way. She didn't care if it had its way with her hips as well; she wasn't giving it up. Sweet tea was her liquid sunshine. And she needed some sunshine in her life.

She picked up a wadded napkin from the floor and opened the garbage can to toss it in. An empty Jack Daniel's bottle lay at the bottom. She dropped the napkin in the can and closed it, then went to the garage and found a box she could carry. She had deliberately used small boxes to pack, knowing this would probably happen—a true sign of how low her expectations had dropped. She set it down in the kitchen and picked up her utility knife, expertly slicing the tape that sealed it. *Dining Room* was written large in black Sharpie across the side.

She could close her eyes and do this, she had done it so many times. She should be a professional mover. In ten years of marriage she had lived in two apartments, one town house, and three different houses—not counting all the remodeling jobs she'd endured in many of those homes. She had the process down pat. That didn't mean she liked it.

This was Tyler's pattern—the same pattern he had with cars and electronics and new clothes. To her it felt like some desperate attempt to fill a vacancy in his soul with something new. When they moved the last time, she'd told him that was it. They didn't need another house. They didn't need another car. And she wasn't moving again.

She *had* told him that, hadn't she?

She put down the knife and wandered aimlessly through the rooms. This house was big—bigger than the two of them could fill up. But it had been a foreclosure, so they had gotten a good deal—something they really needed, considering their experience with their previous house. Tyler had been so excited about buying in a "high-end" gated community on the outskirts of town, going on and on about what a good investment it was. But he hadn't considered the inflated market and the ridiculous mortgage. They'd lost more than Grace liked to think about when they sold that house. But it had been bleeding their retirement accounts dry every month, so at least this move had stopped the monthly hemorrhage.

The new house wasn't that bad, actually. The roof was tin, the floors were pine, and the marker outside declared it was of some historical importance. Being downtown was a plus. And then there was the hope. She always tried to hold on to that hope. Could this be the home that held their healing? Maybe.

Yet every room in this new place still smelled and felt un-hers. It held no memories. She didn't know how to get around it in the dark without hurting herself.

She peeked into the bedroom again. Tyler had rolled over

and started to snore. She walked back down the foreign hall of a home it would take her two years to get used to—just in time for Tyler to want to move again.

A small section of her longer bangs fell in her face. She readjusted the clip. Back in the kitchen, she leaned over to pull a dish out of the box and realized Miss Daisy was staring at her. She couldn't help but chuckle at the ridiculous expression on this dog's face. It was truly a face only a mother could love.

Miss Daisy weighed almost eighteen pounds, far more than most shih tzus. Her eyes looked at times like they might pop right out of her head, and her underbite was bad enough for braces. And ornery—oh my, was she ornery. She never came when she was called. And she made it clear that she would let you know if and when she needed you. Otherwise the world was hers, and you were simply privileged to live in it. She was named after Jessica Tandy's wealthy character in the movie *Driving Miss Daisy* because she, too, pretty much had everyone doing what she told them to do.

Grace and Tyler had bought her a week after they got back from their honeymoon. They'd needed a dog like they needed a hole in the head, and they couldn't really afford her. But of all the money Tyler had spent in their years together, the three hundred dollars they'd spent for Miss Daisy had been the most worthwhile.

Grace rubbed her eyes. It wasn't even noon yet, but she'd been up for nine hours already—a full day. This was what her body had been doing for ten years. It was what she knew. But that didn't make it easy.

She reached for her glass and took another sip of tea. She had already consumed two glasses, one she'd bought for herself from McDonald's on her way to work and another she talked an intern into getting for her during one of the morning news breaks. She had done an entire morning news program and four segments during the *Today* show, and now she had a mountain of boxes to unpack. Forget sunshine—she needed sugar and caffeine.

The thought of that mountain overwhelmed her in that moment. The enormity of the task felt as if it might take her breath away. With every move, she and Tyler seemed to have accumulated more stuff—ten years' worth of it—and not just what awaited her in those boxes. If you could put ten years' worth of accumulated resentment and disappointment into boxes, how high would the mountain rise?

She reminded herself of the online devotional she had read this morning, one she had e-mailed to her every day. "Faith and obedience will move mountains," this morning's entry had said. "Mountains of evil. Mountains of difficulty. But they must go hand in hand." She had always tried to be obedient. But the faith part—well, that seemed to be getting harder and harder.

She tugged at the bottom of the black zippered sweatshirt that hung loosely over the black tank top and pants that served as her pajamas. Tyler liked to keep it freezing in the house when he slept, which usually didn't start until the wee hours of the morning.

She was pretty sure Tyler wouldn't be awake for at least another three hours. There was no telling when he had finally gone to sleep, though he'd been beside her when her alarm clock rang. That wasn't always the case. Some nights Tyler would watch the sun fall and rise before he ever let his head touch a pillow, and she'd have to leave for work before he made it home. You would think she'd be used to his schedule by now, but every day it bothered her. Even if their relationship had been wonderful—which it wasn't—being married to someone you hardly ever saw could take its toll.

When she pulled crumpled newspaper from a moving box, the red corner of a small box that rested inside grabbed her attention, tugging her heart to places she always dreaded going. The Santa plate and mug designed for Christmas Eve and children's magic were nothing but reminders of what her home lacked. There had never been children's magic at Christmas for her. She had never watched her child climb the large rubber-matted steps of a bright-yellow school bus going to a world of learning and laughter as she stood in her robe with a steaming cup of hot tea. She'd never wiped her child's tears after a lost game, a broken arm, or a broken heart. She'd never hung Sunday school artwork on the refrigerator or kept a "mommy's calendar." But with every move, she still packed up the plate and mug as if one day her own Christmas magic would happen and she would have a child of her own.

She swiped hard at the tears, tucked the red box in the farthest corner of the china cabinet, and said a brief prayer. "Please, God, let this be the house that holds the laughter of a child."

Her phone vibrated on the countertop. She picked it up and saw her mother's picture staring back at her. "Hey, Mom." She carried the phone over to the large picture window that overlooked Franklin's quaint Second Avenue.

"Hey. How's the moving going?"

Grace let out a soft laugh. "Like all the rest."

"Anyone coming to help you?"

"After the fourth move, I quit asking people, Mom. I decided I wanted to keep my friends."

She could hear the concern in her mother's voice. "You need me and Dad to come?"

"No, I'm good. I'll have most of it done by the end of the week. And then we'll be back to normal."

"You okay, baby?"

Grace shook at her urge to cry. Her mother had heard enough of her pain through the years. Now, she tried to let her see as little as possible. She didn't want her to hurt too. "Yeah, all good. It really is a beautiful home, and I've always wanted to live in downtown Franklin. Tyler is convinced it's a good investment."

"Have y'all decided where you're going to church yet?"

"No, hopefully we'll visit a few here once we get settled."

"You couldn't get Tyler to stay where you were?"

"No. He just isn't getting what he needs there, Mom. Not all churches are for everyone, you know."

She heard the deep sigh in her mother's voice and hoped a sermon wasn't next. She was too bone weary for that. She was grateful her mother could tell. "You're taking the week off from work, right?"

"No, I'm working."

"Grace, you can't move and work at the same time."

"Mom, it's fine. It will get done when it gets done."

"Well, please take care of yourself. When is the last time you baked something?"

A distant memory of a chocolate cake came to mind, but for the life of her she couldn't remember when she had baked it. With the packing, work, and now the move, the last month had just gotten away from her. "I can't even remember. Can you believe that?"

"Honey, promise Mom that you will do something for you. I'm sending you some money that is for you to go spend. Not on the house. On you."

Grace couldn't help but laugh. She had money of her own. But her mother had been sending twenty-dollar bills in cards since she was in college. She could tell her not to, but it would do no good. "I'm fine, Mom. Honestly."

"Well, if you need us, please call. You know either of us would be there in a minute."

"Sure. I know. I'll call."

"Love you, honey."

"You too, Mom."

She hung up and walked over to the sofa. Her body sank into the green velvet and stretched out. She was so tired. She pulled off her slippers and realized she had forgotten her socks. She always slept in socks, though at some point every night she would kick them off and then find them as a lump under the covers the next morning. Now she was lying here with her body aching, her feet cold, and no clue on the face of the earth where she had packed the blankets. And she couldn't get up if she tried. Not right now.

In a moment she felt something land on the sofa. She looked down to find Miss Daisy staring at her with those large black eyes. "Whatcha doing, girl?"

Miss Daisy didn't respond. She simply walked around as if looking for just the right spot to plop herself. Then she did—right across Grace's feet.

In all the years they'd had her, Miss Daisy had never done

that. Not once. This dog hadn't even wanted to sit close to them when she was a puppy. And now, in this moment when Grace's body was as drained as her soul, this creature as stubborn as kudzu chose to lie across her feet.

A thought brushed through her heart: *This is how much I love you—enough to warm your feet.* She knew it was from heaven. It had blown through her on more than one occasion in her life. And right now she needed it—no, she was desperate for it.

She pulled the sofa pillow up tightly underneath her face. As a deep rush of tears fled to the surface, she pulled it in tighter. She would bury her cries in the down feathers.

Just as she had done so many times before.

{ *Chapter 4* }

SCARLETT JO PULLED at the bottom of her lime-green sweater, the phone against her ear. She loved wearing this color. It made her think of key lime pie, and she loved key lime pie.

The school had called to tell her that her fourth child, Tucker, was sick. She knew he was sick all right. He was sick of school. He had done this every year since he'd started kindergarten, which was five years ago. At some point near the end of the school year, he would report some kind of complaint. One year he'd said he had typhoid fever. Another year he'd tried to convince the nurse he had tuberculosis, which triggered an uproar in the entire school. Truth was, Tucker could be pretty convincing.

Now his pitifully frail voice came on the other end of the phone. "Hello."

"Tucker, what is wrong with you?"

"I'm sick, Mama." His fake cough blared through the earpiece.

She pulled the phone away from her ear. "Well, this is what I have to tell you. If you are sick, this is what your week is going to look like. You ready to hear?"

He hesitated. "Yeah."

"If I pick you up, you will go straight to your room and get in the bed. I'll bring you your dinner. There will be no baseball, no basketball, no football. There will be no dairy because dairy makes coughs worse. And if you forgot, ice cream falls into the dairy part of the food pyramid. Then, if you're still feeling poorly on Sunday when you go to church—and you *will* go to church—you will sit with me in the service, and when it is over, we will—"

That was when she heard a commotion on the phone. "I think I'm feeling better, Mama. Just talking to you has done something for me. Maybe I was just missing you or something."

She shook her head. "That's exactly what I was thinking. I'll see you when you get home."

"Bye, Mama."

The school nurse got on the phone. "Well, I'm not sure what you said, but the color came into his cheeks while you were talking."

"It's a miracle, I guess." They laughed and the nurse hung up. Scarlett Jo pressed the End button on the phone and shook her head again. This was her payback for passing along her drama gene to Tucker. At least that's what Jackson loved to remind her of.

She picked up her pink-flowered key chain, grabbed the

caramel pecan round she'd picked up that morning from Merridee's, and headed out the door. A jogger's dark-brown ponytail slapping against a slim back caught her attention.

The jogger's name was Amanda. She lived a few streets over, had a couple of little ones who rode the bus with Scarlett Jo's boys, and she ran every morning about this time. Dark curls bounced at the end of her long ponytail. A pretty woman, though Scarlett Jo was convinced the child needed food. In fact, one day she had pulled up beside her and invited her to breakfast. The girl's thighs needed biscuits.

But something else about Amanda concerned her. In twenty years of ministry, Scarlett Jo had encountered all different kinds of women. There were those like herself, completely satisfied with the men they had, though not unable to appreciate a fine specimen like George Clooney or Brad Pitt. But there were other women who seemed to walk around with an Open sign. They had that inviting way. And even though Amanda was a wife and a mother, there was something about her that Scarlett Jo discerned as available for more. Scarlett Jo hoped for the day when she could get Amanda over for biscuits or something and maybe get into her heart at the same time.

Scarlett Jo started down the steps, then stopped, turned, and hurried back inside. She pulled a small crystal vase from the cabinet above the refrigerator. She was grateful in moments like this for her height. Her poor mother was just under five feet tall, and the woman practically had to carry a step stool everywhere she went. Scarlett Jo half filled the little vase with water, then grabbed some scissors and went out the door, breathing in the beautiful Tennessee spring morning.

Franklin was pretty quiet today. It usually was this time of morning, right before the lunch crowd took over the restaurants and the streets. Jackson had told her to wait until the weekend to visit the new people on the block, but that seemed ridiculous. Being neighborly meant you were there when your neighbors needed you. These people had just moved in, so they needed food, fellowship, and friends. They needed to know that the people on their street were amiable and inviting.

She clipped a couple of yellow daylilies from the plants that were flowering beside her porch and carried them inside. She stuck them in the vase, grabbed the pastry box again, and headed back outside to make a new friend.

✿ ✿ ✿

A knock on the door startled Miss Daisy from Grace's feet, waking Grace as well. She had fallen asleep hard. She looked at the clock on the newly installed cable box. It was eleven thirty. She had slept for about forty-five minutes, and the fog was still heavy on her head. She was in no way ready for company. She zipped her sweatshirt up a little higher. Her bare feet made their way to the foyer, and she saw her bright greeter through the glass-paned door as soon as she rounded the corner. Miss Daisy was standing at the door with her head thrown back, barking. Her barks came out more as a howl sound. That sound had been one of Grace's favorites for years.

"Hush, Miss Daisy." She nudged the fur ball back with her foot and opened the door to the beaming face of the statuesque blonde in front of her. As soon as there was room, the woman's hand shot out with a vase of yellow daylilies. "Here, sugar, these are for you." The voice came out like any true Southern voice—sweet, more syllables than necessary, and accompanied by an endearment commonly associated with baking products.

Grace took the vase. "Thank you. They're lovely."

The vase's relocation allowed her to catch sight of the huge daisies perched atop the woman's flip-flops. They had to be the largest shoe flowers she'd ever seen. But that might be appropriate since they graced two of the largest feet she had ever seen. Were they tens? Twelves? Bigger? The woman herself was pretty big. She stood a good head and shoulders over Grace's five-foot-three-inch frame. Grace always marveled at how people were fashioned so differently.

The woman's hand was still extended, and her smile widened. "I'm Scarlett Jo Newberry. I live just four doors down from you, and I wanted to come introduce myself."

"Grace Shepherd." Grace offered a smile of her own. She couldn't help it. The woman was so animated.

She also looked a little confused. "But you sound . . . Southern."

Grace laughed. "Born and raised."

"Well, I'll be. I thought—" Scarlett Jo stopped midstream as if catching herself.

"My husband is from New York, though."

The visitor gave an amused nod. "So y'all have a mixed marriage then."

Grace laughed again. She knew all too well how different Tyler's and her worlds were. He still made fun of the way she greeted most people with a hug, and he refused to use the word *y'all*. But he had gotten used to a lot of the things that she loved about the South, especially her cooking. Five years ago, she would have officially pronounced Tyler a naturalized

Southerner. Now they seemed to be back in Civil War territory. Civil. Yet still a war. "Yeah," she said, "every now and then a Yankee will be brave enough to snatch one of us."

Scarlett Jo snorted slightly as she slapped her hand at Grace. "Well, where'bouts?"

"Where'bouts?"

"Yeah, where'bouts were you born?"

"Oh. I was born in Atlanta actually, but my family moved to Knoxville when I was in high school."

Scarlett Jo's eyes widened. "Ooh, I love Atlanta. Oh, and Savannah and Charleston. I swear, if I believed in reincarnation, I would want to be reincarnated as Scarlett O'Hara so I could wear those fancy dresses and corsets and ride in carriages and all."

"Doesn't get much better than the South."

"Only I can't imagine trying to confine all this in a corset." Scarlett Jo gestured toward her ample chest. "Could you imagine being the poor soul who had to strap me in?"

Grace wasn't sure quite how to respond to that. Fortunately Scarlett Jo's mind seemed to wander for a moment, then focus on the item in her other hand.

"Oh, silly me, I brought you this too." She stuck out a white box with a cellophane cutout on the top. Some kind of gigantic sticky bun peeked out at Grace through the window. "These caramel pecan rounds are sinfully good, and I've always thought moving is a perfect excuse to eat sweets." Scarlett Jo's half laugh, half snort came out with no apologies. "That's why I've declared every day is moving day. Hey, I'm always moving something from one place to the other."

"This does looks delicious," Grace offered. "My husband and I will enjoy this."

"Just the two of you?"

Grace shifted, but with her hands full, she couldn't shift far. "Yes, just the two of us. And Miss Daisy here, of course."

Miss Daisy seemed to raise an eyebrow as if to make sure they knew she was listening.

"Well, I have five boys who are completely rentable, and on some days I will be more than willing to send them over for free. If you need lawn services or gutter cleaning or you simply want to be entertained, they are at your service."

Grace smiled. "I'll definitely remember that."

"Do you need anything? I know how hard moving is. I could fix you a meal, get you some groceries—honestly, anything you need."

Grace could use all of the above. "No, we're good, I think."

"All right. But remember, I'm just a few doors down, and I'm always available. Whatever you need—you come get me anytime. I just wanted to let you know you have neighbors who're glad you're here. That's all."

"That's very kind of you. I really appreciate it."

"Okay, well, I'm off to go to Harris Teeter. It's super doubles week."

"Super doubles?"

"Oh, child, do you not know about couponing?" She seemed to stop herself, then laughed as if she realized it was a stupid question. She flipped her hand at Grace. "You don't need to know a thing about couponing if it's just two of you. I'm feeding a pack of wolves at my house. If I didn't know how to coupon, my children would have had to eat me by now. But if you ever want to learn how to do it, you just let me know. It is crazy, girl! I can go to a store and leave and they've paid me money."

Grace did know about couponers. Recently, her station had even aired a clip of a woman dressed in a cute jacket and nice shoes, digging through a recycling bin in search of coupons. She wondered if she'd ever catch sight of Scarlett Jo in a Dumpster. It didn't seem out of the question. "I'll remember that," she said.

"Okay, I hope to see you soon," Scarlett Jo offered as she headed back down the sidewalk. She turned sharply. "You look so familiar to me. Have we met before?"

Grace got that a lot. "No, I don't think so. I'm sure I'd remember." She eyed Scarlett Jo again. There was no way she could forget.

Scarlett Jo shrugged as if she wouldn't worry about it anymore that day—sort of like her namesake. "Well, you have a wonderful day, sugar."

"You too." Grace watched her new neighbor as she walked up the street. She had a sneaking suspicion this wouldn't be the last time Scarlett Jo Newberry knocked on her door. She smiled at the thought. Grace was neighborly by nature too. It was in her DNA. Tyler could be out trimming the hedges and completely ignore a neighbor walking by. Grace couldn't. Making connections with people was one of the ways she kept herself feeling alive.

That's why she still cried at sad news stories, even if she was the one delivering them. Her first two years of being a broadcaster, she'd thought she might get fired for it. But when the viewers started calling in about the new "anchor lady" who shared their sorrow, she'd figured she could let the tears fall if they needed to.

She brought the pastry box to her nose as she made her way to the kitchen. Ignoring the boxes at her feet, she opened the one in her hands. She took out the large round bun and cut off a section, which she placed on a paper towel and stuck in the microwave. The whir of the motor was the only sound in the quiet house. She stared at the spinning pastry through the glass and watched as the edges of the caramel icing began to melt and a few pecans slipped down the side. Then she popped the door open, poured a cold glass of milk, and carried her treat out to the back porch.

Miss Daisy followed closely. The dog could smell food like a reporter could find bad news.

Five boys . . . Grace settled into the porch rocker and curled her feet under her. What would she have done with five boys? She wished she'd had the chance to discover that. The icing dripped on her finger. She licked it off, pulled off a little piece of bun, and stuck it down for Miss Daisy. The dog threw her head back and chomped as if she were eating a pork chop. "You're supposed to savor it, Miss Daisy. Not scarf it."

The door to the porch opened. "Morning, Gracie."

She turned. Tyler's brown hair stuck out all over his head, though that was pretty much how he wore it most of the time. His eyes were bloodshot, his gait slow. He leaned down and gave her a peck on the cheek, his five-day scruff rubbing against her skin and the stale smell of last night's activities as familiar as Miss Daisy's attitude. The disappointment she felt over this new friend he'd invited into their marriage over the past few years was no longer a passing feeling. It was as consistent a presence in her heart as the empty Santa dishes were in her moving boxes.

"Morning," she said. "How did you rest?"

"Good. Good. Whatcha got there?"

"Oh, it's a pastry. A neighbor brought it. She lives a couple of doors down. Sweet lady." She stuck another bite in her mouth.

"Smells good. But I know it can't be as good as the ones you make."

Grace usually made homemade cinnamon rolls every Monday for Leo. They were his favorite. She always left a few on the counter for Tyler. He loved her cooking. And she couldn't deny that her cinnamon rolls were good. On her darker days, in fact, she would make a batch and eat most of them herself—then she'd climb onto the treadmill and work it off for an hour. It was a sad way to self-medicate, though better, she supposed, than Tyler's choice. But she said, "Don't be so sure. This is pretty wonderful."

"I'm going to grab one, then head out to the Sportsplex for some PT," he said. "And I've got that fund-raiser fashion show tonight for Vanderbilt Children's Hospital."

She felt her body stiffen. "Tyler, I can't unpack this house by myself."

His jaw twitched. Then his words came out with a familiar edge—an edge she never got used to, one that turned quickly into seething or an outright explosion. "We'll get it done when we get it done, Grace. You might just have to live with a little clutter for a while."

She hated clutter. She hated undoneness.

He reached down to scratch Miss Daisy's head. "You girls have a good day. I'll be home in a couple of hours, and we can take back the truck. But I won't be able to start unpacking until tomorrow."

"What time is the fund-raiser?"

He ran his hands over his face and through his hair. "I think it's seven. But, Gracie, you don't have to come."

"I already RSVP'd before I knew we were moving this weekend."

"That's silly. You know you go to bed by seven thirty. And you look awful. I mean, exhausted."

His way with words never ceased to amaze her. "I want to come," she said more firmly. "You don't do that much in Franklin, so when you're here, I like to come. You know that."

He hesitated just a second too long. "Okay. Cool." He leaned down again and gave her another peck. "Now I'm going to go eat whatever that is you're eating and then get some therapy for this beat-up old body of mine. I'll see you later."

She didn't respond. He closed the door behind him.

Why did everything have to be an issue? She let out a deep sigh. She hadn't even realized she was holding her breath.

❀ ❀ ❀

Zach walked into the large conference room at his office. He caught a glimpse of the old-but-new Franklin Theatre marquee before turning his gaze to the woman who sat at the table. Her fear was as palpable as the chair he had just pulled back. He extended his hand. "Hello, I'm Zach Craig."

She barely moved. "Marissa Martin. Thank you for seeing me."

He studied her striking blue eyes. They stood out in stark contrast to the white hair that framed her face. It wasn't a gray white, but a frosted white or something. A beautiful woman for her age. Classy. But her expression made it evident she didn't feel beautiful today.

He sat down and tried to be wise with each word he chose. "Would you like to tell me why you're here?"

She shook her head. The tears that filled her eyes made him

suspect that gestures might be all he'd get for a while. "Tough day, huh?"

She nodded this time and dabbed at her eyes with a wadded tissue.

He placed his arms on the table. The sleeves of his white button-down creased in the folds of each arm. "Am I the first lawyer you've consulted about this matter?"

She dabbed again. The nod followed a moment later.

"Well, why don't you just start wherever you need to, and we'll go from there. I'm in no hurry, so take your time."

The corners of her mouth turned down in an effort to hold back the surge that could erupt at any moment. Zach had seen it more times than he could count. They'd try so hard to stop it, but pain wouldn't always bow to sheer will.

She exhaled slowly. "I've been married for twenty-five years, Mr. Craig."

"No formalities here. I'm just Zach."

She brought her hands down, resting them on the edge of the planked-wood conference table. Her fingers laced as if by instinct. He noticed the white tips on her nails. "Zach. My husband and I have walked a long road, a road I would have walked with him anywhere. But I think it's far worse than I ever imagined." Tears raced down her cheeks. She let them fall without apology, then took took a deep breath and collected herself.

"I have one beautiful daughter. She's in college now and will be devastated by all of this, so I am trying to take care of it as quietly as possible."

His leather chair squeaked slightly as he leaned back and listened.

"My husband admitted to me quite a few years ago that he was struggling with pornography. I'd known that in my gut for years—known something was wrong. But whenever I asked, he tried to make me think I was crazy. I've learned since that denial runs pretty deep and wide with such issues. But once he finally told me, I felt like we had a real chance. That we could really put it behind us and heal."

"But it's not behind you?"

She lowered her head and shook it. "Not at all. And it's not just the pornography. I've found some other things. Phone records. Solicitations. Things I never dreamed." She looked up. "I put some spyware on the computer."

"It's not on his work computer, is it? Because it is only legal on home computers."

"No. It's on my computer. Can you believe that? He was using *my* computer." Her voice broke. "My daughter would be devastated. I can't let her know."

He patted her hand. "I understand. I do. But let's not worry about that right now. Right now you're just in my office telling me what's going on, that's all. Let's worry about those things when we get there. Okay?"

She nodded, and he could tell she was grateful for his presence. Her composure returned.

"So you're saying you have tangible evidence that your husband has been soliciting sex on the Internet?"

"Yes. The spyware records a digital image. It takes a screenshot every five seconds, and it also records every keystroke that is made on the computer. So I got the password to his e-mail account and learned he's been hooking up with people from craigslist. I didn't even know you could do stuff like that.

I thought you bought used furniture on craigslist. I'm such an idiot." Her fingers rubbed her temples.

"You're not an idiot. You can find anything you want nowadays. Trust me. You barely have to search. Does your husband have any idea you know anything?"

She shook her head.

"You've been keeping this a secret?"

"Yes. I needed to know two things. I needed to have information to protect myself and my daughter, and I needed to know beyond a shadow of a doubt that there was no retrieving my marriage. I needed all of that before I came here."

"And you believe your marriage is definitely over."

The tears fell now before she could even nod. Her next words came out almost a whisper. "This is my line in the sand."

"Are you able to hang on a few more weeks?"

He saw a slight panic return to her eyes. "What do you mean?"

"I mean don't talk to him yet, keep your secret a little longer. I'd like to take a look at what you have, make sure we have enough to show that he is committing adultery." His next words came out quickly to try to avoid her panic. "You might have plenty. I just want to make sure you're covered."

He could tell she didn't want to wait. He'd seen this before too. By the time people worked up the courage to come see him, they were almost desperate to move forward.

"You're going to need the same strength that got you in my office today to carry you through the next two weeks."

She bit her lip. "He's going out of town this week, so that will help."

"Well, you've done a great job. And if he's going out of town, he'll probably do something else that will give you even more evidence. Let's just see what he does."

"You're sure?"

"Marissa, if you can't make it another day, you can go home tonight and tell him. I'll understand that completely. But since you've kept your secret this long, I think it would benefit you and your daughter in the long run to follow this thing all the way through."

Her eyes cleared and she nodded. "Then that's what we'll do."

"Any questions you have for me?"

"No. I don't think so."

"Okay, well, get me what you have as soon as you can and let me know if anything new develops once he's out of town. Then we'll get the next pieces of our plan ready. It wouldn't be a bad idea to hire a private investigator either." He watched the fear return to her face. "I have a couple of great ones I work with a lot. They could follow him if he's staying within the state."

Her words came out in stutters. "He's going to Memphis."

He walked to the large console that sat against one of the walls and opened the top drawer. He pulled out a couple of cards and handed them to her. "Only if you want to. It's just another layer of protection."

She took the cards slowly as she stood. Then she extended her hand. "Thank you, Mr.—um, Zach. I so appreciate it. Now, what about your fee?"

"I charge two hundred dollars an hour and require a twenty-five-hundred-dollar retainer. Usually it ends up being a little more. But honestly, with all the legwork you are already doing, we will probably end up pretty close to that. I can give you a contract to look over if you want."

She exhaled slowly. "That isn't as bad as I thought. Sure, yes."

He reached into another drawer and pulled a contract from one of the manila folders inside. When he handed it to her, she tucked it into the portfolio she had brought with her.

"Well, thank you again."

"You're very welcome. We'll do this together, okay?"

She gave him the best smile she had in her. He patted her arm and walked her to the door. After he closed it behind her, he moved to the window.

He pulled at his pastel-striped bow tie as he stared at the Franklin Main Street activity. It wasn't lunchtime yet, so most of the passersby were either retirees, visitors, or stay-at-home moms. He watched Marissa climb into her car and found himself wondering what Caroline's words would sound like to a lawyer. He shook the thought off. He didn't have to worry about Caroline. His wife was too wrapped up in her own world to suspect that something could be going on in his. He breathed a grateful sigh. Sometimes narcissism was actually a good thing.

{ *Chapter 5* }

"SLAP HIM AGAIN, COOPER. Mama dares you." Scarlett Jo set the plate of fried chicken down on the counter. "You may be thirteen years old, but you are not too old to be spanked."

Cooper rubbed the top of his head, mimicking his little brother, his hand moving his disheveled brown locks into another state of disarray. He spooned some rice onto his plate without saying a word.

"Mom, I can't eat this." Forrest stood in protest, nodding toward the chicken.

She moved the pot of field peas to a pot holder on top of the island and looked at her secondborn. "Forrest, look at your mother, baby. Tucker doesn't eat fried foods because they make him gassy. He has a legitimate excuse not to eat what's put in

49

front of him. But I happen to know that you love your mama's fried chicken, and it's never disagreed with you. It sure hasn't killed me. And think of your grandparents. Your grandmother is still alive and kicking. Okay, more alive than kicking, but she fried chicken every day for forty years of her life to feed all the men working in Daddy's tobacco fields. If it was good enough for them, it's good enough for you."

Forrest stood there, his plate pressed against his University of Tennessee T-shirt. "But, Mom, it's meat."

Now she remembered. Two days ago Forrest had seen some kind of documentary on TV and announced he was now a vegetarian. Last year he had given up vegetables because of insecticides. That had lasted until she made fried okra a week later. Who knew how long this one might last?

She stuck a spoon into the peas and placed her hands on the counter. "Forrest, I do apologize for forgetting. But you know Mama's got you covered. So get you some extra peas and butter beans for protein, and I'll try to figure out how to chicken-fry tofu. But what I will tell you is that God made the chicken, and he taught us Southerners how to fry it, and I personally am certain he is going to serve it at the marriage supper of the Lamb. And I—"

"Oh my, something smells so good," Jackson declared as he strode into the kitchen, gave Scarlett Jo a kiss on the cheek, and picked up a plate. "Boys, do you know how lucky you are to have a mother who makes this kind of meal for you? When I was growing up, my mother never did this."

"Dad, we know," said Jack, the oldest and his father's namesake. "Your mother never cooked. You ate cereal for dinner. You've told us that story a million times."

Jackson put a chicken thigh on his plate. "I have more where that came from."

"I love your stories, Daddy." Seven-year-old Rhett, the youngest, joined the conversation. Jackson had refused to name a child Rhett four times in a row. When the fifth child turned out to be another boy instead of the girl Scarlett Jo yearned for, he'd finally given in. He'd warned her that one day Rhett would realize he had to live with that name forever and would never speak to them again. But so far Rhett didn't seem to mind. He was as easygoing about the name as he was about the rest of his life.

They all gathered around the table, and Jackson gave thanks. As usual, the discussion was lively and boisterous, and Scarlett Jo reveled in it. This was the best time of her day.

As soon as Jackson finished his meal, the four youngest immediately asked to be excused. The rule was, no one could leave until the last person was finished. Jackson was always the last to finish, so his final bite usually triggered a general exodus. But Jack didn't rush away from the table tonight.

"How was your day, Son?" Jackson asked.

Jack picked another homemade biscuit from the basket that sat on the table, then reached for the jar of King Syrup and poured some on his plate. He talked as he put a spoonful of butter into his syrup and began to stir. "It was good."

Scarlett Jo folded her napkin and put it on her plate, then leaned her elbows on the table. She watched as Jack scooped his biscuit through the buttered syrup and enjoyed studying the man her oldest was becoming. Even though he bore no physical resemblance to his father, he was the most like him in personality—strong, kind, and steady.

"Did you see Sarah today?" Scarlett Jo asked. Sarah was Jack's friend who happened to be a girl. Scarlett Jo secretly hoped they would marry someday.

"Mom, I went to school. Sarah goes there. I see her every day."

"Were you nice to her?" Scarlett Jo prompted, hoping for more.

Jack spooned another large helping of the syrup mixture onto his biscuit and took a big bite. Scarlett Jo couldn't help but smile. She loved nothing more than watching her babies eat her cooking.

Then, before you could blink, Jack crammed the rest of the biscuit in his mouth and stood up from the table. Way up. At seventeen, he was already a few inches taller than her five-foot-eleven frame.

"Mom, I'm charming and a Southern gentleman," he mumbled through his last bite as he scraped his plate into the disposal. "Of course I was nice to her." He put the plate in the dishwasher, then came over and kissed her on the cheek. "But you're the only woman for me. And that was a great dinner. I'll eat your fried chicken any day."

Her heart melted, and she beamed up at him, eyes glistening. He placed a hand on his dad's shoulder. "Want to go look at that car with me? It's a little more than I've got saved, but I think I can talk the guy down."

"Sure, bud. Let me help your mother with the kitchen and we'll go."

"Okay. Just holler when you're ready."

"Will do." Jackson smiled at Scarlett Jo as their eldest left the room. "You are the only woman for me too, and I *love* your fried chicken."

She cocked her head and fanned her face, frantically trying to dry the tears. Her children called her a crybaby. She told them she got it from them.

She picked up the chicken platter, covered it in plastic, and stuck it in the refrigerator. Jackson carried the remaining dishes to the dishwasher and started loading them in. "So how did you like our new neighbor?"

She froze for a moment but quickly went back into motion. He always knew. He had a sixth sense or something. "She was cute. But she looked like I had woken her up from a nap." Before he could say anything, she held up her hand. "I know, I know. You told me not to, but I went over anyway."

"People who have just spent the last two days moving don't necessarily want visitors." He reached in and repositioned a glass. "I hope you at least took her something nutritious."

She scraped leftover peas into a plastic container, then handed Jackson the bowl. "Oh yeah. Super healthy."

"You're pitiful." He fitted the pea bowl expertly next to the plates and closed the dishwasher. "Listen, babe, do you mind finishing up here? I need to return a couple of phone calls, then go look at that car with Jack. And if there's any daylight left, I want to throw the ball with Cooper. We have a baseball game tomorrow night, you know."

"Go, A's!" she shouted. Then she added, "Go. I've got this covered."

He pulled her to him in a big hug. And made her wonder if maybe *this* was the best part of her day.

Jackson made his way to the bathroom to brush his teeth before he left with Jack. Scarlett Jo tidied the counter and wiped it down, their conversation about the neighbor lingering in her mind.

She was sweeping the floor when it hit her. The woman. Her face. The news. No wonder Grace Shepherd looked familiar. She was on TV—on that newscast Scarlett Jo liked.

"Jack!" she hollered.

"Yeah?" he called from upstairs.

She put her hands on her hips. "Yeah?"

He autocorrected. "Ma'am?"

"I need a googler!"

He walked down the stairs from the bonus room. "Mom, you've got to learn how to work a computer."

She stared at him like he had three heads. "Jack, I have five children. You don't have five children because you want to do things for yourself. You have five children so that when they are able, they can be your slaves. So come down here and get to work. I want you to google Channel 4 news in Nashville and show me a picture of the morning newscasters."

The computer was tucked into a small desk area in the kitchen. Jack pulled up a chair and tapped at some keys.

"I still think the word *Google* sounds like a disease."

"Mom, seriously, do you have to say that every time?"

The Internet browser came to life. "Did I tell you the Jeffersons are moving to Alma, Wisconsin?"

His fingers kept moving. "Where?"

She leaned over his shoulder. "It's this little teeny town. Doesn't even have a Walmart."

Jack smirked. "So how can they even live?"

"I know, right? Can you say, 'Hello, Internet shopping'?"

He looked at her and shook his head. "Mom, you are so weird."

That was when she saw it. The face of her new neighbor popped up. "That's her, Jack!"

"Who?"

"That's our neighbor. The new neighbor I met this morning."

"She's hot."

She slapped him on the back of the head.

"Ow." He rubbed his head as he walked away. "Well, glad I could help you with that."

Scarlett Jo leaned over the screen, trying to peer through the finger smudges. That was her for sure. Her new neighbor was the Channel 4 morning news anchor. No wonder the child was tired this afternoon. The woman had just moved, and then she had gone to work this morning before the crack of dawn.

She was going to go see Grace Shepherd again tomorrow, but she wouldn't take her pastries. Tomorrow she'd take her a Starbucks double espresso.

After Jackson had gone to work, of course. Yeah, definitely after that.

❀   ❀   ❀

SOL Restaurant on Main Street offered a refreshing alternative to the chain restaurants abundant in Franklin. The girls loved it, and so did Zach. If he needed a way to make them happy, this usually worked.

"Lacy, would you close your mouth?" Joy's face contorted as she stared at her twin. "It's gross. The way you eat is absolutely disgusting."

Lacy glared at her sister and exaggerated the chewing motions. "At least I eat."

Joy rolled her big blue eyes and nibbled a leaf from her salad. "At least I'm not fat like you."

"Dad, she talks like that to me all the time. She thinks she's all that. You ought to see how she walks around school—like she's too good for anybody."

The whine in Lacy's voice grated on Zach. The last thing he wanted at a nice restaurant on a Monday night was a Lacy meltdown. They could be loud and long and very unattractive.

He looked down at his seafood enchilada and changed the subject. "Why don't we talk about next year? I can't believe that you two are going to high school. I mean, where did my little girls go?" He picked up another chip and dipped it in the tableside homemade guacamole. This alone was worth the trip.

Joy didn't try to hide her disdain. "Dad, this is so silly. We aren't little girls anymore." She ran her hands through her long red hair. It was the same color as her mother's, though Caroline got help with hers these days.

"You'll always be my little girls."

The Lacy meltdown was averted as she dove straight into the conversation, her rich green eyes animated. The animation and the eyes were just like her mother's. "Dad, you seriously are going to have to realize that we're growing up. I mean, we'll be getting our driver's permits next fall."

"Oh no. You two driving? I don't want to think about that right now. Instead, let's think about all the things you're going to do with your father this summer. And how you won't be driving or dating until you're thirty."

"Dad, Mom has a lot of plans for us this summer. She's taking us on an all-girls vacation to the beach. That's why I got this new summer haircut." Lacy patted her brown hair. It was cut about chin length. He hadn't even registered the change. Nor had he heard about their summer plans, ones he apparently wasn't going to be a part of.

"Oh, babe, it's cute. Super cute."

She turned her head. "You didn't even notice. I had to tell you."

Joy saved him from himself. "And Lacy has two summer camps, and I have two summer camps. So I'm not sure what you have in mind, but with all we have going on and hanging out with our friends and stuff, there won't be a lot of time for father-daughter outings."

He cut another piece of his enchilada. "Oh, well . . . okay. It sounds like you have most of the summer planned, then."

"Yep." Joy put her fork down by her plate, leaned back, and folded her arms. She looked at his plate. "Are you done? Can we go now?"

He glanced at her plate. She had hardly eaten a thing.

"I'm not done." Lacy pushed her completely clean plate away. "I want dessert."

Zach wasn't sure how she could have inhaled her entire order of adobo chicken while half his entrée still sat on his plate.

Joy ran her eyes up and down Lacy. "You don't need dessert. You need to start running track or something."

Lacy pushed back hard from the table. "See, Dad. Why don't you do anything about that?" Her volume was escalating. He was grateful the large dining area was almost full and loud conversations were going on all around. "She does that all the time, and you never say anything."

Lacy was right, he realized, but he didn't want to reinforce her whining by saying so. He tried a different tactic.

"Joy, you are way too conscious about weight anyway. You're only thirteen. You should be eating and enjoying life. I want you to be concerned about your health, not obsessed about your weight."

"Right," Lacy huffed. "You don't enjoy anything. You came into this world with your forehead all scrunched up, and you've been that way ever since. How you got the name Joy I'll never know."

"Well, it's hard to enjoy life when I can't get away from you. You have been breathing down my neck since you came out of the womb." Joy was two minutes older and loved to remind Lacy of the nuisance that she was to her.

"Girls, that is enough. Lacy, what do you want for dessert?"

She picked up the menu. He was grateful that she was easily distracted. Joy stood and reached out her hand. "Can I have the key to the car? I'm going to wait out there. I can't stand watching her eat anything else."

Zach was tired of arguing. He didn't have it in him. Nor did he want this restaurant to feature entertainment courtesy of the Craig family players. He reached into his pocket and handed her the key. "Don't turn it on and run down the battery like you did the other night. Just roll down the windows and cut the car off."

She snatched the key from his hand and left without a word.

Lacy ordered the napoleon while he finished his dinner. "Dad, you seriously need to get some therapy for that girl. She doesn't eat anything, and she's always mean and angry—especially to me."

"I know, baby. I wish y'all wouldn't treat each other like that."

"Then why don't you make her stop?"

He looked at his daughter. "Lace, after a while Dad gets tired of fighting with the two of you. It never stops."

"You don't seem to get tired of fighting with Mom. So why can't you fight *for* me once in a while?"

The words fell hard against Zach as the waiter arrived, distracting Lacy once again with her pastry. He had never been so grateful for sugar. It afforded him one more opportunity to avoid the reality of what his family had become.

A reality that was closing in hard and fast.

{ *Chapter 6* }

GRACE PULLED THE BRASS HANDLE of the painted wooden door and made her way into the large ballroom of the Franklin Marriott Cool Springs. As the door opened, she caught a waft of some of the South's finest delicacies: barbecued pork, fried chicken, fried catfish. Puckett's was catering, and Puckett's was one of Franklin's best "meat and threes." She breathed deep as she scanned the crowd for anything or anyone familiar. She and Tyler ran in such different circles these days, they barely knew the same people anymore.

"Grace." A hand darted up from the middle of the room. Grace caught sight of Julie's blonde-streaked head and pushed her way through the crowd to the table where her friend sat.

"Here—you're at our table." Julie pulled out a chair. "Best seat in the house—right next to the runway."

Grace shared hellos with other wives of Tyler's teammates. The guys did the fashion show for charity each year, and with Tyler's extensive attention to fashion's latest trends, this was a perfect place for him.

"I can't believe you made it." Julie curled her arm around Grace's. "You never come to this stuff."

"I know. But this was so close to home, and I do like to support Tyler when I can. Besides, it's a great cause."

"Well, I'm glad you're here. How's the move going?"

Grace felt a dull throb in her lower back, as if the mere mention of the word *move* made her body ache. "Painful," she replied, reaching a hand back to massage it.

Julie grimaced in sympathy. "At least you can sleep in tomorrow. How nice will that be?"

Grace smiled. "I could sleep in if I had taken the week off."

Julie looked at her, stupefied. "You're working this week? I guess that lets you know I don't get up early enough to watch you. But seriously, you can't take a week off to move?"

"Wouldn't matter. My body would still wake up at two."

"Girl, you should hang out with me. I can teach you a thing or two about sleeping." Julie laughed, but her forehead didn't move with the laughter. Julie had been getting Botox for the past three years, though she was five years younger than Grace. Grace had never quite been sure why her friend would want to do that—or for that matter, whether Julie was really her friend. Sometimes she suspected Julie just wanted to be famous and stayed close to Grace in case the station ever had an opening. Grace had never asked if that was true, though. She wasn't sure she'd want to know.

"How's Clay?" she asked Julie.

Julie shrugged. "He's Clay. As reliable as an old shoe."

"You have it made, you know." Grace leaned against the chair, finally allowing her body to relax.

"How is that?"

"That man does anything you ask him to do."

Julie punched her jokingly. "He does not."

"Does too. And you know it."

A mischievous look came over Julie's face. "I know. It's wonderful, isn't it?"

Grace scanned the room around her. The place had people as tightly packed as Leo had her morning segments, and the long catwalk down the middle of the room made it feel even closer. "Yes, it is wonderful, and I hope you never forget how wonderful it is. You'd better not take advantage of him, Julie. He's great."

"But so is Tyler," Julie protested. "That man spoils you, Grace. There isn't a place he goes that he doesn't come back with some gorgeous handbag or piece of jewelry for you. Clay wouldn't even think about those things unless I told him to do it. What I would give for him to actually go out and get me something fabulous like that."

Grace laughed. "First of all, I don't need more jewelry or another handbag. Second, Clay wouldn't have a chance to get a handbag to you before you had gone and bought it for yourself."

Julie laughed loudly. "Well, there is that, isn't—"

The announcer interrupted their conversation, extending a welcome on behalf of the Friends of Vanderbilt Children's Hospital and Belk Department Store at CoolSprings Galleria, which provided the fashions for the show. Then a video began to play on the large screens on either side of the runway, highlighting the beautiful gift that Vanderbilt Children's Hospital was to families all across the Middle Tennessee area.

Grace couldn't help but dab at her tears as pictures of sick babies flashed on the screens. Surely the only thing worse than not having a child would be to have one and watch him or her suffer. Or even worse, to lose a child altogether.

When the food service began, Grace found herself relaxing. She hadn't really been looking forward to the evening, but she was glad she'd come. It felt good to be involved in something worthwhile, to think about something besides work and her own troubles. And good to spend time with friends, she thought with a smile, listening to Julie's animated conversation with the other women at their table. But she was stifling yawns by the time dessert was served. Ordinarily she would be in bed by now. She just hoped she could keep her eyes open until the end of the evening.

The music woke her up, though—a pulsating rhythm that began as the room lights dimmed and white lights surrounding the catwalk lit up.

"Here they come!" Julie squealed.

Wild applause thundered through the room as the first of Tyler's teammates took to the runway stage in their Belk fashions. Grace smiled at the awkwardness of Gary, a right wing for the Predators. He stumbled slightly at one point, only to get increased encouragement from the ladies, to whom he made a slight bow at the end of the runway.

Tyler was next, his self-confidence a stark contrast to Gary's clumsiness. The women clapped loudly as he strode down the runway, his striking good looks undeniable. When he saw Grace sitting near the edge of the runway, he leaned over and reached down his hand.

Her brow furrowed.

"Come here, Grace." He pressed his hand out farther.

She shook her head. Julie elbowed her. "Go. Are you crazy?"

Tyler's smile beamed large and bright enough to be seen in the back of the room, without the cameras that already showed his face in larger-than-life prominence on the two huge screens behind him.

"Come up here," he said.

She took his hand and let him pull her up with him, grateful she had worn slacks and the runway was low. Before she could even get her bearings, he took her in his arms and dipped her, then planted a kiss that made the room go wild.

When he released her, she gave a sheepish smile, raised a soft hand for a hello, and stepped down as quickly as she could. Her face burned with embarrassment. His beamed with pride as he strutted back toward the curtains.

"You are so lucky." Julie elbowed Grace as she returned to her seat.

"Yeah" was all she could offer, hoping against hope that video footage of that moment wouldn't turn out. She was taking a sick day tomorrow if it did. She would not endure the humiliation of having that kiss broadcast. Not knowing what she knew, which was that by the time Tyler's head hit the pillow tonight, he would be as wasted as the scraps on the plates the waiters were collecting. And that the man who had just kissed her ostentatiously in front of a crowded room could barely bring himself to touch her at home.

That was their world—their sad and ugly and secret world. A world of public performance and private emptiness. And she still wasn't sure how she had come to live there.

Tyler had only been the occasional drinker when they got married—a glass of wine here, a cocktail there, maybe a beer with chicken wings. But alcohol had never really been an issue for him until he started to get older and his body took more of a pummeling on the ice.

She knew that was hard on him. Older players on professional hockey teams faced exceptional pressure. But instead of working out harder or playing smarter or simply planning for a second career, Tyler had begun self-medicating. From a bottle.

At first he hid the extent of his drinking from most people. It had simply been their private issue. But lately he didn't seem quite as desperate to conceal it. Grace lived in fear of the truth somehow getting out. And nothing she had tried seemed to make any difference.

She'd asked a couple of his friends to talk to him. That enraged him, and he left her for two weeks.

She'd begged him to come to counseling with her—something that, honestly, they had needed for years. But Tyler wouldn't hear of it. He had his pride. He wasn't about to see a head doctor.

Now, in these brief few weeks he had off between the end of the regular season and gearing up for training, she was planning to reach out to him yet again. She'd been hoping that reduced job stress might make him more open, more relaxed. But the way he'd looked this morning when he got up made her suspect that hoping was all that would be accomplished.

When they married ten years ago, they'd both agreed they would wait to start a family. They were both young and career-oriented and assumed there would be plenty of time. But about the time Grace was ready to try, the drinking escalated, and

Grace learned something she didn't know about heavy drinking. Yes, it could lower sexual inhibition, but it also lowered testosterone levels. Which meant it got in the way of normal marital relations.

The first night Tyler couldn't perform, he was mortified. After all, Tyler was the ultimate performer. She assured him it was okay. But the embarrassment drove him to drink more, and the drinking just made things worse.

It happened four more times that same month. After that, he never touched her that way again.

She had wondered at first if Tyler was having an affair. But there was no evidence of that—at least not when it all began. These days, for all she knew, he could be having a hookup with a different woman in every city where the team played. But when it began, at least, it was all about the liquor. And that was bad enough.

Over time, the situation got worse and worse. The late-night calls for her to pick him up at bars. The explosive rages—though thank goodness he never actually hit her. The secrets from her parents. The excuses to friends. The call-ins on days when he needed to be training but couldn't get out of bed. She had told more lies for Tyler than she had ever considered telling in her life.

Then came the traffic stop. Tyler had clearly been drinking and driving. But the arresting officer happened to be the brother of one of Grace's close friends. So instead of actually arresting Tyler for DUI, the officer simply called Grace to come get her husband.

She considered letting Tyler go to jail, maybe learn his lesson. But the prospect of all that negative publicity led her to accept the officer's gracious offer. Maybe, she thought, the near arrest would motivate Tyler to try counseling or rehab.

It didn't. He refused to even admit he had a problem.

Finally, desperate, she left him for four months—long enough to shock him into getting some help. He confessed his drinking problem to the counselor—the first time he'd ever gotten honest with anyone. He checked himself into a good rehab center the counselor suggested. And when he got out, he begged Grace to come home.

Encouraged, she agreed. But he looked at her that first night they were back together and said, "Don't expect me to just go right back to making love to you."

Though the words shook her, she still held on to hope. They were at a different place than before. Tyler was being honest, working on his problem. They were at a place of possibility.

Two months later Tyler was drinking again. Their place of possibility turned out to be just another a bastion of false hope.

The kiss Tyler had just given her in front of a watching crowd was the first time he had kissed her like a husband in years. Oh, he kissed her—the obligatory small kiss at night, sometimes even a kiss that was soft and kind, but nothing that would allow him to go to any place of desire. He would not fail in front of her. If he was going to be judged by people, he was going to make sure that what they saw put him in the best light possible.

Even if the whole thing was a sham.

"Here comes Clay." Julie interrupted Grace's thoughts. "Oh, my word, he looks ridiculous. He should have taken lessons from Tyler before he got out there." She hung her head. "I can't look. Maybe no one will realize we're married. If he even thinks about pulling me up on that stage, he will sleep on the sofa for the next year."

Clay came near the end of the runway. His expression quickly registered that he had seen Julie's hidden face. Grace gave him her biggest smile. He looked handsome and kind. He gave her his best in return.

"Tell me when he's done," Julie whispered.

"He did wonderful," she reported. "That man is a treasure."

"What he is, is a nerd. You would never know that man slams people into acrylic partitions for a living. I wish he could bring some of that energy to our life."

"You need to cut him a little slack, Julie," Grace said as the houselights came up. She yawned, grateful the charade was over. She remembered now why she rarely came to events. She had spent the majority of the last ten years sleep deprived. She wasn't too keen on willingly putting herself in situations that drained her more.

People began to drift out into the lobby and head home. Tyler and Clay made their way to them.

"Gracie, I think me and the boys are going to go out for a little while."

She knew what that meant, but she saw no point in getting into it with him. Not at that moment. "Okay, well, I'd love to go with you, but—"

"Yeah, I know. Bedtime for you." He leaned over to kiss her. "You just go home and get some rest. We've got a lot of unpacking left to do this week."

Grace resisted the urge to scream. She looked down and fingered the lace edges of her short-sleeved wrap blouse. "What time do you think you'll be home?"

"Who knows? You know how us boys are."

"You should take Clay," Julie encouraged. "He needs to hang with some boys too."

Clay shook his head. "Nope, I'm going home. I worked out hard today, and I want to get this ridiculous makeup off of me—" he wiped his face and crinkled his brow—"and get into bed."

Tyler slapped him on the back. "Yep, that's my Clay. Always doing the right thing. Hey, Julie-girl, you'll make sure Gracie gets home okay, won't you?"

Julie shot him a flirty smile. "Will do."

Tyler extended his hand to Clay. "Good to see you, man. I'll see you later this week, I'm sure."

Clay's face was unreadable. "You too, Tyler. Great job. You're a pro at this."

Tyler threw his head back and laughed. He kissed Grace again and headed for the door.

Grace picked up her red patent-leather bag from the floor and gave Julie a hug. "Good to see you."

Julie still had as much enthusiasm as she'd had when they arrived. "It was a wonderful show."

"Yeah, it was."

"Let's do lunch next week." Julie's words came out quickly.

Grace answered, "Sure," although, honestly, she'd rather have to move again. She waved and hurried away before Julie could remember her promise to see her home.

It was dark when Grace emerged from the hotel. And she was alone—again. She drove the few miles to her new home, a home that felt no more hers than the man who had kissed her tonight. She took Miss Daisy outside to do her business and then walked into the bathroom and studied her face. She didn't see tired. She saw weary. And weary ran to deep-down places.

She slipped into her pajamas and wandered into the kitchen. She didn't really want to unpack, but she didn't feel like sleep either. Three hours later she took the last cardboard box that had held her kitchen stuff out to the garage and stacked it with the other thirty cartons she had emptied that day. Her kitchen was officially in working order, so now she could at least function. As she climbed the few stairs into the house, she rubbed her right shoulder. Her rotator cuff had been giving her a fit for the last three months.

The green fluorescent numbers on the microwave and the stove announced she had worked away most of her sleeping hours. She'd pay for that tomorrow.

Miss Daisy was snoozing in the family room, stretched out on her cheetah-print ottoman in front of the fireplace. Her body operated on Grace's clock, and at least she'd had sense enough to know when to go to sleep.

Grace picked the creature up in her arms and headed to the bedroom. "Come on, Miss Daisy. Let's get an ounce of shut-eye."

She set Miss Daisy down on the end of the bed, then walked into the bathroom. She stared at her reflection again and winced. There wasn't enough concealer in the Deep South to hide the dark circles that had embedded themselves under her eyes. She brushed her teeth, set the alarm for an hour later, and climbed into bed. Alone.

She laid her head on the pillow. Every piece of her seemed to melt into the bed. Her thoughts went to the day she had spent. The early morning. The boxes. The kiss. Disappointment stirred. She pushed it down. She needed to sleep, and she couldn't do that if she stayed angry.

"We've really gotten ourselves into a mess, haven't we, Miss Daisy?"

Miss Daisy only snored.

"Me too, sweetie. Me too." Grace closed her eyes.

She opened them again slowly when she heard the bedroom door ease open. She allowed the illuminated numbers on the alarm clock next to the bed to register. Almost two in the morning.

Tyler spent a long time in the bathroom. Then she felt the mattress yield as his body finally made its way beside her.

She rolled over and snuggled up against him, wrapping her arm around his waist. Somewhere past that disappointment lay the nagging hope that the kiss he'd given her tonight might actually have been an open door. "Did y'all have fun?"

He placed his arm over hers and laid a hand on top of her own. "Yeah. It was great." His words sounded only slightly slurred.

She moved her nose up under his ear and lay there quietly for a while. Finally working up the nerve, she spoke. "Kiss me now, Tyler. Right here. Just the two of us. With no one else here."

He was quiet. Not a word.

A lump climbed to her throat quicker than the pain could get to her heart. She raised her head. Light from the DVR cast a soft glow on Tyler's sleeping face. The sound of snoring followed only a moment later.

She lifted her body from the bed. She hated herself for asking. It was as if she loved to set herself up.

A tear made its way down the side of her face before she

even knew it was coming. She wiped it away quickly. Not now. She didn't have time to cry now. It was time to go to work. She willed the tears to dry as she walked into the bathroom, turned the nozzle, and listened to the water rush from the showerhead. In two hours it would be lights, camera, action. And once again, the makeup, the pretty outfit, and the perfect smile would cover all the pain.

{ Chapter 7 }

SCARLETT JO STOOD at the front entrance of the church, a stack of bulletins in her hand, eyes peeled for her new neighbor. She had visited Grace Shepherd three times this week. By the third visit she had mentioned the church. She hadn't wanted to push too hard. But come to find out, Grace and her husband were looking for a church. So this morning, while passing out bulletins and greeting members and guests, she silently prayed that Grace wouldn't back out.

"Scarlett, I do think your outfit is as orange as my last pumpkin."

Scarlett Jo never let Sylvia Malone spoil her day, even if the woman refused to call her by her full name. She insisted that *Scarlett Jo* sounded juvenile for a grown woman.

"Why, Sylvia, thank you. As I remember, that was a beautiful pumpkin."

Sylvia shifted her glasses to the top of her nose, rattling the dainty silver chain that held them around her neck. "It was *orange.*"

Scarlett Jo scanned her orange sundress and matching orange shoes and confirmed to herself that she looked lovely today. Jackson had told her she did too. So that pretty much settled it for her. "Lucky for me, orange is one of my favorite—"

"Did you see that?" Sylvia whirled around.

"See what?"

"That girl over there has tattoos all the way down her arm." Sylvia pulled at the bottom edge of her yellow suit jacket and then straightened her matching skirt, her lips pressed together in disapproval. "My granddaughter Mary Kate has one on her ankle. It's disgraceful."

Scarlett Jo still didn't know why Sylvia came to their church. She complained about the music and the preaching. She didn't like the old factory building where they worshiped. She fussed about allowing coffee in the sanctuary and believed that if you didn't look like her, you pretty much shouldn't be coming to church.

"A lot of people have tattoos nowadays, Sylvia." Scarlett Jo greeted a visitor and handed her a bulletin. Then she turned to look at Sylvia. "Please smile if you're going to stand here at the door. We want to invite people in, not scare them away."

Sylvia huffed. "Did you know that they are planning a women's event?"

"Yes, it's going to be wonderful."

"Did you know that they are having the women miss church on Sunday for it?"

"It's a weekend getaway, Sylvia. Every woman needs that now and then."

Sylvia's already-wrinkled forehead furrowed more deeply. "You don't go on a church retreat to miss church. No one should miss church."

"You ought to try it sometime. Might do you good. Now here, take some bulletins and pass them out with a smile, or go help in the nursery." Scarlett Jo caught herself. "On second thought, maybe you shouldn't help in the nursery."

Sylvia rolled her eyes at Scarlett Jo. "Why do I go here?"

"Because you love me, Sylvia. That's why."

Sylvia's gray head popped back as she stuck her nose in the air.

Scarlett Jo turned her attention back to those arriving. Ever since Sylvia started coming to church here, she'd acted like she hated both Scarlett Jo and Jackson. Yet she kept coming. Kept engaging. So Scarlett Jo kept believing that Sylvia would find her own heart just as worth examining as she did everyone else's. After all, if God could make a donkey talk and let a man be spit out alive after spending three days in a fish's stomach, surely Sylvia Malone wasn't too big a task for him.

A movement in the parking lot caught Scarlett Jo's eye. "Grace! Over here." She bounced down the stairs, waving wildly.

A smile swept across Grace Shepherd's beautiful face as she approached the church. A tall man walked beside her—ripped jeans, tousled hair, and scruffy beard. Scarlett Jo hurried over and extended her hand. "I'm Scarlett Jo Newberry."

The man's reflexes seemed to set him back at first, but then he took her hand with an awkward smile. "Tyler Shepherd."

"Oh, it's so nice to meet you." Scarlett Jo shook hands enthusiastically. "I'm your neighbor, and I have just fallen in love with your wife." She wrapped her large arm around Grace's petite shoulders and squeezed. "I'm so glad the two of you came today. I think you're really going to enjoy it."

She led the two of them toward the front door, her arm still draped around Grace's shoulders. "By the way, you look just beautiful."

"Thank you." Grace ran her fingers down the tiny strap of the handbag dangling from her arm. The hems of her white pantsuit fell perfectly across her yellow heels. She laughed. "You probably thought I only wore pajamas."

"Nah. I've seen you on TV." Scarlett Jo turned her head toward Tyler. "I hear you play for the Predators. Grace said it's been pretty hard on your body." She felt Grace's shoulders tighten beneath her arm.

Tyler's face wasn't inviting conversation. But he responded anyway. "Yeah. It can be pretty painful at times."

Grace chimed in quickly. "Yes, it's part of the price we pay for what he does."

"I hope once y'all get settled, you can take some time off to recuperate. " She looked down at Grace. "You too, sweetie. You should be taking time off."

Grace gave a nervous smile. "Oh, I'm doing okay."

Cold air from the sanctuary collided with them as Tyler opened the front door.

"Well, welcome to Ecclesia. We're really glad you came." Scarlett Jo gave Grace another quick squeeze, handed them each a bulletin, then showed them where they could sit. Tyler nodded but didn't speak. He didn't have to. Scarlett Jo never needed words to read people.

❀ ❀ ❀

"Well, I still think this is a strange place to have a church."

Zach rolled his eyes as he stepped out of the Range Rover into the church parking lot. His mother-in-law, Adele Whittingham, had come in for the weekend, and he had had about as much of her criticism as he could take. What he lived with during the week was painful enough. Adding Adele took it to Valium proportions. He'd found excuses to stay away from home yesterday, but he couldn't very well refuse to take her to church.

"Mom, I told her not to wear those jeans." Joy's voice rose sharply as she climbed out of the vehicle. "They're mine."

Caroline took a drink from her Starbucks cup. "Joy, would you hush? I don't want to hear anything else out of you."

Zach could hear music as they approached the church doors. It didn't matter what time he got up to start fixing breakfast; they were always late. But there was no chance of sneaking in quietly because the pastor's wife stood at the door.

Great. Zach really liked Jackson Newberry, but he had yet to understand how a man like Jackson could be married to a woman like Scarlett Jo. She was big, loud, and gaudy, and she always seemed to be in everybody's business.

"Hey, y'all. How are you this morning? So good to see you." Scarlett Jo's face beamed about as big as that white belt she had wrapped around that awful orange dress.

"Good morning, Scarlett Jo," Caroline crooned. "Good to see you."

"You too, Caroline. And, girls, you look so beautiful today."

"Thank you, Miss Scarlett Jo," they rang in unison.

Adele gave Scarlett Jo a polite nod as she walked past.

Who are these people? Zach blinked as Scarlett Jo grabbed his hand and pumped it.

"Morning, Zach. I swear, you have the most beautiful family. You should be so proud."

"I am." He looked past her to the front of the sanctuary, where the worship team was already in full swing. "Um, I'm looking forward to the message today."

"It's gonna be a good one. Jackson was tucked away all weekend getting it ready. And the special music's going to be great. I heard 'em practicing earlier."

Zach felt his pulse quicken slightly. "Yeah, the music's always good here."

His breathing slowed once he was out of her gaze. He made his way to the end of the row of chairs where his family had parked themselves. When he glanced at the worship team, shame gripped him as wide and dark as the large beams that held up the old factory where they worshiped.

He lowered his head and held on to the back of the chair in front of him. Every note that came from the mouth of the woman leading worship reminded him of the hypocrite he was. He looked at Caroline's face, fearing she could somehow see it, feel it, sense it in some way. But she was oblivious to him, her head stuck in her bulletin.

He raised his head and waited it out. It would be over eventually. In a little more than an hour he would be out of here. He wouldn't have to be tortured with his own heart for another whole week.

❀ ❀ ❀

Grace closed her eyes as the couple who led praise and worship sang. There had always been something about worship that she loved. It offered a healing of sorts, replenishing her for the week ahead. Between two of the songs she looked at Tyler, trying to catch his eye, wanting to share the feeling.

Tyler was texting. He didn't even look up. And she felt the optimism that this morning, this new church, had brought slipping away.

She pushed down the desire to disconnect too. Staying connected was what kept her sane. Alive. Hopeful. She knew that once hope disconnected, it would be over for her. Giving up was so easy when you faced the same demon year after year, day after day. She hadn't given up, but her hope levels felt as erratic as a thrill ride at an amusement park—some days climbing in abundance, some days plummeting to nothingness.

Church was one way she tried to hold steady. Obviously Tyler didn't feel the same.

They had actually met at a church conference she attended in Virginia not long after she graduated from college. His uncle had pastored the church, so Tyler's entire family was there, along with some of his friends. He was two years younger than she was, but he had never gone to college because he had signed with the New Jersey Devils fresh out of high school.

Grace caught his eye. He caught hers. They talked on the phone for six months before they had their first date. Every chance he had when he was off the road, he came to Nashville to see her. By the time the Predators picked him up, they were already engaged. Everyone said they were meant for each other, that they would have an amazing life together, that their children would be models. Now, at thirty-five, she was still waiting for that to happen.

They'd dated for a almost year before he proposed. His travel schedule and her work made the courtship challenging, but the attraction was palpable. Holding back from making love to him before marriage was the hardest thing she had ever done. But she had fought puberty, first love, and aggressive college men to save herself for this man. For this love. And she'd never regretted that decision. No. That was one out of all her decisions she didn't regret.

She deliberately moved her heart and mind back to the present, to the richness and warmth of this old factory at the edge of downtown Franklin. She had felt it as soon as she entered—that this was a place she could call home whether Tyler made it that way for himself or not. The woman leading worship spoke for a few minutes before she began the next song. As she spoke, her dark hair moved across her shoulders. And as the next song began, Grace let her soul drift away. Again.

When the final chord strummed through the speakers, she and Tyler sat down on the padded chairs. Tyler reached his arm around the back of her chair and rested his hand on her shoulder. She felt her heartbeat quicken, loving his touch. Craving it. She reached her hand up and patted his softly. He leaned down and kissed the side of her head.

For a moment, life was perfect. At least as perfect as their life could be.

❀ ❀ ❀

Scarlett Jo stood in the back of the building as Jackson gave a message unlike any he had given since their church had started.

He was broken and deeply passionate and at times even prophetic. His words came out with a boldness and an authority that only a man who had spent time alone with God could deliver.

Last night after the kids had gone to bed, he had told her he needed some time with the Lord. She didn't know when he'd actually come to bed—or if he'd slept at all. But this morning, he'd said he felt the Lord had a strong message for him to deliver.

Listening to him now, she had to agree. God did have something to say.

She took in the scene before her, all the heads that represented families and lives and hearts. And that was when she felt it. A deep pain in her chest. A pain that took her breath. She hunched over, gripping the large white daisy with an orange center that was clipped to the strap of her sundress. She almost screamed out that she was having a heart attack.

But as quickly as the pain came, it ceased. She caught her breath and straightened, trying to shake off the panic. As soon as she did, the pain struck again, this time harder and deeper. She clutched at her chest, her breathing rapid and short. But right before she broke out in a bad Sanford impersonation, the pain released her.

"God's heart is breaking today, people. I sense that in my spirit. His heart is breaking over your heart." Jackson's words reverberated through the building as if they were coming from a megaphone. "God, help us know what it feels like to have our hearts broken over our own sin."

Scarlett Jo stood upright and knew immediately that was what she was feeling. It wasn't a heart attack. Good thing she hadn't screamed out like she had wanted to. That might have been a little distracting. Then wonder washed over her. God was allowing her heart to sense his pain. His pain for the people in this room. His pain for the people he had entrusted to her and Jackson's care.

"You can only live with your heart shut down for so long. Eventually you will fight for your healing, or you will die. Those are your only choices. 'Today,' the Scripture says, 'I have set before you life and death, blessing and cursing; therefore choose life.'"

With that, Jackson Newberry had said all he was going to say. But Scarlett Jo knew the battle line had been drawn. And she and Jackson had been sent to the front.

{ *Chapter 8* }

BOXWOOD BISTRO HAD a wonderful Sunday brunch. Zach took a bite of his cheese grits and savored the Southern favorite.

"Are you going to eat that?" Adele asked as Caroline stuck her fork in the tiny dollop of cheese grits she had allowed on her plate. "Do you know how many calories are in that stuff?"

Adele counted calories like Mark Zuckerberg counted friends, and it showed. The woman was stylish and classy. Everything about her screamed "put together"—the nails, the jewelry, the clothes, the short brown, highlighted haircut. And she refused to be called any version of *Grandmother*, not even distant soundalikes such as *Gigi*, *Mimi*, or *Nana*. Instead, she'd always insisted that the girls call her Bella. He had no idea where she got the name. Probably googled it and liked it because it sounded remotely royal.

Zach watched the expression on Caroline's face change as she speared a lettuce leaf with her fork. He saw satisfaction in Adele's brown eyes. Caroline scanned the plates at the table. Joy's plate looked just like her mother's and Adele's—practically empty. Zach tried to push down the annoyance that rose at the fact that he had just shelled out sixteen bucks for each of these plates and none of them were eating anything.

"Did Caroline tell you of the changes we're making?" Adele's words stirred him from his consuming observation.

He shook his head and dug into his grits just because he could. "No, she hasn't told me of an upcoming change." He eyed Caroline, whose eyes were on her mother. To be honest, he didn't want to hear what they had up their sleeves, but he also didn't want the hassle of saying so. He glanced at his watch.

Adele's spine was stiff and straight against the curved back of the wooden chair. "I told her she should think about expanding the store. She needs to carry a line of clothes for girls Joy and Lacy's age."

"I can't stand any of the clothes around here. They are so . . . generic." Joy's words came out right behind her grandmother's.

Lacy picked up her glass of sweet tea. "Well, I love Forever 21."

"You would. You want to look like every other girl in school."

Zach sat back in his chair. He studied Caroline's face as it turned from her mother to him. It offered him nothing. She said defensively, as if he had already expressed his disagreement, "It's a great idea for future growth. Investment is always good." She waved her bite of lettuce but didn't actually put it in her mouth.

He felt heat on his face as his anger stirred. He wanted to scream, *When were you going to tell me about this? At what point did you think I might have a say in what we do with our money?*

"Who decided this?" was all he came up with.

Adele spoke first. "We did. This is a woman kind of thing." She spoke as if she were humoring him.

"Well, I don't like it." He turned to his wife. "We should have talked about this together."

She patted his hand as if he were a toddler. "Zach, Mom's right. The store is my issue. The law firm is your issue. I'll take care of what goes on at my store, and you keep the law business doing well. Then Mom won't have to help us any more than she already has."

The jab was real and purposeful, though delivered with the sugarcoating that Southern women were so adept in adding to insults. Adele had lent them some money over the last couple of years, mainly to keep this hobby of Caroline's going. The store lost money most months, not because she didn't sell things—Caroline had a great eye and top-notch sales skills—but because of all she spent on herself and on the girls. There was no boundary. No margin.

Zach put his fork down. "I've told your mother that I appreciate what she has done. If I haven't—" he turned to Adele—"let me say it again. Thank you for how you helped us this year. But this is something we will have to talk about."

It was as if he'd said nothing. It was Adele who patted his hand this time, her patronizing manner infuriating. If he cared more, he would hate her. But he didn't have the energy for that.

"You just don't worry about it. Bella will handle it."

He looked at Caroline, waiting for her to do something. Say something. He wasn't sure why. She never had before.

"Girls, let's go shopping this afternoon," Adele announced with a clap of her hands, the pale-pink polish as perfectly applied as the lipstick she had touched up. "We need swimsuits for our trip to the beach."

Joy placed her napkin beside her plate, her food swirled around as if it had been tossed by a hurricane. "Oh, Bella, that'll be so fun."

"I saw this cute two-piece," Lacy chimed in.

Adele stood and patted Lacy's back as she did. "Well, darling, you need to back off on the sweets if you want to wear a two-piece."

He shook his head in hopeless resignation. It always interested him how Caroline could be constantly concerned about their financial situation yet act as if there were endless resources for whatever she wanted. But then there was an endless resource—standing right there in her pink suit. And she had always been there. A marriage of three, he called it.

Not that he would complain. For this afternoon, at least, she would get Caroline and the girls out of the house and he could do what he wanted. As far as he was concerned, they could spend all the money—Adele's money—that they wanted to.

❀ ❀ ❀

Grace loved Mexican; she could eat it every day. And she especially loved Pancho's, a local Mexican joint located in a strip mall off Highway 96. She loved everything about the place— the burning Coca-Cola, the cheese dip, the chips, and those fajitas. They came out sizzling on the plate. If she were on death row, Pancho's fajitas would be her final meal. A bonus was getting to practice the five Spanish words she actually remembered from four years of Spanish class. The waiters indulged her clumsy Spanish with a smile.

Fortunately Tyler liked Pancho's as much as she did, so it was a Sunday afternoon staple. Now they were on their way home, stuffed to the gills with tortillas and cheese.

"What did you think of the church?" she asked as they made the short drive to their house.

"It was okay. Music wasn't awful. Sometimes the preacher seemed a little too preachy, if you know what I mean, and his wife is kind of ridiculous." He shrugged. "But it was fine."

She leaned her head against the black leather headrest in Tyler's Mercedes G-Class SUV. The vehicle was expensive and big and nothing either of them needed. It was the only compromise they could reach after last year's car war.

What Tyler had really wanted was a convertible. Grace had bucked against that idea with everything she had inside. It wasn't because she hated convertibles as such. If their marriage had been normal by any stretch, she would have bought him one herself. But to her, a convertible represented a mind-set with no thought of children and possibly meant he didn't even want children. So she'd refused, using every argument she could think of to keep that convertible out of their driveway. Which was how they'd ended up with a gas-guzzling monster of an SUV they really couldn't afford.

She'd bought her Prius to compensate as much as she could. She wasn't an environmentalist making a statement. She was simply trying to ensure they had some retirement money left when they grew old. With both their careers, they should have been doing all right, but the last house had bitten a chunk out of them. This had been no time to sell. Even though they'd gotten a good deal on the new house, the stock market and housing market had all but destroyed their savings. And Tyler's insatiable desire for the best of the latest didn't help either.

Tyler's words interrupted her thoughts. "Jeff and Heather are getting a divorce. He told me that last night."

Jeff was a teammate of Tyler's, a drinking buddy. And his wife, Heather, was one of the most self-absorbed women Grace had met. "I'm not surprised," she responded.

"He told me last night. She's whacked, you know."

Grace stared out the window. "I think it's sad."

"Jeff will be better off without her."

She could fight that comment, but it wasn't worth it. She didn't want to start an argument today or give Tyler another reason to get angry or drunk. But it bothered her that no one seemed to fight for their marriages anymore. That was Heather and Jeff's problem as far as she could see. Jeff could be incredibly thoughtless. And Heather definitely wasn't the type to make any sacrifices. No wonder they couldn't hold it together.

But she didn't want to think about Heather and Jeff anymore. She changed the subject. "What do you want to do when we get home? I was thinking I'd bake some bread for dinner tonight. We could have some of that good soup Rachel brought over."

"I'm way too full to even think about dinner. I think I'm going to go to the Sportsplex and sit in the hot tub, maybe get more rehab on my shoulder and ride some on the bike. I'm not going to rush home. But the bread would be great. I could have it when I get in."

She pushed the disappointment aside. At least he was talking about coming home. "Well, thanks for helping me the last couple of days. It made it go much quicker."

He patted her hand, which rested on the console between

their seats. " Hey, I wasn't going to make you move all by your-self. I've never done that." He laughed as if the thought was absurd. "That's why I scheduled the move for my time off."

They pulled into their driveway and went inside. The house was taking shape, starting to look remotely like a home. And as she walked through the door of a place with no painful memories, a piece of hope broke loose inside of Grace and made its way to the surface. They headed to their bedroom, where she set down her purse on the small wicker trunk by the door. Tyler went straight to the bathroom and pulled out his toothbrush. And as he started brushing, Grace felt an unexpected surge of desire run through her. Something about the closeness of their day, sitting with him, being touched by him, talking to him—all of that made her feel connected to him. And deep inside, she hoped it made him feel connected to her.

Her heart sped up. She did everything in her power to slow it down. She joined him at the bathroom counter and pulled out her toothbrush too. She pushed the electric switch and tried to let the brush's humming distract her mind and body. Because her body followed her mind, and she didn't really want to go where her mind was going.

After all these years without intimacy, she was still amazed that she desired it. She had prayed God would just shut down that desire. She'd begged him, *Take it away. Just take it away, and then I won't have to deal with the pain of rejection.* But years of prayers and sheer willpower had failed to accomplish that, so she didn't know how she could make it happen now.

Still, she tried. As she brushed, she tried. She rinsed and wiped her mouth, the ache inside her growing more intense and painful.

Her phone rang in her purse, but Grace let the call go to voice mail. It was probably Rachel. She would call her back.

She looked at Tyler, who was flossing now. What amazed her was that something in her soul still believed this time could be different. Believed that somehow, supernaturally, something had shifted with a touch or a word or an afternoon together that would cause him to desire her. To love her. And that all that was supposed to be would be.

The belief propelled her to his side of the sink. She scooted up behind him and wrapped her arms around his waist, the warmth of his body now against her own. He patted her hand again, as he often did. His touch was familiar, even comforting. But she wanted more. She wanted to be made love to like a young bride, with passion and longing and abandon. But she also wanted it with the beauty of years, with knowing and commitment. She wanted her husband.

Her hand inched down and ran along the edge of his jeans underneath his shirt. Before she could move farther, his hand grabbed hers and pushed it from his waist.

He rinsed his mouth before he spoke. "Grace, would you stop?" His anger was sharp and real.

"I'm sorry. I just . . ."

"I don't want to hear it. Can't you get it? I don't want to make love to you. But you keep pushing and pushing."

His words were loud and clear.

"What does it take for you to get it through your thick skull? I've tried to tell you nicely, and that doesn't work. So you leave me with no choice. I'm not going to humiliate myself again. For whatever reason, sex doesn't work with us. It just doesn't. And you can live in your fantasyland hoping it will get better, but that's not going to happen. I won't live through the humiliation or the look on your face as if I've shattered your world."

He reached for a towel and rubbed his face. "Now I've got to go."

The worst part was that she knew what he was trading her for, what he was always trading her for. Yes, he would go to the training center, get some rehab, and maybe ride the bike. But after that, he had an afternoon of drinking planned. By the time he got home tonight, he would be drunk. Why? Because he could. He was in a season where he could sleep it off before anyone else but her encountered him. And the pit he was digging was getting darker and deeper as the days and months and years ticked by.

She tried to stay soft, to defuse the anger any way she could. "Tyler, I don't think it has to be this way. If you'd just quit drinking, I—"

"I don't *want* to quit drinking." His face was red now, his anger palpable. But he was in complete control as he let the painful words spew. "I like drinking. I like the way it makes me feel, the way it doesn't make me feel. I like everything about it. What I don't like is living with a woman who can't just leave me alone and let me be the man that I am. You can walk around in your goody-two-shoes world and be judgmental about Heather and Jeff, but at least Jeff can breathe now."

He kept ranting as he went into the closet and began to pull his workout gear from a drawer. "What we did here, Grace, was nothing but a huge mistake. We just made a huge mistake."

She followed him into the closet, shaking her head as she did. Tyler had been mean to her before but never this mean. "We didn't make a mistake," she said. "I knew you were the man

I was supposed to marry. You can say it was a mistake if you want, but I will never believe that. Never." She was crying now.

He, however, was seething. He wouldn't look at her as he dressed, grabbed his running shoes and car keys, and stalked out of the closet.

She followed again as he left the bedroom and headed for the garage. "Tyler, don't leave like this. Let's talk. This is crazy. We can make—"

He slammed the door in her face. Her heart pounded in her chest as she stared at the white-painted wood in front of her. This strange door now carried the same familiarity as the doors in every home before it. It didn't matter where they lived or what new start they tried to make—new houses, new cars— none of it made a new life. No, that had to be chosen, didn't it? Just as Scarlett Jo's husband said today, it was all a choice. And Tyler had made it clear what he was willing to choose.

She walked to the bedroom she had set up as her home office. The house was silent, but pain and disappointment clanged through every vein in her body as they made their way to her heart.

Heather and Jeff were divorcing because they didn't try. But she had tried everything she knew. She had prayed. She had fasted. She had believed. She had loved. She had sacrificed herself. And yet here she was with a man who not only didn't want her but was now convinced their life together had been a mistake.

She lay down on the thick wool fibers of the plush carpet and wept. She hated that she was weeping—again. There had been moments when she thought for sure there would be no more tears. And yet each time Tyler rejected her, each and every time she set herself up to be rejected, they fell as fresh and new as if that rejection were the first.

Miss Daisy came up beside her and licked her face. Grace let her hand sink into the soft fur of her faithful companion. Some people wondered how someone could call an animal their child. But she knew how it could happen. When you were forbidden to have children because of a spouse who refused to be a true companion, an animal like this easily became something more. And so she'd let it.

"I can't do this anymore." She wasn't talking to Miss Daisy now. The carpet muffled her words as they poured out to the one true Companion who had faithfully listened to her through each one of these painful outbursts.

"Honestly, I can't. If you would just tell me that there will be a miracle down the road, I'd stay forever. I'd walk this out however I needed to. But you know. You know if Tyler truly desires healing or if this is going to be the cycle for the rest of our lives. And you also know what it would take to release me.

"I can't just leave a marriage—you know that. I can't be Heather. I can't be Jeff. I'm a fighter. I'll go to the bottom of this if Tyler will go with me. But I honestly don't know what you're asking of me here, what you want me to do. So, Father, show me, please. If this is over, give me what I need to let go."

She had never prayed a prayer like that before. And she had no idea if she was prepared for the answer.

{ *Chapter 9* }

"HOW DO YOU DO IT?" Zach studied the silky strands of dark-brown hair laced between his fingers. "How do *we* do this?"

"How do we do what?" She nestled warmly against his side on the couch. His office provided a safe place for Sunday afternoon encounters.

"How do we do our jobs, have dinner with our families, and then come here as if none of that exists?"

She turned on her side and looked at him. He loved her dark-brown eyes, the exact color of her hair. "The same way countless people do it, Zach. We shut out everything else, pretend it doesn't exist. Because this is what makes us happy. It makes me happy, being with you. This is where I feel alive." She leaned in and kissed him.

He returned the kiss, pulling her close, breathing in her scent. He knew exactly what she meant. These moments made him feel alive too. This was what made getting up in the morning worth it these days.

"I make you happy, huh?" he teased her.

She giggled playfully. "Yes. But I have to go."

He tightened his hold. "No. You aren't going."

She kissed him softly and scooted away from him. "I have to. If I'm supposedly at the store and don't come home with something, he's going to wonder how that happened."

Zach raised himself up on his elbow. "Do you ever think he suspects anything?"

She sat on the edge of the sofa and buckled her shoes. They had those pizza slice–looking heels. His daughters called them wedges. "Sometimes," she said. "I'm always the most nervous when I see him right after we've been together."

"You get nervous? You don't act nervous with me."

She stood and straightened the edge of her blue blouse, then leaned over and ran her hands through his hair, brushing it to the side. "I'm not nervous with you. It's out there in the real world where I get nervous." She kissed him softly. "I'll see you soon." With that, she grabbed her handbag and slipped out the door.

In the real world. This wasn't the real world for either of them, was it? There were no bills here. No fussing children. No nagging wife or preoccupied husband. This was easy. She didn't dictate his day or demand explanations. She just enjoyed him. He hadn't been enjoyed in a long time.

But he wasn't stupid. He witnessed the tsunami effect of relationships like this one virtually every day. He knew what they had together was based on illusion.

What would their life look like in the real world anyway? Family dinners. A mortgage. In-laws. All he was doing was acting out a fairy tale that in the end would hold nothing but heartache. Familiar shame spread through him like the cancer that it was, burrowing into the places where some semblance of life remained.

Just a few hours ago he had been sitting in church—a church where he'd invested his time and energy since it started two years ago. And just a few hours before that he'd woken up in his bed with his wife, the woman he'd promised to love and honor.

How did he get from there to . . . here?

He had always tried to be a good guy, do the right thing. He'd even saved himself for marriage, something a lot of the guys in his Fellowship of Christian Athletes chapter at college couldn't claim. He'd been a leader on his college football team, someone his teammates respected. He was a well-thought-of lawyer, a man others came to for advice.

This sinking had happened so gradually. Little by little, he'd found himself seeking comfort in places he'd never dreamed of visiting. And now here he was. Sprawled on the sofa in his office as if he had no common sense, no self-worth, no moral compass. No better than some of the jerks whose marriages he'd helped dissolve over the past few years.

Mental battles like this made him want to tell Caroline—just lay it all out there and let the chips fall. He wanted something to shake her, to awaken her to the fact that he existed. That he wanted to love her—or at least at one point had wanted to love her. Because what they'd had at first was real. When they first met, she was vulnerable and captivating. She was crazy about him and trusted him. But she could never break free from the strong arm of her mother or her own brittle perfectionism, and she could never forgive him for his shortcomings. Sometimes he wasn't sure there was room in her tightly controlled life for him. Maybe she wouldn't even care if she learned the truth.

He knew better, though. She would care. And he couldn't stand the thought of seeing her hurt. Of watching his children realize he wasn't the man he had claimed to be. Or worse yet, of the pleasure Adele would take in realizing he really was the failure she thought he was.

He got up from the sofa and put on his clothes, then ducked down the hall to the bathroom and studied his reflection in the mirror. The blue Izod shirt clung to his chest in the right places and made the blues of his eyes explode—at least Caroline used to tell him that when he wore this color. At forty-two he still had something to offer, and if Caroline couldn't see it, there was someone who could. Someone he made happy.

What amazed him was how he could make someone so happy and feel so miserable at the same time.

❀ ❀ ❀

"Scarlett Jo, did you have more coupons for Tylenol Precise?"

She put her hands on her full hips and gave a big smile to "my Ted," as she liked to call him, the manager of the Rite Aid up the street from her house. "Are you flirting with me or trying to give me a good deal?"

His smile was just as broad. "Scarlett Jo, you know I take care of my couponers. That Tylenol stuff is free this week if you've got that coupon from the newspaper."

"I've got this." She opened her three-inch binder and pulled out the Rite Aid sheet she'd printed off the Southern Savers website. Learning to navigate that site—the full extent of her computer savvy—had paid off big-time. In fact, if she ever met the person who started that thing, she'd pick her up off the ground and plant a kiss right on her. That woman had given Scarlett Jo the ability to feed her family on a preacher's salary without mortgaging her youngest child. Though there were days when she'd be willing to do that with almost any of them.

"I've got me six coupons right here," she said, waving her stack.

"Well, go enjoy yourself. Let me know if you need anything."

"You know I will." Scarlett Jo wasn't what you would call an extreme couponer. She couldn't walk into a store and get a thousand dollars' worth of stuff for free. But she had learned how to pay little or nothing for toothpaste, toothbrushes, and deodorant. And today she would be getting six bottles of Tylenol Precise for free.

She was still flipping the pages of her binder when Amanda, her young chocolate-haired bombshell of a jogging neighbor, rounded the end of the aisle. As soon as she saw Scarlett Jo, there was no denying the slight look of panic on her face.

Scarlett Jo loved a challenge like that. She scooted her cart up next to Amanda and didn't even pretend to avoid the woman's stares at her large binder. "Last week I came in here and got me ninety-three dollars' worth of stuff for six dollars and sixty-two cents."

"With those?" Amanda pointed at the binder as if it had the plague.

"Yep. Have you ever couponed?"

Amanda's expression made it clear she thought Scarlett Jo had just asked the stupidest question ever.

"I know," Scarlett Jo said. "Time sucker, right?"

Amanda raised a manicured hand to her blue-spandex-clad chest, her large diamond catching the fluorescent light above them. "Well, with preschoolers running around my feet, I can't imagine adding anything else to my life."

Scarlett Jo laughed and snorted. "Oh, honey, do I know that feeling. At one point I had four under the age of seven, and I'm telling you, I had sweet tea on an IV drip in those days. If someone had looked at me and told me to try couponing, I would have run down the street screaming like a crazy woman. But I've got to tell you, I have saved oodles. In fact, you want to hear something? I actually put this binder together with all my coupons while I was sitting in first class on my way to San Francisco."

She saw Amanda's hands shift slightly on the blue plastic handlebar of her cart.

"First class!" Scarlett Jo repeated. She punched Amanda's arm and worried for a minute that she might have just broken her humerus or bruised her triceps. "That flight attendant looked at me kind of like you are, and I just told her, 'Honey, it's these coupons that got me up here in first class.'"

Amanda's dark-brown eyes darted right and left as if the woman was seeking an escape, though she kept a fixed smile on her face. Scarlett Jo leaned in closer. She'd learned a long time ago that the people who resisted friendship were often the ones who needed it the most. "Want me to teach you?" she asked. "I'm great at it."

Amanda backed up. Her lips pressed together. "Ah, no, I think I'm good for today. But thank you so much for the offer." She edged her cart in the opposite direction down the aisle.

"Well, you just let me know if you ever want to."

Amanda gave her a nod and didn't even bother pushing her cart in as she made a beeline for the store's exit—itemless.

"I'm here every Sunday afternoon," Scarlett Jo called after her. "If you aren't, the other couponers will take all the stuff and leave you waiting until Ted gets his next shipment on Thursday. They're crazy women!" She raised her hand to wave good-bye. "Still would love to have you over for dinner!"

Scarlett Jo watched Amanda as she left. The woman's black workout pants stretched tightly around her tiny rear end. Scarlett Jo had no idea how she had little ones and a body like that. The woman must jog to Memphis and back every day.

Scarlett Jo patted her own thighs and muttered, "I know, girls. I promise I won't ever put you through that. Now, let's go see what we can get in the chocolate aisle."

❀ ❀ ❀

"Tucker, go get the groceries out of the car for me," Scarlett Jo said as she walked into the house.

His shoulders immediately slumped. "Aw, Mama. Seriously?"

"So serious," she said, dropping her purse on the counter. "Where's Dad?"

"In there." He tossed a hand over his shoulder toward the screened-in porch as he headed for the garage door.

"Hey, Tuck," she said, a slyness in her voice.

He turned his mop of dark curls toward her. "Yeah?"

"There's chocolate in there. You bring the bags in, you can have two pieces."

She wouldn't have to ask twice. She walked out to the porch and was surprised to see Tim McAdams there. Tim and his wife,

Elise, were long-time friends. They'd taken the step of faith with Jackson and Scarlett Jo to start this new church and now served as music pastors. Elise led the singing while Tim played the keyboard and led the band.

"Well, I didn't expect to see you today, Tim. Where's Elise?"

He stood quickly. "Um, she should be at the house."

"You don't have to leave. Sit. I'll make you something to drink. Apparently, Mr. Hospitality didn't offer you anything."

Jackson turned to Tim. "Want something to drink?"

Tim laughed. "No. I would have asked."

"See, that's what I tell her. But she thinks I should offer first."

Scarlett Jo blew air out of her mouth.

"I'll walk you out," Jackson said to Tim before she could ask another question. Both men's body language told her she didn't need to offer anything else.

She went into her bathroom and began to unload the bags that Tucker had put in there for her. All the chocolate was gone, of course. She'd told him two pieces.

Jackson came and leaned against the door. "When have you seen Elise last? Outside of church, I mean."

She opened the door of the cherrywood cabinet. Her couponing stash stared back at her—dozens of toothbrushes, tubes of toothpaste, and containers of deodorant, all stacked in neat rows. If World War III ever broke out and they were sequestered in a bomb shelter, at least they would smell good.

"It's been a while." She answered her husband as she added another toothbrush to the stash. "Why?"

"Nothing. Just wondering."

She stopped what she was doing and turned toward Jackson. "Is that why Tim was here? Is he concerned about her?"

"I told him I'd keep his confidence. Just wondering when you'd seen her last."

She scoured her thoughts. "Quite a while, honey. Honestly. Haven't heard much from her. Just see her at church." She didn't add that she'd check on her. But she would.

"Okay." He walked over and kissed her on her cheek. "So what did you steal today?"

"Today they paid me three dollars and fifty cents to take eighty-two dollars' worth of stuff off their hands."

"If I ever see you diving in a Dumpster, that's it. I'm outta here."

"How about a recycling bin?"

He didn't say a word, just walked from the room. And she left to go get her chocolate back from Tucker.

{ *Chapter 10* }

GRACE CHECKED the caller ID of her ringing phone as she pulled into the studio parking lot. It was Tyler. After he left yesterday, he hadn't come home, still wasn't home when she left for work. His absences these past two weeks had gotten longer and longer, and he had stopped using physical therapy and working out as an excuse. He had used Jeff a few times, but most times he didn't even feel the need for an excuse. When she'd asked, he let her know in no uncertain terms that he was a grown man who didn't need a GPS for a wife.

She sent him to voice mail—a rarity for her, but she just didn't have it in her to talk to him right now. Not before work. Plus, he should be where normal sane people were at this hour—in bed, asleep. So he could endure for a little while what it felt like to be ignored. She grabbed her outfit and bag from the backseat and headed into the one place where she could count on every detail being scripted, organized, and timed down to the minute. The tight schedule made her feel safe. She treasured what she could trust.

She punched her code into the keypad by the front door, a security light on the side of the building illuminating the numbers in the still-black morning. When the lock released with a click, she let herself in. Her flip-flops were the only sound in the quiet hallway as she made her way to her small corner office on the second floor. The station was nestled in one of Tennessee's hills, and she loved the solace of nature her view afforded her, though she wouldn't actually get to see it until after the newscast. She pulled a pink sweatshirt from her bag and put it on over her white T-shirt. Leo kept it cold enough to hang meat in here, and he was still always sweating. She shivered slightly as she sat behind her desk and turned on the computer, waiting for the world to make its way to her fingertips.

She shifted the orange-and-white picture frame that held a picture of Tyler and her from one of the UT–Vanderbilt games they had gone to. The ceramic felt cool beneath her fingers. She studied her grinning face in the picture. She loved football. Then her eyes moved to Tyler's face. He showed the camera his professional smile, the one he reserved for things he endured. She wondered if that was how he felt most days in regard to their life together.

Movement at her door caused her to look up. She saw Leo's stomach first. It was hard to miss because it was always the first thing that entered the room. "Howya doin' this morning, Grace?"

This wasn't a normal "Howya doin'." This was a real question, a question that seemed to include the possibility that she *wasn't* doing well.

She pushed the photo aside. "What is it, Leo?"

He fidgeted with the top of his pants, working to fold down the white lining that his belt pushed to the top. "I was waiting for you to call in this morning. To beg me not to run this story."

She let out a soft laugh, then started pecking on her keyboard. "I don't have time for games today. I've got to work on my script and get ready for the show."

"You haven't talked to Tyler this morning?"

She raised her head quickly. "I'm too mad at Tyler to talk to him. And why would you ask me that anyway?"

"Oh, so you know."

Her forehead scrunched. "Know what?"

He shook his head as if she was making this too difficult. "Have you talked to Tyler at all this morning? In the last two hours?"

She remembered his picture on her caller ID. "No. He tried about five minutes ago, but I didn't want to get into an argument right before I go on the air." She pulled her chair closer to her desk. "That does none of us any good."

Leo shifted in his Reeboks. "Tyler was arrested last night on a DUI. Other networks have already called. They're running the story."

Time stood still for her in that moment.

"Grace—" her name came out of Leo's mouth with a father's tenderness—"we have no choice. We have to run the story."

Then time was unleashed. Her thoughts ran wildly. They were like a bunch of first graders running off a school bus, and she didn't know which one to grab first.

"Hey, I'm sorry," he said. "I thought for sure you'd know."

Her hand came up to her mouth. "I can't believe this. How . . . ?"

He walked toward her desk. "We got word about one this morning. Apparently he was arrested around midnight, and his blood alcohol level was two times the legal limit. Didn't it worry you when you got up and he wasn't home?"

"He's rarely home when I leave." The vulnerable words came out before she thought about them. She scrambled to explain. "He's just . . . he has a friend who's going through a hard time. He's been spending a lot of time with him."

Leo scratched the side of his head, where a small remainder of hair resided. "I can't bury this. It's going to be covered."

Her wits came back quickly. She grabbed for her phone. "I'll call the other producers. This is just common courtesy. Professional etiquette. We wouldn't do this to them."

Leo tugged at his belt. "Actually, we have done this to them. We ran the affair of Callista McIntire's husband last year. You know, Channel 2's evening anchor. Trust me. We won't get a pass here."

Panic surged through her. Her life was about to be exposed, and on television at that. She couldn't let this happen. "You'll have to think of something then." Her throat was so tight her voice came out in a squeak. "Because if this runs on the station I've given the last ten years of my life to, I'm quitting."

His stubby hands rose quickly as if moving them could settle the tremors that had just announced the earthquake. "Now calm down. You're being irrational. This, this is something I don't have any control over. Besides, local news isn't the only thing you have to worry about."

Fear swallowed her whole. "What do you mean?"

"I mean Tyler is a professional athlete. I'll be shocked if the major networks don't run this story, but for sure the sports networks will."

Her feet were moving before her brain could register all the ways her life was about to change. She grabbed her bag, and her words came out laced with panic. "You heard me, Leo. If you run this story, I'm out of here. And if you won't try to get the other stations not to run it, I'll do it myself."

As she hurried down the hall, he ran after her, his feet thudding heavily. "Grace, you're in shock. It's completely understandable. Go talk to Tyler and then get back here, and we'll work this out. You know I couldn't stand to lose you."

Her tone was biting as she grabbed the door handle. "Then make this go away."

Leo held the door as she started down the stairs. "Have you ever stopped to think that maybe this doesn't need to go away? That maybe having to deal with the mess he's made this time might be the best thing that has ever happened to Tyler?"

She turned sharply as she opened the door to the parking lot. "It's not just Tyler here, Leo. It's me too."

She didn't wait for a response. She ran to her car, climbed in, and immediately dialed Channel 2.

Only after all three competing stations assured her they were definitely running with the story did she call Tyler's cell. No answer. She called the Williamson County jail next. Tyler had been there. But his bail had been posted three hours ago.

❀　❀　❀

Tears blurred Grace's vision to such an extreme that she could hardly make out the interstate signs for her exit. The last few years played through her mind like her family's old eight-millimeter videos—jerky, silent, but vivid and real. The first time Tyler came home drunk. The angry rants and sullen hangovers. The spending sprees and bad financial decisions. The heartbreaking rejections in bed and the many nights when she wondered if he'd make it home at all. All those near misses with team management and the law.

Each time she had grabbed hold of their lives in a desperate attempt to conceal all that they truly were because she didn't want their truth to be exposed. She had hurt enough. She hadn't wanted to hurt that way too.

She pulled in to the garage. There was no sign of the Mercedes. Probably impounded. She had called Tyler's cell phone ten times since she left the station. He hadn't answered one of the calls. There was nothing left to do but wait.

The house was as quiet when she entered as it had been when she left. She dropped her keys on the counter in the kitchen and walked toward the bedroom. She found Tyler snoring loudly, reeking of bourbon and smoke and something else—body odor, maybe. Miss Daisy snoozed at his feet.

The sight sent her anger to a new level. Buried fury from deep and dark places rose to the surface with such force that both she and Tyler were caught off guard.

She jerked the duvet off him, causing Miss Daisy to jump down. Then she grabbed Tyler's arm and pulled with all her might, forcing his body to the floor. He jolted upright. "What the—?"

Every blood vessel in her face felt as if it would explode. "You're sleeping? The whole city of Nashville—maybe the whole country—is about to know you're a drunk, and you're sleeping? Have you lost your mind?"

Tyler squinted at her through bloodshot eyes. "Leave me alone." He yanked the duvet from her hand and climbed back into bed.

Grace had nothing left to lose. And there was everything to say. "You will get out of that bed and face me. You are about to make a public spectacle of us, and there is no way you're going to crawl into that bed and act as if nothing has happened. I am through acting as if nothing has happened!"

He flung the duvet off his shirtless body. "What do you want from me, Grace?"

"You've got to be kidding me!" Her arms flew up in the air. "What do I want from you? I want you to be a man, Tyler. I want you to own your stuff. I want you to get help—real help." Her voice betrayed her as it broke. "I'd do anything—*anything*—if you were just willing. I'd walk with you anywhere to get you the help you need and to fix this marriage. Because we're broken. Can't you see that? Can't you see how broken we are?"

He looked at her without expression, a far cry from yesterday's explosion. "I'm not seeing another counselor, and I'm not going to spend my life with you dictating it. If you don't like it, you can get out. I've told you before that our marriage was a mistake. Maybe now you will believe me."

His words cut through her with the precision of a chain saw, leaving a wound gaping and beyond repair. The air rushed from the room.

She had no words to reply to that. He had lied his way through separation, counseling, and rehab, but now there was a resolve in him. He wasn't lying now, and the truth was enough to break her heart.

She fled the room and climbed the stairs to the guest

bedroom. Her body fell across the bed, and she made no attempt to quiet her wails. If he couldn't hear them, it was because his heart was stone.

As silence finally came over her and the heaving stopped, Grace remembered her prayer from the day before. She now knew she had her answer. Her release. All the years she had fought to survive, had prayed for healing, had brought her to this one moment. The line was clear in her soul, the shift deliberate and sure.

This was the end. She had given ten years of her life to a broken, childless, pretend relationship, and she had no intention of giving anything more. Not as long as things remained the way they were.

If their marriage had to end for him to be whole, if Tyler's rescuer had to be removed for him to figure out how to become a man, then that was what she would do. It was now Tyler's time to rescue himself.

❀   ❀   ❀

Scarlett Jo stretched her feet over the side of the bed and slid them into her hot-pink fuzzy slippers. She did her best to stay quiet as she left the bedroom.

She had been doing this for a week now, getting up before dawn so she could watch the news—the early edition, anchored by the local celebrity who had moved in down the street and was coming to their church. Scarlett Jo poured herself a glass of sweet tea and pulled a cinnamon bun from the box she had hidden in the top cabinet where the glasses were. She had picked it up for herself when she went to Merridee's on Saturday to get the boys their own box for breakfast.

She curled up on the sofa with breakfast and turned on the television. You would think she was watching a royal wedding, getting up like this. The news show started, but the woman staring back at her was not her new friend Grace Shepherd—unless Grace had become Beyoncé overnight.

"Doggone it," Scarlett Jo said to the still-dark living room.

"We begin with breaking news this morning," the young woman said, her white teeth almost iridescent.

Scarlett Jo scrunched in tighter against the sofa and took a bite of her cinnamon bun. She loved breaking news.

"Nashville Predators right defenseman Tyler Shepherd was arrested overnight for a DUI."

The gasp Scarlett Jo let out was loud. "Oh my stars!"

A not-too-attractive mug shot of Grace's husband spanned the full screen of her forty-two-inch television. "Oh, that is not a pretty picture," Scarlett Jo offered to the unfamiliar anchor. "He looks drunker than Cooter Brown." She had heard that old expression for years growing up in the South, but she had never learned exactly who Cooter Brown was. "You'd think at least they'd let you go to the bathroom and check yourself out before they put you in front of that camera. Lord knows, you've got to live with that picture the rest of your life."

"He was released on bail this morning. The Predators have yet to issue a statement," the newscaster went on to inform her. "We will make you aware of more details as they become available."

Scarlett Jo took a long sip of her tea, then set her plastic tumbler on the glass-topped coffee table by the sofa. She opened the front door, walked onto the porch, and peered down the street at Grace's new house. All the lights were off. If anyone was home, you'd never know it.

Scarlett Jo would check on Grace after she got the boys off to school. But right now she'd pray. It was still dark as she made her way to the sidewalk, so she decided to just walk and pray in her hot-pink robe. If someone else was up at this ungodly hour, she figured they deserved to have to see her this way.

❀ ❀ ❀

Zach had helped Adele pack up her car. It had been his pleasure. She'd pulled out at six thirty that morning, lingering just long enough to tell the girls and Caroline good-bye before they all started a new week. He hoped it would be a while before he had to endure her again.

As he skimmed a razor blade across his neck, he felt Caroline's arms wrap around his waist from behind. He'd pretended for a moment the gesture was genuine, real. He swished the foam-covered razor in the sink as she peeked her head around his side. She watched him in the mirror. His words took the risk.

"Caroline, honey, why do you let your mom dictate your life the way you do? I watch you when she's here. It's like you revert into this child who has no voice."

Her response was tender, not at all what he had expected. "I don't know."

He let his body relax and brought the razor up for its next swipe. Such receptive moments had been too few and far between. He'd take this one. "Are you afraid of her?"

She was quiet for a moment as she cast her eyes downward.

"It's okay if you are."

She looked back into the mirror. "Maybe a little. I don't know what it is."

"Do you need her approval?"

She let out a cynical huff. "I don't fight for things that don't exist."

He met her eyes in the mirror. "Maybe you should stand up to her. Be honest with her about what you feel. Tell her that we can't afford to expand the business right now—that you're the owner and you'll know when that time is."

She released him and crossed her arms; her gaze turned to a glare. "Expanding the shop is a great idea. My mother happens to be a very smart businesswoman. Look at all she has accomplished."

He steeled his spine as she went on. "Honestly, I think you're just jealous. That's why you play these mind games with me. But if it weren't for her, I don't even want to think about where we'd be right now."

He kept his hand on his neck to make sure he didn't slice his jugular. "Did you have a question, Caroline? Or did you just want to pick a fight?"

She moved to her side of the bathroom. "Do you remember the client I had to style last week?"

He didn't respond, and honestly she didn't need him to. Most of the time her questions were simply information regurgitation.

She continued talking through a second lipstick application. "Well, they live in that really quaint development, Westhaven. They've got a lot of houses for sale there, and so many of the kids go to school with the girls. And I was thinking—"

"No." His answer came out sharp and quick.

Her hands dropped. "I knew you'd say that."

He kept his eyes on the mirror. "Where is the loving wife who snuggled up against me a minute ago? The one who offered me a brief moment of something real?" He didn't try to hide his sarcasm. She paid it no attention.

"This is the best time to buy. I took Mom yesterday to look, and she thinks we'd be foolish not to do it. She's even willing to help."

He had to put the razor down, or it would be a matter of seconds before 911 had to be called. "Caroline, seriously. You had to have this house. Remember? You *had* to have *this* house. You wanted to live in the *historic* area of Franklin. We had a perfectly fine house. And now we have a house payment we can barely afford."

"Well, if your practice did better—"

He stopped her immediately. "If my practice did better? I'm working my rear end off to make sure that we can meet all our demands. Your business brings in nothing. In fact, it has lost money this year, and you're talking about investing another hundred thousand dollars into it that we don't have. Where do you think it all ends?"

She turned toward him, her angry eyes as green as envy itself. "We made the decision to start my business *together*, Zach. Don't act like it was all my idea."

"Well, then let us make another decision *together*. It's not going to happen. Not an expansion to the store and not another move. It may be a good time to buy, but it's not a good time for us. We paid top dollar for this place. There's no way we could even recoup what we've put into it. And we are not taking more money from your mother."

She jerked her three-hundred-dollar handbag off the counter. "You can't tell me what I will and won't do."

He took in a deep breath, trying to release the tension in

his body and in the bathroom. "But why do you need another house? Why isn't this one enough?"

Her tone was still biting. "Because the girls can't just walk to a friend's house from here. They don't have any classmates in this area, so we have to drive all over town for them to have any kind of social life." She found the syrup again. He would avoid getting stuck in it. "Wouldn't it be wonderful if they were right near their friends' houses? This is the age where they are separating from us, and friends are the most important thing. Denying them something like this is just . . . it's just selfishness."

He resisted the urge to laugh. And to scream. He resisted a lot of urges in that moment. He simply shook his head, turned back toward the sink, and picked up his razor again.

"Aren't you going to say anything?"

"How do I respond to that? You know as well as I do that if I move you into that house, in six months you'll want another one. And another car. And another overpriced purse. It's a never-ending cycle of 'another.' There is no response to that."

"You're a jerk, Zach. How is that for a response? You only think about yourself. And I'm so sick of it." Her heels clicked loudly on the hardwood floor as she walked out of the bedroom. Her hypocrisy, however, lingered behind.

{ *Chapter 11* }

"GRACE, WAKE UP."

The voice was distant. Grace tried to open her eyes. Her eyelids felt glued shut. She could almost see the swollen puffs beneath them. Sun trickled in between the tiny slats of the plantation shutters. She still hadn't hung drapes in this room.

"Grace, are you all right?" Rachel's voice finally registered.

"Yeah, yeah." She rubbed hard at her eyes and sat up in bed.

Rachel sat on the edge of the bed. "When you wouldn't answer your phone, I knew it was bad."

Grace blinked and looked around the room. She didn't even know where her phone was. "Sorry."

"It's okay. I just needed to know you were okay."

"I'm okay. I think. It's just . . . Rach, I need you to do me a favor."

Fifteen minutes later, Rachel left to arrange childcare so she could be available later that day. And as much as she appreciated her friend, Grace felt relieved when she was gone. She needed the silence. For now.

Miss Daisy popped up from the foot of the bed. She moved closer to Grace and stretched out luxuriously, waiting to be rubbed. Grace obliged, grateful that at least one of them was unaware of the harsh lines that would define their life from now on.

Grace got up and walked quietly down the stairs, Miss Daisy at her heels. She was finally beginning to get a feel for where everything was in this house. She sighed. She passed the master bedroom, peeking in to see an empty bed. Tyler was gone. Must have had a buddy pick him up.

This was how it always seemed to happen. Another new house, another hopeful fresh start, another quick revelation that it was nothing more than a new address. Then six months of trying to get all the bills to actually show up while living out the same old pain. Would she finally be changing the pattern?

She noticed that Miss Daisy was trotting ahead of her in the hall. "Need to potty?"

The dog's tail wagged and her eyes seemed to bug out even farther, if that was possible. Grace followed her into the kitchen, wondering what time it was. She squinted hard at the numbers on the stove. Ten o'clock. She must have been dead to the world.

She opened the back door to the fenced-in yard. "Go potty, baby girl." Miss Daisy trotted off. Grace left the door open, went into the kitchen, and turned the oven on broil. She pulled a piece of wheat bread from the wrapper and stuck it in the oven. And that simple act triggered a memory of when she'd begun making toast this way.

During her separation from Tyler, Grace had spent a month at her parents' house, then returned home to find that Tyler had taken the toaster. Her morning ritual was a piece of peanut-butter toast, and she'd been furious that he'd taken the one thing she used every morning. Then she'd gathered her ingenuity, stuck her bread underneath the oven broiler, and discovered she liked it much better that way, toasted on only one side. It had been virtually a declaration of independence. She'd never used a toaster again.

She shook off the memory and went to the door to check on Miss Daisy. She noted that their wicker rockers on the back porch looked nice against the deep-yellow siding, but she didn't see a puff of champagne fur anywhere. She ventured farther onto the porch and looked to her right. The fence ran up to the edge of the house, so there was really no place to hide. She stepped off the porch and moved toward the side where the gate was. Her heart dropped when she saw the gate pushed open wide enough for a small dog to get through. Someone had left it open. And Miss Daisy was gone.

Grace's heart pounded as she ran through the gate and into the front yard. She saw nothing but manicured lawns and neat houses, heard only the sounds of cars moving along Third Avenue. Her new house was way too close to the town square for her comfort with Miss Daisy on the loose.

"Miss Daisy!" she called, knowing as she did that the dog wouldn't come unless she wanted to. She never had. When Miss Daisy was a puppy, Grace had gone out one night to find her nose-to-nose with a possum. She had yelled at the top of her lungs for the dog to get inside. But Miss Daisy had just looked up at her, then back at the possum. Finally she'd decided the possum didn't look too interesting and sauntered back into the house.

"Miss Daisy! Come on, baby girl. Want a treat?" Grace was trying to keep calm. She darted around to the other side of the house, praying she'd find her there. No sign of her. She returned quickly to the front. Still nothing. By the time she'd covered every side again, her insides were screaming.

"Miss Daisy! Baby, come to Mama. Oh, God, please help me find her." Now panic was setting in. She walked quickly up the street, her eyes searching madly between the houses as she called Miss Daisy's name. Every few moments she'd glance at the road, praying she wouldn't see a squashed ball of fur. The last thing she needed today was to lose her baby.

The tears began when she finished covering one full side of the street. She dashed to the other side and repeated her search, each section of sidewalk accelerating her fears that Miss Daisy might be gone. She could have been hit by a car, snatched up by anyone. She was yelling the dog's name now and running wildly up the street.

She didn't see Scarlett Jo until she ran into her. The collision almost knocked her down.

"Grace, honey, what is it?" Scarlett Jo's big arms encased her, her own voice urgent.

"It's Miss Daisy." She didn't even try to conceal her heartbreak, tears, or panic. "My dog. I can't find her. I've called and called, and she's nowhere."

"Come on, sugar. I'll help you look." Scarlett Jo grabbed Grace's hand and pulled her up the street. They both yelled Miss Daisy's name as they ran, Grace in her bare feet and Scarlett Jo in the biggest pair of lemon-colored wedges ever sold in Franklin.

It wasn't until they rounded the curve onto Church Street that they saw her—nose buried in an azalea bush, oblivious to her name being called for the last ten minutes.

"Miss Daisy!" Grace screamed.

The dog lifted her head and trotted over. Grace fell to the ground and buried her face in Miss Daisy's fur. Her body shook with heaves. She couldn't help it. Nor did she care if anyone saw. She kissed Miss Daisy's head over and over again, murmuring, "Thank you, God. Thank you, God. Thank you, God."

She felt Scarlett Jo's arm come around her and pull her from her knees. "Let's get you home, sugar."

They walked along the street together, Miss Daisy snug in Grace's arms. As soon as they reached the door, she smelled the burnt toast. She put Miss Daisy down and ran into the kitchen, yanking open the oven door. Smoke rushed out as if desperate for air. Grace grabbed the scorched piece of bread, burning her hand as she did. She hurled it into the trash, turned on the exhaust fan over the stove, and leaned against the kitchen counter.

Scarlett Jo walked into the kitchen and looked at her with sympathetic blue eyes that all but lit up against the yellow floral jacket draping her body like a summer tablecloth.

Grace wondered if she knew. This new friend she had made—did she have any clue what a mess Grace's life had become?

❁ ❁ ❁

Scarlett Jo's words came out quicker than even she had expected. "I watched the news this morning. I'm thinking your life has just exploded."

Grace stared at her. She didn't say a word, but her expression made it clear she knew exactly what Scarlett Jo was talking about.

"How long has he been drinking?"

Grace's body seemed to curl in on itself. She still didn't answer.

Scarlett Jo had wanted to be quiet. She really had. But when there was an elephant in the room, she couldn't pretend she was a circus ringmaster. She simply had to get it out of the way. "I'm not judging him, sweetie. Just asking a question."

Grace's shoulders fell slightly. Miss Daisy trotted out of the kitchen as if they were both an inconvenience to her day. Grace looked up and leaned against the edge of the black granite countertop. "Years."

Scarlett Jo started opening kitchen cabinets. When she found the glasses, she took one out. She pressed the rim against the water dispenser on the refrigerator door, then offered Grace the cool drink. Grace looked at the glass as if the water were a foreign substance.

"Right. Something stronger." Scarlett Jo dumped the clear liquid into the sink and returned to the refrigerator.

"The tea," Grace said. "Sweet tea—in the pitcher."

"Of course, dumpling." Scarlett Jo pulled it out. "Sugar is your friend. Especially when your gingerbread house is crumbling." She pressed the ice dispenser, added tea to the glass, and handed it to Grace. "Wanna sit?"

Grace nodded and moved zombielike to the back door. She crossed the yard to the fence, latched the gate firmly, then returned to the porch and finally sank into one of the rockers. Scarlett Jo took the one beside her. They both stared in front of them at the wood fence and the three large magnolia trees

SECRETS OVER SWEET TEA

that lined it. Miss Daisy came outside and plopped next to their feet.

"Wanna tell me about it?"

Scarlett Jo watched as Grace studied her. She knew the look. She'd been measured on this scale so many times—the can-I-trust-you? scale. People needed to know that their heart was safe, their story was safe.

Scarlett Jo turned her face to the neatly manicured yard, pushed the heels of her fancy new shoes against the concrete of the porch, and set the chair to rocking. "Baby girl, you don't have to tell me a thing you don't want to. I'll just sit here with you and watch the sun move across the sky if that's what you want to do. Whatever you need today is what I'm offering you." And then she waited.

It took a while, but eventually Grace spoke. Almost everybody did sooner or later.

"At first I didn't know what it was. Tyler just started getting angry for no reason. It was like everything I did irritated him. I never knew what I would get when I'd wake up in the morning. Then I started finding liquor bottles. He used to hide them—in drawers, under the car seat, in the bathroom. I'd confront him. We'd argue. Eventually he didn't bother hiding them anymore. He'd just go out and come home drunk. Eventually I got tired of confronting him. It didn't seem worth it.

"Then as I started to get more recognition at work and Tyler's career had more challenges, things got worse. There were days when I wanted to quit my job. I thought if I wasn't so well-known, then maybe he would stop the . . ." Her thoughts seemed to trail off. "You always think you can stop it."

She rocked for a bit before she continued. "But I couldn't

quit my job. Tyler's a spender, and it takes money to keep up our lifestyle, so we needed everything I made. Needed it for houses too—and cars—and counselors. Except we didn't actually have to pay that much for counseling, because Tyler decided the counselor was a quack and dropped him." She smiled sadly. "It's always someone else's fault—especially mine.

"That's the really hard part, you know? The more I tried to help, the more he'd pull away from me. He puts up this big act about being loving in public—holds my hand, kisses me—but at home there's no intimacy at all. He's just not interested."

Scarlett Jo's brow furrowed. "Like . . . no hanky-panky?"

Grace never looked at her. "Like nothing. He doesn't touch me anymore. I thought it was me at first, that I wasn't attractive enough. But the more I researched it, the more I learned about alcoholism and what it does to a body."

"Oh, my side, don't tell Jackson that. He might want to get me some Jack Daniel's." Scarlett Jo leaned closer. "People think Jackson must be really hot to trot, you know, because we have five children. But I will not tell a lie. It's me. That man turns me on quicker than I can spot a pair of fancy shoes." Scarlett Jo's hand shot to her mouth as soon as the words escaped her. "Oh, Grace, I'm sorry. Sometimes my mouth gets out of control."

Grace smiled. "It's okay. I like your mouth."

"Well, that's a good thing because I can't seem to stop spoutin' off with it. But I've got to say, that stuff about alcohol and libido is news to me. I always thought it was the opposite. You know, people getting drunk and—"

"Oh, they get drunk and lose their sexual inhibition, but that doesn't mean they can, um, follow through. And after a while . . ."

"My goodness, that had to be awful for you."

Grace nodded and blinked back tears. "He's a good man, Scarlett Jo. But he has a big problem. *We* have a big problem."

"I'm not judging Tyler."

Grace shook her head. "I know that. I can tell. Honestly, I can. I believe in the soul of me that he loves me as much as he is capable of loving anyone."

"I don't doubt that."

"He's just . . . broken."

"Baby, we're all broken. About the time we start believing we're not, that's when it all falls apart and we realize how bad off we are."

Grace placed her feet on the edge of her chair and wrapped her arms around her knees. Miss Daisy let out a heavy sigh as if she realized that meant they were going to be outside for a while. And that fluffy little thing was clearly not an outside dog—unless, of course, she decided it was a good day for a stroll.

"We actually separated a few years ago. And when we got back together, I thought everything was going to be better. I thought it was the real thing. Tyler was finally honest about the drinking—and I know that when you get something out of the darkness, it loses its hold. We got counseling. We were going to church. We even renewed our vows."

For the first time Scarlett Jo heard anger beneath Grace's words. She was okay with anger. Grace needed some fire in her belly.

"But then it started all over again. He backed off from church. He left the counselor. And we went back to the charade that was our life. I shouldn't have come home. When he told me not to expect him to be intimate with me immediately, I should have looked at him and said, 'Then I'm not coming home.' But I didn't. I just let him convince me."

"So what did you go back to, Grace?"

She watched the tears accumulate against Grace's long eyelashes. The soft blonde hair framing her small face made her look like a child who needed to be cared for. One tear fell quickly before the back of Grace's hand could stop it. "I went back to survival. To what I knew. To what felt safe. Manageable. Mine. But I'm never going back there again." Her voice broke. "Even if I become one of those people. It's over."

"One of what people?"

"One of those failures. I'm getting a divorce, Scarlett Jo. I'm going to spend the rest of my life like all those other people with the big *D* stamped across their chests."

Scarlett Jo felt the thud in her gut that hit her anytime she heard that word. "Baby girl, divorce is a permanent step."

"I know." Grace spoke softly now, her anger swept away with the first tear that fell. "It's horrible, isn't it? You give your life to something. You pray. You fast. You believe. You fight. And then you're left staring at nothing but rubble. But this is where it ends." She turned to face Scarlett Jo. "It's this far and no farther. Tyler Shepherd has been a god in my life since I was twenty-three years old. I have let him dictate virtually every decision I have made in these last twelve years. But I've tried to play his savior too. And it's all got to stop. We're both going to have to be responsible to God for our own souls."

Being a minister's wife, Scarlett Jo had sat across from countless women over the years. She'd heard all sorts of reasons for divorce: affairs, abuse, the ever-formidable and lame excuse of "I just don't love him anymore." And she had said to so many of them the same thing she said to Grace now: "Honey, you know you can release yourself from a marriage all day long. You can find more excuses to divorce a man than you can find cicadas in Franklin when they come out—and I hear that's going to happen any day now. But what you can't and never will be able to do is end a covenant. Only the good Lord himself can do that."

Grace's brown eyes seemed to look through Scarlett Jo. "I know" was all she offered.

And Scarlett Jo believed her. Unlike so many of the women Scarlett Jo had counseled in this situation, Grace Shepherd understood what she was doing and had an inkling of what she would lose. But what Grace Shepherd didn't know yet was how hard she'd have to fight to reclaim her heart—that little-girl heart buried deep down inside that beautiful yet very old soul. She also suspected Grace had yet to realize how deep and rich God's grace was for her. Divorce was sin—this Scarlett Jo knew. But she also knew God had a grace for the divorced heart, just as he had for every other form of human brokenness.

A shrill screaming sound interrupted her thoughts as an enormous insect flew past her head. It landed on the arm of her rocker. She let out a scream of her own and jumped from her chair, flapping her hands so wildly that if she hadn't been top-heavy, she might have taken flight. "What is that? What is that?"

Grace didn't move from her chair. Miss Daisy, however, sat up at the commotion. Grace calmly swatted the creature, which took off loudly. "That is a cicada, Scarlett Jo."

"So they're here." A chill ran through Scarlett Jo, and her entire body shook. She'd lived in the South all her life and never seen one before. "How long will those things be around?"

"Five or six weeks."

She crinkled her nose and pushed up her lips. "They're disgusting."

"Yes, they are."

"They're *huge*."

"They're flies on steroids."

"Did you see its eyes?"

"As red as the devil's."

"You wouldn't care if ten were sitting on you right now, would you?"

"Not a lick."

Yep, that girl was as dead as you could get inside. But Scarlett Jo wasn't worried. Not really. Because sometimes a person has to die in order to really live.

{ *Chapter 12* }

ZACH'S OFFICE WAS QUIET TODAY. He felt it as he walked in the door, and he was grateful. The girls had argued the entire way to the school, and he'd found himself wishing that the Range Rover came with an Eject button. He also wished it came with a return-because-your-wife-convinced-you-that-you-needed-it-and-you-didn't policy. He hated that car and everything it represented. Everything it attempted to represent.

"Hey, Darlene."

His secretary looked up and smiled. Darlene Grant had been with him since he'd opened this practice seven years ago. She was sixty-nine now and embraced each one of those years as the gift it was. She'd let her hair gray and her figure soften, but beauty was so deeply embedded in her soul that it showed through every pore. She had retired briefly when she was sixty-two, just long enough to take care of her grown daughter after a tonsillectomy. But she didn't like retirement or the one week she was home with nothing to do. Zach was the lucky recipient of her inability to retire. He hoped she never did.

"You look a little tired," she said to him this morning. "Did you take the stairs?"

He laughed and poured himself a cup of coffee from the pot she had already made. "Took the elevator this morning. But I am tired. My mother-in-law was in town for the weekend."

"Well, maybe you can relax a little today since you don't have any appointments. Just let me know if I can get you anything."

He looked into her kind face, her hazel eyes soft above her mocha cheeks. If he could invent a mother for himself, it would be her. His own mom had died when he was in college, leaving a huge hole in his heart and a longing for someone to fill it. Darlene helped.

"Thanks," he told her. "Will do."

He spent the next three hours working on his caseload for the week and preparing a motion scheduled for tomorrow. Finally he put down the file and rubbed his tired eyes. His worn leather chair squeaked as he leaned back. He stretched, trying to let go of pent-up anxiety from the weekend. It escaped with a long, heavy sigh.

His office smelled of old books and his late Friday afternoon cigar. His eyes fell on the small Bible perched near the edge of his desk. He wondered for an instant how he would have felt if he had noticed it yesterday when she was here. He tried to recall the last time he'd opened it—at least two months. There had been a brief season after his affair started when the angst overwhelmed him and he said he couldn't see her anymore. Then home got worse, and he needed her. At least he needed something, so he chose her. Or maybe he felt he deserved her. He put his elbows on his desk and his head in his hands. A knock on the door freed him from the train wreck of his thoughts.

Darlene peeked in, her words a near whisper. "Could you see someone?"

He sat up straight. "Who is it?"

"Someone your pastor's wife sent over."

He blew out a large puff of air. "Tell her I'm busy. Have you met my pastor's wife?"

"Zach, stop it. Scarlett Jo Newberry is one of the best people I know."

"You need to get out more."

She pushed the door open a little farther and stepped inside. "It's one of the news anchors from the NBC affiliate in Nashville. I watch her every morning."

She still had to be crazy. If Scarlett Jo Newberry sent her, he was in for torture. But Darlene wasn't leaving. "Okay." He finally yielded, not trying to hide his frustration. "Have her take a seat in the conference room, and I'll be there in a minute."

"Thank you. And be nice." Darlene closed the door behind her.

He turned his chair around and opened the long credenza that stood against the wall beside his desk. File after file of divorce after divorce lined up in neat rows, a stark contrast to the mayhem the divorces themselves left in their wake. He pulled out an empty folder and grabbed a legal pad from his desk. He was at least grateful for the distraction.

He walked through the door of the conference room and nodded to the two women in front of him. He recognized the petite blonde as soon as he saw her. She was something of a local celebrity. Caroline watched her every morning while getting ready for the day.

What was she doing here? Oh yeah, Caroline had mentioned something this morning before their argument ensued. Maybe about a DUI? "How embarrassing," Caroline had said.

She stood when he came into the room. He extended his hand. "Zach Craig."

"Grace Shepherd." Her name was as beautiful as she was. And being this close to her, you couldn't deny her beauty, even with the red nose and puffy eyes. "Thank you for seeing me without an appointment." Her voice cracked with emotion. "This is my best friend, Rachel Green."

"I'm just here to support and take notes," the other woman quickly added.

"Please sit."

He motioned toward the table, then rounded the other side of it and pulled out one of the yellow velvet armless chairs. Caroline had picked out these chairs, said the color was "cheerful." He hated it. Every time he looked at the chairs, he wanted to throw them out the window onto Main Street. But he didn't crave the attention that would bring.

"All right, Ms. Shepherd, how can I help you today?"

"Scarlett Jo Newberry recommended you."

"And how do you know Scarlett Jo?"

"I just moved in a couple doors down from her. We've had several conversations lately, and my husband and I . . ." The catch in her voice seemed to surprise even her. "We visited their church yesterday." She turned to her friend. "Amazing how twenty-four hours can change your life."

Rachel placed her hand on top of Grace's and patted it softly. "It's been years, Grace," she whispered.

Grace nodded, then turned her attention back to Zach and pulled slightly at the sleeves of her green sweater. The color was beautiful on her.

He cleared his throat. "So why don't you tell me why Scarlett Jo recommended me."

"I want to file for divorce." Her words came out flat and certain.

"Okay, well, I have to ask you: are you sure that's what you want to do?"

Grace looked at Rachel, then back at him. She nodded. "Yes, it's time."

"I take it you've thought about this for a while."

"I've fought against it for years."

"All right." He placed his elbows on the table and clicked the end of his blue ballpoint pen. "Let's start with basic information."

He asked names, addresses, length of marriage. Then his questions got deeper, more personal: financial situation, properties owned, children. And with each answer, her voice trembled more. He looked up to see tears pooling in her eyes. He'd seen that plenty of times before.

"Grace, this is going to get even more personal."

She nodded, clearly unable to speak.

"Are you able to give me some insight into what led to the breakdown of your marriage?"

She hesitated a moment, gathering herself. Then she took

a long drink from the bottled water Darlene had provided and began to share her story. Zach always found it ironic listening to stories like this—stories of women whose husbands wouldn't love them. It was far more common than people imagined. And yet he lived with a woman who wouldn't let him touch her. If she did, he had to work so hard at it that it almost didn't feel worth it. She acted like she was doing him a favor and wanted it over as quickly as possible. And yet here was a woman, a beautiful woman, whose husband couldn't appreciate what he had. At least Zach had someone else to make him feel appreciated.

"I'm sorry, Grace," he offered when she was finished. "I really am sorry."

The corners of her mouth turned downward, and for a moment she looked like a child. "Me too," she whispered.

"Well, here are my thoughts." He clicked the end of his pen. "We could proceed by filing under impotence, which is legal here in Tennessee. Or we could file under habitual drunkenness. I think we could get some witnesses, and those, along with the DUI and your husband's failed attempts at rehab and counseling, would give us a real strong case in that regard. We could also see if he is having an affair. I know in many cases where alcoholism is prevalent, so is adultery."

She moved forward in her seat. "I want to file under irreconcilable differences."

He wasn't sure he had heard her correctly. "You want to—"

"I know it might not make sense to you, Mr. Craig."

"Zach. Please call me Zach."

"Okay, Zach, but this is what I feel like I'm supposed to do. I'm going to have a lot of choices to make in this journey, choices to honor or to dishonor. And this is the one I'm choosing to make today."

He shifted in his seat. "I hear what you're saying. But if you're wanting to hire me, I really would recommend that you proceed differently. I think if the judge knows what you've been through, he will make sure you are well taken care of."

"I don't need to be taken care of, and I don't want anything from Tyler. All I want for him is to get help, to be whole. And if he can get well, then maybe, maybe we could remarry one day down the road. Maybe this severing could bring an ultimate healing. But I can't wait for that." Her voice broke completely, and she made no attempt to hide her tears. She simply dabbed them with a tissue her friend placed in her hand. "I've had enough drama in my life, and I simply want this to be as quick and as easy as possible. I want you to file under irreconcilable differences, and I want to get on with my healing—whatever that looks like and however that happens."

He leaned back in his chair. "I won't try to change your mind."

"I'm glad, because my mind is settled."

My, she was a stubborn one. "Okay. I'll get started on your papers and should have them for you in a couple days. Once we file, it will be best if you are able and he is willing to sit down and try to divide your property together. Do you think you can do that? Or do you think you'll need mediation?"

He watched as her wheels turned, and for the first time he saw fear on her face. Rachel must have noticed it too because she spoke for Grace. "Tyler can be a little volatile, Zach. I'm not sure if they can do that together or not."

"If there's any danger of him being inappropriate, then you

need to make sure he doesn't come back to the house," Zach said firmly.

"Tyler's never hurt me," Grace said. "Not physically. He just loses his temper sometimes."

"He's an alcoholic, Grace," Rachel said. "And when he's drinking, he's unpredictable. Zach is right—Tyler doesn't need to come back into that house. You need a refuge. It's time."

"I don't care about that house."

Rachel persisted. "Well, I care about you. And you are not moving. He is the one who loves to move, and you are not moving." Rachel looked at Zach. "She may file under irreconcilable differences, but you need to make sure she gets that house."

"I'll draw up the divorce papers that way. We'll ask for the house. And the rest of the property we can settle through attorneys since he is volatile."

"Okay, then." Grace nodded decisively and then stood. "I'll let you ask for the house. But when you get me the divorce papers, I'll know rather quickly what Tyler and I will and won't be able to do. And when I do, you'll be the first to know."

He watched from the window in the conference room as Grace and Rachel walked across the street and toward the car. Rachel guided her friend with a soft and steady arm, but Grace didn't really need the help. She stepped firmly, with poise, her white slacks emphasizing her lithe stride. She had been named well. Unfortunately Tyler Shepherd didn't need her grace. He needed a kick in the—

Zach stopped himself right there. She didn't need his emotion. She needed his counsel. And she needed a man who loved her. Yeah, she needed a man . . .

❀ ❀ ❀

Scarlett Jo pushed the pedals of the spin bike, willing her royal-blue spandex leotard not to ride up again. A gift to herself twenty years ago, it still fit pretty well, though she'd pinched the tar out of her thighs when she'd tried to tug up the matching pants. But she loved royal blue. What she hated was Sabrina, the sadistic torturer up there shouting demands from her pretty little perch in the front of the class—and barely breathing hard.

"Oh, my heavens, have mercy! I'm dying here, people!" Scarlett Jo announced to the whole class over the rap song that pumped through the speakers, its beat serving as the cadence for the movement of their legs. "Are you trying to kill us?"

"You can do it, Scarlett Jo. Keep those legs moving."

"You can't move what you can't feel!"

The entire back row of seated spinners snickered, but she just ignored them.

Scarlett Jo had joined the Athletic Club of Williamson County last summer to get away from the boys. One day she had had all she could take and decided she'd rather torture her body than her brain. So she'd joined the gym and found out she actually liked to sweat. Most of the time. She'd decided to take a spin class two days a week and reward herself with yoga and Pilates any of the other days. She loved those classes not because she was good at them—though she was better than she used to be—but because they were the perfect place for a nap. Between the mats and the music, they felt like kindergarten.

She had always been a woman who loved her curves, but she also liked the definition of her waistline. She knew too many women who were just a "bip"—a term she'd coined for women who were the same width from bust to hip. Scarlett Jo was no bip. She was simply a full-figured gal—a Marilyn Monroe or Jayne Mansfield, only a little taller—and she was fine with that. But she wanted to stay around for her family too. So she exercised for her physical and mental health.

Sabrina spoke into a small microphone that was strapped over her ear and pressed against her dainty mouth. "Give me one quarter turn to the right."

Scarlett Jo looked at the little knob that rested between her knees, the knob that dictated the tension of her pedals. A turn to the right increased torture. A turn to the left decreased torture. And she did have a choice here. She could increase the torture, which made no sense to her. Or she could *pretend* to increase the torture—just let her hand roll across that knob as if she were adding more tension and let the entire class think she was superhuman. But that wasn't Scarlett Jo. She didn't care what the rest of the class did or thought.

"There ain't no way on God's green earth I'm touching that thing," she said, then grabbed her towel from the handlebars and mopped the sweat from her brow. Before spin, she hadn't even known she could sweat. Now she realized that Southern women actually could do it. That "glistening" stuff she'd heard about for years was nothing but hogwash.

"Last climb! Give it all you've got! Make your work count! Ten, nine, eight, seven . . ."

"Oh, my side. Oh, help me, someone. Oh, have mercy." Scarlett Jo's words came out in breathless staccato bursts. Her legs continued to move rapidly on the pedals as her hand turned wildly at the knob between her knees.

". . . two, one." Sabrina finished the count, and the people atop the bicycles exhaled as one.

Scarlett Jo let out a dramatic moan. "My behind is going to look so good, I'm going to be buried in my casket facedown." She raised her bum off the seat and patted it. "My last words will be 'View this, people! View this!'"

The class erupted. Sabrina couldn't help but laugh too as she climbed off her bike. "Great job, Monday," she said, addressing her class as usual by the day of the week. "Now let's do some stretching."

Scarlett Jo made a vain attempt to get her right foot atop the handlebars to stretch. It swiped the edge and then fell and bounced like a bobblehead by her side. She pulled at it again until she got it perched, though then she felt like she'd just ripped her entire muscle clear up to her behind. She was as flexible as a hammer. By the time they'd finished stretching, she wasn't sure what had hurt worse.

She wobbled out of the spin room and headed for the women's locker room. She walked straight up to the scale, something she loved to do after a workout. She always figured she'd weigh less after sweating out a gallon of liquid. "Not bad!" she noted, then called out the results to whoever was listening. Other women usually tried to cover the top of the scale with their hands. She figured she'd just announce her number so they could feel better about themselves.

"Oh, excuse me," Scarlett Jo said as she rounded a corner and just about took out the woman in front of her. Then she realized who she'd run into. "Elise."

"Hey, Scarlett Jo."

"Honey child, how are you? I haven't snagged you in a

month of Sundays. By the time church is over, you're off that stage and out the door. How in the world have you been?"

She watched Elise fidget with the bag draped across her shoulder. Scarlett Jo had five boys. She never trusted fidgeting.

"Doing great," Elise mumbled. "Uh, really well. How about you?"

Scarlett Jo fought for Elise's lowered eyes, then thought of Tim's visit. It all flashed through her mind as quickly as Cooper could clean out a bag of M&M's. "Good. Good. Well, you and I need to get together for lunch."

Elise stepped to the right, her dark ponytail falling across her shoulder. "Sure, yeah. I'd love that. Let's do that soon. But I need to hurry today or I'm going to be late for my class."

"Oh, I understand. But when can we do lunch?"

Elise fidgeted some more. Scarlett Jo didn't mind. She just let her fidget.

"Soon," Elise finally blurted. "I promise. Great to see you."

That wasn't good enough. "Soon when? I could do tomorrow. How is tomorrow?"

"Um, wow. Tomorrow? You know, tomorrow is crazy. I couldn't—"

"Okay, Wednesday. Wednesday is good for me too."

Elise crinkled her perfect little nose. Which matched her perfect little body. Which matched her perfect little outfit. All of which clashed with her avoidance act. "Wednesday is crazy too, Scarlett Jo." She let out a half laugh. A fake half laugh. "With church and everything and practicing with the worship team."

"Okay, then, Thursday or Friday. Those days are wide open." She'd make sure they were wide open.

Scarlett Jo saw the flash of frustration give way to resolve. "Sure. Yeah. Okay, let's say lunch on Friday. How's that?"

Scarlett Jo's smile stretched so wide she felt her eyes move. "Perfect! Shall we say eleven at Puckett's? Their blueberry cobbler will make you slap your mama."

"Sure, that sounds great. But now I gotta scoot."

Scarlett Jo snickered and shooed her with her hand. "Scoot, sugar, scoot." She watched the dark ponytail flap against the back of Elise's white sleeveless workout top. The contrast was striking. And so was a lot else that hadn't been clear before.

{ *Chapter 13* }

GRACE SAT IN THE FRONT SEAT of her Prius. The package in her hands felt as heavy and deadly as an anchor around her neck. Now, it seemed, she was about to launch it into the ocean. And once she delivered these papers to Tyler, something would die.

She had been strong all week, determined to move forward. Leo had left a dozen messages assuring her that she still had a job and could take off a month if she needed it. She hadn't responded. Neither had she responded to any of Tyler's repeated attempts to contact her after she packed up Miss Daisy and moved to Rachel's for a temporary stay.

He had probably written her absence off to a bad mood and a prolonged pout. But even he knew her well enough to understand that if she handed him divorce papers, she meant it. She had never brought up divorce, never used the possibility to manipulate or threaten him. When he saw her there holding the papers, he'd know this was something she had wrestled with her Creator over. Something she was doing with absolute, if heartbroken, peace. He'd know without a doubt that she was serious. Which was why it was so important to do this according to plan.

She set the envelope that would begin the dissolution of her marriage on the passenger seat, then started the car and pulled away from the curb. She had just a couple hours to do what she had to do and then catch Tyler right before he had to leave for the airport.

He was flying to New York to meet with his agent and publicist to see what damage control needed to be done about his DUI. The Predators had suspended him indefinitely since the arrest. Grace knew he had to be desperate to figure out what he would do next.

Giving him the papers right now while his life was in an uproar seemed a little harsh, but Zach and Rachel and Scarlett Jo all agreed it was the best plan. Tyler was impulsive and easily angered, so he needed time to process the situation without easy access to Grace, and she needed the buffer of physical distance. The trip would provide both—and professionally speaking, he couldn't afford to miss it.

Grace turned in to the parking lot of a downtown bank. Inside, a friendly young woman greeted her. "Can I help you?"

Can she help me? The words bounced around her brain like a pinball. "Sure, um, yeah. I need to talk to someone about opening a new account."

"Let me get someone to help you."

Grace watched the woman walk away, then glanced idly around the small waiting area. Her gaze fell across a copy of *Time* magazine with a photo of the American president and the Israeli prime minister on the front. As she studied their faces, her mind traveled back several years to when she had visited Israel. It was unlike any place she'd ever been. Before she went there, she'd never known she needed to go. After she left, she'd wondered how she could have lived her whole life and never gone there. She wondered when she could go back.

Then her mind interrupted its own mental travelogue. *I just had a normal thought.* She hadn't had what felt like a normal thought since she knew she was headed for divorce.

"I'll help you, ma'am."

Grace looked up quickly. She pressed her red patent-leather handbag against the side of her navy sleeveless blouse and fiddled with the ruffles that ran down the front. She followed the bank officer into a glassed room and took her place in a nondescript chair, feeling her knees collide at rhythmic intervals. She placed her hands on her legs in an attempt to still them.

The round, middle-aged woman scooted her chair up close to the desk and clasped her hands over the desktop calendar, covering countless red markings. "I'm told you want to open an account."

"I actually already have a money market account here. I wanted to take half of that out and open a personal checking account."

A piece of her felt like a criminal doing this without Tyler's knowledge. But Zach had told her that people served with divorce papers often flipped out and started trying to hide money. So she needed to protect herself. She was entitled by

Tennessee law to half of everything she and Tyler owned, so as long as she only moved half, she could and should make sure it was in her name only.

Fortunately for her, Tyler's name wasn't even on the money market account, though half of it was still legally his. She wasn't even sure he knew it existed. Again and again, she had tried to engage him in money matters, set up a budget with him, plan for the future with him. But his single focus always seemed to be how quickly he could spend whatever they made. She had opened the money market account to protect some of their savings. Now it would be her safety net.

"I'd like to move thirty-two thousand dollars," she told the officer.

The woman's stubby fingers moved quickly across the computer keypad. "Let's see here." She clicked a few more buttons. "Okay, let me get just a little more information."

Grace was tired of giving information. She was tired of questions. "Sure. Whatever you need."

The officer worked quickly. In less than twenty minutes Grace had the little bit she owned in this world tucked away and was back in the car, headed for her house.

Tyler had texted her that morning before she left for Zach's office to pick up the papers. His flight left at two, and he wanted to see her before then.

It was the opportunity she had prayed for, laid out before her like a gift. She would meet him right after noon, giving him little time to process before his flight, which she knew Tyler wouldn't miss. He loved being an athlete, a performer. He would want to salvage his career more than his marriage—though, ironically, he was willing to risk both with his drinking.

The closer she got to the house, the faster her heart beat. Maybe he'd cancel his trip. Maybe he'd do something crazy or even violent. Maybe there would be a horrible confrontation. Or worse, maybe he wouldn't even care. But all she could do was what she had planned.

She eased her way onto their street and stretched her head forward to see if she could spot his SUV. He was home just as he'd said he would be. And Rachel, as promised, sat in her car in front of the house next door.

Grace pulled into the driveway behind the Mercedes. She felt her pulse really take off. If heartbeats could be visible, she was certain Rachel would see hers from here.

Rachel met her at the edge of the front walk. "How are you doing?"

She held her free hand in front of her, and they watched it shake.

Rachel grabbed the hand and pressed it between her own. "I would have gone with you this morning."

Grace nodded. "I know you would. But there are certain things I need to do alone."

Rachel released her hand. "I understand. So I'm going to sit right here on the front steps like Zach suggested. And you need to stay in the foyer, okay? Keep the door open. Let him know I'm here. Help keep it calmer."

Grace was grateful for all the reminders, though she had rehearsed this moment in her head more times than she had greeted morning viewers. "I know."

They trudged toward the house at a dirgelike pace, cicadas crunching beneath their feet. Rachel shuddered. "Those things deserve to die."

Grace didn't respond.

"This feels like a funeral too," Rachel whispered.

"It is, Rachel. Unfortunately it is."

Grace gripped the manila envelope more tightly as they reached the steps. She rang the doorbell. Then she and Rachel waited—for what, she wasn't sure, but waiting was all they had left to do. Through the window on the door, she saw Tyler's flustered face come into view. His awkward smile at seeing Grace faded when he caught sight of Rachel, but by the time he opened the door, he had plastered on his familiar, for-the-public grin.

"Gracie. Babe. It's so good to see you." He reached out and wrapped his arms around her. She felt every muscle in her body stiffen as tightly as Miss Daisy's did when Grace tried to pick her up. Rigor-mortis stiff.

"Come in. Come in." He released her and tugged her arm. "I'm so glad you got here before I left town. I've wanted to talk to you all week." His words emerged fast and coated with awareness that he was onstage.

"I'm going to stay out here," Rachel said as Tyler and Grace moved into the foyer.

Tyler turned toward her quickly. "Rachel, that's ridiculous. You know our home is your home."

Rachel's face held solemnity and compassion at the same time. But her words were firm. "No, I'm just going to sit out here on the porch." She looked at Grace. "I'll be right here."

Grace felt fear begin to trickle up her spine. She nodded. Tyler shrugged and started to close the door.

"No, keep that open." Grace's words came out louder than she had intended and slightly more panicked. *Maintain control,* her mind whispered. *No tears. No fear.* "I want the door to stay open." These words were different. Calmer. Steadier.

"Sure. Yeah. Whatever you want." It was evident he knew she wasn't here just to talk, but he didn't seem upset. "Hey, I got you something," he said. "Let me run and get it."

He disappeared down the hall, and in a moment he was back with a box. He held it out to her. She'd know that brown box with the gold monogram anywhere. Boxes like that held expensive handbags. She had five of them already.

Expensive gifts were the consolation prizes Tyler offered her—either as repentance offerings or as excuses for the expensive items he'd bought himself. Or maybe somewhere down inside, they were his way of extending the love he had determined he was incapable of giving in other ways. But no matter the reason, she didn't need or want another bag.

She took the box from his hands and set it on the long, carved table that stretched against the wall beside her. Then she held out the manila envelope in her hand. "This is for you."

He eyed it for a moment. He didn't reach for it, just looked. "What is it?"

For a moment, as he stood there, she wanted to pull it back. Run from the house and forget any of this had happened. Because once he opened that envelope, once he saw the heading "Original Petition for Divorce," this would all be real.

She stuck the envelope out farther. "Take it."

The muscles in his jaw twitched. They always did that when he was deciding how angry he was about to get. He snatched the envelope from her hand and opened the gold-toned clasp. He pulled the papers from the envelope, and his eyes darted across the top page. Then he slammed the whole stack down on the table. Grace resisted the urge to jump. But she did hear movement on the front porch and saw him look past her. Whatever Rachel did out there caused him to tamp his rage down to a sullen seething.

"So this is it, Grace? You wait until I'm—what?" He looked at his watch. "Thirty minutes from having to leave for very important meetings regarding my career, and then you blindside me with divorce papers. You don't call all week. You don't answer my e-mails. You don't respond to my texts. You don't say one word to me, just show up on the doorstep with these papers. Don't I deserve the common courtesy of a conversation with my wife before she goes off and files for divorce?"

Her words came out the way she had practiced, self-assured and calm, though she felt anything but calm inside. "You've had ten years of conversation."

He let out a mocking laugh. "I've had ten years of a mistake is what I've had." His voice wasn't as controlled as it usually was. "This was always a mistake."

"I'm sorry you feel that way. As I told you before, it was never a mistake to me."

He snatched the papers again. "How can you say that? How can you walk in here with divorce papers and then say this wasn't a mistake? If it wasn't a mistake, why would you walk away from it?"

She had wondered how quickly he would try to make it her fault. "I'm not walking away from my marriage. I'm walking away from you. I'm walking away from a man who keeps choosing something he values more than me. I'm walking away from deception. I'm walking away from a man who looked at me a week ago and said he wanted to be left alone to be the man he is. A man who was convinced that his marriage was a mistake. But let me tell you one thing. This may be all you're willing to be, all you choose to be. But I will never— and please hear me when I say this—I will *never* believe it is all you are capable of being.

"So that is what I am walking away from. I believe in this marriage. Even years down the road, I will believe in all that this marriage could be and should be. But I'm walking away from you, from what you have chosen to make it. Not because I don't believe in you, but because I am no longer willing to be the only one in this marriage who does."

He didn't hesitate. He never hesitated. He always had a response. It had taken her a week to figure out how to say what she had just said. "Well, you can perch yourself on your high horse if you want to, Grace, but you *are* giving up. That's all there is to it. I would never have left you."

She didn't remind him that he'd told her to get out. She just nodded. "I know. You would have let me stay here forever. You would have let me die here because that would be easier than confronting who you have become. You're desperate for me to stay because I've spent all these years rescuing you. But I'm not going to do it. Today I am deciding for myself that Grace Shepherd is not going to die here."

She started for the door and then turned around. "When you get back, you'll need to find a new place to live. I'll e-mail you what I feel is an agreeable separation of property, and we can discuss it after your trip. And, Tyler . . ." Her voice wavered. She swallowed hard at the lump that had all but stopped her airflow. "I hope that at some point, healing can come for both of us. Because God knows I am just as broken as you are in so many ways. And my ultimate prayer is that one day we can try again, even have the marriage we were created to have."

He looked at her, the lines on his face as hard as the steel of her resolve. "If we divorce, I can assure you I will never be back. There will be no remarriage. No anything. We will be done."

He wanted her to react. She could tell by the look on his face. He knew how much she loved him. He knew that was his ultimate card. Grace imagined what was going through his head: *Tell her you will never be back and she'll quit this madness. Tell her that if she leaves it this way, whatever she is wishing for, praying for, believing for is nothing but a cruel joke and a wasted effort.*

She finally spoke. "I have no other choice. This has to end. This marriage, what it has become—*this* marriage is over." With that, she walked from the house and closed the door behind her. Rachel stood quickly. Side by side, their steps unhurried, they made their way to the cars.

Rachel stretched an arm around Grace's shoulder. "You did good, baby girl."

Grace let out a long exhale.

"You okay?"

"Yeah. I'm okay."

"Want to come back to the house?"

Grace tucked her fingers underneath the car door handle and pulled. The door opened quietly. She turned toward Rachel. Her friend's dark eyes held all the compassion and depth that thirteen years of friendship brought. Grace shook her head. "No, I think I'm going to spend a little time alone."

Rachel studied her. "You sure? We can go get ice cream. Chocolate. And sweet tea. Do whatever it is people do after giving their spouse divorce papers. We can go do that."

A soft laugh escaped Grace's lips. "Thank you. No, I just need to be by myself for a while. I'll let him catch his plane. Then I'll come over to your place and grab Miss Daisy, and I'll spend the night here."

She could tell Rachel's resignation was hard to offer. "Okay. But call me. I mean it. If he says one word to you. Or if you have a breakdown. Or need ice cream. Please promise you'll call."

"I promise. But I'll be fine."

"You don't need to sleep here alone."

"I *want* to sleep here alone. This is my life now. I have to go in there alone eventually. Might as well start tonight."

Tears glittered on Rachel's long black eyelashes. "You're a stronger woman than I am, Grace. In every way."

Grace shook her head rapidly. "No. I'm just doing what I have to do."

Rachel grabbed her and squeezed tightly, the embrace communicating unquestionable loyalty and love. When she let go, Grace climbed into her car and closed the door.

A few blocks down, she pulled into the parking lot of Landmark Booksellers, Franklin's quaint downtown bookstore. She watched as Tyler's Mercedes passed by in the direction of the airport. And what came out of her after that shocked her. The wails were as loud as the thirteen-year cicadas that screamed from the trees. Her body doubled over the steering wheel.

For the last four days, only she had lived with the knowledge that their ten-year marriage was over. Now they both knew. And if pain could break hearts, she was certain hers had just ripped in two.

{ *Chapter 14* }

SCARLETT JO STOOD by the front counter of Puckett's Grocery and Restaurant. She'd been looking forward to her lunch with Elise, partly because she hadn't been to Puckett's in a while—and she loved Puckett's. What started out as a little country store back in the fifties had turned into a local favorite. Some of the South's best songwriters and musicians used it as a showcase in the evenings. But even when there was no live music, people came for the relaxed atmosphere and the wonderful food—Southern cuisine at its finest.

And oh, that cobbler. Puckett's had the best blueberry cobbler in town. Scarlett Jo knew that for a fact. She knew where the best food was all over the Nashville area. Especially desserts—Scarlett Jo specialized in those. Dotson's made the best chocolate pies. Merridee's was the source for wonderful coffee cakes and cinnamon rolls and those fabulous caramel pecan rounds. Amerigo had the best tiramisu. Loveless Cafe featured delectable homemade biscuits you could slather with peach preserves, while Dalts had the best chocolate malt cake you'd ever put in your mouth. She could go on and on. If you were looking for any kind of sweet treat, Scarlett Jo Newberry could tell you where to go.

She looked down at her watch. Elise McAdams was ten minutes late for their eleven o'clock lunch date. Scarlett Jo shrugged. Might as well grab a table so she could get something to drink as she waited. She ordered sweet tea in a Mason jar because they would do that here if you asked. She always asked. That was how her granny had served tea, and it was her favorite way to drink it.

After another five minutes she went ahead and ordered blueberry cobbler with ice cream. That would be her appetizer. She hadn't had any fruit with breakfast, and this would cover at least one of her fruit servings for the day, plus some dairy. If she decided she wanted another cobbler after lunch—and she might just decide to do that—then she'd be covered for another couple of servings. A giggle slipped out when she thought of that. Sometimes she cracked her own self up.

The window next to her table gave her a great view of the Franklin lunch rush. She caught sight of Elise as she stepped from her car, phone attached to her head, deep in conversation. Elise's wide turquoise necklace bounced as she walked toward the door, still talking. She spotted Scarlett Jo when she came in and waved, quickly said good-bye to the person on the other end, and collapsed in a chair as if she had lived nine lives before noon.

"Whew." Elise set her yellow handbag on the table. "What a morning. I was at the church all morning. Then I forgot our babysitter has to leave early today, so it looks like I won't be able to stay long at all. I'm really sorry, Scarlett Jo. I can't believe school is out already, and I'm not used to our summer schedule yet. You know what I mean? Arranging childcare drives me crazy sometimes."

"Oh, sugar." Scarlett Jo flipped a hand at her. "You'd better be careful. These years will fly by quicker than you can blink. My Jack was two years old yesterday. Now he's taller than me and shaving. Happens before you know it. I mean, when I saw your Hank the other day, I couldn't believe how much he'd grown."

Elise smiled. It was hard for any woman not to smile at the thought of her children, unless she had just spent the entire summer with them. "I know. He and Hailey both seem to be changing overnight."

"And these are such sweet years. Get ready, though. For teenagers you're going to need extra sugar. In fact, considering the way this day is shaping up for you, you might want to start with dessert, too, just to make it through."

Elise looked at the cobbler bowl, then up at Scarlett Jo. "Oh, I'm good. I had some toast for breakfast."

Scarlett Jo shook her head. "What is it about women today? Nobody eats. People look at food as if it has a disease or something. But God made food to be eaten. He made bodies to require it. You are a stick, Elise. You need to eat. Now, if it's money—if the church isn't paying you enough to eat . . ."

Elise let out a nervous laugh and held up her hand. "No, seriously, I'm not hungry. And trust me. I eat. I eat all that I want."

Scarlett Jo pushed her spoon through the velvety ice cream

and crust into the thick fruit filling. She put the entire spoonful in her mouth and chewed slowly, smiling as she did. She wanted Elise to know what she was missing. It worked. She could have sworn that at one point the other woman licked her lips.

She set her fork down. "So shoot straight, Elise. What's up?"

Elise's face showed that she hadn't expected Scarlett Jo's forthrightness. She moved her long dark hair across her shoulder and placed her hands on her purse as if she might need to get out quicker than she thought. Her brow furrowed, revealing the lines around her eyes. "I'm not sure what you're talking about, Scarlett Jo."

Scarlett Jo took a long drink of her tea. "Well, this is how I see it. When you have a friendship with someone and then all of a sudden that friend begins to avoid you, it's either one of two things. One, they might have had a big life change that they are having to adjust to, like a move, a new marriage, a new baby, a new job. Or two, they are avoiding you because they're doing something they shouldn't be doing. So I'm thinking, you haven't moved, there's no new baby, there's no new job, there's no new marriage, yet you've fallen off the face of the earth. You don't stay around after church. You haven't called to get together in months. And I had to all but drag you here today. My best conclusion is that something is up. So what is it?"

Scarlett Jo forked another bite of the rich, sweet goodness and waited with a face that reflected nothing but concern.

Elise looked dumbfounded. "Um . . . well, um . . . I'm just not sure what you're talking about. The church has a lot of demands. My family has a lot of demands. The kids' school, caring for the people in the music department, my volunteer work. I'm just not as available as I used to be."

Scarlett Jo nodded, carefully listening to all that Elise was saying and all that she wasn't. "But these are the same demands you had a year ago. And a year ago we had lunch every other week. We talked about our children, our husbands. How is Tim?"

Elise raised her hand for the waitress. "I think I'll just have some coffee."

Scarlett Jo crinkled her nose. "Sure, honey. Get you a coffee."

Scarlett Jo finished her cobbler and sipped tea while she waited.

The coffee arrived quickly. Strong-smelling coffee. "Tim is good. You know he is." Then her eyes began to water, and Scarlett Jo heard the faint break in her voice. "Well, I'm not sure. He's been acting different lately. I'm kind of worried about him."

Scarlett Jo patted Elise's hand. "Worried why, honey?"

Elise dabbed her eyes. "Well, he just seems to be acting really odd. I don't know—maybe he doesn't love me like he used to. Maybe he's overloaded at work or something. But he just seems real angry with me lately. Like he's frustrated. And I told him I thought he was working too much. You know, with the way the church is growing, it requires more of us, more of him. But he claims it has nothing to do with work, so I don't know. Maybe he's having a midlife crisis. I would just hate for him to do anything foolish if he is."

Scarlett Jo watched Elise take a sip. She held the coffee in her left hand.

"Sugar, it sounds like you and Tim might need to get away together."

Elise took another long drink of her coffee. Her head lifted and she smiled. "That would be wonderful. But right now there just isn't time."

Scarlett Jo leaned over and took Elise's hand in hers. "Honey, you can't afford not to take care of your marriage. Marriage comes first—before children, before jobs, before everything except the Lord. And by 'the Lord,' I'm not talking about doing a church job. Your marriage comes before that too." She beamed. "Tell you what. I'm going to talk with Jackson, and we're going to make sure the two of you get away. I'll even watch the kids." She snorted. "What's two more when you have five?"

Elise shook her head. "No, Scarlett Jo. You can't do that. We're fine. We'll get away with the kids somewhere—camping or something. That'll be what we all need."

Scarlett Jo shook her head, and the large white flower that was attached to her headband shook with it. "I'm not taking no for an answer. You need time without the kids, and the church needs the two of you strong and healthy and happy. And so does your family."

She could see Elise's resignation. "Okay. Well, sure, yes, you're probably right. We probably just need some time alone."

"Trust me, Elise. I know the power of being alone with your man."

"Thank you." Elise glanced at her watch. "Oh, Scarlett Jo, I'm so sorry. It takes me fifteen minutes to get home, so I'm going to have to run. We will do this again soon, though."

She stood, grabbed her purse, then leaned over and gave Scarlett Jo a half hug. Scarlett Jo hated half hugs. Elise touched Scarlett Jo's face. "You are such a wonderful friend. Thank you for listening. But please don't say anything to Tim. I don't want him to think I'm talking about him. He's just going through a rough time, that's all. If you and Jackson offer something to us, let him think it's your idea, okay? Please don't let him know we talked."

Scarlett Jo licked her lips and then moved her fingers across them as if she had zipped them shut.

"You're the best," Elise said. "I've really missed seeing you. I hope we can do this again soon." She straightened and half ran from the restaurant.

Scarlett Jo watched as Elise climbed into her blue Volkswagen Jetta. As soon as she got in the car, the phone was back at her ear.

Scarlett Jo raised the glass of tea and took a long sip. Then she gazed out the window at the traffic as her mouth formed the words, "Lord, help Elise break. Whatever's in her that needs to break to get her whole and out of her lies, break it. But if you could do it as gently as possible, I'd appreciate that too."

❀　❀　❀

Zach shook his head hard. But the image of Grace in his mind was apparently more of the tattoo variety than the Etch A Sketch version. Shaking couldn't dislodge it. She was there. And she seemed to be staying.

Darlene came into the conference room. "I'm going to call it a day."

He spun around, wondering for a second if his thoughts betrayed him. "Sure. Sure. I'm about to leave too." He turned back toward the window. The neon lights of the Franklin Theatre already shone bright, ready to welcome evening movie-goers. "Grace Shepherd." He spoke her name, appreciating the way it fell from his lips.

"Yes? Tough day for her, huh?"

"Yeah, but have you ever seen someone handle a situation like this with, well, such grace? She doesn't get angry. She doesn't talk bad about her husband. She's just determined. And she makes it clear that this is the hardest thing she has ever done."

"It's because she loves him."

Zach let out a puff of air. "Look what he's done to her. How do you love that?"

Darlene walked around the conference table and looked out the window next to his. "You can't explain love. People love broken people all the time, and we are all broken in some way. We see it all in here, Zach. We get them in the denial stage, the anger stage, the shock stage. I think Grace Shepherd has a long road of healing ahead of her. A very long road."

They stood there in silence for a few minutes before she added, "But just like I know God has a beautiful plan for you, I'm confident he has one for Grace. No matter where she may have to go to get there."

Zach turned toward Darlene. Her white dress made her look almost angelic. "How do you know all of that?"

She let out a soft laugh. "I've never seen one living soul who has asked God for help and been refused. I'm not saying help will come the way you want. But I can assure you that from the moment we ask, he has heard and he is moving. Plus, I watch people. I take people in. And to be honest, I learn a great deal about them by what they don't say."

The last sentence came out in a knowing way. Darlene laid a soft hand on his shoulder, then exited the room, leaving him to wonder what she knew exactly.

Zach's paralegal, Derrick, came in a few minutes later. He left a stack of research for next week's court cases on the end of the conference table and said good-night. Zach stood quietly a few more minutes. Then a text message alarm sounded from his phone: **Both girls spending night with friends. I'm doing dinner and a movie with Becky and Lisa.**

That was it. No "What do you have going on? What will you do for dinner? Want to see a movie or maybe spend an evening at home?" There was nothing. Not one thing.

Zach walked into his office and sat in his chair, propped his feet up, and leaned back. He wouldn't even bother to respond to that. He'd show her. Even though he knew she didn't care if he responded. She did what she wanted when she wanted. It was all about Caroline. The rest of them simply existed in her world.

The text alarm sounded again. *What now? I'm sure you're not about to ask my permission.* But it wasn't Caroline.

You alone yet? Can I drop by? Or do you want me to go to that spin class he thinks I'm headed to?

A smile slowly crossed his face. Someone wanted to be with him tonight. Someone was willing to leave her family for him.

He texted back. **I'd love that. Still at office.**

Be there in five.

And she was. Zach never bothered saying hello. The passion between them collided like killer waves on a sun-parched seashore, virtually consuming everything it touched. The intensity between them was so great that for an instant he wondered if this was about either of them at all. Or was it just the desperate desire to escape from what was their *normal*?

But he didn't care. Not in that moment. He simply surrendered. Her presence was all he knew, her breathing the only thing he heard—until the door to his office opened.

Oh yeah, that he heard. And the words that fell from his wife's mouth as he jumped from the sofa.

"What in the . . . ?"

Chaos ruled the next few seconds—expletives flying, Zach and Elise scurrying across the floor like ants on a demolished anthill.

"Elise?" Caroline said, finally recognizing the woman. "You've got to be kidding me. You? You're having an affair with *my* husband?"

Odd that in the moment, Zach was more frustrated by the way she announced him as a possession than the fact that he'd been caught in a compromising position with one of the worship pastors from their church.

Elise was kneeling on the floor, her hands flapping across the carpet as she fumbled for her clothes. "Caroline, I . . . I can explain."

Caroline's green eyes seemed to be ablaze, reflecting the red of her hair. "Oh, do explain, Elise. Explain to me how you accidentally got intertwined with my husband on the sofa in his office." She let out a sarcastic laugh. "I so want to hear that."

"Elise, go." Zach tried to keep his voice calm. "It's best if you just go."

Caroline's head almost seemed to recoil. "Just go? You think I'm going to let this . . . this *home wrecker* walk away? Well, you two have another thing coming. You will both sit here and answer my questions."

Elise looked at Zach, her eyes pleading. He longed to rescue her, to be a man in that moment and snatch her away, then deal with Caroline himself. But what remained of his masculinity had been stripped away when his wife opened that door.

"Sit!" Caroline screamed.

Elise stayed on the floor, tears now evident. Caroline stepped closer, towering over her. "Who do you think you are, going after another woman's husband? A man with children. And you—you're supposed to be all holy, leading the worship at church. But you've made it clear what you really are, so here . . ." Caroline dug frantically into her handbag, pulled out some cash, and threw it at Elise. "Just a little payment for your work. So you can be a prostitute instead of just a slut."

Elise jumped to her feet and grabbed her purse while Caroline continued to scold her like a toddler. "You should be ashamed of yourself! You should both be completely ashamed of yourselves!"

Zach sank onto the edge of the sofa, mutely watching Elise slide over to the half-open door and open it farther. Caroline slammed her hand against it, closing it with such force that the walls shook. Funny he could notice that since everything else was shaking.

"Please let go of the door." Elise's words came out in a whisper.

Caroline's voice cut like a razor blade. "You don't get to tell me what to do. You're not going to tell me anything. You're going to listen to what I have to say."

Zach noticed Elise's white knuckles wrapped tight around the handle. "I've heard all you're going to say," she told Caroline. "I know you're angry. And I'm very sorry. And we can talk, but I'm not going to do it this way."

She looked at Zach again. Caroline followed her glance.

"You think he can help you? He can't help you now. He can't even help himself. What you need to do is get your rear end home and figure out what you're going to do with your own marriage once your husband hears about this."

Elise jerked hard on the door and pushed Caroline back.

Caroline regained her composure, but not quickly enough to prevent Elise from leaving. In a few seconds Zach heard the stairwell door close.

Which left just the two of them. Zach leaned back and felt a brief release wash over him, a gratitude of sorts. The secret was out. The charade was over. There would be no more hiding, no more pretending. He found himself mildly surprised when Caroline ran to him, leaned down, and began beating on his chest like a wild animal. The tears that accompanied her anger surprised him even more.

"I hate you, Zach Craig! I hate you!"

He grabbed her wrists and wrapped his hands around them, pushed her back so he could stand. "I know."

"You know! How do you know? I've never cheated on you. I've never so much as looked at another man. I've given you everything. Our girls." Her hand flew to her mouth. "Oh, our girls. What will they do? They will be heartbroken when they find out."

"I think you're getting way ahead of yourself here. Only three people know about this—you and me and Elise. No one else. We don't have to tell the girls. They don't have to know any of this—especially right now."

The look on her face was a jumble of confusion, shock, fury, pain. Tears had dampened her cheeks, and her shoulders shook as more fell. She jerked her wrists free and ran a trembling hand through her hair. "What am I going to do? What do you do after something like this?"

Zach wrinkled his brow. This seemed to be truly affecting her. To be honest, when he played out this scenario his mind, he had never imagined her caring. In his deep desire to blame

Caroline for what he had done, he had somehow forgotten she might actually get hurt.

"I don't know what to do." His voice was so much calmer than he thought it would be—another difference from his imagined scenarios. He'd always thought he would be more freaked out than this. Had he wanted to get caught? Maybe that was why he'd been so reckless. Or maybe he was as narcissistic as he'd told himself Caroline was.

"Let's just take things one step at a time," he said. "I'll stay here tonight, and maybe tomorrow we can find someone to talk to. I don't know—maybe Jackson and Scarlett Jo."

He regretted saying that as soon as the words left his mouth. Elise was Jackson's praise and worship leader. This news could ruin her and Tim at the church. Tim would be devastated. Funny—until this moment he hadn't thought about Tim at all.

Caroline sank down on the sofa, her tears falling freely now. Zach sat beside her. It was the first time he'd seen her cry like this in a long time. The first time in a long time he'd actually felt sorry for her. But when he wrapped his arm around her, she jerked away.

"Get away from me! Don't touch me!" She stood and started for the door. "And don't come home. Whatever you do, do not set foot in my house."

With that, she slammed the door behind her. And Zach was reminded once again of how quickly open-and-shut doors could change things.

All kinds of things.

{ Chapter 15 }

GRACE CLIMBED FROM THE BED and put on her black slippers. She picked up her white sweatshirt from the end of the bed and pulled it on over her UT tank top, which matched her orange-and white-striped sleeping shorts. Rachel had felt so sorry for Grace, she'd even let her wear the orange and white at her house. But now Grace was home. She moved aside the curtains and opened the plantation shutters, then just stood there looking out, thinking how strange it was to wake up when the sun was shining.

Miss Daisy jumped off the end of the bed and walked out the bedroom door, then stopped and turned as if to let Grace know she needed to follow. Today Grace was almost glad someone was dictating what she needed to do.

"Want to go out?"

Miss Daisy continued down the hall, obviously glad that Grace had gotten the message.

She opened the back door, and Miss Daisy meandered down the steps in a slow saunter. She was so Southern. Grace followed her out and sat on the top step. "I'm watching you."

Miss Daisy ignored her. Grace wrapped her arms around her knees. Her husband would never be back in her bed. The thought had swept over her last night when she crawled beneath the covers, resulting in black stains on her white pillowcase. Now it brought wet streaks down her swollen face.

Miss Daisy bounced up beside her and walked past, returning to the house. Apparently she was finished.

Grace mixed Miss Daisy's food and poured herself a glass of sweet tea. Then she began to walk a small circle through the foyer and into the dining room, down the front hall, and back to the foyer again. Her slippered feet moved at a slow pace, and her prayers came out in fractured bursts.

"I'm really hurting here." Past the dining room table.

"I need you so desperately." The front hall.

"This isn't how I pictured it." Back to the foyer.

"Please help me make it through this."

Then words passed through her heart and across her lips that never bothered filtering through her head because her head held no capacity in this broken state to even pray such a prayer. "And please, please, whatever I've done to get me here, get it out of me. I don't ever want to end up here again."

The prayer wasn't passionate. It wasn't a wailing or travailing kind of prayer. It was gentle, calm, but so desperate. The hurt—this hurt—was far too painful to ever want to feel it again. If she had to go to the deepest places of her personal shame to come out alive, then she was willing to go. She just prayed she'd survive the journey.

She wiped her eyes, walked to the bathroom, and unplugged her phone from the charger. It rang as she picked it up. She checked the caller ID.

Tyler.

The call with Tyler lasted five hours. They both cried. And in the span of that time, they relived every pivotal moment of the last ten years of their marriage. He asked if she was sure about the divorce. She assured him she was. He told her he had done all he knew to fight his addiction, that he had no more fight in him. She reminded him again that he was worth fighting for, but she didn't know if he would ever believe it. And now the fight was his to own.

He promised that when he got home, they could sit down and divide their lives like adults. Whether it would actually work out that way, she had no idea. She knew Tyler too well. But she could hope.

When they hung up, the emptiness of the house and the revelation of how it would be now moved in on her like a hurricane making landfall. It beat her from every angle.

When she was finally able to rise from its aftermath, she picked up the phone again and called her mother. Her parents would be there in a few hours. Then she dialed Leo. He'd be there in thirty minutes.

❀ ❀ ❀

Zach shifted his body and almost fell off the sofa. He cursed the pain in his back as he tried to stand. He had never realized in his past moments spent on that sofa how uncomfortable it could be for a full night's sleep. Maybe he should have thought about that before he got himself here.

Here. He was here, wasn't he? He was here in that place where somehow secretly he had wanted to be. Yet now that he'd arrived, it was the last place he ever thought he would be.

He put on his pants and moved to the window. He stared at the street. Saturday activities were already in full swing, the sidewalks teeming with people who had no idea his life was officially in the toilet. They were drinking Starbucks and walking their dogs and reading the *Tennessean* and talking about things that didn't matter. And he was a grown man who'd been caught with his pants down. None of it felt like he'd thought it would.

He went to his desk and picked up his phone. There were no texts, no voice mails. That never happened. Elise usually texted him multiple times a day, and Caroline did too. Now even his phone was boycotting him. He tapped the small green box in the top right-hand corner. Up popped last night's texts in the order they'd been received, including the final two that had changed his life forever.

He touched Elise's name, and a box for him to type in his message opened. His finger hovered over the screen, but he didn't know where to start. What did you say on a day like this? "How are you doing? Does your husband know yet? Has your world collapsed yet? Are you alive, or did Caroline come over and kill you?"

The last thought might not play out well in court should that be where this ended up. What a stupid thought. Caroline was his wife. There was no doubt where this would end up. It would play out in the very courthouse where he worked every week, but now he'd be one of the Craigs in *Craig v. Craig*. And what a *versus* that would be.

His finger began touching the keys. **Do you need me to come talk to Tim?** He pushed Send before he had the opportunity to change his mind. Then he stared at the tiny screen and waited—for what, he didn't know. For an all-capitals comment? For a response from Tim himself? For a blank screen to still be staring back at him after he had aged another twenty-four hours and twenty-four lifetimes?

I told him last night. We can have no more contact.

And that was all there was. He didn't know what he had expected. But it wasn't this. He hadn't really expected her to tell her husband, and he definitely hadn't expected her response to be "no more contact." If anything, she had acted like she would leave Tim tomorrow if she could. And now, when she could, she was cutting Zach off instead.

There was a stab in his chest. Anger followed. He set the phone down and paced around his desk. In that moment he wished he kept a change of clothes at the office because his wrinkled dress slacks weren't exactly what he wanted to be wearing right now. He wanted running shorts and tennis shoes so he could take off and go who knows where. He just wanted to get away from these feelings and this sense of being trapped and this . . . this *pain*.

He walked to the sofa, sat, and put his head in his hands. He felt the cool metal of his wedding ring press against his forehead. And with that gentle yet real reminder of all that was now potentially irretrievably broken, Zach Craig wept. For the first time in years, he actually cried.

❀ ❀ ❀

"I smell food," Leo said as he stepped through Grace's open front door.

"Of course you do. You are to food like a metal detector is to cheap jewelry." Grace closed the door behind him and then led him into the kitchen.

"You look kinda rough."

"Divorce will do that to you."

He stopped in the middle of the front hall. "I'm so sorry."

She tugged at his hand to keep him in forward motion. "Me too."

She made him sit on a stool at the counter, then picked up a platter of apricot scones. She brought him Devonshire cream, a plate, and a napkin.

"Does this mean you're not mad at me anymore?" His eyes held the same pleading as a puppy's after the fifth accident of the day.

She pulled up a stool beside him. "No, I'm not mad at you. I was hurt. I was scared. And I was really mad at Tyler, at our life, at all that had gotten us to that moment. At me. But not you, Leo."

He looked at her, then back at his plate. She smiled but didn't have the energy to laugh. "You can eat now."

A big grin wrapped around his face as he plucked two scones from the platter and moved them to his smaller plate. The two piles of cream he placed beside them would be considered more scoops than dollops. He crammed half a scone with cream into his mouth. "I'm so glad you're not mad anymore." The words came out as a jumbled mess, but she had spent the last ten years deciphering his words through his food. "Does this mean you're coming back to work?"

She hadn't really thought about work. For the past two weeks, she hadn't thought about much of anything but surviving. She let the question settle on her for a moment. What else would she do? Broadcasting was what she knew. It was her source of income as well.

"Of course," she told him. "But I think I might need another week."

"Sure. Sure. You've got plenty of vacation time accumulated." Small pieces of scone shot out when he said it. "You could take a year. Though for an on-air talent, I don't think that would—"

The sound of the doorbell stopped him from finishing. Miss Daisy was already at the door, announcing her displeasure to the person on the other side of it. It took all of ten seconds to figure out who was there. The fuchsia reflection through the glass in the door gave it away. Grace had called her and Rachel after she called Leo.

She opened the door. "Hey, Scarlett Jo."

Scarlett Jo scooted through quickly. "I need to get in here. I swear a cicada chased me the whole way." She looked at Grace and wrapped her up in her thick arms. "How are you, sugar?"

"Alive." That was the best she could do at the moment.

Scarlett Jo released her from the hug but still held her shoulders tightly. The woman could be a brute. Maybe that's why God had given her boys.

"Tell me all about it," Scarlett Jo commanded, pulling Grace into another bear hug.

Over Scarlett Jo's shoulder, Grace caught sight of Rachel coming up the steps. "How about if I tell you both at the same time."

Grace led them to the kitchen. Scarlett Jo spotted the scones before she spotted Leo. "Oh my, what are those?"

Leo stopped midchew and dropped his scone as if his hand were in the cookie jar. "Y'all ain't ever hath Grathe'th thconth?" he asked.

Scarlett Jo squinted at him as if that would help her make out his words. Her entire body seemed to follow her nose toward the platter of goodies. "No. She makes scones?"

Rachel moved around Grace and opened a kitchen cabinet to pull out more plates. "Does she make scones? Grace Shepherd makes some of the most amazing scones you've ever eaten."

Grace leaned against the counter and watched as the entire room forgot she existed. Leo's brow furrowed and he curled his arm around his plate in case the additional guests got any ideas of snatching something.

Rachel patted his arm. "Leo, you can keep your scone. I promise we're not going to take it from you."

He took another large bite.

Rachel and Scarlett Jo each fixed themselves a plate and started lathering cream on their scones. Then they both looked at Grace as if they suddenly realized why they were here. She saw their torture over engaging her in conversation and having to wait to take the first bite. She motioned toward them. "Eat."

They quickly returned to the food in front of them, and she smiled at their delight. She'd always loved watching people enjoy her food. It was one of the things she found dissatisfying about her job. She liked being a newscaster, especially working with Leo. But with television, it was just you and the camera. You couldn't touch people. You only talked at them. It was so impersonal. You rarely got the gratification of seeing people respond to what you had done for them.

Grace jumped at the sound of Scarlett Jo's hand slapping the countertop. She slapped it again as she chewed. "Oh, my side, that is the best thing I have ever put in my mouth." Then she slapped Rachel.

"Ow. What was that for?"

"Because this stuff is slap-your-mama good. And since my mama is not here, you'll have to do."

Grace let out a soft laugh—and it hurt. Her eyes hurt. Her body hurt. Her head hurt. But that laugh felt good too. Watching her friends sit here and eat her scones felt good.

Scarlett Jo threw her head back in sheer rapture as she chewed. The sounds she made caused Rachel to raise a manicured eyebrow. Scarlett Jo looked at her, and a huge smile swept over her pink cheeks. She threw her arm around Rachel.

Rachel twirled her finger at her temple. "She's cuckoo," she mouthed.

Then Scarlett Jo threw her other arm around Leo.

Leo just smiled and stuffed another scone in his mouth. Rachel extracted herself from Scarlett Jo's grip and gave Grace a you-can't-be-serious look.

"Grace." Scarlett Jo wiped her mouth. "Seriously, honey, how long have you been baking like this?"

Leo shook his head and patted his bulging belly. He'd unbutton his khakis in a minute. "This woman has been cooking like this as long as I've known her. Ever tasted her cinnamon rolls? Her homemade pimento-cheese sandwiches?"

Scarlett Jo moved another scone from the platter to her plate. "Nope. Not yet, anyway."

"Woman, then you have missed out. This girl makes the best stuff I've ever eaten."

Rachel gently touched the corners of her mouth with a napkin. "She makes my kids' birthday cakes too."

Leo raised his hand. "Oh yes, FYI, do not forget my birthday is in two weeks."

Scarlett Jo chewed with her hand over her mouth and nodded at the same time. "Shee'th dointh my nexth oneth."

Grace took the container of Devonshire cream from the refrigerator and put two more big scoops in the bowl that sat by the now half-empty plate of scones. She watched her guests move quicker than paparazzi on a royal. When they had stuffed themselves, she told them about her conversation with Tyler.

It felt good to talk about it finally. But after a few tears, a few hugs, and a good dose of her sweet peach tea, Scarlett Jo stopped the conversation with one question.

"Grace, if you could do anything in this world, what would you do?"

The question sent her sifting through old memories but left her with no answer. She simply shrugged.

Scarlett Jo shifted her top as if all she had eaten had settled on her chest, then leaned on the counter. "So you're telling me you have no idea what would make you the most happy."

All she could do was shrug again.

"I'll tell you when she's the most happy." Rachel leaned over and crossed her arms on the countertop as well. "It's when she's in the kitchen. This is where Grace Shepherd comes to life."

And that was true. "I do feel alive when I'm baking. But I feel even more alive when I watch people eat what I've made."

"Well, good." Leo seemed to dislike where the conversation was going. "Then you should get tons of joy watching me eat your cooking every morning when you come to work. At your job. At the television station where you work. 'Cause Lord knows nobody's going to enjoy it like I do."

Scarlett Jo got up and pushed her barstool under the counter. "Well, I'm going to say this to you. Whatever makes you feel alive, whatever helps you rediscover that carefree childlike heart I know is in there somewhere—" she reached over and tapped Grace on the chest—"that is what you should be doing. Sugar, you act too old for your age, and you don't have to. You're young. You're beautiful. It's time for you to assume freedom and not let all those fears and restrictions hold you back. There is this amazing world out there waiting for you, sugar pie. But you've got to choose to live in it."

Grace looked at her new friend and felt something in her shift. She *had* forgotten what it was to feel alive. Honestly, she wasn't even sure what that meant. But one thing she did know. She had been dead for long enough.

{ *Chapter 16* }

ZACH WAS A WRECK. Caroline hadn't talked to him since she stormed out last night. He had spent most of this beautiful Saturday holed up in his office, trying to figure out who he should call and what he should do.

He'd spent an hour on the phone with one of his attorney buddies who also handled divorces. His friend would set things into motion first thing Monday morning if he needed to. Zach hoped it wouldn't come to that. But he'd been in the business long enough to know he couldn't wait for Caroline to make all the moves. If he did, he could end up sleeping on the office sofa for the next year.

He didn't have any other close friends to call because most of his friends were shared. Their wives were Caroline's friends, and until he knew what she was going to do, he hated to bring someone else in on it. He was just glad he had a bathroom down the hall and enough restaurants around him that he wouldn't starve.

At seven o'clock he called Caroline again. She didn't answer. He hadn't heard from the girls all day, and not knowing what was going on made him stir-crazy.

He ventured out to McCreary's, the Irish pub up the street from his office. He sat down with some fish-and-chips and a cold beer and watched a little baseball, but he never took in any of it—not the food, not the chill of the beer, not even the cracking of the bat on the ball. All he could think about was where his life had evolved to in a mere twenty-four hours—and how he had gotten here.

The thing was, when you lived the kind of life he'd been living, you could develop a sense of invincibility. The feeling that you're good at your game, that you'd never get caught. It was a fantasy, an escape. Yes, there was also the guilt of it, the lying. That awful sense of shame when the realization of what you were really doing settled over you and you were desperate to wash it off. But that just made you even more desperate to escape your reality. More susceptible to the fantasy.

It was a sad and twisted mess, and here he was in the middle of it, all alone. He had no idea where he would end up. For the first time in a long time, he had absolutely no idea what would happen with the rest of his life.

He picked up his cell phone, which sat by his plate of picked-at food. He dialed. The familiar voice came on the other end. It brought both a peace and a dread.

"Hey, Dad."

"Hey, bud. How are you?"

Zach moved his fork across the crispy outer shell of the fried cod. "Not real good. In fact, I was wondering . . . any chance you could come to Franklin?"

His dad would be there in a few hours. And he had agreed with no questions asked.

❁   ❁   ❁

Zach's cell phone buzzed on the mattress in the Marriott Cool Springs hotel room he'd booked for him and his dad. He squinted at the display, trying to make out the name on the caller ID. It flashed in a blur. He wiped his eyes and squinted again. It looked like Caroline. He answered quickly.

"I want to meet at church." His wife's voice was flat but collected.

He sat up in the bed, his mind still not awake but his body shot through with adrenaline. Why church? His mind fumbled for answers, then realized it was Sunday. She wanted him to meet her at the church service. But why?

"Um . . . yeah," he muttered. "Are you sure? What about the girls? Are they okay? Have you told them anything?"

"They actually left to spend the week at my mother's. It was planned before this."

He had no recollection of that, but then he never knew what she was planning until it was time for him to know—which meant whenever she deemed it necessary.

"Oh. Well, sure, I'll meet you. But I need a change of clothes. I didn't have anything with me at the office."

"I'm leaving in a few minutes to go to the store and pick up some things. So you can come by the house after that and get your stuff. Then we can talk after church."

"Okay. Yeah, I guess. Have you talked to Jackson or Scarlett Jo about this? Do they know what's going on?"

"I haven't said anything to them. I did, however, speak to Elise's husband." She said this in a way that let him know she was very much in control. "He informed me that he and Elise are going away for a couple days and he's not going to say anything until they get back in town. Now I've got to go. Just meet me there. We'll talk later."

He ran a hand back and forth through his thick brown hair, the fog still heavy in his mind. "I'll meet you there." He paused. "Thanks, Caroline. Thanks for talking to me."

She hung up without another word.

His dad rolled over in the bed across from him. "What did Caroline have to say?"

Zach scooted down under the covers and laid his head on the pillow with his face toward his father. "She wants me to go to church with her. She said we could talk after that. I'm figuring she's already been in touch with a lawyer. She'll go for the big guns too. Adele will make sure of it."

His dad sat up and took his glasses from the bedside table, where they lay atop his Bible. He had shared some things from it with Zach the night before as Zach unraveled what had been happening. Now he fluffed his pillow so he could lean against it. "Son, I don't know what Caroline is going to do. But at this point it really isn't about Caroline. It isn't about your marriage. It's about you. You can't fix the two of you until you've first taken care of your own heart."

He knew that. His dad had told him that for years. It was sort of his standard spiel, one he said came from living with the consequences of his own shut-down heart. "Once you've had one," he always said, "you have no trouble identifying one."

Zach hadn't exactly ignored those talks, but he'd pretty much brushed them off, thinking they didn't apply to him. Now he wasn't so sure. "Want to go with me?" he asked. "To church, I mean."

"No, I think you need to do this with Caroline. Just go talk. See what she wants."

"Wonder why she wants to go to church. . . . That doesn't make sense to me, especially since the affair was with Elise. It seems like Caroline would just want to see me and let out all of her anger. Let me have it, maybe. And then tell me what she thinks we should do."

"Don't even try to make sense of it, Son. You've got to remember that Caroline is grieving too. She has a right to grieve, and grief like this doesn't have sense. It doesn't have a playbook. It just is. And there is no telling how Caroline's grief will need to express itself. What you have to do is give her the freedom to do that, however she needs to."

Zach sat up and slid his feet from the bed. "You're right. I know you are. She said I could come by the house and get some stuff, so I'm going to head on out." He looked down at his slept-in clothes. "I'll shower and change while I'm there."

"You go. I'll wait right here until you get back."

Zach leaned down and kissed the top of his father's head. "Thanks, Dad. I might need that."

❀ ❀ ❀

Zach waited until Scarlett Jo's neon presence at the door disappeared before he made a beeline for the church. The first strum of music had begun, and he was grateful to know that Elise and her husband wouldn't be here. Otherwise, he was certain there was no way in the world Caroline would have come. In fact, he figured that even if they stayed together, first on the agenda would be a new church.

He spotted her near the front, much closer than they usually sat. That struck him as a little odd. But he walked quickly to her row and scooted in next to her.

He glanced her way, not sure what to expect. She didn't acknowledge him. He wasn't quite expecting that.

As the young man on the platform strummed his guitar, soft worship music permeated not only the farthest corners of the room but, truthfully, some of the farthest regions of Zach's heart. The words resonated.

He had listened to this song a thousand times yet never really heard it. It talked of how God was jealous for him. How God's love was as intense as a hurricane yet full of mercy. He heard that message now, maybe because he needed it now. He closed his eyes, and for the first time in years, real emotion raged in his soul. It was foreign and real and frightening and beautiful. To feel something—really feel something—felt good.

He slid his hand over to try to touch Caroline's. His finger grazed hers, and she quickly moved hers away. He brought his hand back and remembered his father's words. Then he tried to give her permission to feel whatever she needed to. He also gave that permission to himself, and remorse seemed to be the river that was flowing freely.

Jackson came to the platform and began to pray. Other soft voices joined in from sporadic places in the sanctuary offering their agreement.

"I sense the Lord doing something in hearts this morning."

Zach opened his eyes to make sure Jackson wasn't staring at him. Did he know? Jackson's eyes were squeezed tightly shut. Zach's shoulders relaxed.

"I know we don't usually do this, but I'm going to open the altar up to anyone who would like to come this morning. Something tells me that people's hearts need to be ministered to. Encouraged. Healed."

Zach watched as a few people left their seats and knelt on the concrete floor around the platform. Then he became aware of Caroline moving beside him. She pushed past him into the aisle, then began to walk toward the front. He wondered if he should follow. Pray with her, maybe. When she got to the front, he waited to see if she went to Jackson. Fear rushed through him again at the thought of her telling the pastor what he'd done.

But she didn't move toward Jackson. Instead, she turned at the altar. And for the first time that morning since their phone call, she spoke. "I think my husband should be at the altar this morning."

Zach felt the air leave his lungs in one fell swoop. He thought for a moment his knees would buckle. He caught a glimpse of Jackson's face, which now was keenly aware.

Caroline went on. "Because he apparently finds it far more enjoyable to sleep with other women than with his own wife."

Gasps bounced around the room like Ping-Pong balls on a hardwood floor.

"Yes, I caught him Friday night with a woman, and here he is, pretending to be a good Christian." Her words came out like steel. If he were driving a tank, he couldn't have made a dent in her anger. "Apparently he thinks that you can betray your marriage vows and still be a pillar of the church. That a commitment to love, honor, and cherish is nothing more than a suggestion. Well, I have a suggestion for you, Zach Craig." And that was when she looked at him. "You can stay here and face the embarrassment that you deserve for being the hypocrite you are."

With that she marched down the aisle, right past him, and headed straight for the door. Zach's eyes followed her disappearing form; then he turned to find every eye in the house glued to him. How could they help it? Freak shows were like bad car accidents. You had to look. And this was as good as a head-on collision.

Zach's feet seemed stuck to the floor, his body heavier than a *Biggest Loser* contestant at the first weigh-in. He simply could not move.

Jackson spoke quickly. "I'm going to ask everyone to bow their heads. I think this is a time for some introspective prayer. Jared, please come back and lead us in that last song you were singing."

Everyone respectfully and kindly followed Jackson's direction. And before Zach knew it, Jackson was by his side, hand underneath his arm.

"Come on, Zach. Let's you and I get out of here."

Zach was grateful for the hand. Without it, he wasn't sure he would have made it out the door. When the sunlight hit his face outside the darkened sanctuary, it seemed to illuminate every piece of him. And he was certain that every square inch of Zach Craig had now been fully exposed.

{ Chapter 17 }

CAROLINE'S CAR WAS GONE. But now Zach was finding his anger. She had set him up. She had planned this entire thing simply to embarrass him. At least his girls hadn't been there, and as best he could remember, she had never mentioned Elise's name.

He paced in a small circle in the parking lot. Jackson was standing at the front door of the church, talking to the associate pastor. In a minute he joined him in the parking lot.

"I'm thinking you need a drink," Jackson said, his strong hand gently touching the back of Zach's shirt. Zach felt the wetness of his own perspiration as he did.

"Jackson, you can't handle the kind of drink I need right now." Zach's hands were on either side of his head, fingers laced through his hair. Cicadas screamed from the trees as loudly as the voices in his head.

"Come on. Let's go talk." Jackson led him toward his own car and opened the passenger door for him. He asked no questions, simply drove Zach straight to his house and walked him inside to his home office.

"I'll get you some tea." He pointed to a leather sofa across from his desk. "Why don't you sit there and try to catch your breath."

Zach sat, but he felt like his chest would collapse—or explode. The pressure was suffocating. He had never felt this way before.

He had prided himself on his reputation. People saw him a certain way, and that was how he wanted it. He had been the superb athlete and student in college. He was the wonderful father who coached his girls' softball teams. He was the great spouse and the talented attorney. That was who he was—how people knew him. And in one brief span of sixty seconds, Caroline had shot all of that to smithereens.

He got up from the sofa. He couldn't sit. He wanted to crawl out of his skin. To escape, run, hit something. He just needed some way to release this pent-up volcano.

Jackson stood in the doorway, two glasses of iced tea in his hands. He extended one to Zach. "Drink. You look like you're going to pass out."

Zach took the glass, the chill immediately discernible to the touch. He lifted it to his lips and let the cool liquid race through him, hoping to extinguish the upcoming eruption. The ice collided in his half-empty glass as he lowered it to an Ole Miss coaster on the leather-topped side table. He let out a heavy sigh.

He kept his body in motion. Jackson sat on one end of the sofa and watched Zach as he paced.

"I'm wrecked, Jackson."

Jackson pressed his tall, lean frame against the back cushion of the sofa and crossed a foot over the opposite knee. "I'm thinking that's probably an accurate description."

"What am I going to do? My wife just told the entire church I'm an adulterer."

"Yes, she did." Jackson paused. "Want to tell me what's going on with you?"

"Oh no." Zach shook his head wildly. "You should be doing the talking. You should be telling me to repent or something. You're the pastor. So preach."

Jackson leaned forward, elbows on his knees. "I'm just a friend right now, Zach. There will be plenty of time for me to be your pastor. But for right now, I just want to listen. You can tell me as little or as much as you want."

Zach returned to the sofa and finally sat down, calmed by Jackson's solid presence. But he didn't know where to start, what to tell the man. A part of him longed to blurt it all out. Another part wanted to cover for Elise, keep her from experiencing what he had just gone through. But was that even possible at this point? If Jackson knew, maybe he could prevent this disaster from getting worse.

Maybe.

He kept his eyes down, and his words came out measured, as if he were protecting a client. "It happened over time. I didn't set out to cheat on Caroline. We were just in such a yuck place, you know?" He raised his head quickly. "It's not her fault. I'm not saying it's her fault. It's all my fault. I'm the one who couldn't keep my pants up. There is only one person to blame here."

Zach looked at Jackson and studied his face the way a

defense attorney would a jury. It held no judgment, no anger. Nor did it hold pity. What it held was very similar to what his father's had held—a kind of knowing compassion. He didn't understand how Jackson came by it, but it was there. And in this moment he was grateful for it.

"I've ruined our lives, Jackson."

Jackson let out a soft chuckle and leaned forward. "No, you haven't. Not yet. What you do from now on will determine whether or not you have ruined your life."

Those words startled him. He hadn't thought about it quite that way. But Jackson was right. "I've got to go find Caroline. I've got to make this right. I've got to fix this."

Jackson raised his eyebrows and pressed his lips together with a nod. "Yeah, that's probably a good idea—eventually. But I'm not sure Caroline really feels like talking right now. So how about we talk about you? When is the last time you've paid any attention to *your* heart, Zach?"

Zach felt his brow furrow. He didn't understand. "I've *only* been paying attention to myself, don't you think? I'm thinking that narcissism is what has me here."

"Maybe. Maybe not. But you've got to find out. I think what is more important than working on your marriage right now is working on yourself. You can't give Caroline anything of value from yourself until you've figured out what is going on with your own heart."

Zach shook his head. "Have you been talking to my dad?"

Jackson laughed. "No."

"Because my dad is here, and he said basically the same thing."

"Smart man."

"Yeah, well, I'm not sure I know what working on myself means. I don't know where to start with something like that."

"You take one day at a time," Jackson said, "and you go on a search for your heart. Let me ask you this: if Zach Craig could do anything on the face of the earth that his heart desired, what would it be?"

"What do you mean?"

"I mean, when you were a little boy, what did you dream of doing?"

Zach felt the muscles in his face relax. He hadn't even realized the tension they had carried until that moment. He felt the edges of his mouth turn upward. "I wanted to be a football coach. High school. Maybe teach an American history class or something. But to coach kids, on and off the field—that was my real dream. I always wanted a boy." Zach hadn't expected those words to come out. He hadn't even known they were in there.

Jackson gave him a soft smile, his dark eyes as warm as his presence. "I've got five you can borrow anytime."

Zach shook his head. "I don't know where that came from. I love my girls."

"I love my boys, but it doesn't mean I haven't had the desire to hold a little girl in my arms. To have one wrap her arms around my neck and call me Daddy. We all have dreams. My question for you is, when did you give up on yours?"

Zach was quiet for a minute. As he rummaged through the dreams he had mentioned, he realized he wasn't really sure when he'd decided to let them go.

"Okay, let me make this a little clearer. We come into this world with this carefree child's heart. It's open. Alive. It's connected with God and believes anything is possible. It doesn't know much fear, and it has this kind of abandoned wonder. But then at some point—I don't know when, maybe in high school, maybe in college, maybe after we graduate—something happens to us. Maybe we're abused or bullied in school, or we have trouble living up to family expectations and start to worry we don't measure up."

Zach immediately thought of his girls, of Caroline. How Joy perpetually pointed out Lacy's faults. How Caroline lived in such fear of her own mom. Was that what Jackson was talking about?

"So many things can happen to us in the course of our lives," Jackson continued. "Marriage is harder than we thought. Jobs change. Finances shift. People betray us, or we fail at something we really wanted to do. And with each challenge, piece by piece, our hearts begin to shut down. We begin to lose that fearless sense of possibility as we shift into survival mode. We lose track of who we are, what brings us joy. We begin to feel shut off from God because the heart is where we connect with him. And we may eventually shut down to the point that we have to go out and seek some artificial stimulus just to feel like we're alive."

"So you're saying that I—"

"I'm saying that a man who is connected with the heart God placed in him doesn't have an affair. A man who has closed off his heart to such a degree that he doesn't want to feel any-more—that's the man who's likely to have an affair. He does it because he doesn't want to deal with the pain of where he really is and no longer cares about the consequences of his behavior."

"Or just doesn't want to think about them." Zach gave a little growl of frustration. "That's what really gets me. I know better. I see the consequences of behavior like this every day in my office. But I just sort of pretended they didn't apply to me." His mouth twisted in an ironic smile. "That worked out real well, didn't it?"

Jackson's face registered understanding. "Zach, I think more than anything you need to go on a search for your heart. If you don't find that, then you won't have anything to offer Caroline anyway. To go back to her now and try to fix your relationship without first fixing your heart will not do either of you any favors."

"So what do I do instead?"

"You can start with being honest. Tell her exactly what you've done and why you did it. Admit you're a sinner if you want—the kind of sinner you wanted me to accuse you of being—and beg her forgiveness."

Jackson said that with a smile, but then his expression grew serious. "And yes, you do need to confess your sin to God and ask his forgiveness for both the adultery and for not guarding your heart. And here's something else to consider. Until you reclaim your heart, Zach, what you've just done will likely happen again. So if you want to salvage your marriage, the best thing you can do to protect yourself and Caroline from any more pain or humiliation—"

Under his breath, Zach muttered, "Humiliation."

"—is to tell her about the journey you're on to reclaim the man God designed you to be."

"I honestly can't imagine saying something like that to Caroline. She'll think I'm a freak."

"You think she'll have any worse thoughts about you after that conversation than she does right now?"

That was the first time Zach laughed. "You've got a point."

Jackson leaned toward him. Zach noted the deep tracks

embedded at the corners of Jackson's eyes, lines he was certain had been chiseled from experience so rich it couldn't help but leave marks. "I believe in the man you were created to be, Zach. You've just got to decide if you do."

Zach rubbed his hands on his legs. "I don't know. I don't know what any of this looks like."

"You're better off if you don't. You've had enough pictures of how you thought life should end up. Doesn't look like they've done you any good this far."

They kept talking for another forty-five minutes. When Zach finally stood, Jackson followed. "How did you learn this stuff?"

"Let's just say it takes one to know one." Jackson reached over and wrapped Zach in his arms. The embrace was real and strong and sure—everything that Zach wasn't. When it was over, Jackson walked with Zach out to the car and they made the drive back to the church so he could pick up his car.

He climbed out of Jackson's black Tahoe, then leaned inside again. "I'll need you in this."

"I'm not going anywhere."

"I'll call you tomorrow."

"Talk to you then."

Zach closed the Tahoe door and got behind the wheel of his Range Rover. He turned the key in the ignition, feeling the soft motion underneath him. He pointed himself in the direction of the hotel where his father was waiting on him. And wondered if his car would ever head home.

❀ ❀ ❀

Scarlett Jo walked into the kitchen and dropped her large straw handbag with a fuchsia gerbera daisy on the counter. "Cooper,

Mama swears they got it wrong. That old study that says girls have twenty-five thousand words a day and boys have ten thousand—they were sadly mistaken. So could you please, for the next ten minutes, zip it?"

Cooper's mouth started to open, and Scarlett Jo clamped her fingers over his lips. She could tell he resisted the urge to stick out his tongue. "Smart boy," she said and patted his head. He retreated up the stairs, following his older brothers.

Rhett stood by the full white hem of his mama's skirt, his fingers playing with the silk ribbon that hung from the pages of his small Bible. "Mama, what's a fiery furnace?"

"That's what Zach Craig is in right now, baby—"

"Hey, buddy!" Jackson cut her off as he came around the corner and scooped his youngest into his arms. "Have you been learning about a fiery furnace?"

Rhett nodded.

"Well, why don't you go upstairs and change for dinner, and we'll talk about it this afternoon. Sound good?"

"Yep."

Jackson kissed his son's head and set him down on the floor, then watched him disappear in a thunderous tromp up the steps.

"Hey, babe," he said casually to Scarlett Jo, "let's back off on talking about Zach with the kids."

She planted hands on her hips. "I'm not twelve. I'm very capable of knowing what to say to our children and what not to. Remember, I've been a pastor's wife as long as you have been a pastor."

Jackson moved around the kitchen island as he unbuttoned the cuffs of his shirt. He began to roll up his sleeves as he spoke. "You were just saying something to him about Zach."

"I know what I said to him, but it wasn't like I was going to give him all the details. I do have couth, Jackson. My hair may be blonde, but I am not void of thoughtfulness. I do think before anything comes out of this mouth." She winced. "Well, most of the time."

"I know you do." Jackson wrapped his arms around her waist from behind. "And it's a beautiful mouth." When she bent over, he went with her as she pulled out Crisco and flour from beneath the stove top. "Mmm. Mama's making biscuits. Daddy like."

"Well, Daddy better remember Mama is Mama and not one of his children."

"Daddy has heard Mama's request."

She raised a finger. "No, Mama did not request. Mama said."

Jackson laughed and gave her a kiss on the neck. "Daddy heard."

She giggled. "How is Zach?"

He let go and leaned against the island. "In a mess. Caroline just exposed his infidelity to the whole church. Can you imagine?"

"I'm thinking I'd better not have to." She kept her back to him as she pulled a carton of milk from the refrigerator.

He tugged her arm to pull her around, then gave her a peck on the lips. "I wish you could have seen his face, babe. It was horrible."

"You should have seen *hers* as she left the church."

"You saw it?"

"Yes, I was in the back when it happened. She was seething. Not out of control, mind you, but so angry. I tried to speak to her, but that look she gave me—let's just say she was not up for conversation." Scarlett Jo added salt to the ingredients in a large bowl. "I still can't believe she made that announcement in front of the whole church. I'm telling you, if my teeth were false like Sylvia's, I would've swallowed them right there."

Jackson smiled. "I know what you mean. But let's find the pearl here. That whole scene might be a better preventative for an outbreak of adultery in our church than anything I could come up with. Worked for me, that's for sure."

Her hands were covered with dough and Crisco, but she still had her elbow free. She used it.

"Ow!" Jackson laughed, then sobered. "He finally told me who it is—who he's having the affair with."

"It's Elise, right?"

The surprise was evident on Jackson's face. "How do you know?"

"It's not hard to figure out. She's been avoiding me. Tim's been worried about something. And the McAdamses weren't at church today because of a 'family emergency.' It doesn't take a rocket scientist."

Jackson pressed his hands against the counter. She saw the veins protrude from his forearms. "Where was I, babe? Where was I?"

"Oh, honey. You can't blame yourself for this. People can hide whatever they want to."

"But I knew something had changed. Elise didn't come in as much, and when she was there, she basically dodged me."

Scarlett Jo snorted and rolled out her first biscuit. "She dodged me too. Until this Friday, of course, when I left her no choice."

"It's going to be a big mess, you know." Jackson started

pacing. "Something like this is really hard on a church. I mean, when the staff is involved . . ."

She looked up from her biscuits. "I know. God's going to have his work cut out for him. You too."

"But why would she do it? Tim is a great guy. What more could she want?"

"Now, Jackson, you and I both know there are always two sides to a story, and sometimes you have trouble seeing what issues the guy has. You are going to have to dig in with Tim and see what's going on with him too. And I'm hoping you're not having trouble seeing Zach's issues."

He pressed his lips together. "Zach has an issue keeping his pants up, babe. That is very clear. And you're right. Sometimes I cut good guys too much slack. I just can't figure out what Tim might have done to contribute to this. I see him and Elise together a lot. He treats her so kindly."

"Yes, he does—in public anyway. Might be different behind closed doors."

Jackson nodded thoughtfully. "True."

"On the other hand, some women don't understand kind. They interpret it as being a doormat, and then they walk all over it. Don't know if Elise is like that, but it happens." She stuck another biscuit in the pan. "Now, Caroline Craig's something else entirely. I've seen people like her. I know that face."

He laughed. "You do, do you?"

Scarlett Jo patted down the last biscuit. "Jackson, seriously. A woman who will air her husband's sh—" Her eyes shot up to Jackson, knowing how he would be looking back. He had asked her to stop cussing since Jack was a baby, and she did okay most days. Her mouth contorted to form another word quickly.

". . . shhh—*stuff* to an entire congregation of people is obviously not a woman who has a real sensitive side."

"Well, she did just catch her husband with another woman."

"True." She scrunched up her face. "But still . . ."

"How would you tell people if you caught me in the act?"

She leaned against the counter and took his face in her hands. "Sugar pie, honey bunch, we both know I won't have to worry about that because you like all your parts too much." She gave him a peck on the nose and then released his face. "But I can tell you I would handle you myself. It would be a one-on-one encounter, not a staged performance. And I'm thinking, sit her down in your office with Zach and give her your theory on 'one person's dysfunction attracts another person's dysfunction,' and you'll find out really quick what her piece in all of this is."

"Wow, babe. You have an issue with Caroline?"

"Yeah. Sounds like it, huh?" She walked over to the stove, opened the door, and stuck the pan of biscuits inside. "I just think Caroline has some real issues, that's all. I think she hides behind her pretty face and perfect clothes and there is a broken woman in there who doesn't want to admit it."

She planted herself by the counter and studied her husband. He reached out and pulled her into a hug. "How'd you get so smart?"

"I married you. Oh, and I have five sons who know it all. Can't help but be brilliant."

He laughed. "So to change the subject, how's your new friend Grace?"

"A wreck. But she's strong. Even in the middle of this intense pain, she still has a real strength."

"Do you think Grace will find her heart again?"

She smiled. "Oh yes. It's just going to take some time. She still has a lot to discover about herself."

"Did you tell her a heart's a beautiful thing?"

"She hasn't asked."

He patted her arm and walked from the kitchen. "Oh, she'll ask. Eventually they always ask. And then you can tell her how you know."

{ *Chapter 18* }

GRACE SAT ON THE BLACK LEATHER SOFA, the chrome armrest cold against her bare skin. She moved her arm quickly. Her reaction must have caused the secretary to take note.

"Mr. Craig said he is on his way."

Grace was grateful for Darlene's kindness. "Well, I am unannounced."

"It's fine. He knows this is a difficult time."

She put her hands in her lap and stroked her white skinny jeans. Her black T-shirt fit snugly against her petite frame. She guessed she looked all right. But the shirt had been on top of the stack in her drawer, and the jeans had been the first pair of pants she saw. At this point in her life, that was the best she could do. She noticed a small chip in her peach-toned nail polish and made a mental note to fix that. But she knew she'd probably forget.

She forgot a lot of things these days—kept getting distracted. It was a good thing her parents were there to help her keep her life together. They had come in Saturday evening. She had shared the story of her decision, and they had let her talk and cry and do all the things parents let their children do in moments when they still need to be children. They'd spent the Memorial Day holiday with her yesterday and planned to stay the rest of the week, to be there for whatever she needed.

Her attention turned to the door as it opened and Zach rushed in. She wasn't surprised that he looked tired and frazzled. She had been in the back of the church Sunday morning. And that was why she was here.

Zach's worn, overstuffed briefcase hung from his hand. There was no coat and tie this morning, just a pair of khakis and a blue button-down with the sleeves rolled up, one higher than the other. "Sorry, Grace. I wasn't expecting you," he said as his eyes caught hers.

"I only need a few minutes of your time."

"Sure. Yeah." He turned almost in a circle as if looking for direction. A compass.

Darlene saved them both. "Here, Zach, why don't I take your briefcase. You and Grace go into the conference room, and I'll grab both of you something to drink."

"Yeah, sure, that'd be great. I think I'll have a coffee. Black." Zach stood in the middle of the office as if he might need her to escort him to the conference room. A string of pity ran through Grace.

"I don't need anything, Darlene," she said. "But thank you."

Zach turned toward her as if he had already forgotten she was there, but then he motioned to the conference room. "Okay, let's go talk."

She walked in front of him and set down her Italian handbag—one of Tyler's extravagant finds—on the conference room table. "This really won't take long."

He moved to the other side and held on to the back of a chair.

She wasted no time. "I was there on Sunday."

"Sunday?"

"Yes. The church. Your wife. I was there."

He lowered his head, then raised it quickly as if his puppeteer had just demanded performance. "Yes. Well, I'm sorry you had to be there."

Darlene opened the door, and neither of them spoke. Grace saw a rigidness settle onto Zach's shoulders and then disappear when Darlene did. Apparently Zach's secretary didn't know what had happened on Sunday.

"Yes, I was there," Grace went on. "So I'm here to tell you that I'll be looking for other counsel. I don't need my husband and my attorney being the news. That's not something I can handle right now."

He didn't answer. He just stood there.

She waited. But he clearly had nothing. She picked up her purse. "Okay, that's all I have to say. I'll find someone else this week and have them get my file from you."

He still wasn't moving. The silence felt awkward. She walked toward the door.

Then she heard him move quickly. "Grace, wait. Please."

His hand reached for the door. "Look, I may be a failure as

a husband. I'm probably not even much of a man right now, if you want to know the truth. But I am and always have been a really good attorney. You don't have to keep me. I completely understand if you don't. But I promise you that I will help you achieve your goal. I will walk you through this process with as little pain as possible."

"Well, I—"

"You have no reason to trust me. I understand that too. Why would you? But you can ask that woman out there." He pointed toward the outer office. "I'll do a great job for you. Fortunately, in this business, character isn't always a prerequisite." Those last words came out slightly mumbled, but no less convincing. "Will you at least think about it?"

She studied him. He had a sincere face, a kind demeanor. And he could certainly be persuasive, which was a good quality in an attorney. She couldn't believe what she was about to say. "I'll think about it. I'll spend this week figuring out if this is a good idea."

His shoulders relaxed. "Thank you. I really appreciate it."

She gave him a soft smile and nodded. Then she walked past him out of the conference room, said a short good-bye to Darlene, and headed downstairs into the Tuesday morning sunshine.

Main Street was quiet. It was only nine, and most stores wouldn't be open until ten. She headed toward the square and slowed her pace as she did. There was nowhere she needed to be at this moment. She was still on leave from work. Her parents were at the house, so they could take care of Miss Daisy. And in this moment she honestly didn't want to be around people.

Grief was crazy. One minute you needed someone holding

you, just listening. The next minute you had to be alone—to scream, yell, or stare into space. Sometimes you wanted to crawl out of your own skin or jump down someone's throat.

Her mother had let out a smart-aleck comment about Tyler the first night she had gotten there. And Grace had snapped back, "I don't need you to come with opinions. So if that is what you are bringing, you may as well turn around and go home."

The response had come so quickly and escaped so sharply, it shocked Grace into silence. She'd never spoken to her mother that way. She wasn't sure she had ever spoken to anyone like that—claiming what she wanted, dictating how it would be. But she didn't want people talking about Tyler. She could talk about him until the next great Nashville flood, but she didn't want anyone else doing it.

And strangely, that prickly little episode turned out to be a good thing. For one, her mother heard her—really heard her— so the weekend had been peaceful. But the other beauty was that she had said it at all. She had spent the last ten years forgetting how to say what she wanted. So even though she would never want to hurt her mother, realizing she could speak her mind brought a real comfort.

She turned onto the street that circled the town square, the heart of downtown Franklin, and passed a clothing store called Details. She remembered shopping there once. In fact, come to think of it, that was how she knew Zach Craig's wife. Details was Caroline's store. Grace had never made the connection until now. She thought of Caroline for a moment, wondered how she was doing. But few things other than where she was in her own journey right now stayed with her very long.

She continued around the square and past the old courthouse

to Mellow Mushroom, then crossed the street to head back to her car. When she passed the Iron Gate, she paused to look in the window. The beauty of the furniture took her breath away. And for the first time she imagined what it would be like to live in a home that was all about what she liked, to choose it for herself. Not because Tyler had gotten them into another financial bind and they needed to find something cheaper. Not because it was a good investment or a bargain they couldn't pass up or Tyler just needed a change. But simply because she'd found a home she loved, a place that filled her longings. What would she put in it? Where would it be located?

She studied the iron-and-crystal chandelier that hung over an antique wrought-iron bed. That looked like her, like her dreams of what a home should be. Cozy and old and lived-in, with family pictures everywhere and lots of people over to enjoy the place. People laughing over good food and even better conversation. She placed her hand on the window's cool glass and let her fingers trace the letters. Then she continued along the street toward Zach's office, where she had parked.

As she moved around a gentleman washing the windows of a store, he spoke. She returned the hello and passed on to the next window, in the building next door to Zach's. And that was when she saw the sign.

For Lease. The words marinated in her mind. *For lease.* She sort of felt that way herself—in a kind of limbo. Not exactly married, except in a technical sense, but not really free either. It was like being offered for use but still held back. And no one could care for you and make you into a home because they would always know in a deep-down place that you were simply borrowed.

She didn't want to be borrowed. She wanted to be sold outright—completely severed from her old way of doing life. Scarlett Jo was right. She had been around dead things long enough.

She peered past the sign in the window to the space behind it. The whole place looked tired. The carpet was filthy. The walls offered no crispness, no invitation.

She took another step, and something on the counter in the back of the empty store caught her attention. It was a lone blue-and-white porcelain teapot, looking strangely out of place in that drab, empty storefront. As a kid, she had liked those pictures where you had to circle the items that didn't belong. If this were her picture, she'd put a big circle around that teapot.

But something inside her shifted when she saw it. An idea. A feeling. A something. She shook her head and walked a little farther, her eyes never leaving the teapot. And then the something rushed through her again. A what-if. A what-could-be.

She brushed it aside and quickened her steps toward where her car was parked. She needed to get home. Her parents and Miss Daisy would wonder where she was. And they'd be in good company because Grace was wondering that too.

But a few minutes later, as she rounded the corner to her house, the something passed through her again. She dared let the question rumble through her mind. *Could it be?*

She reviewed her life as she climbed the steps to her front porch. Thirty-five years of life. Ten years of marriage. Six moves. No children. Divorce pending. Had someone proposed this scenario to her fifteen years ago, she would have said, "No way. There's no way my life will turn out like that. I've got my life all figured out, and it won't be like that."

But it was. And it had. So as she opened the front door to her home, a thought passed over her. *At this point in life, anything is possible.*

❀ ❀ ❀

Scarlett Jo studied her figure in the mirror, the phone stuck to her ear and Sylvia's voice like a clanging cymbal on the other end.

"It's scandalous," Sylvia insisted. She must have said that five times already.

"What it is," Scarlett Jo answered, "is heartbreaking."

Sylvia humphed. "I don't know where you sent those two. But I sure hope you won't be bringing them back."

Scarlett Jo turned and looked over her shoulder to examine the rear view. "We are working through this with Tim and Elise, hopefully for their healing. And Jackson's facilitated an opportunity to begin that process."

"I sure hope he's not using the church's money to do it."

Scarlett Jo opened her mouth, closed it, took a deep breath, and tried again. "If the church isn't for helping restore the broken, I'm not sure what it's for."

"But I heard—"

"Sylvia, we have a real opportunity to minister to this couple. And I don't think gossiping about them will accomplish that."

"Well, you're my pastor's wife. I should be able to bring anything to you. And what I'm bringing to you is that we need to get this whole music thing settled—soon. I don't like having fill-ins."

Scarlett Jo pivoted and sucked in her tummy. *Not bad,* she thought. *That gym is paying off. No six-pack abs yet, but I might get my two-pack to a four-pack by Christmas.*

"Did you hear me?" Sylvia's grating voice penetrated the phone, and Scarlett Jo pulled it away from her ear.

"Yes, I heard you. We'll get the music situation figured out. It's not like there's a shortage of musicians in the Nashville area. And you *can* talk to me, Sylvia. Anytime you're ready to talk about your stuff, you bring that to me, and we'll talk about it. But I'm not here to talk about Tim and Elise. If I want to do that, I'll do it with them. Now, did you call to tell me your dark and dirty secrets?"

If Sylvia's teeth weren't her own, she had just swallowed them. But in a moment she found her voice, which collided with her pride and came out practically strangled. "I have no secrets."

Scarlett Jo laughed. "When no one has secrets, then those flying pigs we've been talking about for the last umpteen hundred years are going to take off. You may not be ready to talk about yours, but when you are, I'll be right here. Now I've got to go. Bye." She used her long orange-painted nail to click her phone off before Sylvia could spew whatever other nonsense she wanted to spew.

She pulled at the elastic of her Pilates pants and let it snap back around the crease that rested between the two folds of girth she claimed Rhett had given her. Not exactly a model's figure—at least not these days. But she wasn't worried. She could live with being called curvy. Jackson had no complaints. And as long as she did it for him, she didn't need to do it for anyone else. There was enough of that running through the water as it was.

"Jack, let's get a move—" She stopped when she caught sight of her oldest standing at the door, waiting on her. "How did I not have to beg you to do this?"

"Hey, Grace Shepherd is hot. You don't have to beg me to cut the grass of a woman who looks like that."

Scarlett Jo's palm collided with the back of his head, and she grabbed her bright-orange handbag as they walked out the door. "Grace Shepherd is married."

"She's filed for divorce."

"She is way too old for you."

"Haven't you heard of cougars, Mom? They like younger guys. Who wouldn't want some of this?" he said, hands colliding with his chest like Tarzan.

She gave him the mama eye and moved in close. "If I catch anyone getting some of this—" she mimicked his chest pounding—"I will give you some of this." She raised her hand like she was about to slap the stew out of him.

He laughed from a deep place, then leaned over and gave her a kiss on the cheek. "You're funny."

"Yeah, I've got your funny."

He draped a long arm over her shoulder as they headed down the street. "Love you, Mama."

She elbowed him. He let out a fake grunt. She laughed. "I love you too."

Grace opened her door as they came up her walk. Scarlett Jo heard Jack let out a soft and slow "wow."

Grace's blonde hair fell softly at her shoulders, and her warm smile lit up the entry. "You didn't have to do this. I can call a yard guy."

Scarlett Jo cupped a hand around her mouth like a megaphone. "Yard guy! Grace needs you!" Then she pushed Jack forward. "Oh, here he is. Got him. This is the yard guy you need. He is efficient. Reliable." Each word came out more as a directive than a declaration. "And he works cheap. As in f-r-e-e, free. And he is four doors down, so if he oversleeps, you can come wake him up yourself."

"That would be nice," Jack mumbled.

Scarlett Jo nudged him harder than she had earlier. This time the grunt was real.

"Well, I'm very appreciative." Grace turned her brown eyes toward Jack. "Thanks, Jack. Just let me know what I owe you in spite of what your mother here says."

Jack eyed his mama. She eyed him back. He looked at Grace. "No, ma'am. I'm glad to help."

"Well, the mower is in the garage, ready to go. I've got the door raised for you. Let me know if you need anything."

"Will do." And with that he made his escape from his mother.

Grace moved out of the doorway and opened it wide for Scarlett Jo. "You've raised some wonderful boys."

"They can be. Yes." She stepped into the foyer, set her purse down on the bench, and wrapped her arms around Grace. "How are you this morning?"

"Numb, I think." Grace led her down the hall. "I've already had a full morning. I feel like I could crawl into bed and sleep for a week. Want some tea?"

"I'd love it." Scarlett Jo followed her into the kitchen. Grace's mom stood at the counter by the refrigerator as if keeping watch over the coffeepot. The aroma of brewing coffee saturated every molecule of air in the kitchen.

"Scarlett Jo, I'd like you to meet my mother, Lydia Clancey."

Scarlett Jo's mouth flew open. "Oh, my side, you look exactly like Grace."

Grace met her mother's eyes, and both smiled as if they'd heard that for years. No wonder. They had the same blonde hair, caramel eyes, and slender frame.

"I've got to hug you."

Grace laughed as Scarlett Jo pulled her mom in an enthusiastic embrace. "Mom, this is Scarlett Jo Newberry."

"Ooh, you are simply the cutest thing ever," Scarlett Jo enthused. "Grace, how did you and your mom get so cute? I swear, it's like I could just pick you both up and put you in my big ol' handbag."

Grace's mom staggered a little when Scarlett Jo released her, but her smile was warm. "Grace has told me so much about you, Scarlett Jo. And I want to thank you for the gift you've been to my daughter. We had no idea what all was going on, and we are so relieved to know she has such wonderful friends to walk with her."

Scarlett Jo pulled out a stool from beneath the counter and perched on it. "Grace is easy to be friends with."

"Would you like some coffee?" Lydia asked.

Scarlett Jo puckered her nose.

"Don't like coffee?" Lydia said.

She just shook her head and smiled, choosing not to say what she really thought about coffee in front of this complete stranger. And Jackson thought she couldn't keep her mouth shut!

Grace laughed. "I'll get you some tea." She poured a glass and carried it to Scarlett Jo. "I saw Zach Craig today. I went over to fire him as my lawyer."

"You did?"

"Yeah, but he kind of wouldn't let me."

"What do you mean?"

Grace ran her fingers down the side of her glass, where condensation was already building. "Well, he told me he'd understand if I left, but he would fight for me if I stayed. He said he may not be good at anything else, but he's a good lawyer."

"He is good." Scarlett didn't say anything more. She had just reprimanded Sylvia for running her mouth, so there was no way she was going to run hers.

"Anyway, he's got me reconsidering," Grace said.

"So why exactly did you want to fire him?"

Grace found some indignation as she raised her head and looked straight at Scarlett Jo. "He's been cheating on his wife."

"I'd say that's a pretty well-announced fact. I'm thinking she could have posted it in the *Tennessean* and gotten less of a response than by telling a group of Southern churchgoers."

"Anyway, I don't need that kind of drama in my life. But I couldn't help feeling sorry for him."

"Why's that?"

"I wish you could have seen him today. He wasn't his put-together self. He was flustered and nervous. And ashamed—I could see shame."

Scarlett Jo tilted her head. "And that looked kind of familiar, huh?"

Tears suddenly flowed, and Grace didn't seem to fight them. "I've never felt shame like this. I was raised to believe you don't get divorced. My mom and dad have been married for forty years." She nodded toward her mother, who was reaching for a tissue from the box on the island. "My brother's marriage has lasted for thirteen. How do you get rid of the shame?" Her voice broke, and she lowered her head into her hands, elbows on the counter.

Scarlett Jo patted her back. "Oh, sugar, shame is a cruel companion. Don't even try to take a trip with it 'cause it'll snuff the life right out of you." She took the tissue from Grace's mother and handed it to Grace. "See, it's okay to feel ashamed of something you've done and take it to the Lord for forgiveness. But to just walk around in shame is basically to say that God's grace isn't enough for you—that it may be all right for everyone else, but not for you. That's a big ol' lie because God's grace is either deep enough and wide enough for all of us . . . or none of us. And shame carries another lie, too—that we're worthy of something in the first place. That we can act a certain way and that will make us good enough or right enough. But the thing is, you can't ever be good enough or right enough. None of us can. That's why we need Jesus so much. Hey, you need another tissue, baby girl?"

Grace sniffed and nodded. Lydia brought the box over to her daughter.

"Anyway, you've got to move past that shame," Scarlett Jo continued. "You've got to see it for what it is. It's okay to grieve over the breakdown of your marriage. And it's okay to confront your stuff, the pieces you got wrong. All of that is healthy. You probably even have some sin you need to repent of and ask forgiveness for. But I'm telling you, shame can't be a part of this journey. If you want to heal, you've got to see shame for the lie that it is and move forward."

"I just never wanted to be the 'divorced' woman."

Scarlett Jo felt her large gold hoop earrings beat the sides of her face as she shook her head. "When people meet you, I guarantee they're not thinking, *There goes a divorced woman.* They may see a tired woman, a hurt woman. But divorce isn't a banner or a badge you carry. It's not who you are; it's just a piece of your story. And it's not where the story ends. Don't you ever forget that." Scarlett Jo could see that register with Grace. "This is not your defining. It is your *re*fining."

Grace looked directly at her, eyes swollen with tears. "I did play a part in this, Scarlett Jo. It wasn't only Tyler. It was me too. I should have stopped so many things so long ago—stopped covering for him, stopped trying to be his mother, stopped living in such fear. Stopped judging him. I did. I judged him. Thought my way was the right way and he needed to do things differently. At least I told him that a lot in the beginning. Then I finally quit saying anything at all because I was afraid—afraid of people knowing our secrets, scared of how he would respond, afraid of starting a fight. Afraid of this . . ." Her voice trailed off. "The very thing I am living now is what I was so scared of. And if I had known I would be here anyway, I would have let all the balls drop so much sooner. I would have just released them and let them drop!"

Grace's voice was now passionate and sharp. "I want it out of me, Scarlett Jo."

Scarlett Jo raised her eyebrows. "What do you want out, baby girl? Because saying 'I want it out of me' can mean a whole bunch of different things to a woman who lives with six males."

Grace's burst of laughter came through her tears. Her mom laughed too. "Whatever got me here, whatever there is in me that let this happen—that helped this happen—I want it out of me."

"Well, then, that's all you've got to say. Let the good Lord know you want it out, and I assure you he'll give you opportunities to get it out. There are two sides to every story, but God's working on every side."

Grace dabbed her eyes with wadded tissues, her tearstained cheeks still beautiful. "There are probably two sides to Zach's story too."

Scarlett Jo opened her mouth, then shut it quickly. But Grace had seen her. "You know something about that, don't you?"

Scarlett Jo bit her lip, fighting the urge to say anything.

Grace prodded her. "You can tell me."

Scarlett Jo shook her head wildly and spoke through pressed lips. "Nope. Can't. Jackson would kill me."

Grace elbowed her softly. "Come on."

"Grace, leave her alone," her mother scolded.

"No, can't say anything."

Grace smiled. "It's okay. I don't need to know. All I know is, as one-sided as my divorce feels, I definitely played a part in getting us to this point. After living that many years with dysfunction, you can't help but start acting dysfunctionally, or you wouldn't stay. So I'm assuming the same is true for Zach. Which means I need to give him the benefit of the doubt, right?"

Scarlett Jo bit her lip again and shrugged.

"I'll do that."

Scarlett Jo exhaled slower, grateful for Grace's kindness in letting her off the hook. Jackson would like this girl.

{ Chapter 19 }

ZACH PARKED IN FRONT of Jackson's house and let the engine idle. He needed to gather his thoughts and his courage before he went in.

The fallout from last weekend's freak show at church hadn't been as bad as he had expected. At least it wasn't bad so far. Apparently the associate pastor, Stan Hammond, had addressed the congregation after Zach and Jackson left and said he expected what had happened there to stay there. He'd reminded them that the enemy was in a desperate battle for each one of their hearts as well, and he felt this experience had been given to them as a church body to see how trustworthy they were with other people's hearts.

Zach wasn't sure what all that meant. But he did know that no other client besides Grace had tried to fire him, and fortunately she had changed her mind. He flinched every time the phone rang, though.

He was still staying at the hotel. He had called the girls each night at their grandmother's and never let on that anything was wrong. His dad and Jackson had encouraged him to give Caroline some space, so he hadn't seen her since that morning at church. There had been no legal action on either side as of yet. But he was about to see her now.

Jackson had arranged this meeting to at least get them talking. And Zach was more nervous than he had been before his first kiss. And not just nervous. What sat in his gut right now was dread. Fear. Anxiety. Panic. They were all colliding inside him like bad Mexican food.

He turned off the ignition and felt the car come to rest beneath him. If only his pulse could do the same. He stepped out and walked up the front steps. The walkway was lined with the brightest flowers he had ever seen—big bursts of yellow and hot-pink and purple blooms. Exactly the kind of flowers you'd expect Scarlett Jo to have in her yard.

She opened the door before he even got to the top step. "Zach. Hey, sugar, come right on in here. Jackson is in his study." Her smile looked as broad as her hips in that tight blue skirt. She pounded him on the back as he came through the door. If she had played football, she'd have been a linebacker.

"Thank you, Scarlett Jo." He rubbed his hands together nervously. "Is Caroline here?"

"No, not yet, honey. But I'll send her in as soon as she gets here. Can I get you something to drink?"

"Yeah, sure. That would be great."

"You got a preference?"

"No, no. Anything is fine."

She thumped his back again, a little more gently this time. "Well, you go right on in there to the office, and I'll bring something to you."

"Okay." She left him there for a minute. He rocked in his loafers and pulled at the fabric of his blue Izod shirt, which hung loosely over his khaki pants. He walked slowly toward Jackson's office and paused in the doorway. Jackson had his back to the door, looking for something on the bookshelves.

Every inch of the office was inviting. Sunshine streamed in through big windows to the French doors where Zach stood. The walls and thick moldings were all painted a clean white that set off the dark hardwood floor and heavy furniture.

Zach stared a moment longer and breathed a quick prayer. *Please don't let this be a train wreck.* It was the first prayer he had managed all week. He was grateful he still knew how.

Zach spoke. "I'm here."

Jackson turned, his face lit up with a genuine smile. "Hey, man, great to see you." He walked over and gave him a hug, then motioned to the sofa. "Sit. Please sit."

Zach took a seat and rubbed his hands on his knees.

Jackson pulled an armchair over from the other side of the room and brought it closer to the sofa. "Long week, huh?"

Zach let out a small laugh. "Interminable."

"Any backlash?"

"No, not really. A few friends of mine and Caroline's have called, so she is obviously talking to her friends. But around town, it doesn't seem like there's a lot of gossip or anything. I can't believe it, honestly."

"Well, that makes me very grateful. It says a lot about our church, I think."

Their conversation was interrupted by Scarlett Jo. Her large frame loomed in the open doorway, but as she stepped aside, Zach caught sight of Caroline. Their eyes locked on each other as Scarlett Jo announced the obvious: "Fellas, Caroline is here."

Both Zach and Jackson stood immediately. Zach was grateful Jackson had words in that moment because he had just lost control of his ability to speak.

Caroline entered the room. Jackson welcomed her with a quick but kind embrace, and she gave him a tense smile. Then she was beside Zach. He didn't know what to do with her. Did he hug her? Simply nod?

"Hey," he offered.

"Hi" was all she gave in return.

Scarlett Jo clapped her hands together, causing him to jump a little. "I'll be right back with something to drink."

Her absence created a chasm in the room. He wished she'd stayed.

"How are you?" he asked Caroline, reaching out awkwardly to touch her arm.

It was rigid. Nothing new there. "Fine."

He turned his eyes toward Jackson, who read his desperation. "Why don't you both have a seat?"

Zach watched as Caroline straightened her peach-colored sundress. She was perfectly put together, as always. Hair perfect. Dress perfect. Shoes and makeup and smile—all perfect. There had been moments in their life together when he wanted to reach into all that perfection and mess it up. Could that be partly what his behavior was about—a way to make everything less perfect? Or maybe to reveal how fake and imperfect it already was.

He didn't know. Maybe that was an excuse. And he knew it didn't really excuse anything.

Caroline turned her head toward him as if she knew he was studying her in some way. The edges of her mouth set firmly.

Jackson spoke. "Caroline, I want to thank you for coming. I know you didn't have to, but both Zach and I are grateful you did."

Zach didn't feel grateful at all. Caroline just cupped her hands in her lap and gave Jackson another little smile.

"Well, do either one of you want to say anything?" the pastor went on. "I know you haven't seen each other or really talked in a week. And last time you did talk, it was—well, hostile, I guess you could say. So I want to give both of you the chance to say something if you want to, now that you've had some time to cool down and think."

Neither of them moved. Zach felt as if the front of his shirt were stretching. The tightness in his chest all but removed his ability to breathe.

Scarlett Jo came to the rescue. "Okeydoke, here's some sweet tea." She carried a large tray in and set it on Jackson's desk. She handed Caroline and Zach each a glass of tea with a small napkin wrapped around the base. Both gave a soft thank-you. She handed Jackson his glass and kissed him on the cheek. He touched her hand softly, and Zach noted their expressions. The knowing. The kindness. The freedom in the way they loved each other. He wasn't sure he had ever known anything like that.

Scarlett Jo left the room, quietly closing the French doors behind her.

As soon as she was gone, it was as if something loosened his tongue. "Caroline, I'm so sorry. I know I've hurt you in the most horrific of ways. I've betrayed your trust. I've put a wedge in our marriage. But I will do whatever is necessary to make this right."

He stopped abruptly. That was all he had. He waited. She sat there and looked at him but didn't speak.

"Do you have anything to say?" he finally blurted.

Then he saw something odd. What seemed like genuine emotion flooded to the surface. Her eyes glistened with the emergence of tears. But she shook her head, saying nothing.

Jackson nodded. "Well, I understand. Sometimes it's tough to know what to say in situations like these. But I want to share something with you both. You see, as a pastor for some twenty years now, I've discovered there are three parts to most affairs. There is the crisis part, which is where you are now. But there is also what led up to the affair and what happens after it. During the crisis part, the couple's hearts usually want to stay focused on who is to blame. But I care about you both so much I want you to focus on what will get you to a place of healing. So I feel like it is necessary for us to go back and focus on the earlier part. Our goal is to figure out what got *both* of you to this point."

Zach turned toward Caroline and watched as she gnawed at the inside of her mouth. Her eyes narrowed in the way they did when she entered a place of quiet seething.

"Jackson," he said, "what got us here is me. My dysfunction

is obviously off the charts. Caroline had nothing to do with getting us here. Everything I did was my decision."

Jackson nodded. "You're absolutely right. Everything you did with Elise was your decision. But why do you think you made that decision? Pain is often what forces us to places of hiding out, which is usually what affairs are. They are a way to hide from something we don't want to deal with, something that is too painful. And usually both partners contribute to that in some way. So what is it for you?"

Zach hadn't expected a question. And he didn't want Caroline to explode right here in the pastor's office. He knew what her explosions looked like.

"Well, I don't . . . I'm not sure I know exactly why. It's just . . . It's been hard."

Caroline's head snapped around. "Hard? It's been hard for *you*? What are you talking about?" Her anger was still under wraps, but it seeped through her words, as deadly as carbon monoxide.

"I'm not saying you made it hard, babe. I'm just saying . . . well . . ." He dropped his head, and his next words came out more as a mumble. "I don't know what I'm saying."

He raised his head and looked to Jackson for rescue, but Jackson just pressed harder. "What were you running away from, Zach? Because I've learned that with most decisions in life, we're either running *to* something that is healthy and alive or running *from* something that we're trying to avoid. With adultery, you're almost always running from something."

Zach was getting frustrated. He didn't want to say anything bad about Caroline. She was already teetering between explosion and nuclear meltdown. Besides, it was *his* fault. It was *all* his fault. "I guess I was running from me. From my poor decisions. I was running from my stuff." Okay, that all sounded good. But he could tell by Jackson's face he wasn't buying a lick of it.

"Well, sure," Jackson said. "We all run away from ourselves a lot. But let's take this a little further. What in your heart was so broken that you felt like you needed to run away from your wife and to another woman?"

Caroline's knee was moving quickly up and down. One wrong word, one wrong move, and he was certain she would pounce. "I don't know," he said. "I just don't know."

"How about you, Caroline? What do you feel might have gotten you and Zach here? Have you been running from anything?"

He could tell her eyebrows wanted to lift. Botox had rendered them useless. But a smooth brow couldn't mask the anger that perpetually simmered inside. "I don't run from anything, Pastor. I'm more of an up-front, honest person."

Jackson nodded. "Okay, everything is up-front and honest. So how did we get here?"

Caroline's words came out exacting, prickly. "What do you mean?"

"I mean my desire for both of you is your healing. That's way more important than having the right answers. And to get you past this place of crisis and into any kind of future together, we need to unwrap any pretense and get to what is underneath all this hurt."

Then Caroline lost it. "We got here because my husband doesn't know how to keep a commitment. Which I should have known because he never keeps his word to me regarding anything else either. He's always telling me he'll get the car serviced and he never does. He tells me that he'll take care of something around the house and he doesn't do it." She turned to Zach. "I should have known you wouldn't have any respect for a marriage covenant either."

Now she was back to Jackson. Zach was getting motion sickness. "I mean, if a man can't keep his word in the small things, why would you expect him to keep his word in the big things." It was a question, but she spoke it as a statement.

"Do you have trouble keeping your word, Zach?" Jackson asked.

Her last statement had ignited some indignation. "Caroline, how can you compare getting your car serviced to a marriage covenant? I try to get it all done, and I want to. So my first response when you ask me to do something is to tell you yes. But then I'm slammed at work, and by the time I get home, I just want to relax and talk to the girls and such. If you want to call that not keeping my word, fine, but that doesn't have anything to do with why we're here."

"So why are we here, Zach? Are we here so your pastor friend can look at me and tell me I'm just as messed up as you are?" The gloves were off. The control was gone. Her voice escalated. "Are we here so that you can get some validation for cheating on me?"

Zach looked at Jackson, hoping for help. But Jackson simply leaned back in his chair, apparently willing to let this go on.

She wasn't finished. "Or, I know—maybe we're here so you can try to make me as much to blame as you are?" She slammed her drink down on the table next to her and stood. "Well, I can tell you both, I won't sit here and listen to it. If this is the kind of counseling you dole out, Pastor—" the words came out laced with sarcasm, the Southern sweetness gone—"then you can save it for your other church members. And you, Zach Craig, can forget me ever doing this again."

She marched to the French doors and jerked one open. The only thing they could hear as she left was the weight of her steps as she stalked to the door. They listened as it opened and closed.

Zach set his glass down and stood. "We can't just let her leave like that."

"Why not?"

"She's serious, Jackson. She's not coming back. She thought you were saying this wasn't my fault."

"Is it all your fault, Zach?"

"Of course it is. I did it. How could it not be my fault?"

"The affair was your fault, Zach. I never argued that. But you and Caroline both had a role to play in how your marriage got to this point."

Zach stared at him. "Even if that's true, you could have worked that in gradually."

Jackson nodded. "Maybe you're right. Though I'm thinking that with Caroline we might never have gotten there. With Caroline, you need to cut right to the chase."

"Well, you certainly did that. Now *I'm* thinking I need to find an apartment."

Jackson nodded again. "I'll help you."

Zach raised his hand. "No, that will be enough. You have helped entirely enough." He took the same exit Caroline had used. He was pretty sure he wouldn't be back.

❀ ❀ ❀

Zach hit Caroline's number on his iPhone as he got into his car and drove the three short blocks to the parking lot behind his office building. She sent him straight to voice mail—ten times. This wasn't how he'd wanted their talk to go, not at all. Jackson had no business taking the conversation there. Caroline had every right to blame him for everything—including that "counseling" session. He'd been stupid, thoughtless. He let her know this on nine of the ten voice mails.

Then came a call from his friend Tommy Wilson, another divorce attorney in Franklin. He knew. Which meant other people around the city knew. Which meant judges knew. Which meant potential clients knew. Which meant . . . God alone knew what all that meant.

Zach dodged cicadas as he climbed the steps to his office. For the first time, the impact of his decisions and the reality of his life bore down on him with all of their weight. He leaned against the wall because his legs felt too unsteady to hold him up. And there in the stairwell Zach Craig came face-to-face with what his options were. Just like this stairwell, his life offered two directions. The choice was his.

He could walk back down these stairs, go straight to Caroline, and give her whatever she wanted, just to make peace and return to normal. He considered that choice with the intense desire of a thirsty man in a desert.

Then his eyes moved upward. His other choice was to fight—for his home, his marriage, his children, his own life. But fighting would take energy, energy he wasn't sure he had. Energy that, even if expended, might not get him what he was fighting for. He could do everything he needed to do and still come up empty-handed. Years of being a divorce attorney had taught him that lesson many times over.

He leaned his head against the wall and breathed a prayer. Emotion that had been bottled up for years followed quickly. "I don't know what to do. Nothing feels worth it."

The words bounced through the empty, narrow stairwell. He didn't move. He wasn't sure he could. He closed his eyes. And then, as if heaven itself were about to open, he sensed a warmth, a light. He waited, hoping heaven would speak. Something. Anything.

"Zach, are you okay?"

That didn't sound like heaven. And he figured heaven would already know if he was okay or not. He cracked one eye open and saw Darlene's figure illuminated in the open doorway of the offices above him, the sun from the front windows bright behind her.

Well, that wasn't what he'd been hoping for. He didn't try to hide the disappointment. It was pretty much what he had come to expect from his prayers.

Darlene scurried down the stairs, her elegant heels clacking on the concrete. Why was she wearing those shoes on a Saturday, anyway?

"Are you okay?" she asked again. "Come on up here. You look horrible."

"What are you doing here?" he asked as she tugged him upward. He was thinking the downward idea looked better and better.

"I'm going to a wedding this afternoon, and I left the present on my desk. Looks like this is where I was supposed to be anyway. Sit."

She sat him down on the sofa across from her desk and left for the kitchen. In a minute she returned with a bottle of water—ice-cold, just the way he liked it.

He smiled. "You know what I like more than my own wife does." He unscrewed the white plastic top, feeling the click as the top separated.

She sat beside him. "That's not true."

"It is true. Some days I don't know if Caroline knows my name."

"Have you talked to her? Since . . . I mean . . ." Her voice trailed off.

He stretched an arm across the back of the sofa and crossed one leg over the other. "I've talked to her voice mail. And I've been talked at by her. But no, Caroline and I have not really talked."

"She's hurting, Zach. And she's angry. She's all those things."

"I know. I know. I understand all of that."

Darlene pressed her left shoulder back into the couch and crossed her hands in her lap. Zach was grateful for her. She offered him what his mother would have if she were still living—a soft and comforting presence. "But you're hurting too. And you need to give yourself permission to feel it."

"I don't deserve to feel anything but shame. I don't deserve anything but for her to leave me. That is what I deserve."

She smiled at him—a knowing, understanding smile. "Yes, you deserve all of that. We all do. But shame isn't where we're called to live."

"Well, I might have to live there. Caroline's not going to let me come home." He heard the peevish, childish tone in his own voice, and he didn't care. He *felt* peevish and childish.

"Zach, I'm going to tell you something." Her voice took on an authoritative tone—another side to her mothering ways. "Look at me."

He raised his head and looked into her sympathetic hazel eyes.

"This isn't just about your marriage," she said. "It's about who you are. Because you're not going to be any good to anybody until you figure out what happened to Zach. I mean it. You are not the man you once were. When I first started working for you, you were *alive*. You walked through these offices with such energy and zeal. Such ambition. And I have watched over these last seven years as you have turned into a shell of a man."

She laid a gentle hand on his arm. "I love Caroline and the girls. I want your marriage to work. I do. But that isn't what matters most right now. What is most important right now is deciding what you're going to do about you. You've got to fight for what you've allowed to be stolen.

"Now . . ." She raised her petite frame from the sofa, then went to her desk and picked up her package. He watched as those high heels on her sixty-nine-year-old feet made a graceful exit toward the door. She waved a hand over her shoulder at him. "That is all I will say about it."

He looked up. "They're talking about me out there, Darlene."

She turned toward him, one hand on her hip. "Yes, they are. And they will continue to talk until something else happens. But trust me, something else always happens, so that's going to blow over. And you can get all pitiful if you want, but that won't get you anywhere. What you need to do is get started on the hunt for the Zach Craig you used to be." She turned again, the package under her arm. "I will see you on Monday."

And with that she walked out the door. He sat motionless, watching as it closed behind her. Her words clamored through him, seeming to bounce from one gaping hole in his soul to another.

That was what his prayer had been about, hadn't it? Up or down? What to do? Had Darlene heard him? He didn't think so.

He took another long swig from the water and swiped at his mouth. Heaven had listened. And it had sent him an angel.

A sixty-nine-year-old angel in high heels.

{ *Chapter 20* }

SCARLETT JO SAT at a table by a window of the Franklin Mercantile Deli. The air-conditioning and shabby-chic atmosphere brought delight to this suffocating day in late July. Summer had brought with it a shift of routine for Scarlett Jo and given her the opportunity to do more one-on-one things with the boys. And summer was almost over. So this morning it was all about Rhett.

Of all the eating places in downtown Franklin, she loved this one the best. Besides the mismatched chairs and quaint atmosphere, it was the hash brown casserole that got her. Anything with cheese and potatoes came straight from the throne of God as far as she was concerned. So she had ordered the Mercantile breakfast with a double scoop of hash browns.

Rhett sat across from her, digging into his French toast.

"You do know we could have gotten a few more minutes of shut-eye, don't you?" she told him. The child thought sunrise meant everyone in the house should be greeting the day. "That's what summers are for. Children sleep in so their mommies and daddies can have the mornings to get done what they need to get done before you guys wake up and mess up the day."

He stabbed his fork into the syrup-soaked bread, sending up small puffs of powdered sugar. "Mommy, you're funny."

She laughed. "I'm joking, buddy. Mommy was so looking forward to spending this morning with you."

"I know. Me too." Rhett put his fork down and took a long sip of orange juice. "Me and Forrest might be camping out tonight with Dad. And he said that if we do, we can pee outside."

She nodded. "Of course he did."

"Jack says that's what men were created to do. Pee outside."

"He said that, did he?"

He furrowed his brow and took another stab at his French toast. "Yeah. It's what guys do. We sleep in tents and pee outside. And burp. And—"

"That's enough, baby. I get the picture."

She knew it was true. She had raised four boys before him and married one who considered all these things appropriate for boys. There were days when she was grateful no little girl had been forced to endure the sounds, smells, and sights that little boys could produce. "Sounds like a great adventure."

"Yep, and we're going to tell ghost stories," he added, his speech slurred by the mass of egg-and-syrup-coated bread in his mouth. "I mean scary, scream-like-a-sissy-girl ghost stories." He squinted his eyes as he relayed the message he'd obviously gotten from his older brothers.

Rhett could be scared more easily than any seven-year-old she knew. He'd be in her bed before it got good and dark. "Well," she said, "y'all have fun with that. I'll use it as a chance to catch up on my television shows and paint my toenails."

He scrunched up his nose. "Ew . . . girl stuff."

"I am a girl, buddy."

He shook his head. "No, you're not. You're a mom."

She laughed. He had her there. "Yes, I am. Yours. Now quit talking with your mouth—"

The bell on the restaurant door chimed, and Scarlett Jo looked up to see Caroline Craig enter the room. She hadn't seen her or heard from her since Caroline stormed from her house that Saturday afternoon in June.

"Excuse Mommy for a minute." She pulled the napkin from her canary-yellow lap, then stood and made a beeline for the door. "Caroline, honey, so good to see you. I haven't seen you since that afternoon you left in such a rush. And you haven't returned my calls, so I'd love to know how you're doing."

The smile that spread across Caroline's face was about as real as the artificial daisy adorning Scarlett Jo's headband. "Oh, I'm fine. The girls and I are just fine. Thank you. We've been traveling a lot this summer. You know how teenagers are. They don't seem to want to stay put."

"Did you get my calls?" No need to beat around the bush.

"Um, I'm not sure, Scarlett Jo. You know, with everything that has happened in the last couple of months I haven't been able to keep track of things the way I usually do. Please forgive me that I haven't gotten back with you." Her shoulders slumped slightly as she spoke. A moment of vulnerability.

Scarlett Jo saw weariness in Caroline's eyes, even though the Botox kept her brow from showing it. "Oh, honey, that's okay," she said. "I just wanted you to know that Jackson and I care about you. And Zach."

Caroline's expression shifted when she heard her husband's name. Her plastic smile returned. "Thank you, but we're fine. Really, everyone is doing exceptionally well, considering."

"That's good, because if my husband had cheated on me and I'd caught him red-handed, the last thing in the world I'd be is fine. What I'd be is out-of-my-mind mad. And trying to figure out who I was going to shoot with my 12-gauge. I'd have my kids in deep therapy, and I'd be there right along with them. So that you're doing fine is amazing to me. You must be one strong woman, Caroline."

Caroline didn't hesitate. "I come from good stock."

"Yes, you do. I've met your mother. She is always so put-together and gracious. Just a real Southern grace about her."

Caroline looked at her phone as if willing it to ring. "Listen, I don't mean to scoot, but I've got to grab some breakfast before I open the store this morning. So good to see you."

"You too. I've got to scoot too. Please know you're always welcome to call. You can use that phone right there." Scarlett Jo let out a snorted laugh as she pointed at Caroline's cell.

Caroline raised her phone and shook it slightly. "I'll remember that. Thanks." She moved quickly to place her order at the counter.

Scarlett Jo returned to find Rhett leaned back in his chair, plate empty, juice drained. He patted his belly as she passed.

"That'll get me through our adventure tonight, just in case we don't get a kill we can cook on our campfire." He giggled. "Dad says we can always grill us some cicadas."

She grabbed him by the arm and tugged. "Ooh, I hate those things." She shivered. "Now, come on, Daniel Boone. Let's get you home so you can have the supreme joy of peeing in the woods. Goodness knows I wouldn't want you to miss that. Might even join you."

He looked at her as they walked down the street. "Mommy, that is just gross."

She wrapped her arm around him and roughed the top of his head. "I know, baby. Mommy isn't always known for her couth, is she?"

He nodded that she wasn't, though she knew he had no idea what *couth* even meant.

❀ ❀ ❀

"That's it?" Grace clutched her damp wad of tissue and looked at Zach.

He nodded.

"Ten years of marriage, and now the world is going to pretend it never happened."

He touched her arm. The soft fabric of her white linen jacket pressed against her skin. "I'm so sorry, Grace."

Rachel put an arm around her friend, and her mom and dad pulled in close on the other side. Grace could sense their grief. Apparently Scarlett Jo could too because she threw an arm over Lydia's shoulder.

"At least you're leaving with what you wanted." Zach was

obviously trying to encourage her. "You and Tyler worked things out without going to trial. And now you are free."

"Free." The word escaped her lips like something from another language. She batted her eyes to prevent more tears from falling. She had barely been able to answer the judge's questions because of the knot lodged in her throat.

She reached out to shake his hand. "Thank you, Zach. Thank you for everything."

"Thank you for trusting me."

"I'll see you around, I'm sure."

"I have no doubt."

Rachel took her by the arm and led her toward the staircase. They all walked down to the bottom floor of the Williamson County courthouse. Rain pelted them as they hurried between the big white columns toward the parking lot.

"What an appropriate conclusion," Grace murmured, looking up. "Even heaven is crying." But she was grateful for the early August rain that hid her tears and even more grateful that Tyler had honored her request and not shown up. That she could not have handled.

Grace beeped her car open, and she and Rachel and her mother piled in. She didn't know why she'd insisted that Rachel ride with her this morning. Her friend was certainly capable of driving herself to the courthouse. But Grace had wanted to pick her up. And she had quit making apologies for the way she wanted to do this divorce.

The last two months had been filled with a strong sense of how things needed to be done, even when those things were incredibly hard. She kept the car radio tuned to a country station and refused to change it when a love song came on, even if she cried through the entire piece. She made herself spend Saturday mornings in bed with the paper and a glass of sweet tea, just as she used to with Tyler. And she made a point of still eating at Pancho's after church on Sundays. Sometimes she'd only make it through five chips and half a soft drink before she had to leave. Other times she ate every last bite on her plate. But she did it. Giving up was not an option.

Her resolve grew out of a kind of righteous anger that struck the first week after she filed for divorce. She had allowed so many years of her life to be stolen. Tyler hadn't taken them from her. She had given them up voluntarily. By her fear. By her avoidance. She had just handed over her heart as if it held no value.

But no longer. She woke up one morning determined that nothing else would be stolen from her. She had made a kind of pact with her own soul: *You will go through. You won't go around. You won't go under. You won't wish this away. You are going to walk through whatever horrible moment you have to, and you are going to get to the other side.* And for the most part, in the last two months, she had done just that.

Her father drove behind them the few blocks home with Scarlett Jo in his passenger seat. Grace hadn't wanted him to ride alone. Grace pulled into the driveway and turned off the wipers. Through the deluge, they could see Rachel's husband, Jason, sitting in his car in front of the house, waiting to take her home.

Grace's mother turned toward Rachel. "I'm so glad Jason's here to drive you, sweetie. I'd hate for you to have to drive yourself home in this mess."

Grace knew her mother's words were spoken out of parental

concern and care, but they settled on her like daggers ripping through flesh. She gripped the steering wheel with all her might. Rachel leaned up and gave her a kiss on the cheek, told her how proud she was of her and that she would call later that evening. Grace gave her a stiff nod. But once Rachel exited the car and closed the door behind her, the deluge that had been held back by metal and glass found its way inside to leather and chrome. And Grace didn't try to hold it in.

The wails came from a deep place, a place so deep that once it released its pain, you weren't sure you'd ever return to what you were. She wept in frantic, manic bursts. "He'll never drive me anywhere again!" Her words shouted recognition of the finality and magnitude of this moment. "I'm going to drive myself everywhere!"

Her mother reached over the console and stroked Grace's hair. "Baby, I'm so sorry. I wasn't thinking."

"It's not your fault. It's my reality. I'm going to drive myself everywhere. I'm going to be alone everywhere I go. People are going to look at me like I'm half of something. I hate this!" Her hands pounded the faux wood on the steering column. "I hate all of this. It shouldn't be this way, Mom. It shouldn't be this way."

Now her mother was crying too. "I know. It shouldn't. It should not be this way at all."

Grace's body heaved with racking sobs. This morning she had woken up just as alone, but it hadn't been final. Not legal. Not forever. Now it was all of that. And it hurt. In the deepest places where hurt could settle and ache and gnaw, it was there. It was all in there. And she didn't want to hurt like that. She *so* didn't want to hurt.

❀ ❀ ❀

Zach walked into his second-floor apartment and flicked on the light. Sparse living conditions greeted him each night. He had a sofa and a coffee table and a television in the living room, and the bedroom had a box spring and mattress on the floor. No pictures on the walls. No bric-a-brac, as he often called it. Absolute minimum of kitchen stuff.

It was a makeshift habitation, but it was his, and he'd even grown to like it. He dropped the brown paper bag from Bread & Company on the counter and held the phone against his ear as he pulled the key from the door. "I know, Caroline, but I want to see the kids this weekend. Our separation agreement clearly states when they are to be with me."

"Well, they don't want to come over to your apartment. There's nothing for them to do there. And they'll be starting school next week. We've got stuff to do, school supplies to buy, clothes shopping. This is their last weekend to get all of that done."

"They need to see their father. This isn't convenient for any of us, but they need me, and I need to see them. I'm settled enough now that they can spend the night. It will be like a sleepover."

He could envision her pacing. She always paced when she talked. "They're about to start high school, Zach. The last thing they want is a sleepover with their father."

"That may be, but we still need to be together. When can I get them?"

Her sigh came heavy through the phone, but they both knew she couldn't keep him from his kids. That wouldn't bode well for any future arrangement. "I'll have them ready to go tomorrow at five. You can bring them back Sunday night."

"Okay. I'll be there at five." He was about to say thank you when she spoke again.

"I saw Scarlett Jo Newberry the other day. I swear I've never met a woman with more gall—or less tact. And that hair, those clothes—the woman is just plain tacky. I don't know how we lasted at that church so long. She's hounding me to call her back, so you need to tell her husband to have her leave me alone."

"Um, yeah . . . well, okay. But I haven't talked to Jackson much either. Not since that day he said those things to you."

"Well, they are both crazy, and I don't want anything to do with them. You leave them out of our lives, do you hear me?"

"Yeah. Yeah, sure. I'll see you tomorrow. I'll call the girls and tell them good night."

"Fine. And if you are keeping them this weekend, you can take them shopping for school supplies." With that she hung up.

He held the phone in his hand and envisioned a weekend of shopping with his teenage daughters. Caroline wanted to torture him. It was evident.

He poured himself a glass of fruit tea, then picked up the bag from the counter and carried it to the coffee table. He pulled out his favorite sandwich, the Steeplechase—cranberry bread, pulled turkey, honey mustard, apples—and a bag of chips. He sat on the sofa, took a bite of his sandwich, and leaned his head back, savoring the quiet. Guiltily grateful that Caroline's voice wouldn't be pounding in his head all night.

Their phone conversation funneled through him, her words about Scarlett Jo Newberry. Caroline had always looked down on Scarlett Jo. To be honest, Zach had too. And Scarlett Jo was out there; that was for sure. But now he wondered if his attitude had derived mostly from Caroline's perception. Jackson Newberry clearly adored his wife, and despite their disagreement, Zach respected Jackson.

He let his mind ponder the past few months. The forced exit from his home. The legal separation Caroline had insisted on. Accusations flying through town from the stir Caroline was making. And the more time that passed with them living two separate lives, the more distance that time created in their hearts, until there were moments he couldn't even remember why he had married her in the first place.

Then there was work; his cases. Grace Shepherd's case had begun about the same time everything fell apart for Zach. Now it was done, while his situation was still unresolved. No divorce filing. No counseling. Just this bare apartment.

The summer had taken him on an odd and painful journey. And though this was in no way the life he was accustomed to, there were things about it that he craved. He liked the simplicity, the lack of motion, the quiet. Especially the quiet. Life with Caroline and the girls was one of perpetual motion. There was never any place for his heart to settle or his mind to rest, never a moment when they could just *be*. There was always noise. People. Activity. Stuff. Distraction.

He let that last thought linger awhile, and with it came revelation. Wasn't that what he and Caroline had both been doing for the last few years—distracting themselves? Hers was a distraction of the heart with activity and illusive control. His was a distraction of the heart with self-gratification. They *were* both broken, weren't they? Just like Jackson said.

He thought of Grace's quiet poise today, of her compassion and her willingness to give him a second chance. Then he thought of Caroline. Tense and driven. Desperate to be right, to win no matter what, to feel superior to other people. Unable or unwilling to give without getting something in return.

And in that moment he realized Jackson Newberry was right. *It's not just me.* Caroline shared the guilt he had claimed as solely his own. She had come into this marriage with her own stuff—her insecurity, her dependence on her mother, her perfectionism—and it had helped bring them to this place.

Caroline was hurting—he knew that. Beneath all her anger was a deep, undeniable, desperate hurt. But in order for their marriage to survive, they *both* had to be willing to look at their stuff, didn't they?

But what if she won't do it?

The thought hit him hard, followed by an answer: *I have to do it anyway.*

He had to be willing to go on this journey to the unknown, to be man enough to claim what he had done to get his heart into this pitiful shape. He stared at the white walls that surrounded him. The symbolism struck him. He could let this be the start of something new, a clean slate, a true adventure for him too, if he was simply willing.

When his phone vibrated on the sofa beside him, he looked down and saw Jackson's name. He almost laughed. Answering it would mean something. Answering it would mean he was willing to finally confront all the things that got him here.

It rang a second time. He suspected hell itself would freeze over before Caroline Craig ever admitted anything was wrong with her. He had buried one marriage today. He prayed he wouldn't have to bury his own.

He picked up his phone as it rang a fourth time. Zach Craig had a choice to make. No matter what choice Caroline made, this was a defining moment for him.

The phone rang again. And he answered it.

{ *Chapter 21* }

"WHEN YOU'RE ALL HEALED from this divorce thing, please tell me *she* doesn't have to hang around us anymore," Rachel whispered. She motioned with her eyes at Scarlett Jo, who had moved a little ahead.

Grace elbowed her. "I can assure you it's going to take longer than a month."

Scarlett Jo grasped the brass handle of a large black-painted wooden door. She ushered them into the Red Pony restaurant, which was nestled between the Heirloom Shop and Walton's Antique Jewelry, its boundaries marked off by red-painted brick. Dark walls encased them as they entered, and a metal screen painted in a pussy willow pattern stood at attention across from them. The dim lighting and dark woods brought a nighttime effect indoors, even though the sun was still a few hours from setting.

"Can I help you ladies?" the young hostess inquired.

"Newberry. For three." The large white bow wrapped around Scarlett Jo's head bounced as she said it.

"I swear, she needs that ribbon to keeps all her brains together," Rachel muttered.

"Stop it," Grace warned. "You're—"

"What in the world are you doing?" Rachel stared as Scarlett Jo patted her body all over and shook like a dog after a bath.

"I'm making sure I don't have any cicadas on me."

"You can't be serious. The cicadas all keeled over weeks ago."

Scarlett Jo did her habitual nose-crinkle thing. "You're kidding. They're gone?"

Rachel walked to the door and opened it. "Listen, Scarlett Jo." She stuck her head out. "Can you hear anything?"

Scarlett Jo tilted her head, listening. "Well, I'll be. I can't believe I've wasted precious weeks of my life hiding from those things."

Grace could see Rachel's brain working. She was certain Rachel would use this exchange to her advantage at some point.

The hostess called them and led them toward a staircase to the second floor. They maneuvered around the bar, where many patrons had already deposited themselves for the sweet hour that declared the weekend had arrived. Two men on the end turned their heads, and Grace felt their eyes follow the three of them as they headed up the stairs. Her thumb instinctively rubbed her empty ring finger, and her heart ached.

On the second floor, a server ushered them into a large room. Two wood-and-mirrored-glass serving tables occupied the room's center, each adorned with a soaring flower arrangement that practically touched the ceiling. The three women were shown to a beautifully set four-top nestled against one of the brick walls.

Grace allowed the soothing atmosphere to calm her. She was going to enjoy an evening out with the girls. It was just what she needed after another grueling week of learning how to survive.

As Rachel slid her black napkin into her lap, she posed a question. "Who would name a restaurant Red Pony?"

Scarlett Jo didn't miss a beat. "It's from a Steinbeck novella."

Both Rachel's and Grace's eyebrows went up. Grace smiled. Rachel mouthed, "She reads."

Grace rolled her eyes. Fortunately Scarlett Jo was already facedown in the menu. The girl saw eating as a lifestyle.

"Oh, my word, they have the best shrimp and grits ever here." Scarlett Jo poked her finger at the middle of the menu.

Grace picked up her menu and glanced through it. Nothing caught her eye. She hadn't had an appetite in six months.

"Ooh, and their blue cheese risotto. Oohwee, that stuff is slap-your-mama good." She raised her hand toward Rachel.

"You better not slap me," Rachel shot back. "I'm telling you now. You have been warned."

Scarlett Jo laughed and flicked her menu at Rachel, then looked at them both as if the best idea had hit her. "I know. Let's get three different things and share." She bounced in her seat. "That way we can all get a little taste of everything."

Grace put her menu down. That was one less decision she had to think about. "Sure," she said. "You pick."

Rachel nudged her. "I want to pick something too."

Scarlett Jo clapped her hands together. "Okay, yes, you pick.

I love surprises." She placed her hands on the table and leaned forward. "Do you know I let each one of my boys be a surprise? I mean, the fact that they were boys. I never let the sonogram lady tell me they had wingadingas."

Rachel slapped Grace's arm. "She did not say that!"

Grace couldn't help but smile.

"What?" Scarlett Jo looked back and forth between them. "What? What do *you* call them?"

Grace shook her head at Rachel, who had opened her mouth to speak. "You don't want to know."

Scarlett Jo flapped her hands. "Anyway, I just waited until they popped out. Never knew what a one of them was going to be." She leaned back. "So you pick, Rachel. Surprise us." She said the last two words in a husky, spooky voice.

Rachel rolled her eyes and picked up the menu. She gave Scarlett Jo both her requests, the shrimp and grits and the beef tenderloin with the blue cheese–sweet corn risotto. Then she added the Red Pony BLT—bacon, lobster, and tomato over Yukon Gold ravioli. Scarlett Jo licked her lips with sheer excitement as Rachel gave their order to the waitress.

Grace was grateful for her two friends because their banter kept her from having to make conversation while waiting for their food. And despite Rachel's attitude, Grace could tell she was beginning to like Scarlett Jo. Scarlett Jo wasn't afraid to ask or say anything. She was a straight shooter. She asked Rachel about everything from race to religion and multiple topics in between, and she didn't bristle at the answers. Scarlett Jo would declare her love for Sarah Palin, Rachel would pretend to gag, and Scarlett Jo would just laugh. There was no taking offense, no high-maintenance personality to soothe. And because Rachel was such a straightforward person herself, she appreciated that. They were an odd combination, these three. But they were becoming a sweet one.

Rachel kept the conversation going even as the waitress arrived with the food. "Scarlett Jo, where did you go to school?"

Grace had never even thought to ask.

"Ole Miss. I majored in philosophy."

Rachel moved her glass to make room for the tenderloin platter. "You majored in what?"

"I know. Crazy, right?" Scarlett Jo speared a shrimp with her fork. "Most people would have me pegged as an early-childhood education major or a dropout. But there's stuff up in there." She tapped her head. "Past the big hair and big headbands and underneath all that bleach, there is something up in there."

Grace smiled. "I can see that about you."

Rachel shook her head. "Then you are a bigger woman than me. I wouldn't have pegged that for anything."

Grace elbowed her, but Scarlett Jo laughed. "Grace, it's okay. It's not like I go around ruminating on the great mysteries of life or anything. Truth is, I find it more interesting to ponder life as it's being lived."

Rachel looked at Grace and shrugged. "Who knew?"

Forty minutes later, Scarlett Jo pushed away the remnants of her chocolate demise cake and unfastened the top button of her black walking shorts. "Oh, girls, you're going to have to roll Mama out of here."

Rachel stood and took Scarlett Jo by the arm. "Come on. You can do it. Just squeeze those cheeks together and push yourself out of there."

Scarlett Jo raised her head with a haughty sniff. "Philosophers do not partake in such childish banter."

Rachel laughed. "Well, it's a good thing you're not a philosopher, then."

Scarlett Jo snorted and slapped her. "Ain't it though."

Grace yawned hard. The richness of the meal and her early morning hours since going back to work made eight at night feel like midnight. She placed her hands on the edge of the wooden table and forced her body out of the chair. She got to the top of the stairs and wished for another way down, one that didn't pass the bar. Scarlett Jo and Rachel were in front of her, laughing and carrying on, so she just kept her head down and followed them out.

They headed down the sidewalk, the Friday night crowd as thick as the August humidity. They could see people milling around outside Mellow Mushroom at the end of the street by the square, waiting for a table with cold drinks and good pizza. As they passed the building next to Zach's law firm, Grace couldn't help but peek.

Scarlett Jo and Rachel both noticed. "What are you looking at?" Rachel asked.

Grace had stopped. She couldn't help it. The For Lease sign was still up. She leaned close and squinted, trying to see into the darkened building. She couldn't make out a teapot any longer. "I just think this is a quaint space."

"A quaint space for what?" Rachel goaded.

Grace shrugged.

Scarlett Jo let out one of her melodramatic gasps. "Oh, my side, Grace. This would be a perfect space for you to open your restaurant." She bounced excitedly as she spoke as if she were going to do it herself.

Rachel sidled up next to her. "Is that what you're thinking, Grace?"

Grace shrugged once more and cocked her head slightly, still looking inside the building. "I don't know. I was kind of . . . dreaming. About a tearoom."

"It's okay to dream, you know."

"Yeah, I know."

Scarlett Jo leaned in close to them. "A tearoom would be perfect. You could serve those scones. Oh, mercy, those scones." She used that voice again, that ecstasy-ridden, deep growl thing she had that always made Grace a little concerned about her mental health. "And that cream. Oh, boatloads of that cream. And little finger sandwiches."

"How can you get excited about food right now?" Rachel asked. "I'm not sure I ever want to eat again."

Scarlett Jo was already lost in her new world. "And we could decorate it in canary yellow and tangerine and teal!"

Rachel raised a hand. "Hold on there, chief. The only one living in the exploding Crayola box is you. Me and Grace here are chocolate and vanilla kind of girls, not rainbow sherbet, if you get where I'm going with this."

Scarlett Jo clapped her hands together again, her excitement not in the least bit drained by Rachel's insult to her color palette. "Well, you can do the interior. That's fine. But I want to be the tasting expert. And I can taste everything first and then greet customers and tell them what they should order."

Grace started walking up the street again. "I'm glad y'all have such grand plans for my money. Which I don't have enough of to take a huge risk like that."

"Banks have money," Scarlett Jo suggested.

Grace chuckled. "Yes, they do. They also have strict regulations, and I'm sure they wouldn't lend me enough to start a business."

Rachel grabbed her arm, stopping in the middle of the sidewalk. "I'd lend it to you."

Grace heard the seriousness in Rachel's tone and saw the solemnity of her friend's face. "What? You don't have that kind of money."

"Jason does."

Grace so loved her friend in that moment. "Rach, I know you and Jason would do anything for me. But I'm not taking your money or his money to start a business."

"But we've been looking for something to invest it in. And this town could actually use a tearoom. You know how people hated it when Homestead Manor closed down. And Lillie Belle's is no longer a tearoom. There is no tearoom around here, which is a shame because we're Southerners. We love tearooms. And your food, Grace. No one I know cooks like you. Everything you make is so good."

Scarlett Jo ran her tongue across her lips. "Ooh, so good."

Rachel pointed a finger at Scarlett Jo. "Stop it! Seriously, you have to get control of yourself. You're freaking me out."

Scarlett Jo clapped her hands together and straightened her back. "Sorry. Yes, go ahead. You were talking about how we are going to start a business."

Rachel shook her head adamantly. "No, I am not talking about how *we* are going to start a business. I am talking about how *she* is going to start a business. I will be a silent partner and financier. And you, Scarlett Jo, will be even more silent."

Scarlett Jo got a pouty look on her face. "But I want to do something. I want to work. Wait tables. Greet customers."

Grace put a hand over her mouth to hide her smile. Rachel wagged her finger at Scarlett Jo. "No, no greeting customers. But maybe we can find something for you to do."

"I'm going to have a job!" Scarlett Jo screamed. She ignored the strange looks from a gaggle of teenagers skirting them. "A real live job!"

Rachel glared. "There will be no job if you don't learn how to control yourself."

Scarlett Jo grabbed one of the kids and whispered, "I'm going to have a job."

The girl slid from her hands and ran down the street.

Scarlett Jo straightened herself up again. "Okay. Yes. Complete control."

Rachel moved closer to Grace. "Seriously, Grace, think about it. If there ever was a time in your life for you to do something that you want to do, it's now. Not because it's smart. Not because it will make someone else happy. Not because it's practical or makes sense in the long run. But just because you want to do it. You want that for you."

Grace studied her friend's eyes. Rachel meant every word. Simply knowing that was almost overwhelming.

Scarlett Jo sidled up beside them, her eyes glistening with tears. "I don't know two women in the whole world who are better friends than the two of you. I want in on it. Can we be best friends forever?"

"Do we have to?" Rachel asked.

Scarlett Jo punched her with a snort. Rachel rubbed her arm. Grace was certain it would leave a bruise.

"I've only known you a few months, Grace," Scarlett Jo said. "But until this moment I have never seen this kind of light in your eyes."

"This is the light she used to have," Rachel added. "Before . . . well, just before."

"It's time for it to come back on," Scarlett Jo said.

Rachel shook her head. "I can't believe I'm about to say this, Grace, but listen to her." She pointed to Scarlett Jo. "Listen to her."

{ *Chapter 22* }

SCARLETT JO LEFT Landmark Booksellers with a new book under her arm and big hugs from Joel and Carol, the owners. She knew most people didn't think of her as a reader. They looked at her head of big blonde hair and her other rather looming parts and figured her for a shallow kind of gal. But she'd devour this biography of Steve Jobs in a week, even though it contained more words than one of Sylvia's tirades.

Scarlett Jo read so much, in fact, that her kids said she needed one of those e-readers. But she liked real live books, the kind with paper and ink—which was why she liked Landmark. They still sold real books, and they always had great recommendations. Plus, they knew her name, and she liked that too. There was just something special about a bookstore that wasn't one of those chains or on the Internet.

She'd read about a woman in Texas who had a bookstore inside her beauty salon. One minute that woman would be teasing your hair, and the next minute she'd be telling you about the latest Pat Conroy novel. And she sponsored a book club where all the members wore tiaras and animal prints when they got together to talk about books.

Scarlett Jo loved the idea so much that she'd started her own book club last year. She'd even invited Eugenia Quinn, who let her know in no uncertain terms that she didn't do either tiaras or animal prints. But Eugenia had shown up every week anyway and brought several of her friends. They'd stopped meeting for the summer and had never quite gotten started again, but maybe it was time—

"It's official! We are going to hell in a handbasket. I'm saying that, and I don't cuss."

Scarlett Jo looked up to see Sylvia stalking toward her. "Who's *we*?"

"Me. You. This world." The frantic tone in Sylvia's voice was unusual even for her.

"Now, Sylvia, why don't you get hold of yourself and sit down. You need to tell me what is going on." She pulled a wrought-iron chair from under a table in front of the bookstore.

"I don't want to talk about it." Sylvia tried to scoot past Scarlett Jo.

But Scarlett Jo was fast and broad, and nobody scooted around her. She stopped Sylvia dead in her tracks. "Tell me," she repeated, her voice calm and kind.

Sylvia's permanently furrowed brow wrinkled deeper. "I will not. Now get out of my way."

Well, she had forced her. "Sit!" Scarlett Jo's words barreled from her chest low and loud.

Poor Sylvia about jumped right out of her patent-leather pumps. But she sat.

Scarlett Jo straightened the hem of her pink floral sundress and pulled it down as she sat across from Sylvia. "Now . . . talk."

Sylvia set her matching patent-leather handbag on the table in front of her. "It's my granddaughter. You know, Mary Kate?"

"I know. Keep talking. What about Mary Kate?"

"She's—she's gone and gotten herself . . . pregnant." She barely whispered the word.

Scarlett Jo felt a twinge of heat rise in her face. She tried not to let Sylvia's ignorance make her too angry. She leaned over and whispered back. "People say that out loud these days. It's okay."

Sylvia humphed. "It isn't okay. We don't do such things in my family. And she knows better. She's just sixteen years old, and she's ruined her entire life, not to mention the whole family's reputation. And she won't even marry the boy. Says she doesn't love him. Well, she should have thought of that before she went out and . . ." She didn't finish the sentence. Apparently she couldn't form the words.

Scarlett Jo leaned back in her chair. "Well, you're right. She should have thought first. But she didn't."

Sylvia's eyes narrowed. "People will think she's white trash."

Scarlett Jo felt herself twitch. "Yep. And they may think awful things about you too."

Sylvia's expression made it clear Scarlett Jo wasn't helping. "People are nasty. Mean. I mean, her own father's talking about kicking her out of the house, and he'd have the perfect right."

She fumbled with her purse. "Never did think much of that man, even if he is my own son-in-law."

Scarlett Jo crossed her legs and let her foot rhythmically dangle in front of her. "So let me ask you, then, what in the world can you do about it?"

"We can hide it. Send her away."

Scarlett Jo rolled her eyes. "I guess you could, like they did in the Stone Age—although there is the question of where you'd send her. I don't think they have homes for unwed mothers anymore. But come on, Sylvia, I'm asking a thoughtful question here. What can you *really* do about it?"

That was when she saw Sylvia's lip quiver. Or thought she did. But the woman got up so fast it was hard to tell. She snatched her purse and took off past Scarlett Jo's still-sitting body. "I'll tell you what I can do, Scarlett Jo Newberry. I can make sure I never tell you anything else again. As liberal as you are, you would probably want to take her in yourself."

Scarlett Jo stood. "No, I'm thinking that might be what God's asking you to do. And I think that might be why you're so angry—because you're resisting his voice."

Sylvia turned on her one-inch square heels. "I can't have that kind of . . . *person* in my home." And she was gone.

Scarlett Jo couldn't help but wonder how long it had been since Jesus had been invited into Sylvia Malone's house either.

❁   ❁   ❁

Zach's talks with Jackson the last few weeks had created an awakening of sorts—an awakening to events from his past. The tragedy of his parents' divorce. The performance-driven personality he had developed and the deep wounds that remained. The way he and Caroline had entered into marriage, vainly trying to complete one another in ways that left them both undeniably unfulfilled. How they had learned to cope. And how, little by little, they had both shut down their hearts.

"Do you know what I mean when I talk about a shut-down heart?" Jackson had asked him one night as they strolled through downtown Franklin. With the cicadas finally gone, the sweet sounds of a Southern summer had returned.

"Honestly, I don't think I do."

"Think about our kids again. You know, like we talked about that first day in my office."

"I was kind of a wreck that day, remember?"

Jackson clapped him lightly on the back. "How could I forget?"

"So your point was?"

"That our kids didn't come into this life jaded. They started out with full hearts—fully alive and fully themselves."

Zach felt a stab of guilt as he thought about Joy and Lacy. They were the ones who suffered most in all of this. And he still wasn't sure what he could do about it.

"Think about when your girls were little," Jackson was saying. "They probably danced with this reckless abandon when music would come on. They played dress up and had tea parties or did whatever girls like to do."

"Well, one of them did. The other is more a soccer-playing tomboy kind of girl. And for the record, they still dance in the kitchen with the music turned up loud—I mean loud."

Jackson laughed. "My boys came out of the womb making truck noises and wanting to shoot something. And not much has changed with them either. Now it's airsoft guns and video games where they're virtual soldiers. Long way from our BB guns and Swiss Army knives, huh?"

Zach laughed. "Yeah, a whole new world."

"But my guys still play outside until Scarlett Jo hollers for them to come in. And you know I mean it when I say she hollers."

Zach pretended shock. "No. Scarlett Jo?"

Jackson chuckled. "I know—right? But my point is, those kids are *alive*. They're here, present, in the moment. We throw them in the air, and they yell, 'Do it again, Daddy!' They cry when you take away their crayons or make them leave a friend's house. They feel their feelings. They don't try to be something they're not."

"I'm not sure I agree with that," Zach said. "My girls are trying so hard to be like everyone else. You know—skinny, popular, right clothes."

"And what are they, thirteen?"

"Just turned fourteen."

"That's exactly what I'm talking about. They're starting to experience what can happen to us when we let life shut us down. We're meant to stay connected to our hearts, you see. Feeling our feelings, present in the moments we're given. But we don't do that. And that's when we get in trouble."

"But we're not supposed to stay kids forever, are we? Shouldn't we grow up? You know, put away childish things?"

"Of course. We mature and take responsibility for ourselves and others, and that's a good thing. But we're never meant to lose that alive quality, to get cut off from our true hearts. Growing up isn't the same thing as shutting down."

"But it happens. That's what you've been telling me."

Jackson nodded. "It does happen, but it's not inevitable. We can fight it. We have to fight it. Because when our hearts shut down, we become mere shells of who we once were. We don't laugh—not honestly, not from the heart. We don't dream. We don't feel our feelings or use our gifts. We end up trying to just survive instead of live. It's like we've handed our hearts over to the enemy of our souls and said, 'Here, you can have it. I'm giving up.'"

He stopped and looked at Zach. "Am I making any sense at all?"

Zach gave a rueful smile. "Too much sense. That's when we have affairs, right?"

"Not all of us. The thing is, shut-down hearts don't always look the same. I've seen this in my own life and when I've walked it out with others. Some people try to control everything in their life. Some fall into pointing out everyone else's issues instead of dealing with their own. Some try to please everybody, make everyone happy, or play perpetual rescuer. And some people act out sexually."

"Like me."

Jackson nodded. "Like you. This thing has a thousand different faces, Zach."

"That makes sense too, I guess. But it doesn't really tell me how to get, well, opened up again. I've lived this way for a long time, and I don't have a clue how to be different. Where do you even start when everything around you looks broken?"

Jackson stuck his hands in the pockets of his madras shorts. "Okay, this is the way I see it: you start with the lie."

"Come again?"

"You have to ask yourself, what is the lie you've believed— about life, about yourself, about God?"

Zach considered this as they rounded a corner and started down yet another street. "I don't know, Jackson," he finally admitted. "I don't know what lie I've believed."

"Then that is where you start. Ask him, Zach. Get curious with him. He's a big God. He can handle your questions."

"I guess I never thought we could do that. Question God, I mean."

"Why not?" Jackson said. "Abraham asked God questions and was called a 'friend of God.' And Jesus was always asking questions. You ever wondered why?"

"Probably not because he didn't know the answers."

Jackson laughed. "No, probably not." He stopped walking and faced Zach. "I believe it's because he knew that if he asked questions, we'd start asking questions too—questions about our own hearts. Because that's what Jesus was always concerned with—people's hearts. Remember when he talked about adultery? He said if we even look at someone with lust, we've committed adultery in our hearts."

"Well, then—" Zach stuck out his hand—"meet Mr. Perpetual Adulterer."

Jackson laughed. "It's in all of us, Zach. That's part of Jesus' point, that we all have sin in us. But he was also saying that sin begins and ends with the heart. Actually, that idea runs through the entire Bible. As a man 'thinks in his heart, so is he.' 'Out of the abundance of the heart his mouth speaks.' In other words, what is in us is going to come out of us. And 'above all else, guard your heart.' Do you hear that, Zach? Out of everything we do, protecting our hearts is the most important thing.

"We've got to guard them especially from anything that could come in and set up a lie about our God. Anything. I mean, even doing my work—and I'm a pastor—could convince me that God needs me in some way. That would be the perfect way for the enemy to set me up to wear myself out and shut myself down. And it would all start with a lie. The devil will try to convince us of anything—he's the father of lies, remember. And that is why we have to guard our hearts so carefully."

Jackson put a hand on Zach's shoulder. "So maybe that's a place to start. Ask yourself what lies you've been believing."

Zach had dug into that conversation for weeks. And he had asked. He had asked God, "What are the lies I've believed about you that got me here?"

Possibilities came in flashes. With his parents' divorce during his teenage years, he had shut down. He had convinced himself that if he'd been a better athlete, a better student—just better—then maybe that wouldn't have happened. So he'd thrown all his energy into becoming the best at everything he did. That had led to top honors in academics and athletics. And he'd learned to perform his way through conversations with adults, convincing them of his deep reservoirs of understanding. He'd been one impressive kid, even though his heart wasn't in any of it. Then, when he met Caroline, he had performed for her too. She was beautiful. Smart. Came from a family that he wanted to validate him. Her parents were still married. He hadn't really offered her his real heart. He'd given her what he thought would impress her and make her love him.

The truth was, he'd believed God hadn't written his story well enough, so he needed to write it himself. He needed to write a story that would make other people respect him, that would attract a Caroline and a perfect family. He needed to be the best so people wouldn't discover all his flaws—because, deep inside, he thought God had made a mistake with him. That was another lie he'd swallowed—another lie that had gotten him into this mess.

❀ ❀ ❀

Zach sat at a four-seat table in Saffire Restaurant. He looked into the faces of his teenage daughters and, at that moment, saw them differently than he had before. He saw them through the lens of all he was discovering about himself—and he was asking questions about issues he'd never even noticed.

Why, for example, did Lacy eat as if she were desperate? Where did that come from?

"Lacy, hon, the food isn't going to run off the plate. You don't have to eat like it will. Slow down."

Lacy looked surprised at his comment, but she slowed her chewing .

But then Joy weighed in. "Close your mouth too. It's gross. The way you chew is disgusting."

And why was Joy always bossing her sister around like that? Did her life feel so out of control that she tried to control everything else around her? Was it anger at him and Caroline that made her so hard on Lacy?

Zach put down his fork. "Joy, I'm looking around, and I only see one parent here at the table. Want to point him out to me?"

Joy rolled her eyes and took a small leaf from her salad.

Lacy stabbed at the fried fish on top of grits. "She always acts like that. I swear, she thinks she's thirty years old or something."

He decided to distract them. "Why don't you tell me how school's going so far?" He put another piece of pork chop in his mouth. It tasted so moist and delicious, he found himself making an appreciative noise as he chewed. When was the last time he had really tasted food?

Joy sipped water. "Fine."

"Good," Lacy added.

"So how about if we go away for the weekend?"

Joy's eyes widened. "Dad, no. We're supposed to go to Abby's church tomorrow for their cookout, and I promised Jenna we'd go to the mall."

"Yeah—" Lacy spoke through a mouthful of food—"and I have to meet Sarah at the library to study for a test."

"But this is your weekend with me. I don't mind if you do one thing with a friend, but we're going to spend the rest of the time together."

He saw a quiver start in Joy's jaw. She cried when she got mad. "I have plans with my friends, and I'm not changing them."

They sat there looking at each other while Zach pondered the best response. "Joy, let me ask you a question. At what age does a daughter no longer need her father?"

"Twelve," Lacy answered as if she had read it on a fortune cookie. Then laughed.

"I'm being serious, Lacy. So I'll ask both of you—when do you think a daughter no longer needs her father?"

Joy caught on quickly. She stiffened her jaw. "It's not that we don't need you. We'll always need you." He heard the manipulation in her words as soon as they came from her lips, and his heart cringed at how quickly kids took on the traits of their parents. He wasn't going to let her get away with it. A couple months ago he would have. No, he *had* done it. But now that he was beginning to see—really see—what was going on in his life, in their lives, he knew he had to start making changes somewhere, if only incrementally. And this was where he chose to begin.

"That's not what I asked you. At what age?"

Joy stiffened her back and put down her fork. "There isn't any age. A girl always needs her father." Her words were laced with frustration.

"Yes, she does. I just read recently that it is scientifically proven that a father emits chemical signals that can actually delay you from maturing too fast sexually. They are called pheromones. They're basically hormones that I give off and you pick up somehow. You don't know you're doing it, and I don't know I'm doing it. But just by walking in the room, I affect your growth and maturing process. Did you know that?"

"Okay." Lacy's face indicated she found this fact rather interesting. "That's a little weird and a little cool."

"And did you know that if I wasn't present in your life or didn't care about what was going on with you, you would mature more quickly sexually?"

Joy's face reddened. "Tell me we're not going to talk about this."

"Well, you've been acting all grown up, like you can make all the decisions and tell your sister what to do and inform me how we're going to spend our time together. So if you're that mature, we do need to talk about things like this."

Lacy stuffed another piece of fish in her mouth. "Mom says we're supposed to talk about sex with her, not you."

That was news to him. Apparently he and Caroline needed

to do some talking too. "This is what I will tell you. No two girls are loved by their father more than you two. I won't always get it right. In fact, I've made a lot of mistakes already." He knew that was true. "But I will always be your father. I will be present in your life, and I will be a voice in your ear. So—"

"How will you do that when you're living somewhere else?" The emotion in Joy's voice surprised him. Until this moment the girls had said nothing about his being gone. It had seemed the girls had hardly noticed his absence, and the few times he'd tried to bring it up, they had avoided the topic. This moment made him very aware that his girls did miss him. And it made sense. He had been a stable presence for them. Many nights it had just been the three of them eating dinner together. He should have pressed in harder. Quicker.

"Do you want to talk about me not being home?"

Lacy put her fork down and stopped chewing.

Joy bit her lip, clearly refusing the tears that were desperately trying to make their way down her cheeks. Just like her mother. "I don't want to talk."

"Honey, you need to talk. It's okay to talk. I'm a grown man. I can handle anything you want to say to me."

"Mom talks about it all the time."

"Shut up, Lacy," Joy scolded. "Don't talk about Mom."

"Well, she does. She says you hurt her, Dad."

"I'm afraid she's right."

"What did you do?"

He looked into Lacy's innocent and searching green eyes. How should he handle this? He and Caroline hadn't discussed how they would talk with the girls, and they definitely needed to have that discussion. At least Caroline hadn't told them about his infidelity, and they didn't seem to have heard the gossip. That was something to be thankful for.

"I just didn't treasure your mother like I should," he answered carefully. "Sometimes married people forget how they need to take care of and protect each other. Mom and I forgot that."

"Mom didn't do anything," Joy snapped. "It's all your fault." Angry tears raged to the surface.

He was grateful for them, even though her words stung deep and real. "Sweetie, I've made some huge mistakes. And one mistake I've made is that I haven't been the father I should have been. I haven't been present with my girls the way I should, even when I lived at home. And I can tell you right now, that's going to change. I'm not here to put blame on your mother. I'm here to figure out how to put my family back together. But first I have to put Daddy back together."

Lacy reached over and put her hand on top of his. "Daddy, I love you just the way you are."

He turned his hand to clasp hers. "I love you too, honey."

"I want you to come home," she said, her eyes filling with tears of her own.

"I'm going to try my hardest."

Joy wiped her nose with her napkin. Lacy got control of herself and picked up her fork again. And Zach finally exhaled. If change went forward in baby steps, he had just taken one tonight. All he could hope was that a lot of baby steps made for one giant one. Because he had a long way to go.

{ *Chapter 23* }

GRACE LOOKED at the teleprompter, but this time the screen was blank. There were no notes for this. No scrolling white letters. Just her and the camera. She was surprised that her only feeling was excitement. Well, a touch of anxiety, nervousness about what lay ahead. But she had expected sadness, tears maybe, and there were none. Just a feeling in the very soul of her that something beautiful was on the horizon.

"I want to thank you for being faithful companions over these last ten years. I have enjoyed waking up with you and meeting you on the street, at the mall, and in restaurants. You have made getting up at an ungodly hour actually enjoyable," she said with soft laughter. The guys behind the camera smiled at her words.

"But I am starting a new adventure," she went on. "I am leaving the station to fulfill one of my dreams. Not someone else's dream for me. Not what seems practical. Instead, I'm jumping off a cliff into a great unknown. I seem to have been doing a lot of that lately. But I truly believe you can't get anywhere in life without some leaps of faith. So if you're ever in the Franklin area and need some sweet tea, hot or cold, some warm conversation and Southern hospitality, and maybe a scone or a muffin, I hope you'll come by and visit me at my new tearoom downtown. Watch for my ads; we're opening this fall. Thank you again, and God bless each one of you."

With that a montage of Grace's years as a reporter and news anchor began to play on the monitor—everything from an interview with the governor and coverage of a devastating Nashville flood to a kiss from a monkey during a visit to the zoo and her falling out of her chair at the anchor desk. Leo had done an amazing job putting it together. And as she watched, tears fell. The staff had thrown a sweet surprise dinner for her the night before and given her a handsome plaque and a gift card to a spa. Leo said she deserved to be pampered.

"Great job, Grace," he said as she walked off the studio floor.

She looped her arm through his as they made their way to her office. "Thanks, Leo."

He put his chubby fingers atop hers and patted them gently, his rough palm rubbing her knuckles. "What if I asked you not to go?"

"I'll still make you free food anytime you want it. I'll just have a larger kitchen." She let go of his arm and entered her office. She pulled a box out of the pile by the wall and set it on her desk. She unsnapped the middle button of her orange-and-white geometric-patterned sweater and draped it across the back of her chair.

"It's not about the food. You know that." He sank down into a chair across from her desk.

"I know. I'm joking. I don't want to cry, Leo. I did enough of that last night." One thing she was learning was to be present wherever she was. And apparently right now, being present with Leo meant talking, even if it hurt. "You've become a wonderful friend to me. I'll miss you."

His eyes didn't leave hers. "Is there anything I can do to make you stay? More money? Bigger window?"

She laughed and perched herself on the edge of her desk. "You know why I'm leaving."

"I do. And I want you to be happy. I've seen a light come on in your eyes even when the cameras are off."

His words struck her. *Even when the cameras are off.* "Is that what you saw? That I was able to turn on a spark for the camera?" It wasn't an accusation. It was a sincere question.

"Sure I did." He tried to cross his ankle across his opposite knee, but it slid right off. He tried again, grabbing his ankle and holding on to it. "I'd see you come in here some mornings looking ten years older than you are. It was a tired so deep that sleep couldn't fix it. But when that red camera light came on, you would come to life. I never knew how you did it."

Grace had never really thought of herself as a performer. Not until that moment. Not until those words. Newscasting was her job, a job that demanded professionalism no matter what went on at home. But Leo's description was true, wasn't it? She had come in some mornings hurting badly, but she'd never let on.

Rachel was the only one she'd shared her pain with. To

everyone else, her world had seemed perfect because that was what she had wanted them to believe. Or at least that was what she thought she'd convinced them of. But Leo knew. He saw. "I guess I've been a phony."

He swatted his free hand at her. "Nah. You aren't a phony. You're as sweet as that sweet tea you're always fixing. You just never wanted anyone knowing all your stuff."

He was being gracious. It was more than that, and she knew it. It wasn't that she didn't want people to know her stuff. She didn't want people knowing she *had* any stuff. That's why she'd always worked so hard to put up a good front—stylish clothes, chic hair and makeup, winning smile, happy marriage. She'd had this desperate need for people to think she had it all together. And thinking of how untogether her life had been for so long made the whole thing feel like a charade.

Shame in that moment threatened to capture her again. But these days she wasn't giving in to that relentless pursuer.

She slapped her hands on her legs. "Leo, I'm messed up."

He showed her a wry smile. "We're all messed up."

"But I'm messed up, messed up."

His belly shook when he chuckled, and his hand lost its grip on his foot. He let it fall off his knee. "Grace, I'm telling you—so am I."

"Yes, but you've told me about all your stuff. I know that Helen kicked you out of the house and why. I know about Darius's issues with pot and him being arrested. I know about the financial challenges you've had and what happened at your last family reunion when you found out your niece is really your baby sister."

He shook his head. "Oh, that was nasty. I mean, as ugly as you can get."

But she wasn't through. "I know what your favorite foods are. I know what your favorite color is. I know where you buy your pants, Leo. I mean, seriously, I know everything about you."

He crinkled his brow. "Guess you do, huh?"

She put her hands on top of her desk. "What do you know about me?" She felt her turquoise earring rub against her neck as she moved. "What do you know about me?"

He moved his lips back and forth as if that helped him think. "I know things, Grace."

"What's my mom's name?"

"Seriously? Lydia."

Yeah—he would know that. "That was a dumb question. She comes to the station every time she's in town. What's my favorite color?"

"Red."

"That was a dumb question too. You see me almost every day. Where's the last place I went on vacation?"

He raised his finger. "Ha! You don't go on vacation."

"I did three years ago with Tyler for our anniversary. We went to Seaside, down in Florida. But those are too easy. Did you know I desperately wanted children?"

He hesitated before answering. "No. I figured you were more interested in your career."

"Did you know I wasn't fulfilled here at the station?"

"You gave this job 150 percent. You worked when you shouldn't have. I thought you were addicted to this place."

"Did you know I've spent the last six years praying for a miracle in my home? See? I let you in on so little. I only offered what I wanted you to know." The personal revelations kept coming. "I could have spent the last ten years of my life offering people more than I did." She felt the impact of that statement, and her hand rose to her mouth. "I could have had ten years of offering my own life, my own failures and life lessons, my *honesty* to people. And all I've given them each morning was a smiling face and white teeth to look at."

Leo shook his head. "You're being too hard on yourself."

Maybe. She was good at that.

"You did give them something. You gave them real emotion. When you were moved by something, they knew it. That was real, Grace. You can't fake that. Besides, a lot of them needed a smiling face. I mean, have you seen Buster the cameraman's wife? I mean, oohwee, that brother needs someone smiling at him after waking up to that every morning."

"That's awful." She leaned over and gave him a playful punch. "But the thing is, I could have done more. Revealed more of myself."

"I guess you could have. But I did know a lot, Grace. I knew you were tired. I knew things with Tyler were hard. I knew things had been tough. You may not have said it all, but I knew."

"You knew because you're such a great guy. You're discerning."

He shrugged. "I just see what I see. And what I see is that you can do things differently from now on. Go out there and do what makes you happy and offer people more than you have before."

"So now you're giving me permission to leave?"

"As long as you promise you'll still bake for me, I am giving you permission to go."

She smiled. "Anytime. Promise me you'll come in."

"Every time Helen lets me. She thinks I'm on a diet."

Grace raised an eyebrow. "You still haven't told her you've been giving your lunches to the intern?"

"Are you insane? She kicked me out once. She'll do it again. The woman's a beast."

"You're pitiful."

He stood and walked to the door. "You know me so well. Now don't leave without saying good-bye."

She wouldn't. She couldn't.

❊ ❊ ❊

It took her two hours to pack all her boxes. She kept getting sidetracked by memories that overwhelmed her as she was packing, so it was a miracle she finished that quickly. It didn't help that colleagues kept stopping by, but she was glad to see them. There were a lot of hugs, a lot of tears, but she kept insisting they all knew where to find her.

Two of her coworkers carried the boxes out to her car, and once they were stowed, she climbed into the driver's seat. She brought the car to life beneath her and couldn't help but feel a slight sense of panic as she pulled from the parking lot.

The panic increased when her phone rang and she saw Tyler's name and face pop up. She had to get his number off of there. But Accept or Decline were her options now, and she vacillated between them. They hadn't spoken since the day before she went to court. He had given her space to do what she needed to do, and she was grateful. She had no idea what he wanted now.

Accept won. "Hello?"

"Hey, Gracie. It's T."

T. was his friends' nickname for him. She had never liked it, never called him that. "Hello, Tyler."

There was an awkward silence. Then his words rushed out. "I just saw you on television. You looked beautiful."

What could she say to that? "Thank you."

"Yeah, and I hope this is a wonderful move for you. I just wanted you to know I wish you all the best."

She felt a pain in her gut. It would be so much easier if this could be ugly right now. If he were yelling at her. Threatening her. Drunk out of his mind. At least she thought it would be easier. Because to have the man you love be so nice to you and yet know in your heart that he was content with his brokenness was one of the saddest and hardest places to be.

"Thank you. I appreciate that." She refused to cry on the phone. "Anything else?"

"No. No, that's all. Just happened to be awake and caught it."

He meant he had never been asleep.

"Well, thanks for letting me know. I'll talk to you later."

She clicked End Call before he had a chance to say anything else. Her hands gripped the leather steering wheel tighter, and she rolled her shoulders to loosen them.

She might be driving off into her future. But in order to do that well, she really needed her past to leave her alone.

❀ ❀ ❀

Zach needed coffee. The day had been brutal. Fridays could be like that. He spent hours in a divorce mediation with a client whose wife was trying to clean him out. She wanted the house, the retirement account, the cars, and the children. At one point he had to ask for a ten-minute break, and it hadn't been for his client's sake. It was one of those odd moments when the reality of all that could be ahead for him sank in—or, more accurately, crash-landed on the nerve endings in his brain and overwhelmed him.

Besides, he had nothing to rush home to tonight. Caroline had insisted the girls stay with her that weekend because of school. He had spoken to the girls every night since their last visit. Their attention spans gave him two minutes apiece, max, but he made a point of not missing that phone call.

Sidewalk traffic had already picked up. The workweek seemed to be getting shorter and shorter these days. Everyone, it seemed, needed the weekend before five o'clock ever arrived. It was only four forty-five. By the time he reached the Starbucks at Five Points, he knew that whatever kind of coffee drink he bought, it was going to be cold. He could feel his undershirt wet against his back and under his arms.

He looked at the familiar menu. Since he moved out, it had practically become his pantry. He had Starbucks for breakfast almost every morning—coffee plus a breakfast sandwich or sometimes a pastry. He was sure he had gained five pounds. He was eating out for every meal, drinking sugary drinks like they were water, and didn't have a huge desire to run. It was strange to think about how motivated he had been a couple months earlier. That almost seemed like a lifetime ago.

He ordered a grande mocha Frappuccino to go and sipped it as he wandered down the street, looking idly into windows. He walked more slowly these days. For some reason, even the hurry had left his step. And yet his senses seemed unusually acute.

That was something he had noticed recently. When life swallowed you whole, it did something to your perceptions.

There were moments when your senses were sharp, alert, when you caught the slightest nuance in a gesture or picked up a sound three streets down. And then there were times when you missed it all. The train wreck in your life could be such a force of energy that it blew away awareness of anything else.

He was in one of those acute awareness moments when he saw her. Grace Shepherd. Through the window. She was standing in the middle of an empty store.

He walked up to the window, and she looked up. Her blonde hair was piled in some semblance of a bun gone wild. She wore white shorts and a University of Tennessee T-shirt.

She gave him a huge smile. He returned it.

She came toward the front and opened the door, then poked her head out, her brown eyes shining. "Want to meet your new neighbor?"

He lowered his drink. "What?"

"Yeah. Come look." She stepped back and opened the glass door a little farther.

"I can't."

Her face fell. "Why not?"

"I don't associate with people who have such poor judgment in football teams."

She looked down as if she had forgotten what she had on. When her head lifted, her smile had returned. Her beautiful smile. "Shut up. Who is your team?"

"I'm a Georgia fan."

"Bulldogs are ugly."

"Excuse me? What is a Volunteer?"

"A very fine person. Now come look."

He scooted past her into the store. It was nothing but a

wide-open space. She walked into the middle of it and flung her arms open. "It's all mine."

He nodded and turned a full circle. "Wow. And you wanted all of this?"

She dropped her arms. "I quit my job."

"You what?"

She laughed. He wasn't sure he had ever heard her laugh. And he knew he had never seen her like this. Smiling. Younger. Freer. Alive. She covered her mouth. "I know, right? It's crazy."

He usually warned clients against making big changes so soon after a divorce. He must not have had that talk with her. "So what are you going to do?"

"I'm opening a tearoom. A place where women and little girls can come in and put on hats and drink from fancy china and eat finger sandwiches and pretend they are in a London hotel or a charming English village."

"Hm. Have you ever owned a business before?"

She twitched her nose. "No. But—" she raised a finger— "I have been owned by some painful stuff for the last ten years of my life. And I have decided I'm not going to do that anymore." She stopped. Her shoulders dropped. "I am crazy, aren't I?"

He saw it immediately. The self-doubt, the fear—all of it settled on her in that instance. He didn't want that. He wanted the Grace of just a few seconds ago back. Here. With him. He touched her shoulder. "No, you're not crazy. I'm proud of you." And he was.

She smiled. "Yeah, me too. This is huge for me, Zach."

He nodded. "I know."

She paused and cocked her head slightly, kind of like Lacy did sometimes when a lightbulb was going off behind her eyes.

"You do, don't you. You know all my story, every dark and ugly and painful detail."

"I know I'm very glad you don't have to live that way anymore."

"Well, sometimes it's just a different kind of torment these days." She lowered herself to the dingy carpet and crossed her legs like one of his girls would do. She patted the floor in front of her. "Sit."

He looked down and crinkled his nose. "That floor's nasty."

"It'll wash off."

He pulled at the pleats in his navy suit pants. He had shed the coat and tie hours ago. "So how are you doing?" he asked as he joined her on the floor.

She reached up to readjust her loose topknot. "You know, it's crazy. The way I feel seems to change almost every moment. I'll be with people and can't wait for them to leave. Then I'll be by myself and just want people around. Sometimes I'm panicky and I can hardly breathe. And every now and then, there is a moment where I feel really good. You know. Alive."

She lowered her head and wiggled her red-painted toes in her flip-flops. "There are a thousand moments when I have to remind myself of all the things that got me here. And then there are those moments when I realize all the things *I did* that got me here."

He raised his mocha. "Wait just a minute. I know your story. You didn't do anything to get yourself here."

"You're sweet, Zach. But a well person would have never let her life get to the place I let mine go. I put up with too much and rescued Tyler from himself more times than I can count. And you know what? Honestly, I don't think I did all of that just because I cared so much about Tyler."

Zach raised his eyebrows.

"No. The more I dig into all my stuff, the more I realize that I didn't want to hurt. So I avoided conflict. I avoided anything that would have exposed where we really were. I was never completely honest with anyone. I couldn't stand the shame of having the whole world know what our marriage and our lives really were like. Shoot, I couldn't stand knowing what it really was, so I wasn't even honest with myself most of the time. I just kept running around, trying to keep all those balls in the air, never even questioning if that's what I was supposed to be doing. And I regret that, Zach. If I hadn't been so concerned with what people thought about me, who knows where I would be today."

"Where do you think you'd be?"

She shook her head slowly. "I have no idea. But I have a lot of regrets, and that may be my greatest."

"You shouldn't have regrets, Grace. You did far more than most women I know would have. Caroline wouldn't have—" He stopped himself.

Grace's hand flew to her face. "Oh, Zach, forgive me. I've been going on about my pain and forgetting that you have yours too."

"Don't worry about me." He shook it off. "I made my bed, gotta lie in it now."

"But how are you?"

He bent his knees and let a hand fall across each one. The mocha sat at his side, incapable of staining the carpet any worse than it already was. "Oh, I'm all right."

She tilted her head again. "Excuse me, but I was in church that day. So . . . bull. And I can add more to that if you'd like."

He felt his shoulders sag. Why did he do that—insist on

acting like everything was fine and that his life hadn't exploded in front of hundreds of people on a Sunday morning? Force of habit, he guessed. He had spent his life being the one who asked the questions, keeping other people's secrets and never having to reveal his own. Until Caroline revealed his for him, that was.

"Yes, and you still kept me as your lawyer after that—that's a miracle." He let out a soft half laugh. "But please tell me a beautiful Southern lady like you doesn't talk trashy."

She placed her hands on her hips. "I can if I need to."

He laughed. "I'm pathetic, Grace. Living in a tiny apartment, drinking liquid sugar for dinner and having it again for breakfast. My wife won't talk to me. My girls are complete wrecks. My mother-in-law, well, God alone knows what she has said or thought. I've lost three clients. I get looks from women I'm certain Caroline has shared our little secret with." He used air quotes to highlight the word *secret*. "Oh, and each day I'm learning more and more how messed up my life is."

Her words came out as soft as the nudge against his knee. "Isn't it painfully beautiful?"

He let out a puff of air. "I'm not sure I'd call it beautiful. But painful? You've nailed it."

Grace leaned in so close he almost felt he should lean back. "Zach, if you could do anything, anything in the world, what would it be?"

He looked at her in surprise. "That's what Jackson Newberry asked me."

"So what did you answer?"

He studied her face, realizing she genuinely wanted to know. "I'm not quite sure. Be a football coach, maybe? I loved football in high school and played some college ball. I'm pretty sure I'd be a good teacher. What I do know is if I had a choice, I wouldn't be doing divorce law. But it's where the money is, and money has always been a necessity in my family."

"What if you let all the balls that you've been keeping in the air all these years just fall?"

He shrugged. "I'm thinking I have. Last I checked, my mattress and box spring were on the floor instead of in a bed frame."

She leaned back and placed her palms on the floor, stretching her long legs out beside him. "Well, all I know is that if you would've told me even six months ago that I'd be sitting here in a storefront that was going to be my very own tearoom, I would've said no way. I couldn't do that. My job was secure, about the only secure thing I had left. I could have just kept on the way I was going.

"But I dropped the balls, Zach. And here we sit, in my future tearoom. I don't have a paycheck. I barely have savings, and I'm in debt to my best friend. But what I do have today that I didn't have a few weeks ago is a heart that feels something. Really feels something."

"I'm very happy for you, Grace."

She gave him a warm smile. "Thank you. And I want the best for you." She nodded toward the plastic cup on the floor. "You're welcome to quit drinking that stuff and come drink my tea anytime."

He lifted himself up from the floor, realizing he needed to leave. It was a Friday night. His marriage was in a shambles. He was lonely. And this was one of the kindest, purest, loveliest women he had encountered in a long time. With his track record, not a great scenario.

"I may take you up on that," he said as she got to her feet. "Once you get the place going, of course."

"I'd love that." She touched his arm as they walked toward the door. "Have a great weekend."

"You too," he said before he headed down the street again. But he wasn't sure how good a weekend it was going to be when all he could think about was Grace Shepherd, and the person he needed to be thinking about was Caroline Craig.

❀ ❀ ❀

Grace closed the door behind Zach and moved back into her space. Her space.

She danced around like a five-year-old, holding her hands out as if she held the edges of a flowing skirt. She twirled until she was dizzy, and that got her tickled. She leaned over her knees and laughed until she could finally stand up. She slowly raised her head . . . and let out a scream.

A man stood with his hands cupped against the window. Now she knew why people put brown paper over their windows when they remodeled—to avoid heart attacks. He had scared the living daylights out of her.

Then she caught sight of the squeegee in his hand. He held up a card, and she returned to the door. She opened it and stepped out onto the sidewalk, where people were heading to movies, dinner, or ice cream.

He handed her his card. "I'm Fred Parton. I clean a lot of windows around here and thought you might be interested." He nodded toward the window. "I saw that the For Lease sign was gone. Didn't know if you were the new renter or not."

She studied the name, wondering if he was related to Dolly.

She didn't see any family resemblance, but then again, she wasn't really sure what the original Dolly looked like. "Owner, actually," she said. "I don't like to rent."

She had told the Realtor it was the only way she would take the space. The plan was for Grace to eventually buy out Rachel and become the sole owner. The Realtor's wife had recognized her from television. Gratified that she still had loyal fans, Grace had promised the woman special treatment when they opened.

"Well, I thought I'd leave you my card, in case you start needing your windows done. I'm living with an aunt over in Spring Hill, but I do windows in Franklin and Brentwood too. Give me a call, and we can work out a schedule."

Right now she was still trying to figure out how to afford toilet paper. "Thank you, Mr. Parton. I will certainly remember that." She looked up at how high her windows went. "I'm thinking this might be a job better suited for someone other than me," she said.

His chuckle accentuated the deep creases in his face. The sun hadn't been kind to Mr. Parton, nor had the years, it seemed. "Well, I do have everything I need to do a good job, and I'm real reasonable. So if you decide you need some help, just call."

"I'll do it. Thanks."

He nodded and walked away.

She went back inside and found her little pad and pen. *Buy window paper!* she added to the top of her list.

❀ ❀ ❀

Zach saw Caroline in the distance as he made his way up the street toward Baskin-Robbins. He realized he had two choices in that moment. Hide. Or seek. It took him a while to decide, but he chose seek.

She had avoided him since that day at Jackson's. When he went to pick up the girls, she was nowhere to be found. When he dropped them off, she was not to be seen. He left voice mail messages most days, and she responded in texts or ignored them altogether. And even though they both worked downtown, she had somehow managed to keep from bumping into him.

Until now.

She was in front of her store, struggling to drag a huge box through the door. He hurried to the other end and lifted it. She looked up, and for an instant her face said "thank you"—until she realized who he was and the "thank you" gave way to disdain.

She set down her end of the box. "I don't need your help, thank you very much."

He shifted his grip and picked up the entire box. "Desire and need are two totally different things. You may not desire me, but you do need me right now." He carried the box inside and set it down in the back. "Why did they leave a box in the front?"

Frustration was evident in her tone. "New driver."

She wasn't going to make this easy.

He straightened. "Where are the girls?"

"Home."

"Do you need help opening it?"

"No." She just stood there.

"Do you want to grab a coffee? Ice cream?"

Her jaw pulsed. "No."

"Want me to leave?"

He could have sworn he saw her eyes twinkle at that. "Yep."

He pressed his lips together and nodded. "Okay, well, I can take a hint."

"I wasn't hinting."

He let out a soft laugh, though it wasn't really funny. He headed toward the front door, reached for the handle, then turned back to her. "I'm really sorry, Caroline. I wish I could rewind it all and put Humpty Dumpty together again. But we still need to talk, get counseling . . . do something."

She offered nothing.

He turned and walked out the door. He might get the triple scoop.

Ten minutes later, the chocolate-mint ice cream made its way to the edges of the napkin wrapped around his cone as he started back to his office. He crossed the square and realized he had to pass Caroline's store again to get there. He rounded the edge of the building and peeked inside the windowpane of the front door, just to make sure everything was secure and okay.

What he saw shocked him. Caroline sat on the floor in a heap. And from the way her body was shaking, he knew her pain was fierce and hard.

He wanted to ditch the ice cream and run inside. But Caroline wasn't ready for ditched ice cream and extended arms. And honestly, if his healing was affording him any insight, it wasn't his place to rescue her from what she needed to feel. The sad thing was, the walls inside her were as old and stubborn as the stone walls that lined so many of Franklin's back roads. He didn't know how long it would take her to breach them—if she ever did.

But seeing her there, weeping, took him back to when she had broken down right before their wedding. That had been a tense time. Her mother had dictated every detail of the planning, down to the color of the bridesmaids' dresses, and her constant criticism of Caroline's choices had finally been too much. He didn't remember what the argument had been about—probably something small—but it had left Caroline in tears. Zach had held her then and suggested she appease her mom, that it was just a day and they would have the rest of their lives with each other.

That was now officially one of the dumbest things he had ever said. Who knew what would have happened if in that moment, before they were ever man and wife, he had stood up to Adele and said, "Here is the line. You can only cross it if we invite you." But they'd both known that if things didn't go her mother's way, she wouldn't pay for the wedding. Another thing he should have realized back then—money was a powerful motivator.

So here they were, fifteen years later, with Adele still telling them what to do and Caroline trying desperately to hang on to control. In all their years of marriage, he hadn't seen her come apart like this, and he thought it was a good thing. Maybe it would help her come apart in a different way—break free from those old patterns that had robbed them of so much. He had to do that too. Because until they dismantled what had been put together so poorly, they could never hope to reassemble it the right way.

{ Chapter 24 }

SCARLETT JO LEANED over the open box and pulled out another china cup. She rubbed the lower part of her back. "If I weren't so big on top, this wouldn't hurt so bad."

Rachel stood on a ladder on the far side of the room, holding a strip of pink toile wallpaper. She aligned the top edge of the wet paper at the ceiling, straightened the strip, then pressed hard with her smoothing brush. "If you weren't so big on top, you'd be up here on the ladder instead of me. Don't want to risk you toppling over or anything."

Scarlett Jo glanced down at her grimy smock. "Well, I say we all need a break. I'm craving ice cream."

Grace came around from behind the counter that had been built last week. Constructed from distressed white beadboard, it provided just the girlie, shabby-chic look she was going for.

She raised her eyes to Rachel and waited. It wouldn't take long.

Rachel scooted down the ladder, pressing the wallpaper strip firmly against the wall as she did until she got to the molding. She slid the razor across the bottom until she had the perfect edge. Grace had given her exacting friend the best job for her personality.

"I hate you, Scarlett Jo," she said. "You know I can't refuse ice cream."

"Oh, I knew it." Scarlett Jo jumped up in the air and clapped her hands together.

Rachel eyed her bouncing figure. "You jump much higher, you're going to give yourself a black eye."

Scarlett Jo made her hand a claw and swiped at Rachel while letting out a bobcat-style hiss. "Kitty likes to scratch."

Grace laughed. "Rachel doesn't always play well with others."

Rachel went to the counter and grabbed her purse. She stuck her tongue out at Grace.

Grace rolled her eyes. "They're so cute at that age."

Rachel walked straight for the door. "Well, come on, you two. We don't have all day. If you're forcing me to go get ice cream, let's make it snappy."

Grace and Scarlett Jo picked up their handbags and snickered as they followed her out into the pleasant September night.

"So where to?" Rachel asked. "Baskin-Robbins or Sweet CeCe's?"

Grace loved them both, though Baskin-Robbins's plain chocolate was still her all-time favorite. That and the chocolate-dipped vanilla cone from Dairy Queen. Both of those reminded her of childhood.

Scarlett Jo raised a hand in the air. "I vote for Sweet CeCe's. I want toppings!"

Rachel wrapped an arm around Scarlett Jo's waist. "This isn't *Braveheart*, honey. You're not William Wallace leading your men to war. It's just ice cream."

Scarlett Jo put an arm over Rachel's shoulder and pulled her tightly up under her, so tightly that Grace was concerned Rachel's right shoulder might be permanently dislocated.

"Good grief, woman." Rachel shook herself loose. "What do you eat in the morning? An entire box of Wheaties?"

"I've been lifting children since Jack was a baby." Scarlett Jo flexed her bicep. "That's how I got these." Scarlett Jo gave Rachel a push, and she tumbled sideways, almost knocking Grace over. "You're so jealous."

Rachel laughed. "Yep, you found me out."

They crossed Fifth Avenue when the little green man on the crosswalk sign told them they could and made their way to Sweet CeCe's. "Please do not hurt the children on your way to the ice cream," Grace said as she opened the door. "That's all I'm asking."

Rachel gently shoved past Scarlett Jo, who countered with a flick of her broad hip. "That's cheating," Rachel protested.

"All is fair in love, war, and ice cream." Scarlett Jo laughed and reached for the stack of large plastic cups that sat next to self-serve frozen yogurt dispensers.

Grace loved the decor in this place. Everything in the room screamed childhood magic. The hot pinks. The bright greens. The big flowers. The Willy Wonka–style array of candies, nuts, and other toppings. It all invited you to feel free, like a child. Which was a good thing because the two women she had brought with her had no problem acting like children. She watched as Scarlett Jo dispensed a tubful of red velvet cake yogurt. Rachel followed behind, filling hers with the cake batter variety.

"Remember, Grace, assume freedom," Scarlett Jo advised as she licked some ice cream from her finger.

Grace got herself a bowl. She pulled the nozzle down on the sugar-free chocolate dispenser and watched as a large swirl wrapped once around the bottom of her plastic cup and then began its second rotation. She stopped before it made its way fully around and then moved on to the vanilla. She let it make one full rotation, then stopped it. And then she assumed some freedom and let it make one more round. Scarlett Jo and Rachel were already casing out the toppings by the time she finished.

"I'm craving Froot Loops," Scarlett Jo announced. She turned a silver dial to release an avalanche of cereal onto her mountain of frozen yogurt.

"Appropriate," Rachel cracked as she covered hers with chocolate chips.

Grace turned the nozzle for crushed Oreos and watched in horror as Scarlett Jo went on to crushed Reese's peanut butter cups. Scarlett Jo proceeded to the chocolate sauce and caramel sauce, then finished with a cloud of whipped cream and took the whole thing to be weighed. Before the cashier could announce that the bowl cost almost seven dollars, she had a spoonful of it in her mouth.

Rachel had her beat, though. The pieces of cheesecake and brownie she had crammed into her bowl brought the total to right around eight dollars. Even Grace's came to just over six—the most she had ever paid at Sweet CeCe's. They were apparently all assuming some freedom.

As Grace went to pay, Scarlett Jo stuck her Sweet CeCe's punch card in the cashier's face. "Can you give me her punch too?"

The woman eyed Grace, who nodded. "It's fine. I don't come here enough for a punch card. She has five children."

Scarlett Jo took her punch card back. "I can almost fill up a punch card in one visit with my boys."

"If we had been more strategic, we could have done two cups apiece, and you could've gotten two more punches," Rachel informed her, placing her bowl on a table.

Scarlett Jo's lips twisted over her spoon as she sat down. "Now why didn't I think of that?"

Grace pulled up a chair beside them and sat down. She dipped her spoon into her cup, listening to Scarlett Jo and Rachel banter and watching idly as a young mother maneuvered a stroller through the door.

Pain shot through her without warning. It ran swift and fierce, taking her breath away. Tears stung her eyes, and the lump that lodged in her throat made swallowing virtually impossible. She set her spoon down, grateful that Scarlett Jo and Rachel were too preoccupied to notice.

She remembered the first time she'd ever come to Sweet CeCe's, and the memory now flooded her with the impact of a class IV rapid. She had dreamed of what it would be like to bring her children here and watch them act like Scarlett Jo and Rachel over being allowed to create whatever their hearts desired. She had dreamed of their wide-eyed wonder, their hands in hers as they walked to a park bench across the street from the post office and watched the world go by. She'd dreamed of talking with them about preschool and puppies and all the things a mother talks about with her own children.

Thinking of all those lost dreams made her soul ache.

"Excuse me. I'll be right back." She pushed her chair away from the table.

Scarlett Jo raised her hand in acknowledgment but never looked up. Rachel didn't even acknowledge her.

Grace hurried to the bathroom and locked the door. She stood over the sink and turned on the faucet to cover the sound of her cries. Her grief mixed with the water running down the drain. But she simply let it surge, surrendered herself to it. Surge and surrender—there was nothing else to do. When it finally let her go, she looked in the mirror.

"Please don't let this pain last forever," she whispered to the heavens.

The ache subsided enough for her to wipe her face and gather herself. By the time she returned to the table, Scarlett Jo's pants were unbuttoned and her own ice cream was virtually a puddle. But it didn't matter. She had lost her appetite.

"Where'd you go?" Rachel asked, dabbing a napkin at her mouth.

"Just had to go to the ladies' room."

"You've been crying."

"Yep." She had no intention of hiding it from them.

Scarlett Jo touched her arm. "You okay, sugar?"

"Yeah, I'm good. Just have to get it out when it sweeps over me like that."

"That's good, honey. That's real good."

"I can't believe you're crying over him. He's a jerk, Grace. You should be nothing but angry."

Grace felt anger all right, but not at Tyler. Not in that moment. Words came out of her mouth before she could restrain them. "Rachel, you can't tell me how to feel. Don't tell me when I should be angry and when I shouldn't. I'm doing the best I can. And if I want to feel sad, I'll feel sad. This is my journey to walk, not yours, and not anyone else's. And last I checked, there was no book called *Being Divorced for Dummies*. I promise you, there'll be days I'm angry with Tyler, but right now I'm sad, and if you're my friend, you're going to have to accept that."

Rachel's shock at the outburst was evident, but her apology was immediate and genuine. "Grace, you're right. Forgive me."

Grace shook her head. "It's okay, Rach. Nothing to forgive."

"You've never spoken to me like that before."

"It wasn't planned," Grace assured her.

"Hey, I liked it," Rachel said. "You need that feisty in you. You've always said you admired how I was able to tell Jason whatever I felt. But you've never done that, Grace. You've just sat there and taken whatever was thrown at you. Unless of course it had to do with your faith. Now, don't let someone attack that. You're like a pit bull with that one. But anything else, you'd give them all the ground they wanted. I'm proud of you. This was a huge step for you."

Grace smiled. "It kind of was, huh? Maybe I'll yell at you some more. Want me to?"

"Don't get crazy. I can still whoop you. Come on, we've got more work to do. Get up, blondie." Rachel motioned to Scarlett Jo as she stood.

Scarlett Jo pushed herself from the chair, her pants still unbuttoned.

"Oh no," Rachel said. "I'm not walking down the street with your pants like that."

Scarlett Jo threw her cup away and looked at Rachel. "Let me tell you something, my sweet sister. I'll wear my pants on this street however I want to. You can walk three steps in front of me or four steps behind me. But sister ain't buttoning these pants."

Rachel shook her head as they walked out the door. "Great. Now I get two of you with attitude."

Scarlett Jo snorted and punched Grace. "That was good, wasn't it?"

"I couldn't have done it better myself."

"Scarlett Jo, what is that on your back?" Rachel's voice was suddenly urgent. "I think it's a cicada!"

"What? Where?" Scarlett Jo's hands started slapping at her shirt as she danced in frantic hops down the street. She finally stopped when she heard Rachel's belly laugh.

They ambled back to the store in a comfortable haze of sugar and freedom. Grace was pretty certain she couldn't think of two better companions.

❁ ❁ ❁

Zach closed the sunroof and moved the visor to the side to block the glare of the setting sun as he drove north past stands of trees that were just beginning to change colors. He flipped on the radio and searched the channels. He wanted music. He usually listened to sports talk radio, but this evening he felt like a change. When the dial landed on a country station, Brad Paisley's voice came over the speakers, and he turned it up. He liked that guy because, well, he was a guy. Had a song about it and everything. But this song he hadn't heard. It was all about finding yourself.

That was what he was doing. He was finding himself. He exited at CoolSprings Galleria and pulled his car into a parking space in front of the Belk store. On any other day he would hate the mall. Boycott it entirely. But he needed it tonight, just like he needed music. Another piece of finding himself.

He opened the door and stepped into a vortex of high-priced jeans and slip-on shoes. The sights and sounds momentarily overwhelmed him. He didn't shop for clothes. Oh, he had before he and Caroline were married and for a while after. But gradually, over the years, he'd let Caroline take over. He'd convinced himself he was too busy to shop for clothes, that he didn't want to do it. But in this moment he knew that wasn't it. The reason he didn't shop was that Caroline had convinced him he couldn't dress himself. That what he picked out wasn't good enough, cool enough, right enough for wherever it was she wanted them to go or how she wanted them to be perceived.

He fumbled through the polo shirt section in Macy's like a teenager on a first date—excited, unsure, and hoping no one was paying too close attention. He picked up a shirt that caught his eye. Yeah, that was right—*his* eye. It was blue-and-white striped with a little orange man on the left side of the chest. He held it out in front of him. Studied it. He didn't know what else to do with it. So he just stood there holding it. Looking at it like a teenage boy staring at his date when she first opened the door. Wondering, *Now what am I supposed to do with this?*

"Can I help you?" a man asked, his hot-pink tie suggesting that Zach didn't want his help.

"Nah, I'm good. Just browsing." *Oh, my word, I just said* browsing.

"Well, let me know if I can get you anything."

"Sure. Yeah. I'll do that." He sounded twelve. He felt twelve, like a child in a grown-up world. How did he get to this, not knowing what kind of clothes he liked or how to choose between a polo and a button-down?

He spotted a sign featuring a golfer and headed that direction. He loved to golf, but he hadn't done it much in recent years. Caroline always complained that it took him away from the family. Thinking about that now made him almost want to laugh. Caroline was the one who was rarely home—not just with work, but with the gym, with meetings, with her friends. She was the one who took long vacation getaways with the girls. And yet he was guilted over an afternoon of golf?

He ran his fingers across a soft golf shirt. It was light blue. He loved that color. The one next to it was a kind of orange. He picked them both up. He noticed two mannequins nearby that were wearing some great pants. He searched the tables next to the mannequins and pulled out two pairs, one in black and one in a light khaki. By the time he made it to the dressing room, he had ten different items draped over his arm and was pretty sure he and the pink-tie man were going to be lifelong friends.

He tried on clothes and shoes until the lights blinked to indicate the store was closing. By then he had six shirts, three pairs of shorts, two pairs of slacks, two pairs of shoes, and a pack of underwear. And he had picked every item out himself.

When the pink-tie man rang up the total, Zach almost gasped. He never spent money on himself. There was an awkward pause as the associate held out his hand and Zach debated leaving all those clothes right there on the counter. Money was tight. His wallet felt heavy in his pocket. Pink-tie man's smile was starting to collapse.

Finally Zach pulled the debit card from his pocket and handed it to the man. And instantly felt fine about the purchase. Tonight freedom had no price.

He walked out smiling into the now-black evening. Once in the car, he pushed the radio button and began to think through what the last few hours had done for him. He had lost some self-doubt and some insecurity. And he had found a few things as well. He had found that he liked shopping for himself. That he liked Sperry shoes and golf shirts in colorful shades of blue and orange and green.

Yeah, he was finding himself. He was finding himself so much that he might actually admit to someone that he had been shopping. In fact, he wanted to tell someone.

He texted Caroline. She didn't respond.

❀ ❀ ❀

"Mom, I think I want to cuss," Rhett declared as he climbed into bed. His Spider-Man underwear revealed the superhero's ability to swing from a web that shot from his hands.

Ten-year-old Tucker ran in and jumped onto Rhett's bed. Rhett pushed a hand toward him. "Get off, Tuck."

Tucker bounced up and down just to torment his little brother—until Scarlett Jo popped him on the backside. "Get to your bed, Tucker." She reached for the edge of the brown blanket that lay beneath Rhett's green, brown, and blue patchwork coverlet.

"I want to cuss again, Mom," Tucker announced as he threw himself across his bed and his feet collided with the wall.

Scarlett Jo had to laugh. The whole cussing issue had begun the other day in the car, when Cooper was tattling on Forrest for taking God's name in vain. Cooper had been a rat the entire day. Everything out of his mouth that day was either thoughtless or downright rude. So Jackson had asked him, "Cooper, what's worse—taking the Lord's name in vain or having a nasty attitude like you've had today and saying ugly things to your brothers?"

Cooper hadn't even needed to think about it. "Taking the Lord's name in vain because that's a Ten Commandment!"

Scarlett Jo had hurried to cover her mouth and nose so she wouldn't snort. But her shoulders were shaking so hard she was certain her seat was moving.

"That's where you're wrong, bud," Jackson said. "Jesus looks at our hearts. We tell you that all the time. Now I'm not saying you *should* take the Lord's name in vain. But I've got to tell you, I know a lot of men who would never, ever say a bad word, who go to church every Sunday and don't miss paying their tithes, but treat people as mean as anyone I've ever met. They get angry if they feel like they've been slighted even a little. And their words can be cutting and cruel. Do you understand what I'm saying?"

Cooper wasn't sure he did.

Jackson decided to help him some more. "It's like saying a cussword. Some people make a big deal out of not cussing, but they'll treat the cashier at Walmart like she has no value. So what is worse, Cooper? Saying a cussword if you're joking or you just forget? Or treating someone badly?"

"Um, treating someone badly?"

"That's right. Mom and I have tried to teach y'all that God is most concerned about the condition of your heart."

Forrest wanted to explore this some more. "So if I am in a boat with my friends, and we almost tip over, and I say a bad word—that's okay?"

"I'm saying if your heart has evil intent in anything you do, Forrest, that is sin. But I'm not recommending you go out cussing with your friends."

Scarlett Jo had looked back at her youngest boys, who were following the conversation with rapt attention. Maybe it was time to defuse the whole issue. "Tucker, do you want to say a cussword?"

Tucker let out an almost-feminine giggle. "Sure." He stuck out his chest and let one fly. The entire car erupted.

"Cooper, do you want to say one?" she prodded.

Cooper shook his head.

Rhett blurted out, "I'll say one!" as if it were the coolest thing he could imagine.

Scarlett Jo caught Jackson's eye and snorted. "Okay, buddy. Go ahead."

And off he'd gone. The word he chose had surprised everyone, including himself, and they'd all burst out laughing. Which was obviously why he was bringing it up now.

She swatted his rear end in a playful way. "No, no cussing tonight. Though I'm glad you have the freedom to say anything to us, I'm thinking we don't need to be known as 'the cussing preacher's family.'"

"But cussing's fun, Mommy."

She laughed and picked at a chip in her orange-painted

fingernail. Renovating Grace's future tearoom was fun, but hard on her manicure.

"I agree it can be fun every now and then. But tonight let's just say our prayers. Mama's pooped." She pushed the blanket underneath his chin in a wadded mess. Jackson would have folded it neatly, which had never made any sense to her. Rhett would have it wadded in a few minutes no matter what.

Rhett folded his hands under his chin. She turned and looked at Tucker, who had his eyes closed too. "Lord, thank you for this day and for food and for the poor people in Haiti and Africa. Bless Mommy and Daddy and Jack and Forrest and Cooper and Tucker. And, Jesus, I pray that when we cuss, you'll know our heart. Amen."

Scarlett Jo leaned down and kissed him on the cheek. "Amen, baby boy." She walked over to Tucker and kissed the top of his freckled head. "Love you, Tuck."

"You too, Mom."

She moved toward the doorway. As she did, an unmistakable—and rude—sound ripped through the room. Tucker burst out laughing. Rhett responded by producing one just as loud. "You boys are pitiful." Scarlett Jo reached to flick off the light. But as she left the room, she let one go that put theirs to shame.

She could hear them howling all the way down the hall as she headed to her bedroom—and thanked God that she didn't have a houseful of girls. Because her boys thought she was the coolest mom ever.

{ *Chapter 25* }

GRACE THREW ANOTHER BAG of trash into the Dumpster behind her store. She was a little more than three weeks away from opening, and the place already looked amazing—everything she'd wanted it to be. The pink- and white-checkered tile floor matched the pink in the toile wallpaper. Light fixtures with large paper shades and dangling crystals hung in four different sections of the store. The kitchen was fully equipped.

With all the decorating basics in place, now she was into the fun stuff. Scarlett Jo had unpacked the gift items that had arrived—packaged teas, cups and saucers and teapots, gourmet chocolates. Shopping bags with her logo and the store name, Sweet Tea, would be there any day now. Each time she held an item, she felt like she was holding another new piece of her life.

"I don't know what you want me to say. I can't apologize anymore." The voice she heard coming from nearby was familiar.

She peered through the slatted wood divider that separated her parking place from the building next to her. Zach Craig stood by his car, talking on the phone. His words came in spurts and sputters as if he couldn't get through to the person on the other end of the line.

Grace leaned against the boards and listened, not to what he was saying, but how he was saying it. She knew that tone, the desperation in it. Why wouldn't she? She had felt it so many times herself. She also heard exasperation. Weariness. All of it was so familiar. And she hurt for him. In spite of the mistakes he had made, she hurt for him in this moment.

"Were you listening to my conversation?"

She hadn't heard him come up beside her. She jumped, and her hand flew over the Izod logo on her short-sleeved red shirt. "Oh, my goodness, you scared me half to death."

"That's what you get for eavesdropping." His words weren't angry, but they weren't warm either.

Her hand slowly slid from her chest. "I wasn't really eavesdropping."

He put a hand on the beam that ran along the edge of the divider, the cuff of his blue button-down rolled up close to his elbow. "What do you mean, 'wasn't really'?"

She pressed her lips together. "I came out here to throw away some trash and heard you talking. But I wasn't listening to what you said. I was listening to how you said it."

His eyebrows lifted. She had never noticed how pretty his eyes were until this moment—all open and alert and completely focused on her. They were blue and clear . . . and clearly not happy.

She wanted to run and hide. She wanted to pretend she hadn't heard anything. She wanted to do what she had always done, which was pretend. She stood up straighter, as if that would give her more confidence. "I know your tone."

"Oh, you do, do you?"

She was getting a little indignant herself now. "Yes, I do. I've had it."

"And what tone is it exactly that you've had and you think I have?"

"Well—" she shifted slightly—"it sounds kind of desperate."

He moved his hand and let out a puff of air. "You think I'm desperate?"

She shook her head. "No, that's not what I'm saying."

"It's exactly what you said."

"Those were my words, yes. Not necessarily my meaning." She was getting flustered, and he wasn't helping. "I just mean I can hear what is underneath your words."

"So now you're a shrink." The words came out with a bite. He noticed too. He ran his hands through his thick brown hair. "I'm sorry, Grace. I'm tired."

She stuck her hands in her jeans pockets. "It's okay. I didn't handle this the best way either."

"The thing is, you're right. I am desperate, in so many ways."

She pursed her lips and rocked slightly on the toes of her flip-flops. "Well, it takes one to know one. That's why I could identify it."

"Listen, I need some caffeine."

"I've got tea, but we're not really open yet."

"I need more than tea. I'm going to Starbucks." He started walking, then turned. "You coming?"

Apparently she had missed the invitation. "Sure. Yeah."

She grabbed her purse, and they walked through the alley-way and parking lot toward the rear entrance of Starbucks.

He ordered some kind of hyped-up espresso drink, and she got a green tea Frappuccino. "That looks like baby poop," he observed as they returned to the alley.

She pulled the straw from her mouth. "Well, you make me really want to drink it now."

He laughed. "Sorry. But it does. It looks like one of those smoothies they've put spinach in. Something that looks that nasty has to be good for you."

She talked through another mouthful. "It's topped with whipped cream. Trust me. It's not good for me. But I'm sure it's better than that liquid speed you're about to consume."

"I confess. I'm an addict." He took a long drink. "Look, I'm sorry about earlier. My tone and all."

She shook her head. "It's okay. I'm not usually that forth-right. Huge step forward for me."

"Aren't our friends lucky?"

They both laughed.

"How's the new space coming, by the way? The brown paper on the windows keeps me from spying on you like you spy on me."

She started to protest, then stopped. "I was so spying, wasn't I?"

"Shamelessly."

"No, I was ashamed, but I was still spying. I haven't done that in years."

"I'm glad I can help you break out of your old patterns of behavior."

SECRETS OVER SWEET TEA

"Zach, I'm really sorry."

He fiddled with the brown cardboard sleeve on his coffee. "Well, it's not like I wasn't having a rather loud discussion in the middle of a parking lot."

She furrowed her brow. "True. So I wasn't spying." She took another big swig of her Frappuccino. "I feel so much better about myself now."

He laughed.

"Do you want to come see how it looks?" she asked.

"What looks?"

She elbowed him. "My store."

"Oh. Right. Yeah, I'd love to see it."

She unlocked the back door and took him in through the kitchen. They passed the restroom and her office. She pulled back the toile curtain and looped it over a scrolled iron hook that held it back. Then she studied his face as he took it all in.

"Wow." His eyes widened and he lowered his coffee cup. "It's . . . pink."

"I know. Great, isn't it?" She still couldn't get over how good it looked. Every time she walked through the door, she smiled.

"Yeah, but it's so girlie."

"It's a tearoom, goof. What do you expect?" This ease she felt with him was nice. "Guys usually don't visit tearooms. That's why there's a pub a few doors down."

"Yeah, for beer drinking and cigar smoking and crass conversations."

"Yes, for men. Here we'll have tea sipping, scone eating, and hat wearing. Plus, I imagine, a lot of women talking about girl stuff."

Zach looked at her, studying her almost. She fidgeted

beneath his gaze. "You look so happy, Grace. And I'm so happy for you."

She smiled. "It's true. I didn't know this kind of happiness was even possible." She paused, not sure if she should share what had just popped into her brain. The old Grace would have bitten her lip. Nodded. Thanked him for coming. But this Grace had something else to say—or rather, ask.

"Since now I'm an eavesdropper and all . . . how are things with you?"

He lowered his shoulders and set his drink down on one of the glass-topped tables. In a few weeks they would sport blue tablecloths over bold pink- and white-flowered skirts. "It's not good. Caroline won't talk to me. Well, let me rephrase. She talks at me, not with me. There's so much that needs to be said, so much that we need to go through. But she just puts up this wall."

"She's got to be really hurting."

He ran his hands through his hair again. "I know she is. And she has every right to hurt. But we can't get anywhere if we can't communicate. We've been separated for months now. She threatens divorce but doesn't pursue it. But she doesn't pursue me either. I've tried to get her to go to counseling with me. I've tried to get her to go to counseling by herself. But she won't do anything."

"Maybe she can't. What y'all went through was huge. I mean h-u-g-e."

"Yes, I get it, Grace."

"Sorry. I'm just saying that sometimes that kind of pain can get you stuck."

"Well, she's got to get unstuck if anything is going to happen."

"I really am sorry. And I do understand on some level. I understand your pain, and I understand hers too."

"I just can't fix this. I can't. At least I've come to terms with that."

"That certainly sounds like improvement. From one fixer to another, I'm thinking there's some freedom in that for you."

"There is." He smiled. His teeth were white and straight, and his smile was kind. And genuine. "I've started shopping. By myself."

"That's a good thing?"

"I hadn't bought my own clothes in ten years."

She crinkled her brow. "What?"

"Caroline bought everything. Even my shoes."

Grace was shocked at that. Tyler would never have dreamed of letting someone else buy his clothes. The problem was, he never knew when to quit buying them for himself. "You didn't even buy your own shoes? Who lets someone else buy their shoes?"

"A man who has no idea who he is or what he wants or what he was created to do. But . . ." He ran his hands down the front of his outfit. "I bought this all by myself."

She stepped back and studied him. "I'd say you never need to let a woman do your shopping again. You have done perfectly fine by yourself."

"So what about you?"

"What do you mean? I buy my own clothes."

"No, I mean, what are you doing that is different from what you used to do?"

Her eyes scanned the room. "I'm opening a business. And eavesdropping. And apparently beginning to say whatever is on my mind. I even let Rachel have it the other day. Not one of my better moments, but it was good for both of us."

"That's not the Grace who sat in my office—what was it, five months ago?"

"Something like that. And nope, I'm not the same—not in the least." She motioned toward two white folding chairs that sat on either side of a table. "Want to sit?"

"Sure." He pulled out a chair.

She pulled the other out for herself and smiled as she sat. She was glad he had stayed.

He leaned forward, knees on elbows. "So tell me, how did you know?"

He must have noticed her puzzled look. "How did you know when it was over?"

She pulled her feet up onto the chair, wrapped her arms around her legs, and thought for a minute. How could she describe it? "It's hard to explain. It was something deep inside, like I'd finally been released. Like God had released me. I didn't make a move toward divorce until I was sure of that. I prayed some very specific prayers. And God answered them."

"Like, just . . . answered them?"

She shrugged. "It's not like I heard this deep voice from heaven. But yeah, he definitely answered. He knew what would release me. He knows me better than anyone."

She paused, remembering. "I would have stayed, you know. If I believed that was what God was calling me to, I would have stayed with Tyler forever. But that wasn't what needed to happen. It was clear. My marriage was over.

"No one has to tell me why God hates divorce," she added. "I know. I hate it too. And there are still days when my heart longs for nothing more than for my marriage to be put back together. But Tyler has made it clear that he cannot or won't deal with his stuff, and I can't do that for him, and I can't live the way we were living. So I am doing everything I can to deal with my own stuff and heal my heart and learn how to find my voice again, and I will trust God to write the rest of my story as he's written the beginning."

He looked down and ran his fingers along the sides of his cup. "I don't know if I trust God like you do. I certainly don't feel released, but I can't see how Caroline and I can ever patch things up either. I just don't know what I need to do next, where to go from here."

"So what is the worst that can happen?"

He looked at her and narrowed his eyes. "I don't know. I was outed in public by my wife—in church, no less. I am living alone. My children are broken. My wife is broken. I'm broken." As he spoke, she could see the revelation in his eyes. "I just don't want to see my girls grow up in a broken home. I know I don't want that for them."

"I'm sure you don't. No one wants that for their children."

"But I'm a better dad now. I do know that."

She smiled. She couldn't help it.

"What? What are you smiling at?"

"The way you said that. There is an innocence about it, Zach. About you."

"Me?" He laughed. "That's ridiculous."

"No, I mean it. It's like you are discovering so much for the first time. Just like I am."

He leaned forward, the blue in his eyes even brighter. "It's true that I've learned more about myself these past few months than I have in years. I think that's one reason Caroline's so worked up these days. She doesn't know what to do with me."

"Is that a bad thing?"

"For her it is. She's used to me giving in just to keep the peace." He must have noticed her smirk. "Takes one to know one."

She raised her hand. "My name is Grace, and I am a people pleaser."

He laughed, but she shook her head.

"Look where avoiding conflict got me, Zach. Worked out real well, didn't it? I wish I had found my voice years ago. The voice that said, 'No, this isn't okay. No, we're not doing it this way.' But I didn't. One of the best things that can happen to you or Caroline, at least I would think, would be for you to find your voice and not worry about making everyone happy."

He sighed. "It's all totally and royally jacked up."

She leaned toward him. "But it's totally freeing, right?"

He did that narrowing thing with his eyes again, the one that clearly communicated he was thinking. Then, slowly, a smile stretched across his face. "Yes, it is."

They sat there for a moment. Silence surrounded them.

"I was tired, Grace."

"I understand." She paused for a moment. "You're a good man, Zach Craig."

The air came out of him in a puff. "I'm an adulterer."

"Not anymore. And that's only a piece of your story. I am certain this is not how your story is going to end."

She saw what her words did to him. It was written all over his face. And she meant them. He stood, and the chair made a scraping noise against the tile as he did.

"Ooh, I'll have to fix that," she said.

"You just need those little felt pads to put on the bottom. Or the kind that slide. Either will work."

She smiled. "Thank you, Mr. Handyman."

"Thank you, Ms. Grace."

They stood there for an awkward moment. Did they shake hands? Hug? What? Finally she reached out and hugged him, and he hugged her back.

"Thanks for the Frappuccino," she said as he made his way to the back door.

"You shouldn't thank me for that. That was gross."

She was still laughing when he left. She grabbed her purse and keys and decided to head home. She had done enough damage for the day.

As she locked up and climbed into her car, she couldn't seem to shake him from her mind. And she needed to. Blue eyes or not, Zach Craig was still married.

❀ ❀ ❀

How did you feel like a stranger in your own home?

Until now, Zach had never thought that was possible. But he stood there on the Oriental rug in the foyer, sweeping his gaze through the small area, and it all looked foreign to him. Unfamiliar.

He had never noticed that pattern in the rug before. He had never noticed the gold scrolling on the antique console across from him or the way the shade flared out over a blue-and-white porcelain lamp. He picked up a framed photo that sat on the small side table next to the door and took in the faces of his family. *His* family. They all looked so young. So happy. Filled with such illusion that life would be easy and doable. Now their lives were a disaster.

Adele was in the house. He heard her voice in the other room. "You'd better not let him get away with anything. You stand your ground. You are a Whittingham, and don't you ever forget it."

"I won't," Caroline replied in that familiar compliant voice. "I know."

Had he known his mother-in-law was here, he would have chosen another spot to meet. But he hadn't, and here they were. That woman was a classic. She loved to quote Scripture, but apparently she thought the piece in the Bible about the three-stranded cord not easily broken meant a daughter, her husband, and her mama. He'd done a terrible job of challenging that misconception. But no longer. He was ready to take that bull by the horns.

Caroline walked into the foyer tugging at her ear, trying to get her red hoop earring through that little hole. He still had no idea how she did that. Or why. But then she probably couldn't fathom why he spent hours trying to hit a ball into another kind of hole.

"We can talk in the family room," she said as she walked past him. She had agreed to meet with him tonight, while the girls were at the library. But her demeanor was as cold as the "breakup" letter he had gotten from yet another client yesterday.

She sat on an upholstered armchair across from the sofa. He had never realized how much red the floral pattern had in it.

"I'm not sure what you want to talk about, Zach."

He lowered his body onto the sofa. "I want to talk about us, Caroline. In the past few months we've done very little of that. It's going to be the holidays before we blink. I just want to know where your head is and—" he paused and looked at her—"where your heart is these days."

She folded her hands and brought them to rest on her designer jeans. He had been shocked when she first opened her store and he saw the price of those things. For a man who was content with the single pair he had in his closet, from a store he couldn't remember, the idea of spending a car payment on little pieces of denim was simply preposterous.

"Where my heart is? That's an interesting question coming from you." Caroline raised her head, her eyes now fixed on him. But he could tell she was aware her mother was listening. "Since when did you decide to take *my* heart into consideration?"

He knew anger was a direct manifestation of her hurt. He had sat with couples in this same situation time after time. But apparently his experience hadn't taught him much. He leaned closer to her and lowered his voice. "Babe, I know this is awful for you. I know you feel betrayed. And I'll tell you again: I'm so sorry. I am. I really do want to fix this. But you and I have created some really horrible patterns of behavior, and we can't continue to do things the way we've done them in the past."

"Well, I'm glad we've got that cleared up." Her tone was biting. "So you're saying adultery won't be part of our future together?"

He took a deep breath. "I'm saying that my adultery isn't the only poor decision I've made through the years. One of the biggest mistakes I've made is shutting down my voice with you. I've been afraid, Caroline—afraid of arguing, afraid of telling you no, afraid of standing up to your mother. But not anymore. For us to move forward, which I truly want to do, some things are going to have to change. And that includes your mother's influence in our marriage and on your decisions."

He didn't care if Adele heard that.

Caroline pulled her head back. "Excuse me? Are you really sitting in this room telling me what has to change? What I need to do about *my* mother? I'm sorry, but last time I checked, I wasn't the one who messed up this marriage."

He'd known he would get resistance, but he didn't know how else to say it. He softened his voice and leaned closer toward her. "It's absolutely true that I've messed up. Big-time. But it's also true that your mother has been in this marriage from the beginning. I watch you when she's around. Everything you do changes. Like just a minute ago—I could hear it in your voice when you responded to her. It's like you turn into this little girl, and the beautiful, strong woman that you are just melts away."

He noted familiar signs of her growing anger—the straight back, the pulsing jaw, that tightly wound stillness—and fought the urge to back down. But he didn't. He couldn't. "For most of our marriage, you've been more concerned with her opinions than you have with mine. And if we're going to stay married, I need you to be *my* partner, not your mother's. It is time for this to be our marriage. Just us. We've got to do this thing together—raise our girls together, make decisions together about our money and our—"

"Let me tell you something, Zach Craig." She bolted from her chair and started pacing. Her voice was loud, but Adele was not showing her face. "My mother has been there for me when you couldn't be bothered. She's held me when I cried over you. She's been faithful when you couldn't even spell the word. So you have some nerve, telling me my mother's to blame for what *you* did. Jackson Newberry may be telling you to set boundaries or to start leading me or whatever it is you're trying to do, but I can assure you that isn't what is going to put our home back together."

Zach was feeling a little frantic by now. "Caroline, babe, what I'm saying is neither of us have been living the way we were created to. Not me and not you. I'm doing everything in my power to change that on my end. But I just need you to see that the way we interact, the way we treat each other, the way we do life together isn't healthy."

"There is nothing wrong with the way I do life."

He threw his hands up. "So what is your idea? You seem to have a reason why none of my ideas are worth talking about. What are your ideas? How do you propose putting our home back together?"

She walked to the other side of the chair and turned her head sharply. The ends of her red hair swung around to the side of her neck. "The first thing you'll do is leave that church and stay away from the Newberrys. Then you won't be at your office unless Darlene is there with you. And you'll give me your phone bills every month and your e-mail password. And—"

He raised his hand to stop her.

She glared at him. "See, now who doesn't want our marriage to work?"

He stood too. "I'm rediscovering my heart, Caroline. I lived with it closed up for years, and it wasn't good for either of us, much less our marriage. The man who was married to you wasn't a man. He was a coward. A shell of a being. Nothing like he was created to be. I will never be that man again. And part of no longer being that man means loving you enough to look at you and tell you that things have to change. I cannot and will not live like we have lived in the past. So you can tell me all your demands if you want to, and I'll do my best to do whatever is necessary to help you trust me again. But I will not let you put me back inside a box that I am fighting with all my heart to get out of. And I will continue to pray that you find your heart is worth fighting for too. Because this is a battle I will fight with you wherever it takes us. But I can't do it for you."

Her jaw flicked, and he saw the tears well up. She didn't want him to see, but she wasn't quick enough to hide them. He moved close and put his hands on her arms. What did he have to lose? "It's okay to hurt. You don't have to be strong. You don't."

She stood there not moving, but her tears had a life of their own. They fell down her face in rhythmic bursts.

He pulled her toward him. "We loved each other once. We really did. That's why we got married. And for a brief season, years ago, you trusted me to be your husband. We can get back there. I can be the man you married again, and you can be the woman I fell in love with."

For a moment her body was soft in his arms. For a moment he could tell that what she wanted was something completely different from what she was saying. He could see it in her face and feel it in her body. Then he felt the rigidness slowly make its way back through her. She extricated herself from his hold and turned, glancing around as if concerned that Adele had seen her weakness. She tossed her words behind her as she left the room. "Show yourself out. Now."

He walked out the front door and headed toward Main Street and his office. He was horrible at this. He didn't know how to connect with her. He didn't know how to reach her. He didn't know what it would take for her to let go, to accept that she wasn't perfect and didn't have to be, to be okay with falling apart.

He didn't even know how to love her right now. All he wanted to do in that moment was shake her and scream. And he didn't even want to put into words what he'd like to do to Adele. He found this especially frustrating because he was making such progress in other areas of his life. He was laughing. He was humming, for pete's sake. He had bought his own clothes. He was playing golf. And he was paying attention to his heart. For the first time in a long time, he was paying attention to his God-designed heart.

His mind was still recounting its recent victories as he passed Grace's tearoom. Her business name and logo had been stenciled onto the glass. Sweet Tea. It was official. Her dream had a name. His mind ran back to their conversation. No one had bothered to know him, to listen to him the way she did.

Caroline didn't know him. Not really. Elise certainly had never known him.

Elise. It suddenly occurred to him to wonder how she was doing. Jackson said she and Tim had moved back to their hometown in North Carolina. And Zach wished them the best. He really did. But he realized in that moment that she hardly ever crossed his mind these days.

Grace did, though. She crossed his mind more than she should. He wished Caroline was like her. He wished Caroline cared the way she cared.

He wished . . . he wished he didn't think about Grace Shepherd so much.

{ Chapter 26 }

GRACE UNPACKED the last three boxes in the stockroom. The grand opening was in nine days, and then Sweet Tea would be in business.

Rachel and Scarlett Jo had been working nonstop with her to get the shop ready. Grace loved what they had produced. There was nothing Victorian about the place, nothing smelling of mothballs or dust. The atmosphere was vibrant and alive, just like Grace was starting to feel inside.

One small thing kept gnawing at her, though. She couldn't get Zach Craig out of her mind. She had avoided him for the last two weeks. He seemed to be avoiding her too, and that was probably good, but it still made her sad.

Zach was the kind of man she desired. Well, the man he was

becoming was the kind of man she desired. The trouble was, he was married, albeit unhappily. He didn't need her as a distraction, and she didn't need him as one either. She shook her head at the thought and put a white teapot and teacup with the Sweet Tea logo up on the shelf with the others. And that was when the horrific crash happened.

Grace and Rachel came running from opposite doors—Grace from the stockroom and Rachel from the office, both headed toward the front of the store where the crashing noise had come from.

"I'm going to kill her," Rachel said. "I swear that woman has broken more stuff. You're going to run out of inventory before opening day."

"I should probably quit letting her carry breakables," Grace said as she followed Rachel.

"You think?" Rachel snapped.

As they entered the front of the store, the sun illuminated the beautiful toile-patterned walls, the antique red armoire that sat behind the beadboard hostess stand, the shelves of delicate teacups and teapots. Scarlett Jo stood in the center of it all as if she were glued to the pink-and-white tile beneath her. Shards of several bone-china cups lay forgotten around her feet.

"Scarlett Jo, why can't you keep from breaking stuff?" Rachel scolded. "Can't you make it through one day without your hands dropping something or your chest knocking something over or those hips of yours bumping into something? Just one day? I swear . . ."

Scarlett Jo wasn't listening. She just stared out the window toward the street, where Fred, the window cleaner, was standing. Grace had hired him to do the windows before the store opened. She'd felt it was worth the investment. But Fred wasn't cleaning at the moment. He too stood frozen in place, his eyes locked on Scarlett Jo.

Moving closer, Grace noticed that Scarlett Jo's hands were shaking violently. Tears flowed down her face. But she remained motionless, her eyes glued on Fred.

Then, in an instant, Fred was gone. Grace grabbed one of Scarlett Jo's arms, and Rachel grabbed the other. "Scarlett Jo, sit. Baby, sit." They maneuvered her over to a chair, and Scarlett Jo slowly sank into it. A soft cry came from her lips, and her tears flowed like a leak from a broken faucet.

"What is it?" Rachel asked. "What happened?"

Grace patted her leg. "Was it Fred?"

Scarlett Jo looked up at Grace, her eyes wide. "Fred." The name came out in a whisper.

Grace turned to Rachel. "Go call Jackson. Then get her some water."

Rachel ran from the room, and Grace knelt beside her friend. "Do you know him—the man at the window?"

Scarlett Jo nodded.

"Can you tell me about it?"

Scarlett Jo shook her head.

"You're scaring me a little, honey. Has Fred hurt you or something?"

Scarlett Jo bit her lip, and that painful cry seeped out again.

"Okay. It's okay," Grace told her. "Rachel is calling Jackson, and we'll get him to take you home."

Rachel came around the corner with the water. "Jackson's on his way. He was at Zach Craig's office for some—"

Before she finished her sentence, Jackson and Zach rushed

through the front door. Jackson ran over and knelt beside Scarlett Jo. "Hey, baby doll, what's wrong? Did something happen?"

Scarlett Jo looked at Jackson, her blue eyes still streaming with tears. She nodded slowly.

"Want to tell me what happened?"

Her words came out in a pained whisper. "It was . . . Fred. He was here."

Jackson glanced at Grace, and his jaw twitched. Obviously he knew who Fred was—and wasn't happy about Fred being there. He stood and took Scarlett Jo by the arm. "Okay, honey. It's okay. Let me just get you home."

Jackson looked at Zach when he finally got Scarlett Jo to her feet. "Make Grace lock the door."

Grace stood too. "Jackson, what is it?"

Jackson turned to her. "It'll be okay. She just needs to get home right now."

"Okay. Sure."

Jackson and Scarlett Jo walked out of the building. Zach turned toward Grace, deep concern on his face. "Grace, who is Fred?"

She felt flustered. "He's just a guy. He washes windows."

Rachel interjected. "She hired him to get them clean before the opening."

Zach started toward the door. "I'm going to see if I can find him. What's his last name?"

Grace followed, shaking her head. She knew it. She just couldn't remember it. "I don't know . . . It's—" she searched her memory—"like a country singer."

Rachel left the room and came back. "Here, Zach. This is his card."

"I've never seen Scarlett Jo like that," Grace murmured, tears now coming to her eyes. "I don't understand what happened. One minute—"

Rachel just stood there. "Whatever it is, it's got to be bad."

"I've got to go now. I'll be back later. But you lock this door. Both doors. Lock up tight and then go stay in the back."

Grace protested. "Zach, that's ridiculous. He's a window—"

"Grace, don't argue with me!" His hands were on her shoulders, his eyes anguished and urgent. "You've got to do what I said. Lock this door. If anything happened—"

He stopped himself. "Lock the door, Grace." Then he was gone.

Grace didn't move. She just stared at the door. Finally Rachel walked up from behind her and twisted the lock. Then she turned to Grace.

"Something strange is going on around here. I don't know what it is, but I'm going to find out—starting with you and Zach Craig. Grace, I saw the way he looked at you. Are you going to deny it?"

Grace lowered herself into the chair Scarlett Jo had been sitting in and looked up into the eyes of her friend. A friend she had shared everything with. Until . . . well, until Zach.

❁ ❁ ❁

Scarlett Jo drank an entire glass of water before she came up for air. This was crazy. It couldn't have been him. But it had to be. She would never forget that face. Those eyes. Those eyes . . .

"Are you sure it was him?"

She shook her head wildly and stomped her feet on the kitchen floor. "Jackson Newberry, do not ask me that again," she said through her tears. Scarlett Jo was a soft soul. She wept easily at movies where dogs died or when her kids were sweet. But she rarely cried over her own pain. Now she couldn't seem to stop. Seeing that man had dislodged something she thought was over. Dead. Dealt with.

"I'm sorry," she said when the tears finally slowed. "It just seems so odd that he would be here. I mean, Mississippi is a long way from here."

Her eyes suddenly widened as panic raced through her again. "What if he knew we were here, Jackson? What if he came here for me?"

His look made it clear he had already thought about this— which sent her fear soaring. Then he obviously realized what his expression had done to her. He pulled her into his arms. "Babe, that can't be. I'm sure it isn't like that. Maybe there's a perfectly reasonable explanation. But I can assure you, I'll find out."

She held tightly to his strong neck. She always felt safest in Jackson's arms. He'd loved her back to life years ago. They had fought their way together through all of that pain. And they'd both thought it was behind them—until today. Until she saw his face in that window and all the fear returned—as real as the bile in her throat.

She released Jackson and ran for the bathroom. The sweets she had consumed that day were quickly expunged from her gut. She could only pray the fear would go with them.

※　※　※

The sun was getting low in the sky when Zach phoned Grace from outside her store. The front door opened, and Zach instinctively wrapped his arms around Grace. He noticed she was shaking. "It's okay," he whispered.

"Did you find him?"

"Not yet."

"Who is he, Zach?"

"I'm still not sure. Everyone I talk to says he has worked for them for the last six months and never done anything but clean windows really well."

He heard the sound of someone clearing her throat, and Grace immediately removed herself from Zach's arms. Rachel stood close by, her face stern.

"Hey, Rachel." He nodded to her. "Listen, why don't y'all close up shop for today and go home."

"Yeah, I'm thinking home is good." Rachel emphasized the word *home*. Zach figured she was making a point.

"I'll check in with Jackson and see if I can get some more information. And if I need to go talk to some of my friends at the police station, I can."

"You think he's a criminal?" Grace asked.

"I think he's something. Jackson was definitely worried for your safety, and he's not prone to overreacting. He knows something about ol' Fred the window washer."

"My word." Rachel shook her head. "Do we have to do background checks on everyone these days?"

Grace turned toward her friend. "Let's go check on Scarlett Jo."

"Grace, why don't you just stay home tonight?" Zach asked. "Jackson has Scarlett Jo, it'll be dark soon, and y'all don't need to be out walking around."

"Zach, I'll be fine. I'm a big girl. I've lived virtually alone for a long time. I can handle walking up the street to check on my friend."

Rachel put an arm around her. "I can take care of Grace. I pack."

Zach let out a soft laugh. "Of course you do." Rachel had been by Grace's side from the moment they met. "Okay, well, be careful. And I'll let you know what Jackson and I find out."

Rachel looked directly into his eyes. "How about you call me, and I'll tell Grace."

He picked up on the note of protectiveness in her voice. Was he that obvious? He hadn't even realized how deeply he cared about this woman until just now. But apparently his feelings were clear enough that Rachel noticed them. And clearly disapproved.

"We'll let you know" was all he offered. Women had told him what to do for long enough.

❀ ❀ ❀

Grace curled up beneath the covers. Miss Daisy was already snoring at the foot of her bed. That dog's snores could rival a roomful of men after Sunday dinner. Usually Grace could sleep through the noise, but tonight she kept tossing and turning, thinking about everything that had happened that day and looking up multiple times to make sure she had activated the house security alarm. Each time, the red light blinked back the assurance she needed—until she had to look again.

When Rachel and Grace had walked over to the Newberrys' earlier, Scarlett Jo had already gone to bed, but Jackson had said they could come see her tomorrow. Grace had insisted that he let them know if they could do anything, and he'd assured them he would. Rachel had been as worried as Grace was. The poor girl was crazy about Scarlett Jo, no matter how she talked about her.

But Scarlett Jo's mysterious trauma wasn't the only thing keeping Grace awake tonight. She pulled the sheet up around her neck and felt the ache in her soul. It was a deep-down kind of ache that hurt in places your fingers couldn't touch and medicine couldn't heal. Her heart was so torn, so confused.

She still loved Tyler—she knew that. Some days she missed him so much that it was all she could do not to find him, wrap her arms around him, and beg him to come home. At the same time she knew her life was better now. She treasured the peace, relished the deep undercurrent of excitement and anticipation that ran through this new era of her life. But she couldn't help but be haunted by questions and worries.

Would she ever be loved again? Would she ever want to be loved . . . or touched? Could she ever be comfortable with another man? As broken as she and Tyler were, being with him still felt familiar. And it was all she had ever known because she had saved herself for him. Her wedding night had been the first time she had ever been intimate with a man. No man except Tyler had ever seen her naked—at least not since she was a child. Only he knew about the cellulite that all those glasses of sweet tea had contributed to. Would another man be able to handle that? And what about the stretch marks that she now bore, courtesy of her divorce? She had lost so much weight when it happened. And then, when the weight came back on, it had brought these new little white lines on her thighs. Who would love that?

Could Zach love that?

The thought came unbidden. She knew she shouldn't be thinking about him, but she couldn't seem to help it.

Zach had sat on the floor across from her and listened to her. He had shared his frustrations with her and encouraged her dreams. And he had been so worried about her today. His concern had really touched her.

Tyler used to leave the house with her in bed and the door unlocked. He'd go on the road for days and never think to ask if she was okay at home. She'd drive to work when it was still pitch-black night, and he'd never tell her to be careful. But today Zach had been petrified that something might happen to her. That kind of caring was utterly foreign to her—and so what her heart craved.

Tears flowed onto the pillow. At times the possibility of loving again seemed a world away. At other times she could practically feel it waiting to emerge, terrifying and exhilarating. She had so much healing left to do. And here was this man who was healing in all the same parts and places, who was becoming everything she longed to have. Yet he was in no way available.

Her sobs shook the bed. And she let them, hoping they would bring her that much closer to the other side of her pain.

{ Chapter 27 }

SCARLETT JO CLIMBED OUT OF BED and made her way to the kitchen, her pink robe pulled tightly around her. Jackson already had the boys up, and they were scattered across the kitchen eating breakfast.

"Morning, honey." Jackson kissed her on the cheek. "Jack is going to get the boys to church, so you can stay home today if you want. It's up to you. I can take them out for something to eat afterward."

She felt panic rising inside her. She didn't want to be alone.

Jackson took her elbow and pulled her out of the kitchen into the hallway. "If you want me to get Stan to fill in this morning, I'll do it. I won't leave you alone if you're scared."

She shook her head at the fear and bit her lip to try to stop the tears. "No, I'll be okay."

"So do you want to stay here or come to church?"

Her shoulders slumped. "I don't know what I want to do."

"Well, if I'm going to preach, I need to go on. So can you decide and just go with the kids if you want to go?"

She nodded. He pulled her into his arms, and she laid her head on his shoulder. She loved this man who had walked with her through everything. They didn't come any finer, any better, any kinder or wiser than Jackson Newberry.

He released her and gave her another kiss. "I'll see you later, babe. Whatever you decide is fine with me."

He headed out the garage door. She pulled her shoulders back and swiped at the tears on her face before returning to the kitchen. The conversation, as usual, was wild and loud.

"She's crazy!" Cooper hollered.

"No, you're a hoodlum," Forrest offered.

"I'm not a hoodlum," Cooper protested. "I'm a guy. And guys like guns, don't they, Mom?"

She picked up a dishcloth and used it to wipe up the crumbs from the cinnamon rolls Jackson must have gone out and bought. She had no idea how she had slept that long. "Mm-hm."

"See?" Cooper raised his hand. "She's going to make Garrett a sissy boy if he can't play with guns."

Jack, who was sitting at the end of the table, let out a laugh.

Scarlett Jo turned quickly to her oldest. His eyes were bright this morning. She looked into that face every day. It was nothing like Jackson's. Jack had his name but not his face. Still, there was so much of Jackson in that boy, so much that blood couldn't put in him.

"You shot her screen door with your airsoft gun, Cooper," Forrest reminded him. "That's why she won't let you come over."

Cooper got up from the barstool where he had been perched. "I did *not* shoot her screen door or her mailbox or her son like she said. That lady's crazy as a coot. And now she told me I can't even come into her yard with my airsoft gun. And I need to go through her yard to get to Jeremy's."

Jack came over to the sink and leaned toward his mom's ear. "Mom, you've got to talk to him."

She jumped slightly. "Oh. Yeah. Cooper, stay out of Mrs. Patterson's yard with your gun."

Cooper stuck his lips out in the smart-aleck way he had. "Mama, I told you—I *need* to go through her yard to get to Jeremy's."

Jack reached out and swatted him softly on his head. "Put your dishes up and brush your teeth. You can smell your breath in the other room."

Cooper blew hard on Jack. "It's just cinnamon rolls. Who wouldn't want to smell that?"

Jack herded them all off to the bathroom for their final hygiene exercises. When he came back into the kitchen, he walked over to Scarlett Jo.

"Mom, what's wrong? You are acting like a space cadet."

She touched his cheek. "Do you know how much I love you?"

He patted her hand, then gently moved it from his face. "Yes, I know."

"I think I'm going to let you take the kids this morning if that's okay."

Jack's brow furrowed. "You haven't missed church in . . . I don't know. Have you ever missed church?"

She kissed his cheek and walked from the kitchen toward

her bedroom. "Thanks for taking care of the boys this morning." She waited until she heard him leave with the younger kids, then went into the family room and curled up on the sofa.

She had lived with the pain of her past and overcome it. Or so she'd thought. It had almost kept her and Jackson from getting married. But he had loved her so well. And she had fought so hard for her heart. And she had won. She had found her heart and discovered what it meant to be truly free. That was what allowed her to be irreverent. And sassy. And alive. Her real self.

Until now. Until yesterday, when she came face-to-face with the man who had stolen so much of her heart from her.

She had forgiven him a long time ago. That wasn't the issue. The issue was the fear he evoked. Apparently that wasn't behind her—not by a long shot. And she wasn't sure she had the strength to fight that battle again.

❀   ❀   ❀

"Well, what is Jackson saying?" Rachel asked again.

Grace stood on top of the ladder, adjusting the toile curtain that separated the eating area of Sweet Tea from the kitchen and the office in back. She looked down at her friend, who was driving her crazy.

"Rachel, I've told you the same thing a thousand times. I've been over there every day for the last four days, and every day Jackson tells me the same thing. Scarlett Jo just doesn't want to see anyone."

"And you really have no idea what this is about?"

Grace stepped down from the ladder and studied her work. Then she shook her head slowly as a thought swept through her. "No, I don't know. I've never asked Scarlett Jo her story." She went to the hostess counter and leaned against it. "I have been so consumed with my life and my problems and my own pitiful story that I have never once asked Scarlett Jo Newberry to tell me hers." She looked at Rachel. "So, no. I'm ashamed to say it, but I have no idea what this is about."

Rachel walked over and laid a hand on her shoulder. "Give yourself some grace here. You have spent years only talking about other people and their stories. Even in your own home, it was always about Tyler. It's okay for this to be a season that is all about you."

"But I should know, Rachel. I need to know." Grace pushed the curtain aside and headed to the back of the store, past the kitchen and into the office. She picked up her purse and returned to the dining area.

"I won't ask where you're going," Rachel said. "But just remember, we have a to-do list bigger than the bows in Scarlett Jo's hair. And that new chef, cook—whatever it is you call her—is coming in tonight to talk through food prep before the opening."

Grace winced. "I'm sorry, Rach. I'll try to be back by then."

"Go." Rachel shooed her with a hand. "Tell her to get her rear end back here." Her next words were mumbled, but Grace heard. "I've kinda missed it."

Grace smiled at Rachel and left the store, then strode briskly toward Scarlett Jo's. As she walked around the town square, she spotted Caroline Craig standing in front of the Details window, apparently studying a new display. A teenage girl came out and talked with her for a minute, then kissed her on the cheek and headed across the square.

The exchange made her heart hurt. She was at an age where she could have a teenage daughter too—a daughter who kissed her on the cheek, called her Mom, talked to her about boys and all the stuff that mothers and daughters share.

Grace let out a deep sigh to avoid the tears that seemed to fight desperately for release. She didn't want to talk to Caroline. She didn't want to like her—to anything her.

All the more reason she needed to say hello.

She walked over. "Excuse me. I'm Grace Shepherd."

Caroline turned at the sound of her voice.

"I'm going to be your new neighbor. I'm opening the tearoom a couple streets over."

Caroline smiled and extended her hand. "So nice to meet you—and welcome to the neighborhood. I saw that you're opening on Monday."

"Yeah, I can't believe it. We still have so much to do."

Caroline laughed. "The work never ends. But it's worth it—working at what you love."

Grace smiled and nodded. "That's a whole new way of doing life for me." She turned toward Caroline's window. The youthful-looking, faceless mannequins would have been staring at her if they had eyes. "Those are cute outfits."

Caroline looked back at them. "Yeah? You think so?"

"Oh, absolutely. Makes me wish I had a daughter to buy them for."

"I just started carrying this teen line. I have two girls of my own. It felt like a good fit."

"Well, they should do well. They're adorable."

Caroline kept her eyes on the window. "Thank you. I think so too." She turned to Grace. "If you need anything, let me know. The first year can be difficult, but I'm sure you'll make it. The place looks great."

"Thank you for that. Well, I need to go check on a friend. Nice to meet you."

"You too, Grace. Nice to have you in the neighborhood."

Grace walked on toward Scarlett Jo's, feeling a little disgruntled. Caroline was nice. Grace didn't want her to be nice. She wanted her to have horns, breathe fire, spin her head around. But she didn't. Probably under other circumstances they would be friends.

Under other circumstances. There should be no other circumstances.

She got to Scarlett Jo's door and discarded her thoughts. She knocked. No answer. She banged. Still no answer. But she knew Scarlett Jo was there. Jackson had told her she was.

"I'm not leaving!" she announced loudly to the closed door and then banged on it again. "You were the one who wanted me to get fire back in my belly. Well, I've got it, and you're going to deal with it!" She banged again.

She saw a streak of bright pink race past the paned window in the door.

"Scarlett Jo Newberry, you answer this door right now. You are not avoiding me one more day!"

She saw the top of Scarlett Jo's hair peek out from behind a wall in the foyer.

"Keep it moving."

Then her eyes.

"I want more."

Her chin came into view.

"I want all of you right here opening this door. Now."

Grace wasn't playing. And apparently Scarlett Jo realized it. She shuffled her feet toward the door.

"You're a bully," she said as she opened the door. Her pajama bottoms hung out from beneath the hem of her hot-pink robe. Some animal was printed on them, but Grace couldn't tell whether it was pigs or dogs.

Grace came right on inside. "You're too old to avoid people, Scarlett Jo. Now you can tell me what is going on, or I'm going to force it out of you by making you scones."

"You wouldn't dare."

"I would. Come here." She took Scarlett Jo's hand and walked her over to the sunporch on the side of the house. A large swing hung by the windows. She sat Scarlett Jo down on one end of the swing.

"There's no way you're going to balance this thing out." Scarlett Jo spoke in a monotone. "You know that, don't you?"

"Well, at least you still have your sense of humor." Grace sat down. "Look at me," she ordered.

Scarlett Jo's big blue eyes looked into her own. They looked tired and sad. Grace had never seen them like that before.

She stuck her hand out. "Hello. I'm Grace Shepherd."

Scarlett Jo crinkled her brow. "I know who you are, dummy. I haven't been out of touch that long."

Grace waved her hand in front of Scarlett Jo's face. "Go with it. Hello. I'm Grace Shepherd."

Scarlett Jo raised her hand and barely shook Grace's. "I'm Scarlett Jo Newberry."

"Oh, it's so nice to meet you. How long have you lived here?"

Scarlett Jo crinkled her brow again. Grace raised an eyebrow, and Scarlett Jo answered. "Two years."

"Two years? So what brought you to our city?"

"My husband felt like we were called to start a church plant here."

Grace pulled her sneakered feet onto the swing and wrapped her arms around her knees. "Oh, really? Do you have children?"

Scarlett Jo let out an exasperated puff of air. "Grace, you know I have children. This is as stupid as all get-out."

Grace stopped. "I know you have five boys, but I still have trouble putting all their names with their faces. And that's not the only thing I don't know. There are countless others. But I want to know. I want to know your whole story. And I want to know what role Fred Parton plays in it."

Scarlett Jo stood abruptly, causing the swing to wobble and bang against the windows. Grace had to drop her feet to keep from tumbling off. "I don't want to talk about this."

Grace had suspected that. "We're not talking about anything in particular. All you're doing is telling me your story. A story I've been way too self-absorbed to even ask about."

Scarlett Jo pulled her robe around her tighter.

Grace got up and walked over to her. "I have only known you about five months. But you know every piece of my life, all the ugly details. Now I'm asking you to trust me with yours—not because I want to know your stuff, but because I want to know you. What made you this amazing woman that you are, this woman I've grown to admire and love. I want to know her story."

Scarlett Jo let out a heavy sigh. "Don't open a can of worms unless you want to go fishin', Grace Shepherd."

"I'll go fishing with you anytime, Scarlett Jo Newberry."

Scarlett Jo's shoulders slumped, and she dissolved into tears.

She pulled Grace to her as she sobbed, and in a few moments Grace started kicking at the ground in an attempt to free herself.

Scarlett Jo released her and pointed to the swing. "Go sit down."

"I will if you promise to warn me before you get up next time."

Scarlett Jo half laughed. "I promise."

Grace would take that. Right now she'd take just about anything from her.

They both sat and started to swing. Slowly, quietly, until finally Scarlett Jo began to talk. From the beginning.

{ *Chapter 28* }

ZACH HIT A PERFECT SHOT off the fourth tee at the south course of Vanderbilt Legends Club. He had joined the golf club quite a few years back. Its rolling lines were as voluptuous as a beautiful woman, the Tennessee hills serving as a handsome backdrop. He loved the quiet here. It didn't get any more peaceful than this.

"Wow," Jackson said, following the ball's long arc.

Zach smiled and put the driver into his bag. "I've had a lot of free time lately."

Jackson came up to the tee box and stuck a tee in the soft soil. "Well, it's paid off, at least for your golf game." Jackson hit a ball long but to the right and in the rough. "Obviously I need to cut back on my preaching."

Zach laughed as he waited on Jackson, and then they slung their bags over their shoulders and walked on. Zach liked to walk golf courses instead of using a cart. For him that was part of the experience, an experience he'd almost forgotten how much he enjoyed.

In fact, Zach had always been more into experiences than into stuff. If he bought a gift for someone, he preferred it to be some kind of activity, not another gadget or piece of jewelry or a bigger car. The same was true for what he bought for himself. He wanted a memory. And this golf course had given him quite a few memories over the past several months.

"Jackson?" Zach's voice was about the only sound other than the birds and squirrels in nearby trees.

"Yeah?"

"How's Scarlett Jo?"

"She's doing all right. She made me come, you know."

"You needed it. Except for church Sunday, it's the first time you've left her side since all this happened. I'm glad she made you."

They walked on for a bit before he continued. "Jackson, we've known each other now for close to two years. And I know a fair amount about you, especially stuff you've shared with us at church meetings and such. Your vision, how you got started pastoring, what brought you here. But after Saturday, it's clear there's something big I don't know about. You don't have to talk about it, but if you want to, I'm here to listen. You've done enough listening to me over these last few months. I'd be honored to return the favor."

Jackson laughed. "What? You think my wife having a breakdown is something peculiar?"

Zach laughed too as he approached Jackson's ball and put his bag down. "Well, that was a little dramatic even for Scarlett Jo."

Jackson set his bag down too and pulled out a club. "I've always been honest with you, Zach. Remember I said that I understand what you've been going through because I know what broken looks like?"

Zach nodded. "I remember."

"Well, there was a time when Scarlett Jo and I were severely broken. It started when we were still in college and had just gotten engaged."

❋ ❋ ❋

Scarlett Jo twisted slightly in the swing, causing it to move sideways. "It was the most beautiful ring you'd ever want to see. And I'd never been happier in my life because Jackson loved me for me. I mean, Mama and Daddy loved me to pieces, but it seemed like guys only ever wanted one thing from me." She glanced down at her chest. "I had these in college too. And maybe my judgment wasn't the best. But anyway, I just seemed to attract these horrible men."

"Until Jackson?"

Scarlett Jo nodded. "Then Jackson came along, and he was a man." Her voice went into that low throaty thing she did.

Grace laughed. "Yes. Jackson is a fine specimen."

"You should have seen him back then. And that man loved me. I mean loved me like my mama and daddy did. I was so happy you could butter me and call me a biscuit." She stopped for a minute and licked her lips.

Grace covered her mouth to hide her smile.

Scarlett Jo lowered her head, and her voice softened. "But

about two weeks before graduation, I was hosting my last big hurrah with all my college friends. I'd agreed to host since my apartment complex had this party room by the pool. It was supposed to be all of us girls together for one last time, and it was supposed to be alcohol free. But we had a few boozers in the group, and they brought some bottles and invited some guys. Two of them we didn't know—rough guys from across town. They didn't go to the school or anything.

"I got kind of frustrated with the girls for letting the guys come, so I told them they had to leave, that this was a girls-only party. Well, they acted all nice, like they were leaving. But a little while later, when I went up to my apartment to go to the bathroom—"

Her voice broke, and Grace reached out instinctively for her arm. "Scarlett Jo, if it's too much, it's okay. You don't have to say anything."

Scarlett Jo patted her hand, then pulled a tissue from the pocket of her robe. She blew hard and loud—freight-train loud. Grace felt her brow furrow. She had no idea how a sound like that could come out of a lady, even a lady with as big a personality as Scarlett Jo's.

"No. It's okay," Scarlett Jo said. "I know your stuff. You can know mine." She stowed the tissue in her pocket again and continued. "Anyway, when I got to my room, I went to close the door, and one of those guys pushed it back open. I could smell the booze all over him. And he smelled like oil and gas, like he worked around cars or something. And he started calling me these horrible names. Telling me I thought I was better than him and he was going to show me who was better.

"And then . . ." Her voice trailed off to a whisper. "Then he raped me."

❀ ❀ ❀

"I wanted to kill him," Jackson said, the emotion in his voice as rich and real as Zach had heard it on Sunday mornings time after time. "I looked for that guy everywhere. But I guess the Lord knew I'd ruin my life if I found him. Anyway, I never did." Then Jackson looked up. "But I blamed her too, Zach."

Zach shifted and leaned against his club. "You did? Why?"

"I don't know. I guess because I'm a man. And I'm an idiot. And I just wondered. Because you know Scarlett Jo. She can't walk past you without touching you or calling you a pet name. She can be so sweet and warm and inviting, and she's got this, this amazing figure, and part of me wondered if all of that had led him to believe she was available for something more."

"But she said she kicked him out."

Jackson shook his head. "I know she said it. But I still struggled with all this anger, and I didn't know what to do with it. There we were, three months from getting married, and this happened. And I knew I needed to be there for her, to take care of her and love her. But I was just so angry, and some of it got aimed at her."

"How did she handle your anger?"

"Not well. She cried all the time. She kept begging me to believe her." He rubbed the top of his head. "She shouldn't have had to ask me that, Zach. She is the most honest person I know, the most loyal. She would have never come on to that guy. And I know now that there is nothing a woman can do that makes it okay for a man to rape her."

Jackson lifted his head and stared off toward the next hole. "What I discovered as we went through counseling later was that I was really angry at myself. Angry that I hadn't been there. That I hadn't protected her. That someone had taken a piece of what I considered mine. Except she isn't mine—I've had to learn that too. She is ultimately God's, and I am simply a steward of her heart for a season. And I was angry at God too. I wanted to know where he was in all of this. Why hadn't he stopped it? How could he let someone as kind and loving as Scarlett Jo be violated like that?"

"I'm so sorry, Jackson. I'm so sorry you and Scarlett Jo ever had to go through this."

Jackson looked at Zach. "Well, there was more."

❀ ❀ ❀

"His anger was bad enough. And I didn't know what to do with that. I mean, here I had tried to get that scoundrel out of the house, and he had raped me, left me with what felt like a mark of shame, and now the man I loved could hardly look at me. I just couldn't handle that. And then, two months later, I found out I was pregnant. I was going to have a baby. And it wasn't Jackson's, Grace. No, we'd been saving ourselves for marriage. I had been looking forward to my wedding night ever since I met Jackson Newberry. But some drunk had stolen that from me, and now I was pregnant one month shy of my wedding."

Grace tried to hide her shock, but Scarlett Jo noticed. "Don't even act like this isn't a horrible story. It's as awful as it sounds."

"What did Jackson do?"

Scarlett Jo scratched beneath her wild blonde curls. "You know, it was odd. When he found out I was pregnant, his whole attitude changed. Maybe it was because I was so freaked out. I all but had a nervous breakdown. I knew there was this life growing inside me, but I wanted it out. It wasn't mine. It was some stranger's. It was like someone was forcing me to take something I didn't want. And I just collapsed in all that grief and pain and trauma."

Grace leaned back harder into the swing. In that moment, she had no words.

❀ ❀ ❀

"When I found out Scarlett Jo was pregnant, Zach, it was like something in me shifted. All that anger just kind of drained away. She was hurting so bad. And I knew that the God of the heavens was either God in the middle of all that pain or he wasn't. Even at that young age, I knew deep down that if there was a life growing inside her and if God is the giver of all life, then he had a plan in all of this. And even if I didn't understand what it was, I was no longer going to question him."

Zach felt overwhelmed by all that he'd been hearing. "But what about Scarlett Jo?"

"She was a wreck. She basically begged me to leave her. One minute she wanted to rip that baby out of her, and the next minute she grieved over the fact that she would even think such a thing. She was so confused, so sad. But I made the decision then and there that this was the woman I wanted to spend the rest of my life with, and this was the baby we'd been given. However it got here, it was ours now. And we were going to fight our way through this."

"Where do you even start with something like that?"

"For me it started with deciding to trust God in the middle of everything that was going on."

"And for Scarlett Jo?"

"Well, you know my wife." Jackson laughed. "She's not the type to give up easily. But it took her a long time to get to a better place. She never enjoyed one moment of her pregnancy. We got married on our scheduled day, and she'll tell you to this day if it weren't for the pictures, she wouldn't even remember it. Then when Jack was born, she could barely look at him. Her face in those pictures, Zach—her face tells the whole story. She'd completely lost her heart."

"But you didn't feel that way?"

"Oh no." Jackson shook his head and smiled, remembering. "When I saw my son's face for the first time, I knew I wanted him to have my name. He looked nothing like me. But he's so much my son, Zach—so much inside him is mine. Scarlett Jo pretty much let me care for him for the first year. She could barely take care of herself. She didn't laugh. She barely smiled. She didn't do any of the wild and irreverent things that made me fall in love with her. She just did stuff."

"What do you mean, 'did stuff'?"

"Well, she'd clean the house. She'd do the laundry. She'd go to the grocery store. She volunteered at the library and the hospital. She didn't care what she did as long as it wasn't with Jack. But all the time, she was running from her pain."

❀ ❀ ❀

"Then one day I came home and saw Jack in Jackson's arms, and I heard that baby say *da-da*. And something about hearing that word come out of his little mouth was like a sword to my gut. I looked at my Jackson and saw how great he was with the baby. I mean, here was a man who wasn't even related by blood, and he'd loved Jack from the moment he saw him."

"Oh my."

"And I thought, that child is part of me. And I have done everything imaginable to avoid dealing with this pain that I've gone through, and it has stolen so much from me. My wedding. The birth of my first child. The first year of my boy. It took so much . . ." Her voice trailed off, and now her tears were falling. "And I let it."

"But you fought through that, Scarlett Jo. That's so apparent."

"I did fight. Hard. And I vowed that I would never let anyone steal from me like that again. That once I'd reclaimed my heart, no one would take one more day from me. No one would keep me from enjoying my family and enjoying my life."

❀   ❀   ❀

"What happened to the guy who raped her?" Zach asked.

"They caught him. He was a kid from town who had way too much to drink and a crummy enough life not to care. But Scarlett Jo faced him head-on at the trial, and they sentenced him to twenty years in prison."

❀   ❀   ❀

"I didn't think I'd ever have to see him again. But then—"

Grace's hand shot over her mouth as it all came together for her. "Oh, Scarlett Jo! Fred?"

Scarlett Jo nodded. "I'll never forget that face."

"Oh no. I'm so sorry. I had no idea."

Scarlett Jo stood quickly, and the swing wobbled again. Grace went to plant her tennis shoes on the ground, but one of the wooden slats caught the cuff of her jeans and jerked her leg. She pulled it free before she could fall off.

"Well, you couldn't have known," Scarlett Jo said. "But what's done is done. And now I need to go make dinner."

Grace grabbed her robe. "Wait, Scarlett Jo. Wait. You can't go back to hiding."

When Scarlett Jo turned, tears had left wet streaks down her face. "I don't want to go through any of that again, Grace. I'm too old for that."

"Scarlett Jo, you're forty."

"That's halfway to death. I don't want to go through another court case. And I don't want Jack to know anything about that man being around here."

"Jack doesn't know?"

"Yes, he knows how he was conceived. He even knows his biological father's name. But he has never tried to contact him. And I don't want him to."

"You can't protect Jack from this forever."

Scarlett Jo's face reddened. "Well, I sure can protect him from this for now." With that she walked into the house and closed the door. Hard.

❀   ❀   ❀

Jackson hit the white ball into the hole on the seventh green, then pulled it out. He and Zach picked up their bags and began to walk again.

"But she's bad right now, Zach. I think it's mostly about Jack. She had thought we'd be able to protect him from that man for at least twenty years; then suddenly he was right here in town. I don't think Jack has any desire to talk to him. We've been very honest with him, and he's never shown the slightest interest in meeting his biological father. But something about seeing him made all of it real again for Scarlett Jo, and now she's just . . . scared. Seems like she's scared of everything."

Zach readjusted his bag. "And what about you, Jackson? How are you in all of this?"

"I want to know why he's here. That's all. I don't need to kill him anymore, if you're concerned about that."

Zach laughed. "I guess that's a relief. I don't usually do criminal law, and I'd rather not change over because of you."

Jackson clapped him on the back. "No, all I'm really concerned about is that Scarlett Jo might let this take her down another horrible path. I've been there, done that. And we worked too hard to come back to life."

"She's an amazing woman, Jackson. I didn't fully appreciate her for a long time."

Jackson's chuckle came out in a burst. "Scarlett Jo can definitely be an acquired taste."

"Well, the more I've seen of how, um, vibrant she is and how great you two are together . . . it makes me see how messed up Caroline and I are." Zach stopped. "I just brought this right back to me, didn't I?"

Jackson shoved him. "Shut up."

Zach sidled up to the tee box of the next hole. He took a tee from his bag and pulled out his driver. "Grace Shepherd is that way now, Jackson. She's so brave and authentic and passionate about life. It's beautiful to look back to where she was and see where she is now. Such a contrast to Caroline."

Jackson tilted his head and looked at him through narrowed eyes. "You been thinking about Grace a lot?"

The words held no accusation. They simply asked a question. But Zach still felt convicted. "Too much," he answered.

"How is Caroline these days?"

"She's like a brick wall wrapped in barbed wire."

"Ouch."

"Yeah, right. But Grace—" Zach heard the shift in his own voice—"Grace listens. She laughs. She wiggles her toes like this young girl who's open to life. And I have to admit, I love being around her."

"You've been around her a lot?"

Zach shook his head. "Not so much lately. I've been trying to avoid her—honest. And I've been pursuing Caroline, trying to connect with her. It's just . . . Caroline doesn't offer me much to want to pursue. I'll catch this brief glimpse of openness or warmth, and I'll think maybe there's hope. But then she pulls it back with everything she has."

Jackson took out his own club. "You can't make Caroline find her heart, you know. You'll just have to wait and see what she does with it. She may do nothing. She may walk away from you and this marriage. And honestly, if she isn't willing to confront her own issues, I don't know if you'd even want to go back. But—" he stopped and looked Zach square in the face—"you are still married to Caroline. Whatever interaction you're having with Grace needs to stop."

Zach let out a heavy breath of air. He pulled at the collar of the black V-neck sweater that fell loosely over his white polo. "I know. You're right."

Jackson laid a hand on his shoulder. "I am so right."

"What I really want is for Caroline to be that way too, Jackson. I mean, she's never been what I'd call a free spirit, but when we first got married, she wasn't nearly so rigid. She could be spontaneous, even laugh at herself, and the way she looked at me in those early years—" he exhaled a sigh—"I wish she could be that way again."

Jackson took a practice swing. "The thing is, that may never happen. She may choose to live the rest of her life the way she's living it now. But you can't let that stop you from doing what you need to find your own healing. And who knows? Maybe watching you heal and change and discover your heart in an entirely new way will be enough to make her go looking for hers. Now can we please finish this game? If we don't get going, we're going to be playing in the—"

They were interrupted by Jackson's buzzing phone. It was the church secretary. Fred Parton had just entered the church building.

{ *Chapter 29* }

ZACH CLIMBED INTO BED exhausted from the round of golf, his mind still pondering all he had heard and felt throughout the day. The ceiling fan swirled above him, blowing cool air across his face. He pulled the sheets over his chest and placed his hands behind his head.

He wasn't sure he could ever do what Jackson Newberry had done. Raise a boy who wasn't his. Love his wife through all that depression. Care for a baby more or less by himself in that season when a child needed his mother so much.

Not kill Fred Parton.

Without a doubt, Jackson was a good man. Grace had called Zach a good man too. But she didn't know he felt things for her he shouldn't feel. That he thought about her more than he should.

Like I did with Elise. And then I did more than think.

Jackson had told him from the very beginning that if he didn't deal with his own sin, his own heart, he'd be right back where he was. Right back in another affair, making a royal mess of someone else's world. But that wasn't what was happening with Grace, was it?

Am I fooling myself again?

He knew he wanted his family, wanted them to heal. In the deepest places of his soul, he longed for them to be together again. But most days, in all honesty, he couldn't imagine that happening. Caroline was this unmovable piece of stone. She could be the fifth head on Mount Rushmore. And he didn't think he had it in him to chisel his way back to her.

Is there any point in trying?

He lay there in silence, just lay there. It felt like he was waiting for something, though he didn't know what it was.

Without warning, he felt his face flush with heat despite the air that swept continuously through the room. Tears choked his throat and burned his nose. They had hit the pillow on both sides before he could stop them. And somewhere deep inside, he felt something click into place. A realization. And a desire— a ravenous hunger—to be the man God created him to be.

If he and Caroline were going to rebuild their marriage, that's what had to happen.

If Caroline refused to work on their issues or pay attention to her own heart, it was still necessary.

If their marriage didn't make it and there was someone else down the road, that someone deserved a whole man too.

But more than any of that, he wanted it for himself.

He slipped from the bed and knelt beside it, pressing his

burning face against the rumpled sheets. "I'm a mess, you know." He spoke into darkness that somehow felt alive. "I mean a real mess. I don't even know where to begin with all of this. But I don't want to live like I've been living."

The presence moved in—thicker, stronger.

"God, I've already told you I'm sorry for my affair and all the people I've hurt. And for shutting down my heart. And Jackson says I need to trust that you've forgiven me, so I'm going to try to do that. The thing is, I really do want to reclaim my heart. But I think I may be in danger of messing up again. And I'm pretty sure I'm going to keep on getting stuff wrong more than I get it right. And . . ."

He stopped. He didn't know what else to pray. So he waited some more.

It's reclaiming . . . *not* reclaimed. The words fell softly in his soul. And in that moment he remembered something about Paul in the Bible saying he had to die daily. Jackson had said the same thing.

Reclaiming . . . Zach felt relief flooding in.

"I want to be a husband to Caroline. I do. But you've got to help me close this door with Grace. She deserves an amazing man, a good man. Send her one. And while you're at it, please make me one too. My girls need that. Caroline needs that. And I want it. I want to be a good man."

Deep sobs were all he had left. He'd wept just one time through this entire season. But all the tears that should have been shed refused in this moment to be denied.

Zach Craig would cry. And Zach Craig's heart would never be the same for having done it.

{ Chapter 30 }

GRACE SCOOPED FLOUR into the bowl. She and JoEllen, the cook she'd hired, were fine-tuning her cranberry-and-almond scone recipe, making sure it worked in the new kitchen. Sweet Tea opened in two days.

Rachel came into the kitchen with her hands on her hips. "She's not answering the phone, Grace."

"I know. I've done everything I can think of to do." She reached up to rub her nose with the back of her hand. Why did it always decide to itch while she was elbow-deep in flour? Her mother would say an itching nose meant someone was coming to see you. Today she honestly didn't need company.

"Well, she needs an intervention," Rachel said.

"Yes, she does. Because we need her here with us."

Rachel walked over to the metal worktable that filled the center of the kitchen and reached for a scone from the previous batch. Grace slapped her hand.

"Ow. I'm hungry."

"You're always hungry."

"And I miss her. I admit it. I miss that snorting, sugar-talking, bow-wearing Amazon. We need to go get her."

Grace wiped her hands on her apron. "Okay, we'll go get her. But if this gets ugly, it's all your fault."

Rachel grabbed a plate and started putting scones on it. "These will at least get us in the door. And if you'll give me some cream to go with them, we might even get her out of the house."

"You're incorrigible."

"Yes, I am. Now, about the cream . . ."

❁   ❁   ❁

It was only eight o'clock, and the morning was chilly. Grace zipped her khaki sweater for the four-block walk to Scarlett Jo's. Fifteen minutes later they were knocking on her door.

"We're here too early for a Saturday." Grace shifted in her red Converse sneakers.

"We are here to save our friend. And if you ever tell her I said this, I will kill you, but the business needs her. She is oddly captivating—*odd* being the key word in that phrase."

Jackson answered the door. Grace was thankful he was dressed and not in his robe. He immediately noticed Rachel's plate of scones. "Oh, y'all are sneaky."

Rachel smiled. "We're through playing nice."

He chuckled. "She's still in bed."

Rachel raised her eyebrows. "We don't have a problem with that. So if you do, you'd better let us know."

He stepped aside and opened the door wider. Rachel walked in with a smile and turned back to Grace. "I knew I liked this guy."

Grace shook her head. "Sorry, Jackson."

"It's okay. A swift kick in her beautiful derriere might be exactly what that woman needs. Here, let me show you where to go."

Grace and Rachel followed his directions down the hall past the kitchen. Rachel opened the bedroom door, flicked on the lights, and walked straight to one of the windows. "Wake up, Sleeping Beauty," she proclaimed as she threw open the shutter. "Your chariot has arrived."

Grace came in behind her and thought for a second that she would just enjoy the show. But Rachel was right. It was time for this to be over. She went to the other window and opened another shutter. "It's time for you to face the world. It's a new day, and we're here to make sure you don't miss it."

Scarlett Jo let out a loud groan and flopped over, burying her head beneath a pillow. All that stuck out were some wildly mangled blonde curls.

Rachel approached Scarlett Jo's side of the bed and pulled the covers back. "Now get up."

"Get out." Scarlett Jo's muffled voice came from beneath the pillow. Her pajama-clad self was sprawled across the bed. Fuzzy hot-pink socks hid her feet.

"What grown woman wears pig pajamas?" Rachel asked. "Seriously, Scarlett Jo. For that alone you need an intervention."

Scarlett Jo kicked her feet against the bed like a two-year-old having a tantrum. "Leave me alone."

Rachel tugged at the pillow with her free hand, her other hand still holding the plate of scones. But Scarlett Jo had too much strength in her. The pillow stayed in place. Rachel jerked. Scarlett Jo jerked harder. Rachel jerked again. But Scarlett Jo still won.

Rachel finally straightened and looked at Grace. Then she slowly removed the plastic wrap from the scones and lowered the plate close to Scarlett Jo's pillow. She moved it back and forth, and her voice came out in a luring singsong. "It's your favorite. Cranberry-and-almond scones."

Scarlett Jo's body went stone still.

Rachel turned back to Grace and raised an eyebrow. The woman was wicked. "And I've got Devonshire cream with a dollop of cream cheese. We know how you love that with your scones."

Scarlett Jo wiggled slightly beneath her pillow.

"They're still warm."

But she didn't move again.

Rachel's exasperation was evident. Grace let out a loud sigh. "This is ridiculous." She snatched the pillow from atop Scarlett Jo's head, grabbed her by the arm, and in one fell swoop turned her over. "Now listen to me. No one has died here, and it's time you got back to living. We open in two days. And if you're going to be part of it, you'll be much more effective in a standing position with a smile on your face. So rise and shine and go brush your teeth. And brush your hair while you're at it."

Grace hadn't expected her words to come out quite that loud. Her hand popped up to her mouth, and she turned and looked at Rachel. Rachel's eyes were as wide as a hoot owl's.

Scarlett Jo crossed her arms over her chest. "You two are harassing me."

Grace sat on the edge of the bed. "No, we are not harassing you. We are showing you love because we do love you. Don't we, Rachel?"

She heard nothing behind her. She turned and stared at Rachel, whose brow was completely furrowed. Grace spoke through gritted teeth. "Don't we, Rachel?"

Rachel raised the side of her lip, sounding like Little Orphan Annie to the orphanage matron. "Yes, Scarlett Jo. We love you."

Scarlett Jo huffed. "See? Listen to her. She doesn't mean it."

"Scarlett Jo, this visit was Rachel's idea. She's the one who said she misses you."

"I will kill you," Rachel mumbled from behind Grace. Scarlett Jo looked in Rachel's direction, and Grace whirled around. Rachel gave her biggest beauty pageant smile.

"She did?" Scarlett Jo said.

"She did," Grace confirmed. "Now scoot over." She shoved Scarlett Jo to the center of the bed. "Bring those scones over here," Grace ordered Rachel.

Rachel walked to the other side of the bed and climbed in, wriggling herself into position. One leg had to hang over. "Good heavens, this is the littlest bed in the world for two ginormous people like you and Jackson. What size is it?"

"It's a full."

Rachel jerked her head toward Scarlett Jo. "A full? Woman, do you know how big you are? You gotta be six-foot-four."

"I am five-foot-eleven."

"Whatever. Y'all should have a king—at least!"

"We like to touch each other."

"That's enough." Grace reached over and took the plate of scones from Rachel. She stuck it in Scarlett Jo's face. "Here. Eat."

Scarlett Jo pursed her lips together and shook her head.

"You're acting like a spoiled child," Grace said. "Open your mouth, or I promise I will open it for you."

Scarlett Jo's eyes widened with surprise at Grace's words, but she picked up a scone. "Put it in the cream," Grace ordered.

Scarlett Jo dipped the scone in cream, then bit off a chunk. She leaned her head against the padded headboard and chewed slowly. Grace decided she'd join her. Rachel didn't waste a minute once she knew it was okay to dig in too.

"Oh, there is a God," Scarlett Jo finally announced.

"Wow! These are good." Grace grabbed another, then realized both Rachel and Scarlett Jo were staring at her. "What?"

"Nothing. Just that I've never seen you eat the way I do." Rachel turned to Scarlett Jo. "Okay, sister, it's time for you to get your rear end out of this bed and back to whatever it is you do. Talking too much. Bugging us. Making bodily function sounds. Walking down the street with your pants unzipped. All of that. It's time for you to start acting like yourself again."

Scarlett Jo took another small bite of scone. "I know. I do. It's been crazy. It's like I haven't been able to snap out of it. It just caught me so off guard."

Grace took another bite and groaned with pleasure.

"Good grief, woman, get a room." Rachel's words came out from her scone-stuffed face.

"I have one, thank you very much."

Rachel focused on Scarlett Jo again. "Well, listen—and I promise you will only hear this once. We need you. Yes, I said it. We need you. I will deny I ever said it if you try to mention it outside this room. But we do need you."

Grace watched the corners of Scarlett Jo's mouth slowly begin to quiver and contort.

Rachel wrinkled her nose as if she were smelling something putrid. "Oh no. Do not do the ugly cry. That I do not have time for."

Scarlett Jo couldn't seem to help it. She sniffed. "You need me?"

"I'm an idiot." Rachel flounced back against the headboard.

Grace took her turn. "Yes, we need you. And Jackson needs you. And the boys need you. You can't let Fred Parton steal from you again—and that is what you are doing."

Scarlett Jo wrinkled her forehead, making almost all of her blonde locks move. "I am, aren't I?"

"Yes, you are." Rachel grabbed another scone. "Now stop it. I'm tired. I'm overworked. I'm underpaid. And this man is not worth frittering away one more day of your life."

Scarlett Jo sat up a little taller. "They found him, you know."

Grace and Rachel looked at each other quickly, then back at Scarlett Jo. "What?"

"Well, Fred actually found Jackson. He came to the church."

"He came to the church?" Rachel almost dropped her scone.

"He said he didn't even know we lived here, but once he saw me, he looked us up. And when he worked up the courage, he went and found Jackson. He said he'd served eighteen years for what he did to me. Said he'd been drunk when he did it, had started drinking with his dad when he was only in middle school, but he'd gotten sober in prison. He told Jackson he was a changed man and said the window-cleaning business is a way to start putting his life back together."

"And what do you think about that?" Grace asked.

Scarlett Jo lowered her head. The remains of her hot-pink manicure stood out boldly against the white sheet she was playing with. "I don't know. I do know I don't want him here. And Jackson told him that."

Grace laid a hand on Scarlett Jo's leg. "What did he say?"

"He said he completely understood, that he could wash windows anywhere."

"Where is he now?" Rachel asked.

"On a bus to Georgia. Jackson bought the ticket."

Grace let out a soft laugh. "I love Jackson."

Rachel punched Scarlett Jo in the shoulder. "Then why in all that is holy and sacred are you still in this bed?"

Scarlett Jo shook her head slowly. "I don't know. I don't want to be here. Each morning I wake up and say, 'I'm getting out of this bed and facing the world.' And then I change my mind. It just feels too hard. I already reclaimed my heart. Why should I have to do it all over again?"

Grace shook her head. "I don't know how you did it even once. I feel like I'm doing it every day—fighting for a little piece here and then another little piece there."

"I wanted it to be over and done with."

A snort came from Rachel, and she threw her hand over her mouth. "Oh my goodness, I did not just snort."

"You did." Scarlett Jo nodded solemnly.

"Well then, listen to my great wisdom. Life ain't fair, sister. Not one piece of it. And you might have to go back over the same mountain a thousand times until it is torn down. But what if you quit on the 999th time, and you get to those pearly gates, and Jesus tells you, 'Well, one more time would've done it'? What would you say to that?"

"Doggone it!" Scarlett Jo snapped her fingers with a dramatic sweep of her arm.

Rachel rolled her eyes. "Of course that's what you would say."

Grace reached out and turned Scarlett Jo's face toward her. "You've got to get out there and let all the Freds of the world know that they'll never have you again. That you will live in spite of them. And honestly, Scarlett Jo, I don't think living with your heart open is a destination. I think it is a daily journey—sometimes a moment-by-moment battle."

Rachel sat up and slid off the mattress. "I am so buying you a new bed."

Grace got off her side as well. "Scarlett Jo, it's time for your morning walk. It's still early. You've had breakfast. Now get out there. The world needs you and your bright colors and your beautiful smile and your prayers. And you—it needs you. So that's the place for you to start."

Rachel pulled Scarlett Jo's arm until she was out of the bed. "And do not wear those pajamas in public, whatever you do."

Grace and Rachel walked to the door. "We will not leave until you are dressed and walking," Grace said.

And they didn't.

Chapter 31

ZACH HELD THE WRAPPED GIFT in his hand. It was crazy, he knew, but something he felt he needed to do. He had gone to pick it up after church.

He had spotted Grace at the service from across the sanctuary, though they hadn't spoken. But he knew she'd be at Sweet Tea by now. She rarely left the restaurant these days, though he had been trying not to notice as much. He only hoped Rachel wasn't with her.

He tested the handle of the back door. It was locked. He was glad. Even in small towns, you never knew what you'd find or what could find you. Last week's events had proved that.

He knocked, hoping she'd hear. She did. When she opened the door, he sucked in air. He couldn't help it. Even in her jeans, sweatshirt, and Converse tennis shoes, her hair pulled up in a ransacked semblance of a bun, she was beautiful. Stray blonde strands waved around her face. Her hot-pink apron was covered in flour and who knew what else.

Her smile was hesitant. "Zach. Hey. I didn't expect you."

He stood awkwardly in the doorway, the gift in his hand. "Yeah, I know. Um, I won't take long. Promise."

She stepped back and opened the door wider. "Come in."

He walked inside and was overcome by a wave of wonderful aromas. "Wow. Whatever that is, if it tastes as good as it smells, you are going to bust the bank in here."

She laughed as she closed the door. "Is that a hint for me to let you taste something?"

"You can feel free to let me sample anything you want."

She moved past him and motioned for him to follow. She led him into a large kitchen. The appliances were double the size of any he had ever seen, with more knobs than he'd know what to do with. Platters of food lined the long table in the middle of the room, all of them looking as appetizing as they smelled.

"Sit." She pointed to a stool, and he took it, watching as she pulled a dainty dish from the cabinet.

"That's a girl plate."

She turned toward him and raised her eyebrows. "If you insult the plate, you don't eat."

"I've always been fond of pink and white," he replied.

"That's what I thought." She set the plate down and began to fill it with different midget sandwiches. He'd never seen sandwiches so tiny. "Okay," she said. "These are samples we worked on today. We want to make sure tomorrow is perfect. This one is a BLT."

He leaned over to inspect it. "That is the smallest BLT I have ever seen."

"It's a tearoom, Zach, not a sports bar."

"Touché."

She began pointing. "This one's pimento cheese—my grandmother Packer's recipe. And this is the tomato sandwich."

He studied the round piece of bread, spread with what seemed to be mayonnaise and topped with a tomato slice. The tomato was the perfect color of ripe red and sprinkled with salt and pepper.

Zach's stomach growled. He set the gift-wrapped box on the table and instinctively reached for the sandwich. She slapped his hand. "Ow," he said as he jerked it away.

"And this last one is a mini Reuben. My personal favorite." She moved the plate in front of him. "Now you may sample."

He wolfed down the tomato on white bread in one bite.

"Zach, you don't inhale them. You savor them. Otherwise, you won't even know what you ate."

He nodded as he chewed. "I so know what I ate." He shook his head rapidly. "That is unbelievably good. How did your husband let you go?"

Her laugh came out nervous. He wiped his mouth with the white linen napkin she had set beside him. "Sorry. I shouldn't have said that. In fact, that's why I'm here."

She stepped back slightly. "Zach, we can't . . ."

He stood. "You don't even have to say it. We're not children, and we're not stupid either. We both know that what we've gone through has left us vulnerable. But that's not the whole story here, is it? The thing is, what we've experienced in the past months has changed us. It's made us into what we both desire in a spouse."

She flushed and lowered her head, and he knew immediately that he'd said the wrong thing. He walked around the table to where she stood.

"Oh, Grace, I'm so sorry. If I can get my foot out of my mouth, I'll try to say that a little better."

She looked up at him, tears glistening in the corners of her eyes. "It's okay. I understand what you were trying to say. And you're right. What I see in you now is what my heart desired all those years with Tyler."

He leaned against the counter beside her. "And you're experiencing the kind of freedom I long for Caroline to know. And it just . . . it makes you so beautiful to me."

She moved away again as the tears started to flow. "Zach, don't . . ."

"I'm not. That's what I'm trying to tell you. Look, you know my story, what I'm capable of. It would be a lie to say I haven't been tempted. I mean, look at you. But I've been there, done that. I've already taken two women and devalued them—Caroline and Elise. And my greatest mistake with both of them was I didn't see them. Not really. Not their hearts.

"But I see you, Grace. I really do see you. I value your heart too much to wound it. And you know what? For the first time in maybe my entire life, I value my heart too much as well.

"So today is just about coming by and telling you congratulations on your new place. You've completely transformed it from that empty storefront with the nasty carpet I had to sit on the first day I was in here."

She pulled her apron up and wiped at her tears, leaving a fresh splotch of flour on her cheek. "That carpet was nasty."

"Rancid. But look what you've done with it. How far you've

come. What you've created." He chuckled. "Granted, it's a little pink for my tastes, but it's going to be great. And I want you to know I admire you—not just for what you've accomplished, but for what you've become. For your beautiful, brave heart."

She wouldn't lift her head to look at him. So he reached over and brushed the flour from her cheek. "In another life, another world, this . . . this connection we share could have gone somewhere. But that's not the way things are. I have a wife out there. I have no idea what she's going to decide about herself or our marriage, but she's entitled to my whole heart. And that's what I intend to give her, if she'll have me."

She looked up now. "It's the right thing. You know it is. And I really do hope that your marriage becomes everything you've ever dreamed it could be."

Now he was the one to lower his head. He rubbed one Sperry against the other. "Me too. But even if it doesn't, I've got to focus on my healing. Which means I need to—"

She laid a gentle hand on his arm. "Zach, no matter what mistakes you've made in your past, I know the man you're becoming will make a wonderful husband. Any woman would be privileged to love you."

He half smiled, half grimaced, those words so bittersweet. And final. "Thank you." He looked back down at his little plate of sandwiches.

"You can finish those before you leave if you want."

"As long as you promise you'll never tell my male friends I was in a tearoom."

She chuckled. "Your feminine side is safe with me."

He ate the Reuben in two bites and remarked with each bite. She did nothing but smile—that warm and beautiful smile.

When he finished, he caught sight of the gift still sitting next to his plate. "Oh, Grace, I'm an idiot. Here." He pressed the gift toward her. "This is really why I came."

She tilted her head to the side. "Zach?"

"No, take it. It's a restaurant-warming gift. Or whatever you call something like this."

As she pulled the pretty ribbon from the box, it released in one tug. Then she did what women do—daintily pulled at the wrappings instead of tearing into them like a guy would. Zach could have eaten another plate of those mini sandwiches in the time it took her to open it. When she lifted the lid from the box, her eyes widened. And there came the tears again.

"All right, seriously. How can you cry over that? It's a sign."

She pulled the sisal rope handle out of the box. From it hung a hand-painted wooden sign with the word *Open* in hot pink on one side and *Closed* in hot pink on the other. "Oh, this is so thoughtful. I haven't even thought about needing one of these."

"Well, I saw it in a shop window and thought it was perfect for you."

She pointed to the lettering. "You know this is pink, don't you?"

"Hot pink, actually. And shopping for pink isn't exactly my thing. But I do have two girls, remember. So it's not the first time, I assure you."

She got that giddy-girl way about her that he'd seen before when she was excited—a kind of hop and a really big smile and dancing eyes. "Let's go hang it up."

He inclined his head toward the covered plates on the table. "If I help you do that, can I come back and sample some of these desserts before I leave?"

"I'll send you home with a goodie bag. How's that?"

He motioned toward the door. "Lead the way."

They walked to the front of the store, and she flitted toward the entrance. A small pink toolbox sat on one of the front tables. "You've got to be kidding me" was all he could say.

She ignored him. Reaching into the box, she pulled out a nail and a hammer with a pink handle.

"Scarlett Jo has brainwashed you."

She kept walking toward the door. "She gave me this. She said every woman needs her own toolbox." She took the small nail and positioned it near the top of the glass-paned door. When it was where she wanted, she hammered it in, then lifted the handle and hung her sign up proudly. She went outside and closed the door, moving out farther to study her handiwork. She tilted her head to each side as if that would make it look different. And then she smiled. Wide. It made him smile too.

She came back inside, closing the door behind her, then walked straight toward him and wrapped her arms around his neck. She pressed her mouth close to his ear, and her words came out whispered and true. "Thank you, Zach Craig. Thank you for everything you've given me."

He wrapped his arms around her and held on for a moment too. They stood there in the quiet of the store, the aromas of tea and fresh paint and food from heaven filling every crevice. She patted his back in a kind way. As he started to release her, he looked toward the window.

The expletive flew out of his mouth before he could catch it.

"What?" Grace asked as she let go. Then she realized he was staring out the window and turned toward it quickly.

Caroline's face was in clear view. Before either Zach or Grace could say another word, Caroline's hand was on the door handle and she was in the store. "I knew it was all a lie, Zach Craig. I knew you could never do it. So what are you going to do, sleep with every woman on the block?"

He felt that little boy in him wanting desperately to hide. He moved back. He had done it for so long, it just came naturally. Grace turned and looked at him, clearly more concerned for him than for herself.

"How dare you tell me all the things in me that need to change when you're still a lying coward of a man? And you!" She turned to Grace. "You're nothing but a—"

"That's enough, Caroline." Zach gently moved Grace to the side. His voice came out stronger than even he had expected.

"What do you mean, that's enough?" Her tone was snide and mocking.

"You won't talk to Grace that way. She has done nothing, and you won't accuse her of anything."

Caroline glared at him. "I will say whatever I want to you and to her."

He moved closer to her, and this time he would make sure he wasn't offering a discussion. "No, you won't. You will not say anything else to her because your accusations are wrong and unwarranted. She was a client who became a friend, and she is opening a business, so I gave her a grand opening present." He gestured toward the sign. "That is what happened here."

He stepped closer still to his wife. "Caroline, I love you. You are the woman I gave my heart to, what seems like a lifetime ago. You are the woman I want to spend the rest of my life with."

Her stunned expression made it clear she had no idea what to do with his words. He wasn't finished. "So you can deal with that however you want to, but you won't—and let me make this very clear—you will not stand here and accuse me and Grace of anything because we weren't doing anything wrong here."

She just stood there, obviously fuming.

He said it again, a little more loudly. "Do I make myself clear?"

She turned on her three-hundred-dollar heels and walked out, slamming the door. The new sign beat against the glass. Zach and Grace both stood there for a minute, too stunned to say anything.

Finally Zach turned toward Grace. "Can I have that goodie bag to take with me?"

Her brown eyes darted up at him. "Um, yeah. Sure."

By the time he left Sweet Tea, Zach Craig felt freer than he had ever been.

{ Chapter 32 }

SCARLETT JO HADN'T WALKED before church this morning—
quite honestly because she hadn't wanted to. She hadn't wanted
to walk yesterday either, but Grace and Rachel had hounded her
to death, and she was a sucker for those scones. Holding them
in front of her nose had been downright evil.

Anyway, she had finally gotten out to walk after Sunday
lunch.

She passed Fifth Third Bank and couldn't help but wonder,
as she did every time she passed it, what happened to the first,
second, third, and fourth third banks. That name didn't make
a lick of sense to her.

She left the bank and its issues behind her and thought
about her own. She realized she hadn't really prayed through

371

this current situation. She had cried out some accusations a few times, but she'd never tried to engage God in dialogue or even stopped to listen to what he might be trying to say to her. That was something else she hadn't really wanted to do. She just hadn't felt like talking to him.

"I'm a little peeved, you know," she said to the October day, the air still warm in the dots of sunshine that filtered through the red and gold leaves overhead. "I hadn't counted on all this. I thought he was gone for good, like a bad hemorrhoid or something." She caught herself and chuckled. "Lord, have mercy. I wonder if you ever get tired of my crude analogies. If you had given me a girl, maybe I'd be a little more refined."

She felt as if heaven laughed at that. She swatted her hand toward the sky and said, "I know. Wouldn't have made a lick of difference."

Her pink-and-white tennis shoes moved quietly across the solidness of the concrete. "I just didn't realize I'd have to fight that battle again."

Over and over. The words came like a flash to that quiet place deep inside her.

"But I want it to be done. Finished. Finito. Bon voyage. Arrivederci. Poo-poo."

Nothing followed that.

"I tell my boys all the time how valuable their hearts are, how they need to fight for them and keep them connected to you and listen for what you're saying. I haven't been doing that for the last week or so. But I'm doing it now. So what are you saying?"

She walked in silence for a few blocks. Her heart desperately wanted to hear something from God. Anything. She read street signs, plaques on houses, historical markers—anything to try to get a "thus saith the Lord." But she didn't get a thing except more frustrated.

As she rounded the corner to Church Street, she caught sight of Caroline Craig headed for her front door. Her steps were determined across the brick courtyard. And she was obviously crying.

Scarlett Jo didn't feel like checking on Caroline any more than she felt like staying up with Tucker and his stomach issues after a fish fry. But she felt that familiar tug.

"I'm not gonna do it," she muttered back to the sky.

It tugged harder.

Caroline's sobs grew louder. Or at least they seemed to.

"Oh, for all that is Southern and sweet, if she says one stupid thing, I swear I'm going to slap her." Scarlett Jo marched to the gate and crossed the courtyard to Caroline's front door. She and Caroline reached it about the same time.

Startled at Scarlett Jo's sudden appearance, Caroline tried to stifle her cries. She sniffed hard, multiple times, then began to rummage through her purse. "Scarlett Jo, what are you doing here?"

"I have no idea" was all she could muster.

"Well, if you're going to ask me to come back to that church of yours, you can forget it."

Caroline finally fished out a tissue and blew her nose— rather unattractively for someone who acted so refined.

"Wow, that was loud," Scarlett Jo blurted out.

Caroline's brow furrowed. "If you're here to insult me, I'm not in the mood. In fact, I'd rather spend the rest of my life without encountering you or that husband of yours who dishes out his two cents' religion and psychobabble hogwash."

Scarlett Jo started to bristle. Then she heard: *Hurt people hurt people.* She'd preached that to her boys a thousand times, but she was now hearing it for her own life, her own pain—and for Caroline's.

"Your husband is a thoughtless jerk," Scarlett Jo said.

That stopped Caroline cold. It was apparently the last thing she had imagined Scarlett Jo would say. She sniffed again. "Yeah . . . yeah. He is."

"What if he's always a jerk?"

Caroline dabbed her nose with the tissue. Her forehead wrinkled. She shook her head slowly, thoughtfully. "I don't know."

"What if he never changes? What if he continues to make decisions dictated by what's in his pants?"

Caroline's frown grew deeper.

"I'm serious. What if for the rest of his life he makes decisions that he shouldn't, and there you are? What do you do then?"

Scarlett Jo watched Caroline's eyes narrow and twitch and imagined her mind searching wildly to figure out what Scarlett Jo was trying to get at. "I don't know."

"What of that can you control, Caroline? Truly control?"

She watched as Caroline's jaw started to pulse. She could see fury building.

"Get mad if you want. But get mad at what needs to be gotten mad at, sugar. And last I checked, I'm not it."

Caroline started digging into her purse again, obviously looking for her keys.

"How long are you going to run?"

Caroline's eyes narrowed into slits, and her words came out in an angry whisper. "I have nothing to run from."

"Oh yes, you do. You have been running from yourself for who knows how long."

Caroline dug harder. Scarlett Jo prayed she wouldn't find the keys until she was through saying what needed to be said. "Caroline, you are one of the most beautiful women I know—on the outside. You are. But, baby girl, that beauty has been swallowed up by all the ugly you're toting around on the inside. So how long are you going to wear yourself out trying to control everything?"

"I am so sick of this!" Caroline threw her purse down in frustration.

Scarlett Jo took that as an answer to prayer. "That's good," she said. "What are you sick of?"

Caroline's hands clenched into fists as tears rushed down her face. "I'm sick of everyone trying to tell me what is wrong with me! What I've done wrong. What I need to change."

"Okay. Good. What else?"

"Ooh!" she let out in an angry burst. "There's nothing else."

"Nothing?"

"My husband is an adulterer."

"Yes, he is."

"He cheated on me." Her cries were coming out in waves.

"Yes, he did." Scarlett Jo's voice grew softer as Caroline's anger gave way to grief.

"He hurt me. Humiliated me."

"I know he did. In the deepest way." Scarlett Jo stepped closer.

"I don't know what to do."

A little closer. "You can let go."

Caroline raised her green eyes and looked at Scarlett Jo. She shook her head slowly. "I don't know how to let go. I've always been the one to hold things together, make sure everything works the way it's supposed to."

"You like to be in control."

Caroline's defensiveness flared again. "I guess so. Nothing wrong with that."

Scarlett Jo pressed in. "But why is being in control so important to you, honey?"

Scarlett Jo watched as Caroline made a desperate attempt to figure out the answer to that question. And then, slowly, revelation spread over her face. Her shoulders dropped. "Because my mom still controls me. And if I can control everything else, those are places that she can't."

"Yeah." Scarlett Jo nodded. "Might be true." She motioned toward the two Adirondack chairs on Caroline's porch. "Mind if I tell you a story about a broken woman?"

Caroline shook her head and they sat.

For an hour Scarlett Jo shared her story, all the way down to her seeing Fred and having Grace and Rachel visit yesterday. When she was done, Caroline's face looked like an interstate full of skid marks, she had cried so much.

"I've thought you were tacky," Caroline offered after Scarlett Jo was finished.

"I know. I've thought you were a prissy pants and a control freak."

"Prissy pants? You've got to be kidding." Then Caroline laughed. "But control freak? I am so that."

Scarlett Jo stood and pulled at the hem of her pink velour sweatshirt. "We can be friends if you want. I won't tell."

Caroline smiled. "I think I might want you to tell."

Scarlett Jo snorted. She hadn't snorted in over a week. It felt so good.

"And about church . . . well, I wasn't going to invite you back. In fact, I didn't even want to walk over here at all. But you should know we have a new worship leader. It's a man. He's single." Scarlett Jo added the last two words with emphasis just in case Caroline now had a permanent fear of female worship leaders.

Caroline gave her own little snort-laugh. "Good."

Scarlett Jo couldn't help it. She reached out and gave Caroline a big old hug. Caroline took it pretty well, considering that she was Caroline. And for the first time since she'd spotted Fred Parton through that plate-glass window, Scarlett Jo felt like her old self.

As she rounded the corner of her street, she caught a glimpse of Sylvia and her granddaughter as they walked up Sylvia's front steps. The body language communicated everything she needed to know—the girl's hand on her rounded stomach, her lowered head, Sylvia's wagging finger. That finger wagged until the door closed behind them. Sylvia had agreed to take the girl in, and that was enough to keep Scarlett Jo's hope for her alive. But clearly Sylvia still had a long way to go.

Scarlett Jo took a full breath of the October air and exhaled loudly, stretching her arms out in a broad sweeping motion like they did at yoga. When she released her second breath, she thought of how this life never allowed a person the opportunity to take a respite. As long as she lived, she'd have to continue to fight for her heart—and for the hearts of others.

That was when she heard it—finally heard it.

That's what I've been trying to say.

❈ ❈ ❈

Zach picked up another scone and dipped it in the cream Grace had packed in his goodie bag. He sank down into his sofa and took a bite . . . and thought his eyes might roll back in his head. Now he knew why women loved tearooms, and he was finding it harder to figure out why men would rather have beer and buffalo wings than this. If Grace would put a big-screen television in her shop and show SEC football on Saturday, he might be able to get some of his friends in there. He laughed at the thought.

He jumped when he heard a knock on the door. No one visited him here. He got up slowly, contemplating grabbing something to protect himself. But he figured a burglar or murderer wouldn't knock, so he was probably safe.

He looked through the peephole. It was Caroline. He opened the door. She looked beautiful, softer somehow. The rusty-orange sweater wrapped around her subtle curves and made her auburn hair more vibrant. Her green eyes looked slightly swollen, yet strangely bright.

"Mind if I come in?" she asked.

For a moment it felt awkward. He wasn't sure he wanted Caroline in here. In his space. His new, simpler world.

"Sure. Yeah," he said. "Come in."

There was an immediate awareness of the sparseness of his surroundings. The single sofa. The bare coffee table. The television that sat on the floor. The place was uncluttered. Spare. To her it probably looked downright primitive.

She walked in, her hesitancy apparent as well. "So this is it, huh?"

He swung his arms out, then dropped them at his sides again. "Yep, this is my humble abode."

She turned quickly, tossing her hair to one side. He noticed tears had welled up in the corners of her eyes. "Zach, you were so stupid." Her voice was full of emotion. Not anger. Just weighted emotion.

"Yes, I was." He had nothing to hide. "Really stupid."

"You broke my heart."

He nodded. "I can see now that I did."

That seemed to surprise her, at least for a moment. Then her shoulders dropped. "You didn't think you mattered to me?"

He shook his head. "No. Honestly, Caroline, I didn't."

She walked over to the sofa and sat on the edge of it. The light-brown leather moved beneath her. He sat on the other end. She rubbed her hand across her jeans. Then she raised her face to his. He wasn't prepared for what she said next because he wasn't sure he had ever heard it before.

"I'm sorry, Zach. I am. I'm so sorry." She didn't even try to hide her tears now. "Today, when I saw you with Grace and the way you responded to me—you've never responded to me like that. And it just made me realize how much you've changed. You're like . . . like you were when we first got married. All opinionated." A little laugh bubbled out through her tears.

He couldn't help but laugh himself.

"I've missed that," she said.

Now he was confused. "How could I have known that?"

"I know it's crazy because I just seemed to take over."

"It was your way or no way. That's how it got to be with you. And my sin was that I let you. Well, one of my many sins. I just shut down and hid and let you do whatever you wanted to because

I didn't want the conflict. But I'm getting better with handling conflict, Caroline, even if it is with you." He laughed again.

"I don't know what this means for us, Zach."

But he could tell by the way she was speaking to him that she wanted to know. In her own way she was asking him to lead her. Maybe she had wanted that all along.

He scooted closer to her and took her hands in his. "Babe, I've done such a poor job of loving you well, and I'm so sorry about that. I've tried, in some seasons harder than others. But you're a strong woman, and you don't like to hear no. In fact, you fight pretty hard against it."

She gave another little laugh. "I know."

"We can't always do things your way, Caroline. And when you don't respect my opinion about what needs to happen, it clearly communicates that you don't respect me."

She hesitated, and a tear ran down her cheek. "Zach, this is how I've been for a long time. I don't know how to do life differently or even how to figure it all out. But I can see I've hurt you, and I really am sorry for that. And I have no idea what comes next, but I'm telling you I'm willing to do whatever we need to do to work this out."

He raised his eyebrows. "You are?"

She nodded. "Yes. I am. I don't want to live without you. I don't want the girls to grow up without you in the house."

"What if it means making changes—changes that won't be easy?"

"Like standing up to my mother?"

"Or allowing me to—whichever works best."

Her tears fell harder. "I don't know how to do that. I can't imagine doing that. I love her."

"I'm not saying she has to be out of our lives or that we want to hurt her. I'm saying we need some boundaries. And you have to let me lead you in this because that's one way I can love you. And I do love you, Caroline. I do. I always did, even though there were days I forgot how much. But the love has always been there."

She wiped the tears from her face, her words coming out as vulnerable as a child's. "Even when you were with Elise?"

He shook his head. "I've done a lot of thinking about that. And honestly, that affair wasn't about love or even sex. Not really. It was an escape from what we had become. I was just trying to get as far from our reality as I could. And my heart was so closed off by then—that was the only way it could have happened. But I've done a lot of work these last few months while we've been apart. When I look back at my choices and see the progress I'm making—I'm just not the same guy. I would have to really shallow myself out to go back there again. I'm not willing to do that."

"And what about Grace?"

He hadn't really expected that. He thought he had settled it. But he wanted to be truthful. Finally he said, "Grace is a wonderful woman. I know her entire story, and I've walked with her through a lot. But like I told you this afternoon, nothing is going on between us, and nothing is going to happen. I really hope you can believe that because it's true."

Caroline was watching his face closely. He watched hers too. Finally she gave a cautious little nod, and he continued. "Grace has been fighting desperately to heal, and she's come so far. Watching her has shown me what it looks like to come back to life. And honestly, seeing how much she's changed, how happy she is, is what convinced me we could do that too. She's shown me what we could have together."

She bit her lip. "I don't know how to do any of that."

"Me neither. But I'm learning. And if I could pick anyone in the world I'd want to do it with, it would be you. That doesn't mean it's going to be easy. We've lived this way for a long time, and I am certain we are going to prick each other's painful places a lot." He emphasized those last two words. "But I'm willing to work on it if you are."

"Should we start with you coming home?" she said, the emotion in her voice almost more than he could stand.

He leaned over and kissed her on the head. She rested her head against his mouth.

"How about we do a little dating first? Maybe remember what it was like to fall in love and why we did it in the first place." He thought for a minute. "I'd like to pick you up tomorrow morning after you drop the girls off for school and before you open the store and take you to breakfast. How is that for a date?"

She sat up, and he saw the heaviness that had sunk into her brow release. "Actually, the girls are sleeping over at the Conners', so I'm free a little earlier. Do you still like to go running in the mornings? Maybe I could join you." She gave him a soft smile. "I've taken up running too. Does wonders for stress. Now I know why you did it so much."

He laughed. "Running would be good. And breakfast afterward."

He walked her out to her car, kissed her again softly, then shut the car door. And reflected that a much bigger door had been opened tonight.

The door to his wife's heart.

He hadn't known that would ever happen. But it had. And he had no idea what was on the other side of it, but he was going to walk through.

Yeah, he was going to walk through.

❀ ❀ ❀

"You've got to get home and get some rest." Rachel rubbed her eyes as she stood in the doorway that separated the restaurant from the kitchen.

Grace wiped the checkout counter. "You want me to do that so *you* can get some rest."

"Absolutely. Us beauty queens need sleep."

"You won the Miss Watermelon Seed Spitting title. Does that really qualify?"

"Hey, sassy, I had a sash and a crown. If there's a crown, then you are a queen."

"Yoo-hoo, girls! Scarlett Jo is here." The last word came loud and in multiple syllables from the back door.

"Oh, brother," Rachel mumbled.

Scarlett Jo pushed against Rachel as she barreled through, depositing them both in the center of the restaurant. "I am alive, and I'm all yours." She clapped her hands together. "So what do you want me to do tomorrow?"

"Retire," Rachel offered.

Scarlett Jo punched her and snorted.

Rachel looked at Grace. "Slap me for saying I missed her. Please. I deserve it."

Grace slapped her on the shoulder.

"That didn't help. She's still here."

Scarlett Jo moved past her and toward the other side of the counter. "Yes, I'm still here, and I am ready to work."

Grace walked over to give her friend a big hug. "And we are so glad you are. This has been waiting for you." Grace pulled out a hot-pink apron with the Sweet Tea logo on the front and stood on her tiptoes to pull it over Scarlett Jo's head of blonde curls.

Scarlett Jo looked down and immediately got emotional. She fanned her hands in front of her eyes and bounced lightly on her toes. "Oh, Grace, I love it. It's my favorite color."

"Who would have guessed?" Rachel retorted, eyeing the hot-pink jumpsuit under the new apron.

Grace ignored her. "I want you to be my hostess, Scarlett Jo. I have to help cook, at least for the next few months, and we need Rachel to facilitate orders and run the register. Besides, I think you'll do a wonderful job greeting our guests."

Rachel cleared her throat. "Grace, first impressions are everything."

Scarlett Jo looked at Rachel and stuck her tongue out. Rachel reciprocated.

"Yes, they are," Grace answered, "and Scarlett Jo makes wonderful first impressions. She will keep everyone smiling and happy."

Rachel frowned. "Well, remember that they are here to eat, not for a Scarlett Jo therapy hour."

"Sounds like someone didn't take her happy pill this evening."

Rachel muttered and reiterated her position. "Seriously. They don't need a therapist. They need to be seated, and then the servers and I will do the rest. You are the hostess. A hostess seats them and leaves them."

Scarlett Jo's wheels were turning. Grace could tell by the contortions her face made. "Seat and leave," she said solemnly. "I can handle it."

Grace patted her broad back. "Of course you can. I am confident of it. Now, breakfast starts bright and early. Then we have lunch and afternoon tea, so it will be a long day. So you two need to go get some rest."

When they had all the lights turned off, Scarlett Jo ran back into the kitchen, claiming she'd left her purse—though a bag big enough to stash a small child dangled from her arm. She reappeared with a petit four crammed in her mouth.

"I'm taking that out of your salary," Rachel informed her.

Scarlett Jo stopped midstride. "I'm getting paid?" The words came out along with small flecks of cake. That led to an entire song-and-dance routine.

The whole way home, Rachel kept lamenting that she'd even mentioned it. She hadn't known she had free labor. Grace just laughed as they walked down the streets of Franklin together. It was that deep-down kind of laugh that only alive people could do.

{ Chapter 33 }

GRACE WALKED INTO her tearoom and looked around. It was almost seven, and everyone was ready. The food was prepped. The staff was in place. Scarlett Jo was practicing her greetings, and Rachel was critiquing her. Every detail she could think of was about to find its place on the stage of her new life.

In less than a year, everything she had known, all that was normal to her, had disappeared. Her old life was over. Closed. And over the last few months, each day she had taken another step into her new life. Back to the heart that she had once shut down. Given away.

She went to the front door and leaned against the door-frame. The sun had yet to fully rise, so people were still more shadows than faces. But she recognized Zach as he walked down the street in workout clothes. The woman next to him, dressed as if she'd also been running, was clearly Caroline. He reached over and took her hand as they strolled quietly in the direction of the square.

Grace felt a slight twinge of pain. Not because Zach and Caroline were together—that was as it should be—but because they would have what her heart desired, what she had yet to fully know. Yet even with that pang came the quick realization that it was out there for her somewhere. So much was out there for her.

She reached up to the sign Zach had given her and traced the *O* and then the *P*, followed by the *E* and finishing with the *N*. Then she turned it over slowly. Sweet Tea was open for business. And Grace Shepherd's life was now fully and completely open too.

a note from the author

I thought of the title *Secrets over Sweet Tea* about five years ago. I even attempted to write another novel with the same name. However, I was in such a broken place at the time that all I could write were miserable, lifeless characters, and the book was rejected multiple times. That was the season when I was walking out my personal healing and learning the revelation of what it meant to reclaim my own heart.

I had spent years telling people that college was the best time of my life—basically implying that "Life right now stinks. Oh, how I wish I could go back." But when life hit me square in the face with my deepest, most personal pain and shame, I was confronted with a choice. I could stay in my broken place with this fractured, malfunctioning heart, or I could fight with everything I had to reclaim it. I chose the latter. That is why you hold this book in your hands and why I wrote its nonfiction counterpart, *Reclaiming Your Heart: A Journey Back to Laughing, Loving, and Living*.

Reclaiming my heart was one of the most painfully beautiful

things I have ever done. I had to go into some of the darkest places of my own soul, confront some of my poor choices and broken patterns of behavior, and begin to understand why I had operated the way I had for so long. Then I had to start breaking those patterns and learn to engage life in a new and healthy way. The journey was at times excruciating. The joys, however, have been breathtaking.

I always count it a privilege to share stories with you. This one is more personal than any we have shared together. May it challenge you, encourage you, and remind you how valuable your heart is, that it needs to be guarded "above all else" (Proverbs 4:23, NIV).

about the author

DENISE HILDRETH JONES has spent the last eight years writing fiction that has been hailed as both "smart and witty." Her ability to express the heart of the Southern voice has led to her being featured twice in *Southern Living* and receiving the accolades of readers and reviewers alike, but it is the simple joy of writing stories that keeps them coming.

Denise makes her home in Franklin, Tennessee, with her husband, five bonus children, and her dog. And on her days off, she will settle for a long walk or a good book and a Coca-Cola.

Visit Denise's website at www.denisehildrethjones.com.

discussion questions

1. Would you call Scarlett Jo nosy or neighborly? Why? Do you know anyone like her? Would you like to have her as a friend?

2. At the end of chapter 3, Grace receives a small blessing—what she calls a gift from heaven. Have you ever experienced something similar—a small, unexpected blessing either from God or a friend that helped get you through a particularly tough time? What was it and how did it help you?

3. What finally pushes Grace to a decision about Tyler and their relationship? Do you think she made the right choice? Why or why not? Have you ever faced a difficult, life-changing decision? If so, what was the deciding point for you—or are you still struggling with it?

4. In Matthew 19, Jesus says divorce is not what God originally intended for man. But we all know that divorce is rampant in our society. What contributes to this trend?

What else does the Bible say about divorce? If you have come out of a broken relationship or know someone in a similar situation, what have you learned from that? How has divorce affected your other relationships?

5. At the end of chapter 11, when Grace is grieving her divorce, Scarlett Jo says she's not worried because "sometimes a person has to die in order to really live." What do you think she means by that? Do you agree?

6. Rachel encourages Grace's dream, "not because it's smart. Not because it will make someone else happy. Not because it's practical or makes sense in the long run. But just because you want to do it." What dreams do you have that you would like to explore with this kind of freedom? What is holding you back? Is there anyone in your life to whom you can offer this kind of encouragement?

7. Have you ever experienced shame the way Grace and Zach do? Or do you know someone who may be ashamed of the way their life has turned out? In chapter 18, Scarlett Jo tells Grace that wallowing in shame is wrong for two reasons. What are they? How could her advice apply to you or someone you know?

8. When Zach's affair is first exposed, he takes the blame for the demise of his marriage entirely on his shoulders. While he alone bears the responsibility for starting an affair, do you think Zach is right about *all* of his and Caroline's problems being his fault? What are some of

the warning signs that their marriage was in trouble
that he and Caroline should have recognized earlier?
What are some of the ways each of them contributed to
the problems between them? What healthy steps could
they have taken to turn their marriage around? If you
are married, how can you apply some of these lessons to
your own marriage?

9. In chapter 20, Zach reflects on the frenetic pace of his
and Caroline's lives over the past several years. Have you
experienced times or seasons of life where things run at
a frenetic pace and you can't find peace? What steps can
you take to cut out distractions and let your heart "settle"?
What are some of the dangers if we do not make that
effort?

10. Jackson talks to Zach about the concept of a shut-down
heart and how that can look different for different people.
What are some of the examples he gives in chapter 22?
Did you see any of those characteristics match up with
the characters in the story?

11. When Scarlett Jo comes face-to-face with someone from
her past, that experience seems to ruin her though she
thought she had processed her emotions over him. Have
you ever had a similar experience? How did you handle
it? Do you think the process of reclaiming your heart is a
one-and-done thing or something you need to do on an
almost-daily basis?

12. How does the need for control affect the characters in this
story? Do you identify more with Grace, who figured out

early on that she needed to let go? With Scarlett Jo, who thought you only had to deal with your issues once and forgot that sometimes living means dying daily? Or with Caroline, who felt like she was under someone's control for years?